WAGING WAR

BOOK FOUR
THE IMMORTAL DESCENDANTS

APRIL WHITE

CORAZON
ENTERTAINMENT

The Immortal Descendants Series

Marking Time
Tempting Fate
Changing Nature
Waging War
Cheating Death

Waging War. Copyright 2016 by April White
All rights reserved. Published by Corazon Entertainment
Palos Verdes Peninsula, CA

Edited by Angela Houle
Cover design by Penny Reid
Cover images by Shutterstock
Quote from *Daughter of Smoke and Bone* used with permission from Laini Taylor

ISBN 978-0-9885368-9-0
First American edition, January, 2016

"Have you ever asked yourself, do monsters make war, or does war make monsters?"
– Laini Taylor, *Daughter of Smoke and Bone*

TABLE OF CONTENTS

The Immortal Descendants

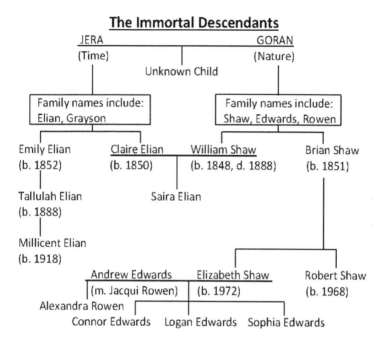

JERA
(Time)

GORAN
(Nature)

Unknown Child

Family names include:
Elian, Grayson

Family names include:
Shaw, Edwards, Rowen

Emily Elian
(b. 1852)

Claire Elian
(b. 1850)

William Shaw
(b. 1848, d. 1888)

Brian Shaw
(b. 1851)

Tallulah Elian
(b. 1888)

Saira Elian

Millicent Elian
(b. 1918)

Andrew Edwards
(m. Jacqui Rowen)

Elizabeth Shaw
(b. 1972)

Robert Shaw
(b. 1968)

Alexandra Rowen

Connor Edwards   Logan Edwards   Sophia Edwards

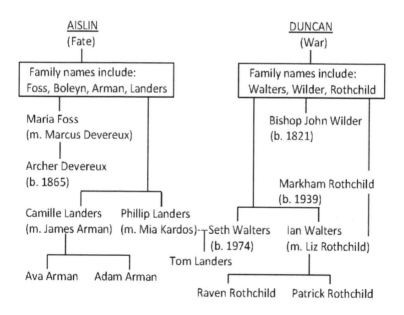

AISLIN
(Fate)

DUNCAN
(War)

Family names include:
Foss, Boleyn, Arman, Landers

Family names include:
Walters, Wilder, Rothchild

Maria Foss
(m. Marcus Devereux)

Bishop John Wilder
(b. 1821)

Archer Devereux
(b. 1865)

Markham Rothchild
(b. 1939)

Camille Landers
(m. James Arman)

Phillip Landers
(m. Mia Kardos)

Seth Walters
(b. 1974)

Ian Walters
(m. Liz Rothchild)

Tom Landers

Ava Arman   Adam Arman

Raven Rothchild   Patrick Rothchild

SHIFTER TRAINING

A twig snapped behind me, and I caught the faint trace of Connor's Wolf.

I'd been studying up on Shifters, and animal facts scrolled through my brain. *Wolf. Carnivorous predator. Average travel speed – five miles an hour. At full sprint – thirty-eight miles an hour. Average number of teeth – forty-two. Strategic scent-trackers that hunt in packs.*

Connor's Shifter Wolf was alone though, and if I stayed ahead of his forty-two teeth, he and I would have a better chance of remaining on speaking terms.

I was free-running in the forest outside the boundaries of Elian Manor, where there were more hiding places and better escape routes for the keep-away portion of this game. But there was the small matter of *forty-two* Wolf teeth somewhere in the undergrowth behind me.

Also, the Wolf and I weren't the only players in this game of get-back-to-Elian-Manor-unscathed, and if I left the woods, I might as well paint a target on my back. My camouflaging abilities would be totally useless in the manicured fields and wide open spaces immediately surrounding Elian Manor.

I caught wind of him again, which was odd, because wolves hunt downwind from their prey. Connor's Wolf was deliberately revealing himself. He kept pace behind me, but stayed back out of sight. I'd need a better plan when the woods thinned out near the

1

old apple orchard, but for now, keeping myself out of reach of his Wolfy grin was the best one I had.

He howled suddenly, and I felt the Cat rise up inside me as if she'd been woken from hibernation by the sound. I pushed her back down the only way I knew how – by mental chat. *No! I decide when to Shift, not you.* In England, "mental" was another word for "crazy," and talking to the feline Shifter part of oneself was pretty *mental*.

Cat grumbled at me. *I can take down the Wolf.*

We are not taking down Wolves today. I said, as if taking down wolves was *ever* on a list of things to do in a day.

She huffed. *It's a dog.*

It's an Alpha, and he's my friend, so sheathe your claws. I attempted to convince myself it was only a little weird to argue with a Cougar alter-ego.

Go ahead, fight me, she smirked. *You'll be defenseless, and when you need me, you'll have to beg me to come.*

Gah! It was a lot weird.

Another twig snapped, then a deep grunt. And suddenly a massive, dark figure loomed up ahead near the edge of the woods. My courage shredded and I almost stopped in my tracks, but fortunately I had a razor-sharp sense of self-preservation that overrode the pants-wetting instinct a Bear usually inspired.

Bear. A solitary omnivore. Able to scent food up to eighteen miles away, with a sense of smell seven times better than a bloodhound. One swipe of a paw could disembowel or decapitate a man. Top speed – thirty-four miles an hour.

I couldn't outrun Mr. Shaw's Bear in human form.

The Shifter bone was around my neck, tucked down in my t-shirt. I was only half-Shifter, so I needed the Family artifact to unleash my Cougar. It was on a long leather thong, and the ancient bone itself felt alive against my skin.

I shuddered. If I decided to do it, the Shift itself would be intense and glorious, like scratching chicken pox with a wire brush. It was the inevitable post-Shift internal battle with my Cat that I dreaded.

2

So instead of Shifting, I changed direction and headed for the stone wall that separated the apple orchard from the rest of the fields.

The Bear followed at an easy lope, and when I leapt to the top of the wall, he swerved around to the orchard side. It was a bold move designed to trap me between the orchard and the woods, or to put it in real terms, to trap me on top of a six-foot-high stone wall between forty-two teeth and a decapitating paw. So I had that going for me.

The wall was only about fifty feet long, and ended in a laurel hedgerow that stood taller than my head. Shaw's Bear had outpaced me and was now at full height on the right side of the wall, about ten feet in front of me. A standing bear was a curious bear, and I'd know he was aggressive if he tensed and dropped to all fours. My legs locked up and I practically skidded to a halt.

"Whoa, Bear," I whispered, frozen in place. From the top of the wall I scanned the woods again, hoping some new escape option would suddenly reach out and embrace me. I almost jumped down to take my chances in the forest, until Connor's Wolf stepped out from between the trees and howled a bone-chilling call of the wild.

And then Shaw's Bear dropped down with a deafening roar full of a challenge my Cougar couldn't ignore. I knew I was screwed even as I tried to rip my t-shirt over my head. There was a Wolf on one side of me and a Bear on the other, and they'd both just called my Cat to defend herself.

And she answered.

I was going to miss that t-shirt.

I hadn't been fast enough to control the Shift, and now I was mad - at the Wolf and Bear for provoking my Shift, and at my Cat for disintegrating my clothes. The jeans and boots had been old and could be replaced, but I probably wouldn't be going back to San Pedro Muffler for another shirt any time soon.

The Wolf exploded forward, and my Cat's first instinct was to leap off the wall and fight. *NO!* I yelled at her in my mind. *I'm still the boss of you.* I yanked her around and we took off across the top of the wall at a full sprint.

I was effectively pinned in place on the narrow strip of stone that divided the woods from the orchard. If the Bear stayed low, I might have a chance to get past him. If he stood up again, I was going to have to leap off the wall into the Wolf's territory. It didn't matter that this was a training game. In our Shifter Animal forms it was real, and it could be deadly.

It's only one Wolf. We could hide in the woods. Cat was pushing her will forward. She wanted to leap off and fight, but I wasn't going to cave on that, so she was trying to appeal to my basic instincts for survival.

I know we could, but that's not the game.

There was an edge of fear in her thoughts. *Too close to the Bear.*

I wrestled control from Cat as she tried to hurl us off the wall. *He'll let us pass.*

He could swat us off this wall like rodents.

He won't. He's testing my fear. The instant I thought it, I felt my control over my Cat slip into something calm and confident, and Cat's nervous anxiety seemed to melt away.

The Wolf was closing in from my right side, but the Bear stayed on all fours as I passed above him. The Bear began to run alongside me, easily keeping up as I sprinted across the top of the wall – the wall that was going to end in twenty feet at the hedgerow.

How are our jumping skills? I asked Cat. She huffed again, clearly insulted, and I laughed. Confidence was overriding fear for both of us. There were two big ash trees on the wild side of the wall, within jumping distance of the hedgerow. If I could get to them, I could climb up to clear the hedgerow, and no animal would be able to catch me. But the trees were outside my human leaping range so I couldn't rely on my own experience; I had to trust my Cat. I was glad to feel her understand what I wanted and add her burst of speed to my own.

4

The Bear was running full-out, but my Cougar could sustain a sprint longer than he could, and I sensed he was near his limit. The Wolf could still outrun me, but he seemed to hold back just a little to see my plan. Good. I needed any extra seconds I could get.

The Wolf finally figured it out when I didn't slow at the end of the wall, but even his thirty-eight miles an hour wouldn't matter now if I caught the biggest branch right. No matter how fast Connor's Wolf was, he couldn't climb.

The Bear roared as I bunched my muscles and leapt. I was at full speed, and I would have to dig in when I hit the branch so momentum didn't carry me right off the tree. I landed perfectly and my claws bit into the bark. It hurt, but not as much as falling would have, and I changed trajectory up toward the higher branches.

The Bear was now trapped on his side of the wall, and the Wolf would have to go around another stone barrier to get me when I made it over the hedgerow. The Bear roared again, on principle maybe, and the Wolf added a short bark to the noise. I reached the height I needed to clear the laurels, and I allowed my Cat a moment to savor the view. I'd be able to make it back to Elian Manor before either of them could catch me now, and if I'd been in my human form, I wouldn't have been able to resist the "na, na, na-na, na" that sang in my head. Yeah, I was mature like that.

It was a good jump, I told my Cat.

She preened. *It was a great one.*

They can't catch us now. We won. I tried to keep the smugness out of my own mental voice, but winning a game of ditch against a Bear and a Wolf was pretty cool.

I coiled my Cat's muscles to leap over the hedgerow and down to the field. Cat was dominant and bossy, and yet I hadn't let her take over. I was the one in control, and a surge of strength made the leap from the tree almost as spectacular as the one that got us there.

Right up until the moment a Falcon attached itself to my back on my way down.

My Cat roared and tried to spin in mid-air. The Falcon screeched, dug it's talons into my fur, and hung on. *NO!* I yelled at her, as she pulled her legs in to roll and crush the Falcon. *Don't hurt him!*

I wrestled with her to keep control, and I stuck my landing.

So did Logan's Falcon.

Get it off! Cat was shaking with fury and she tried to turn her head to snap at the predatory bird. I clenched every muscle we had and fought her command. The Falcon's talons were tangled in my fur, and I could feel their pinch, but they hadn't actually broken the skin, so my own fighting instinct was starting to calm.

And then I began to laugh.

I laughed, and I ran, and the Falcon hunkered down on my back to keep his balance. I could picture him up there, riding my Cat like a windsurfer, and I laughed harder.

It's not funny. He caught us in mid-air like a flying squirrel. She was still mad, but my laughter was infectious and her tone was starting to lighten.

Let's make him earn the win, shall we? I could sense her immediate agreement, and our stride lengthened. I'd never run so fast, and the Falcon struggled to hold on. Finally, even my Cat began to have fun as we sped across the field back to Elian Manor.

CONDITIONS

Liz Edwards hadn't batted an eyelash when her younger son came into their garage flat riding the back of a Cougar like a skateboard. He flew into the rafters, Shifted into a Spider Monkey, and scolded me with chatter before he sped off to throw on a pair of shorts. A phone call to the main house and a cup of tea later, my mom arrived with my clothes to find me sitting with Liz in her kitchen, wrapped in her bathrobe, recounting the day.

When I was back in my uniform of jeans and a stormtrooper sugar skull t-shirt, I joined my mom and Liz in the kitchen. Claire Elian and Liz Edwards had become friends while Connor and I had Clocked around medieval France trying to repair time with Archer and Ringo, and it was always an honor when they included me in their conversations like an equal.

"As far as I know, Jane Simpson is planning to open St. Brigid's for start of term as usual," my mom said.

"But so many Families have withdrawn their children. There won't be anyone left to teach, apart from my mangy lads," answered Liz with a head-toss toward Logan, who followed me in wearing his human skin and a pair of shorts.

"Connor's the mangy one," he said absently as he ducked out of range of his mother's intended hair-ruffling, and reached for a slice of cake she had just cut. She smacked his hand away without even looking.

He turned to me with a cheeky grin. "Had to try."

I shrugged. "Naturally."

Once the cake was plated, Liz slid it across the counter to him and shot him a teasing glare. "You can do better."

"Thank you, Mum," Logan said with a formal, mannered voice, then popped a piece of cake in his mouth with his fingers when his mother's back was turned. He retreated to the table and began flipping through a book of endangered animals while the moms continued their previous conversation.

"The drop in enrollment at St. Brigid's is due to fear of Monger reprisals against anyone who dares stand up to them in the Council. It scared a lot of people when they took Bob right out of his office," my mom said.

"What about the mixed-bloods they've kidnapped?" I asked. "What's the Council going to do about finding them?"

My mom shook her head. "Unfortunately, the Council's problem is that they very likely *are* mixed-bloods."

I stared at her, shocked she could even think that. "Mom!"

"Not because of the moratorium, don't be ridiculous, Saira. You know where I stand on the subject, and obviously the Seers are with us." The Seer Head was Camille Arman, the formidably stylish and powerful mother of my friends, Adam and Ava.

"What about the Shifters?"

My mom gave a wry smile. "The MacKenzie is a bull-headed stick-in-the-mud who refuses to stand with anyone on any issue brought before the Council. If he can abstain, he does."

Liz spoke quietly. "I assume it goes without saying that Rothchild and the Mongers are holding firm in their stand for the old laws?"

"What old laws?" Logan asked from the table.

I appreciated that Liz didn't even hesitate before she gave him an honest answer. It said a lot about how much she trusted her kids. "There are old Descendant laws that don't allow mixing Family lines. The laws assert that mixed-blooded Descendants are abominations because of the unpredictability of their skills."

8

"That is *such* a weak argument," I said, annoyed. "We're all unpredictable in our skills. I mean, look at Millicent – a full-blooded Clocker who can't Clock."

Logan rolled his eyes. "And don't even get me started on that Edwards kid who can Shift into any animal he wants." He was talking about himself, of course, as if the grin on his face didn't give it away.

Liz laughed. "Definitely don't get me started on that kid."

My mom redirected us back to the conversation. "The problem the Council has with the missing mixed-bloods is that because of the moratorium, their Families have never officially claimed them as Immortal Descendants. Without that designation, the Council has no jurisdiction or power to force their return."

Liz added, "We don't even know why the mixed-bloods were targeted, and we certainly can't confirm it was Mongers who took them."

"Of course it was Mongers," I said in disgust. "It's always Mongers."

"Careful, Saira," my mom cautioned. "No one is all good or all bad."

I snorted. "Seth Walters is all bad. Bishop Wilder was all bad. Jack the Ripper, definitely all bad. And guess what Family they all came from? Oh, that's right ... Mongers." I snorted, and Logan giggled at the sound.

My mom sighed in the way moms do when they're too tired to argue. "My point is that the Council's hands are tied on the issue of the mixed-blood kidnappings. If families were willing to come forward to us, or if something definitely tied the Mongers to the disappearances, then we could step in. Otherwise, there's nothing we can officially do."

"Do any of the Seers have information about the missing people?" Liz asked.

"If there have been any visions about them, I'm not aware of it. The Armans have just returned from France, and in fact they've invited us to tea tomorrow, so we can ask them," said my mom.

9

Connor loped into the room wearing jeans and a Tardis and Link t-shirt. "The Seers *should* know something. There's at least one Seer among the missing people," he said.

"How do you know that?" I asked.

"You remember the last person we heard had disappeared – a guy called Tam that Olivia knew? Well, I saw your very small Pict friend the other day when she came to visit her aunt Sanda, and we talked about Tam. He's part Seer, apparently, and he was with some friends of Olivia's the day he was taken. But these friends, a brother and a sister, lied to the police about being there when it happened, and they won't tell anyone what they know."

"Has Olivia tried to talk to them?" I was the closest to the teapot, so I poured Connor a cup.

"Not since the girl, Melanie, first called Olivia. She told Olivia they had seen Tam get taken, but didn't give any details, and now the friends have stopped answering their phones."

I looked sharply at him. "Could they be missing now too?"

"That's what Olivia's worried about, but she can't go to London by herself to check on them." He shrugged. "She gave me their names and an address and asked if I would try to find them."

Liz came over and squeezed some lemon into her son's tea. "I'm not so wild about any of you going into London. If the Mongers catch you outside the protection of home or school, they'll have very little compunction against taking you."

"I could go as a Philippine Eagle." Logan said, pointing to a page in his book. "It's the largest eagle there is, and I could probably fly to London in under an hour, pop in to chat with the friends, and fly back home."

Connor scowled at his little brother. "It's also one of the rarest birds on the planet, and you'd be less conspicuous on a broom. If Mum has a problem with me going to London, it's pretty much a guarantee you can't go."

Logan looked equal parts crestfallen and defiant, and before he could launch a verbal attack on Connor I slid onto the bench next to him. "Scooch over and show me."

Logan was eleven and looked like something out of a Dickens novel, with shaggy blond hair and a boyish scruffiness that never went away no matter how often he bathed. His brother, Connor, was already tall for his age, with lean ranginess that reminded me of his Wolf. Connor was fifteen, with darker hair, and a quietness that spoke of too much responsibility too soon. Since they had come to stay at Elian Manor, when it was clear the Mongers were looking for Connor, I'd spent a lot of time with the brothers. And for these last weeks of summer, since we'd gotten back from medieval France, they had worked with Mr. Shaw to teach me the fine art of Shifting.

I pointed to the Philippine eagle. "Could you actually Shift into that?"

He shrugged. "Sure. So could you."

He meant because I wore the Shifter bone nearly full-time now. I tucked it under my shirt and shook my head. "No. It lets me Shift into *my* animal. Only real Shifters can do the any-animal thing with this." The Edwards family and Mr. Shaw were the only Shifters who knew I had the ancient Shifter bone, because it was clear to us all that I'd get no access to it if anyone else knew it had been found.

Connor sat across from Logan. "Show her the bush viper," he said to Logan before looking at me. "And by the way, you *are* a real Shifter."

I wasn't going to argue with Connor, so I turned back to his brother, who quickly flipped the pages to a striking blue and yellow snake. "Cool, huh?"

"It's beautiful," I said. "But Indiana Jones is a snake-lover compared to me."

Logan's grin turned sly and Connor shook his head at me sadly, like I'd made the *dumb ways to die* list. "Really? You just gave him *so* much ammunition."

I winced at the look of an evil mastermind that had taken over Logan's features, which he instantly schooled into something benignly angelic. Yep, I was going to pay for that.

Connor spoke to his mom. "By the way, Uncle Bob said he won't be in for dinner. He wants Saira and Archer to meet him in the lab when Archer gets up." He rinsed his mug in the sink, then turned to me. "I'm heading back to the manor. You coming?"

I nodded. The light outside was dimming and Archer would be up soon. "I'll grab a sandwich or something from the kitchens, Mom. And Liz, thank you for the tea." My mom looked settled in for conversation with Liz, and I had the feeling Millicent might be dining alone tonight at the manor.

"Where's Ringo?" I asked Connor as we stepped outside the flat. He slid down the stair rail, and I jumped over the side to land at the bottom. It should have been a tough landing, but I'd gotten better at them since I'd been training in Cougar skin.

Connor ticked off his fingers. "Either at the archery range, in the garage, or in the lab. But most likely, he's with my uncle."

"Which means in the lab." Mr. Shaw had set up a makeshift laboratory in an unused greenhouse on the grounds of the manor, because my mom and Liz didn't want him working on campus at St. Brigid's during the school holiday. "He's turning into a science geek like you, isn't he?"

Connor grinned. "Worse. He's becoming a tech geek too."

"What do you mean? You guys aren't sitting around playing video games in the lab, are you?"

"Don't be daft. We moved a television into the east wing library for that."

Because … boys.

Connor continued. "Ringo found some old radios in the attics, and between those, the toaster oven, the stereo receiver, and the Walkman, he could practically build a robot to clean the house at this point."

"I thought he was just fixing that stuff."

He scoffed. "Like anyone would ever fix a Walkman. Did you know there was a VCR *and* a Beta machine up there? I mean, come on!"

I grinned at him. "That's pretty cutting edge for Millicent, don't you think?"

We entered the manor house through the kitchen door just as Jeeves, Millicent's driver and all-around house manager, was leaving.

"Ah, Connor. There's enough light left for another lesson if you'd like." Jeeves was probably in his late forties, though his hair was shot with enough silver that I forgot he wasn't old until he smiled. Which he did as he held the door for us.

Connor's face lit up. "Really? That would be fantastic!"

"What lesson?" I asked.

"Jeeves is teaching me to drive a car," he said with a grin as he followed Jeeves outside.

I laughed and waved him away. Ever since Jeeves had given Connor's family his flat over the garage, he had spent a lot of time with Liz and her kids, and the happiness potential made me smile.

I grabbed a couple of carrots from the cutting board and headed up the back stairs, then slipped out a third floor window and climbed up a dormer to the pitched roof above it. I sat with my back to a chimney and watched the sun dip behind trees. The sky here was never the vivid orange and red that exploded across Venice Beach. The English sky was more polite than that. She'd blush, flare a little warm with embarrassment, and then finally turn away, her pink and coral dresses blending into the blue night until her light dimmed altogether. Sunsets here were always pretty, but I missed the fire and passion of the California sky.

A hand caressed the back of my neck and I looked up to find Archer kneeling next to the chimney. A flush of heat filled my chest.

"You found me."

"Always." His voice was quiet, but his tone had edges, and when he sat beside me on the roof, his fingers twined with mine.

"How?" I leaned my head back on his shoulder. "How did you find me?"

He was silent a long moment until I turned to study his face. His deep blue eyes found mine and he searched them as if he was deciding how honest to be. "I felt you."

"Felt me?" Archer was part Seer from his mother's side of the family, and that Seer blood had saved his life when he was infected with the porphyria-like mutation that killed normal humans but turned Immortal Descendants into something resembling mythological vampires. "I didn't think Seers were empaths."

"I've never had the true skills of a Seer, beyond my own ability to sense lies. But since we were in France, my sense of *you* has grown stronger, and continues to the more time we spend in each other's company."

Maybe that should have freaked me out, but I'd become pretty immune to freakouts about special skills. So instead, I looked up at the evening sky and considered how lucky I was that someone could find me in such vastness.

"What are you thinking?" he murmured into my ear.

I smiled at the shiver his voice sent across my skin. "I'm thinking that could be useful for the times I forget to leave a note." It was supposed to be a joke, but too much about that statement was layered in things we didn't talk about. "Sorry. Forget I said that."

Archer turned me to face him. "Why? Why is that uncomfortable to discuss?"

I took a breath. This wasn't going to be easy or smooth, because I wasn't really sure what I was going to say. "Leaving a note is generally something people do on pillows or nightstands, and pre-supposes that I sleep where and when you sleep. Which is something you've emphatically resisted since we've been home."

"That would be mitigated if you would marry me." The softness of Archer's voice was in direct contrast to the words he had just spoken, and I stared at him as if he had just shouted across the rooftops. Maybe because with those words, he had.

"Marry you? I'm eighteen years old, Archer. I'm not getting married right now, or maybe even ever. What does marrying you have to do with getting to sleep next to you?" My heart was pounding and I wasn't sure why. It didn't matter though, my brain was overriding anything my heart might have to say in the matter.

There had been something vulnerable and searching in his eyes when he had spoken so quietly, but whatever that was had quickly shuttered. "I apologize, Saira. That was clumsy of me."

He was backing away – not physically, which would have sent him off the roof – but he was building a quick and effective wall against whatever emotions had just been raw, and I didn't like it.

"Stop it, Archer. Clumsy is falling off a bike. Clumsy isn't tossing a marriage proposal into the wind to see what sticks."

He took a breath. "It was clumsy of me to challenge you with it, rather than present it as a hope and a wish that you might someday fulfill. Saira Elian, I would stand by your side until the end of time, and it is my deep desire to one day do so as your husband."

Cue the pounding heart again. I inhaled to steady my emotions, which raced in every direction at once, then took a breath and tried to explain myself in a way that didn't hurt him. "I feel too young to be married. It feels like a thing settled people do when they're ready to have a house, and a dog, and kids." There was an argument starting on his face and I cut him off. "Be clear. You are my future. I don't want any other future than one where I'm standing right next to you."

A huge, unspoken conversation sat there between us, but instead, he kissed me. "I've always moved too fast with you. I apologize."

I smiled at him and kissed him back. "Not always. But when you do, you do it spectacularly. But back to my original point, when do I get to sleep next to you?"

Archer had been resting during daylight hours in the Elian Manor keep, which was a windowless room in the center of the manor house. It also had the benefit of being warded, so when it was locked, he was protected from anyone who would do him harm. The arrangement worked pretty well for his safety, but since

Millicent and my mom had keys to the place, there wasn't a lot of privacy that could be counted on if I wanted to join him for a nap.

He looked very serious as he answered me. "You know my feelings about this. It is inappropriate for me to come to your bedroom in your mother's house. The keep belongs to the house, and it is only through her generosity that I'm welcome to sleep there. And unless our commitment is formalized, I am uncomfortable asking for another bedroom where you could visit me."

"You're so Victorian," I whispered, as I bit his lip softly.

He kissed me with an intensity that left me breathless. "And you make it very, very difficult for me to be honorable."

The kissing went on long enough that I was ready to drag him into the attic just so I didn't accidentally fall off the roof. When he finally pulled away from me, I could tell he was trying to get a grip on his feelings, and it made me glad I could ruffle his perfect Victorian composure. He studied the view over fields and forests while I studied the hard lines of his jaw, the softness around his mouth that was so quick to smile at me, and the deep blue of his eyes that matched the nighttime sky.

"Have you ever …" I shut my mouth quickly. What kind of idiot asks her boyfriend about the love life he had before her?

He turned a confused gaze to mine. "Have I ever … what?"

I winced. I was going to do it. It was like watching myself dip my hand in boiling water, knowing it would burn, but also knowing if I didn't, the unasked question would burn just as hot.

"Have you ever … been with anyone else?"

I looked away, horrified at myself for having asked the dumbest question on the planet. The man was more than a century old. We had only known each other for a year, which left a whole other lifetime – several lifetimes – for him to know other women.

I buried my face in my hands. "Ugh. Don't answer that. I don't want to know."

Archer gently pulled my hands away and cradled my face as he looked at me. "Saira, no matter what else has happened in my life, I've only ever loved you."

I cracked my eyelids open and returned his gaze, suddenly feeling very young, and oddly, a little annoyed too. "I'm sorry I asked that question. It's not my business, and it would be ridiculous for you to have been celibate your entire life. Just forget I asked."

He touched my cheek gently. "You are the woman of my dreams." He helped me to my feet and I sank into strong arms as he kissed me. "Come. Shaw's been waiting for us. He left me a note."

The cheeky grin on his face made me want to poke him, and it wasn't until we were almost to Mr. Shaw's lab that I realized Archer hadn't answered my question.

Experiments

The greenhouse glowed like a beacon under the tarps Mr. Shaw and the gardeners had rigged to keep the hot sun out during the day. I was suddenly very happy for the security cameras and extra groundspeople Millicent and my mom had installed around the property as Monger deterrents during the past couple of months. I hadn't seen Mongers or their minions at all since we'd come back from France, but that didn't mean they weren't out there watching us.

Archer held the door for me, and I stepped into a space that was like a cross between Mr. Potts' workshop in *Chitty Chitty Bang Bang* and the mad scientists' laboratory in *Young Frankenstein*. Ringo sat in one corner at a table that was covered in radio and television parts, while Mr. Shaw, surrounded by test tube holders and trays of glass slides, had his face buried in a microscope. Both of them looked up at the sound of our entrance.

"'Eard young Logan took down a Cat tonight." Ringo grinned.

"He didn't quite take me down, so much as rode me like I was a skateboard." I couldn't keep the sigh of resignation out of my voice.

Archer barked a laugh. "He rode you? As what? A Meerkat or a baby Monkey?"

"No, as a Falcon." I demonstrated with an action pose, and all three of them cracked up. "The kid needs his own theme song; he's that good."

"He's fearless," said Mr. Shaw, "which is as astounding as it is horrifying. My sister thought it was difficult to keep Connor out of trouble from boredom – but keeping Logan unscathed is going to take an act of God."

"Or manacles," said Archer.

I shook my head and shuddered. "Nope. He'd just turn into a snake and slither out. He wants to go to London to talk to some possible witnesses in the Descendant disappearances, and he's probably the stealthiest of all of us."

Mr. Shaw was already shaking his head. "He's eleven."

I raised an eyebrow. "So was Harry Potter when he went to Hogwarts."

Mr. Shaw glared at me, and Ringo looked surprised. "Who's 'Arry Potter?"

"Dude, you've got some reading to catch up on." There was no hiding the disgust in my voice. No one who read as much as Ringo did had an excuse to skip those books.

Ringo winced at Archer. "I got duded."

Archer shrugged. "It's required reading. I'd dude you too if I didn't sound the idiot doing so."

I ignored them both and turned back to Mr. Shaw. "Eleven is young, but you and I both know the Edwards brothers haven't really been young since their dad died."

This time it was Mr. Shaw's turn to wince. He sat up and rubbed the back of his neck. "We also both know that neither Liz nor Connor would ever forgive themselves if something happened to Logan."

I sighed because I knew he was right. "I'm actually not arguing for him to be allowed to go. I just think he's the type of kid who's going to do what he does, regardless of what other people think."

"Like someone else I know." Archer's voice was quiet near my ear.

"Maybe," I whispered back with a smile. I'd gotten a lot better about thinking first before I jumped, but I knew how lucky I was every time I landed on my feet.

Mr. Shaw's shoulders slumped. "If he was the adventurous child of anyone else, I'd feel exactly as you do. But you know, perhaps better than most, that loss makes for some oddly irrational fears, and I'll tell you, Jeeves moving Liz and the kids here while you were in France with her son was the thing that saved her from letting the barely glued bits crumble."

He seemed to shake off the heavy weight of those thoughts and suddenly looked around. "Speaking of, where is my eldest nephew?"

"Getting driving lessons from Jeeves."

Mr. Shaw looked startled for exactly one second before his expression turned thoughtful. "That doesn't actually horrify me as much as it should. Well, then, I'll proceed without him." He sat back and invited us both to sit on the tall stools that were arrayed around the table.

"You both know that Connor and I have been doing extensive research on Archer's blood for the past several months." We nodded mutely. Archer had basically been a human pincushion for them, and I'd called them the Vampires more than once. They hadn't thought that was as funny as I did.

Mr. Shaw continued. "The development in France of Archer's injury spectrum has given us a new direction into which to look."

I shuddered, still a little shocked at the memory of how every wound Archer had ever gotten had begun blooming on his body each time he got hurt. It hadn't always been that way, but since I'd known him, each time he'd been wounded it got a little worse. Mr. Shaw continued.

"We now believe we understand Archer's relative immortality. The key is in his debilitation while the old injuries resurface and the longer healing time afterward."

That was news, and I held my breath.

Connor's voice came from behind me as he entered the lab. "Am I too late? Can I give them the news?"

Mr. Shaw smiled affectionately. "You discovered it. It's yours to share."

Connor stood next to Mr. Shaw, his cheeks flushed from running, and his eyes bright with excitement. "You have extra-long telomeres." He was looking at Archer.

He grinned. "Is that a compliment?"

I giggled, mostly because of nerves. Connor didn't even rise to the bait. "It is if you don't want to age."

"Okay, what are telomeres?" I asked.

"They're the caps on the ends of your DNA chains that protect the chromosomes. Normal aging happens because the chromosomes don't regenerate all the way to their ends during the DNA replication cycle. Telomeres protect the information in those chromosomes; telomerase is the enzyme that activates the telomeres to replicate and replace themselves as they fall off. You have extra-long telomeres protecting your chromosomes, which might have already been genetic, or it might have come with the porphyria mutation when you were infected. We think that infection locked onto your DNA and has super-promoted your telomerase. So even if your telomeres were inclined to fall off as they normally would – a process that would allow the chromosomes to alter and change – your rocket-fuel telomerase makes new telomeres so fast there's no time for apoptosis." We must have looked stupefied because he tried again. "Apoptosis is cell death. Your cells don't have a chance to age."

I looked at Mr. Shaw. "I think I get it, but can you translate what wonder-boy just said?"

Connor smirked and shook his head at me as Mr. Shaw laughed. "Okay, you know our super-promotor for our rock star Descendant genes? Well, Immortal Descendant genes are just one of the bands in the whole music industry that is human DNA. Now imagine that some garage band fails every day, and the fact that they fail keeps the whole music scene in a constant state of change. You don't want to be the next band to fail, so you're always innovating, taking risks, and making new music. What if a high-powered music producer came along and halted the failures. No matter what, bands wouldn't fail. There would be no reason to change, no reason to take risks, and no reason to innovate. Music would become a static industry that would have no reason to evolve to stay alive. That high-powered music producer is the infected telomerase in Archer's DNA. It has stopped the death of garage bands and caused the music to go static."

I grinned at Mr. Shaw's analogy. "So, Mr. Shaw, what instrument did you play?"

He chuckled. "I had a drum kit. And I was very good."

Connor scoffed. "Not according to Mum." He turned back to Archer. "We also believe your need for blood protein and your vitamin D intolerance is a product of the need to fuel the telomerase. Shut down the factory and the fuel requirements disappear."

Archer was looking from Connor to Mr. Shaw intently, and I noticed that Ringo had moved his seat closer.

"Can you shut down the telomerase so that it returns to normal levels?" Archer asked quietly.

Mr. Shaw's expression turned serious. "We're still working on it, but we think so, yes."

"How?" I asked.

"We're looking at a couple of viruses to do the trick."

I stared. "An infection to fight an infection? But won't the porphyria-lock fight it?"

"Not if it's busy fighting something else."

My heart sank. "You mean like an injury." They'd brought up the old wounds that had bloomed the last few times Archer had been hurt, so that had to be what they meant.

Mr. Shaw sounded grim. "It's what led us to telomeres in the first place. If the sheer magnitude of Archer's accumulated injuries is resurfacing with each new one, perhaps it's like the kick-back on a discharged weapon. When the telomeres get kicked into re-growth, there's an instant of pure weakness just before the shot of telomerase. Perhaps if the virus attacks during the 'porphyria-lock's' moment of weakness, it might have a chance to shut the telomerase down."

I could see a whole host of issues with that idea, and I opened my mouth to protest, but Archer cut me off. "What do you need from me?"

Connor answered. "For now, just keep giving us blood. We're narrowing it down, but there's still too much theoretical and not enough practical information."

Mr. Shaw gazed steadily at Archer. "We're working up a list of risk factors to mitigate the surprises. We'll try to be as thorough as possible."

Archer nodded. "That's all I can ask for." He turned to Ringo as he reached for my hand. "I need to talk to you both. Can you come running with us?"

"'Course." Ringo set down the tiny screwdriver he'd been using and brushed invisible dust off his perfectly clean jeans as he stood.

Archer nodded to both Mr. Shaw and Connor. "Thank you for everything you're doing."

Mr. Shaw reached out and clasped Archer's shoulder. "It's not just a research project, you know that."

"I know." Archer's gaze was direct, but there was something very guarded in his eyes. We left the greenhouse quietly, and he started running the moment the door closed behind us.

The old barn two fields over was our unspoken destination, and the moonlit run was silent except for the crunch of grass and the sounds of our breath. It wasn't until we were all sitting on the roof of the stone structure that I spoke.

"I don't like it."

But Archer was already talking. "I want to find Tom."

That wasn't at all what I thought he was going to say, and I felt the air whoosh out of my lungs. I had spent the last few weeks since we returned from France trying very hard not to think about Tom. The guilt and regret that laced my memories of him made my soul ache and my conscience itch, and his name was definitely not a comfortable topic of conversation.

"Ye think a cure can save 'im from 'imself?" Ringo didn't sound surprised.

"What does Tom have to do with anything?" I said.

"I don't trust the Monger in him."

I turned to Archer. "You think now that he's a Vampire he'll suddenly turn into a bad guy?"

Archer gazed back at me without blinking. "He's full of Wilder's blood, Saira. He's everything that Wilder was, and more. I think he's angry, and I think he could be stronger than Wilder was too. He started as a mixed-blood and that makes him a wild card."

"Tom's not a power-hungry maniac bent on ruling the Immortal Descendant world." I refused to accept that he could ever be anything other than the lonely and misunderstood boy who had been my friend.

"Saira, Tom put 'imself on the path to 'is own destruction when 'e sent Léon back to kill 'is 'uman self. And 'e's a ball of self-loathin' for 'avin' murdered the one person 'e loved, which means 'e's either curled up in a corner somewhere waitin' to die, or 'e's engineerin' that death." Ringo's voice was quiet and confident, as if he'd figured all of this out long ago.

Archer spoke calmly. "He tried to commit suicide in France and failed. I'm afraid the only people strong enough to end him permanently are other Mongers or Vampires, which means he'd have to go looking for that kind of trouble - or causing trouble to come to their notice." His voice held such certainty it made me flush with anger.

"Why don't you believe he could have found some peaceful place in time to live out a life of books and art and whatever else doesn't involve heights?" I believed that was possible. I had to.

"Because *he* doesn't believe he deserves happiness." Archer's simple words were like a punch in the gut.

"So, you want to find Tom and get him whatever cure Mr. Shaw and Connor have cooked up?"

"Yes." Archer's gaze didn't waver from mine.

"And if the cure doesn't work, or he doesn't want it?"

Archer said nothing, but his eyes said everything I didn't want to hear. I turned to Ringo. "Have you already been looking for him? Is that why you don't seem to be surprised by all this?"

Ringo shrugged. "Yeah, I've been lookin'. I'm startin' to think 'e could 'ave made 'is way to World War II."

I stared at Ringo. "Why?"

"Every war 'as its legends. A couple of the ones in Russia and Germany might fit a self-'atin' Vampire."

"That could be any Vampire," I said angrily. Then my eyes shot to Archer's face as I realized what I'd said. "Not you." My heart clenched. It was too much all at once, and I was handling it badly.

Archer reached out a hand to my face. "Wherever Tom is, he's only half Monger. We know there's good in him too."

I shifted backward, away from Archer's hand. "There are Mongers here, now, who are taking Descendants. That should be our priority."

But Archer wouldn't let me out of range of his touch, and he twined his fingers through mine with a wry smile. "Because we're the only ones who can find them and save the day?"

I huffed dramatically. "You know what I mean."

Archer's expression became serious again. "Yes, I do. Your self-sufficiency has become a finely-tuned sense of responsibility, which I share."

"I don't," Ringo smirked, "but I'm not lettin' either of ye do yer rescuin' without me."

I shot him a perfect twelve-year-old sneer, and he crossed his eyes back at me. Because sometimes adolescent behavior is a necessary part of one's repertoire, and at least it lightened the mood.

Archer gave me a pointed look. "But we have allies in the search for the missing Descendants – people to help share the burden and responsibility of it."

I finished the part of his sentence that he didn't say. "And if we locate Tom, we're the only ones who can go back for him."

Archer didn't even need to agree. I saw the certainty of it in his eyes. I sighed. "Okay, fine. But I'm going to London tomorrow to find the brother and sister who witnessed Tam's kidnapping. They must have seen something that could help us out. The Armans are back from Paris and they've invited Mom and I to tea, so we can detour to the address Olivia gave us before that."

Archer gave me a sharp look. "Jeeves will drive you?"

I barely held back an eye-roll. "As if he'd let anyone else drive Lady Elian anywhere."

Archer schooled the concern out of his expression and stood to help me up. "Be careful, Saira."

I knew what it cost him not to mention the fact that it would be daytime, so he couldn't go with me even if he wanted to. I kissed him lightly on the lips. "Last one back's a rotten egg."

Because sometimes adolescent behavior is the only thing that trumps fear.

A Trap

After we got back to the manor house, Archer left us to go back into London. He wanted to scout Olivia's friends' address before we went, and would stay the day at Bishop Cleary's unless there was a problem. He and Ringo discussed random car stuff that Ringo had helped Jeeves do to service the Aston Martin, and then they made a plan to explore St. Brigid's before school went back into session. The mood I was in, I could barely follow their conversations, much less contribute more than a distracted goodbye kiss when Archer drove away.

Ringo turned to head toward the library, and I followed him. The big room had floor-to-ceiling bookshelves, complete with wheeled ladders and massive wooden tables, and was one of my favorite rooms in the manor.

When the door was closed behind us Ringo turned to me. "Okay, spit it out."

I almost denied anything was wrong, but the look on his face was already impatient so I didn't bother sugar-coating it.

"I don't want to find Tom."

He crossed his arms in front of him. "Why not?"

"Because if he's bad, Archer will kill him."

"Not if the cure works and 'e can become 'uman again."

My voice dropped to a whisper. "I don't know if I want Archer to try the cure."

Ringo stared at me in shock. "But 'e wants it."

"There are risks—"

"There are always risks, and ye know it. Saira, ye can't deny 'im this. If 'e's willin' to take the chance, ye 'ave to support 'im."

"What happens to me if something goes wrong?" I could barely get the words out.

He looked me straight in the eyes. "Ye'd go on and live the life ye were meant to live." Ringo gripped my upper arms and made me look at him. "Ye 'aven't told 'im any of yer fears, 'ave ye?"

I shook my head no.

"Good. Ye can't."

"Why not? We're supposed to share things that matter to us. He'd understand."

Ringo let go of my arms and ran his hands through his hair. "Saira, it's like the man who admits to 'avin' an affair. The admission makes 'im feel better for tellin' the truth, but 'e 'ands it to 'is wife to carry around as 'er own. It isn't fair. Ye know Archer'll never do a thing to 'urt you, so ye get to walk around feelin' just fine, but what 'e wants gets buried in makin' sure yer 'appy. Ye don't get to tell 'im this one. I'm tellin' ye, it isn't fair."

I really didn't want to hear this, not from Ringo, not at all. I spun away and headed toward the door. But guilt made me angry and I turned back to him. "You didn't fight for Charlie, and now you're telling me I can't fight for Archer? Go wipe your conscience on someone else, Ringo, because *that's* not fair."

The door was too heavy for me to slam behind me effectively, but it wouldn't have made anything better anyway. I passed Sanda on the landing as I raced up the stairs to my room.

"It's hard t' outrun yerself, lass."

I wanted to keep going until I could shut myself away in my room, but somehow I couldn't do that to Sanda. I turned to face her. "What about fear. Can you outrun that?"

"Only if ye stand still and face it do ye have a chance against fear."

I made myself square my shoulders and walk the rest of the way to my room.

After a couple of hours of very fitful sleep, I finally gave up the idea of rest as a waste of time. It was still dark outside, and I guessed dawn was only about an hour away. I dressed quickly and slipped down the hall to the other wing where Ringo slept.

I knew he'd hear me the minute I opened his door, so I didn't bother knocking. His eyes were open and looking at me as I sat on the end of his bed.

"I'm sorry," I whispered.

He looked at me in silence for a long moment. "Ye lash out when yer scared, ye know? Like a wild thing, ye are."

"It wasn't right, what I said about Charlie. And I'm so sorry I said it."

He finally sighed and sat up, wrestled the bedside light on, and scrubbed his palms across his eyes. "Wipe *my* conscience?" he scoffed. "Ye pick an ungodly time to wipe yers, ye wench."

I bit back my smile. We were good, but I still tread carefully. "I think about Charlie all the time, and how she's doing as Valerie Grayson's protégé. No matter how clever Charlie is, the sixteenth century isn't easy to navigate, and Henry Grayson's death in France hurt his mother in ways I can't even imagine."

I tried to picture what it would be like to live in a noble house in Tudor times. Hygiene issues alone were enough to send me running, not to mention court politics and Immortal Descendant intrigue. I shuddered.

"Charlie's braver than I know how to be."

"Ye might say that. Though sometimes bein' alone becomes what ye know, and choosin' otherwise is the 'ard part."

I looked into his gray eyes and saw the pain in them. "Did she run away from a life with you, or run toward one with Valerie?"

He watched me for a long moment, then finally shrugged. "Doesn't much matter, does it? We'll either find each other in the end, or we won't."

"How can you be pragmatic about that, Ringo? It sounds so lonely."

He smiled gently. "We've all been alone in our lives. Ye've 'ad yer mum, but ye've only relied on yerself. I 'ad a mum for five years, and Archer never 'ad a mum at all. But all of us 'ave known what it is to be loved, and that makes us lucky. But the thing about love is it's like the wild thing ye are – when ye 'old on tight ye frighten it away, but when ye open yer 'ands and yer 'eart and trust it, ye can always find it no matter 'ow far it flies."

"I trust Archer."

"No, ye don't. If ye did, ye would trust 'im to do what 'e needs to do for 'imself, and ye'd take yer own fears out of it."

I looked away from his eyes and searched the room for something else to focus on that didn't see me so clearly. There were bookshelves against every wall, and they were bursting with books and parts of electronics. Tools covered the desk under the window, and a diagram of an engine was pinned to a corkboard. "What are you going to do with your life?"

"Learn everything I can."

"And then?" I looked back at him curiously.

"I'll know when I've done it, I think."

I nodded and stood up to go. "I'm sorry about before."

He smirked at me. "But not sorry about wakin' me?"

"Nope. My conscience is all clean now."

He hurled a pillow at me and I ducked out of the way, laughing, before I left his room.

My mom agreed to leave a little early for our tea with the Armans so we could stop by the address in Pimlico where Tam's friends lived. I could tell Jeeves didn't like it, but he just clenched his jaw and took us into town.

I told my mom what Mr. Shaw and Connor had said about the cure, and she'd already heard much of it from Mr. Shaw directly. She said he'd been proud of Connor for discovering the telomere anomaly, and it had set them on a whole new course of research. Even better, they weren't focused on mixing Descendant blood anymore, so the Council couldn't condone Monger action against either of them.

"The Mongers have to be stopped, though, Mom. You guys can't let them be the Descendant police force."

She frowned. "We know that, Saira. As I told you, it's one of the things I've been discussing with Camille, and we hope to engage MacKenzie in as well."

"The Shifter Head seems like kind of a bully."

She smirked because it was true. The current Head of the Shifter clans was a Highland Bull, and everything about him screamed it. "He is, but one of his sons seems reasonable."

The car glided to a stop in front of a small mews house. In the eighteenth and nineteenth centuries, rich Londoners lived in terraced houses with mews at the back which opened onto a small service street. The mews included horse stables, a carriage house, and upstairs living quarters for the stable staff. The advent of cars and the world wars saw the end of stables, and they were eventually converted into housing called mews houses after the original King's Mews at Charing Cross where the king's falcons were kept. Ringo had been the source of that information, though in his thieving days the mews were still smelly horse stables at the backs of the grand houses.

Olivia's words ran through my mind as I walked up to the front door. Her friend Melanie Thomas and Melanie's older brother, Cole, were distantly related to Tam through his mom. They had all been at St. George's Square park when a lady's little dog got off leash, and Tam crossed over to the river side to help her. The next thing Cole and Melanie saw, a white van with no windows screeched to a stop in front of them, blocking their view of Tam and the woman. After a few moments, the van sped away. Neither the woman, her dog, nor Tam was seen again.

"What do you know about these two?" my mom asked quietly as I rang the bell.

"Nothing of any substance."

Jeeves stood outside the car like a statue, and I knew that if I'd been inside the house, the sight of him outside would have kept me indoors and away from windows. "Hey, Jeeves. Could you take the car for a spin around the block, please? You're pretty intimidating in your uniform."

He looked startled at that, but my mom smiled and nodded her agreement, and he reluctantly got back in the Range Rover and pulled away down the narrow cobblestone street. When the car was finally out of sight, I rang the bell again. This time I heard someone on the staircase, and a moment later the door opened cautiously. A black guy about my age, built like a broody Adam, looked at us with suspicion.

"Hey," I said with a nod. "Sorry about the driver."

"Who are you?" Despite his surly tone, there was a rolling West African lilt to his voice that sounded much nicer than his words.

"Friend of a friend. Is Melanie in?"

His eyes narrowed. "Why?"

Something about the guy annoyed me, but I knew that was just unreasonable, so I added a smile to soften the snark he inspired in me. "Because I'm here to talk to both of you about what you didn't tell the police about Tam. It's just easier if I don't have to repeat myself."

My mom tsked next to me. "Saira, that's just rude."

The guy I assumed was Cole tossed his head at my mom without looking away from me. "She your mum?"

"Yeah."

"Why'd you bring her?"

I shrugged. "Because she's the Clocker Head and Tam's not the only one who's gone missing."

I knew I was taking a calculated risk, but if I was right and this guy knew anything at all about the Families, he'd know better than to shut the door in my mom's face.

32

The guy did shut the door in our faces. Not slammed. Shut. And just when my mom was about to ring the bell again in impatience, I held her arm. "No, wait. They're coming."

The door opened again, and a girl about fourteen with short braided hair pulled on her coat and led the way outside. She held out her hand for me to shake. "I'm Melanie. Who are you?" Her West African lilt was softer than her brother's.

"Saira Elian. I'm a friend of Olivia's from school." I shook her hand and Cole followed his sister outside.

Melanie started off down the street. "Come on. We'll talk in the park."

My mom gave me a startled grin. I just shrugged and followed Melanie as she headed toward the river. St. George's Square was a block away. Melanie waved to some nannies playing with toddlers at the far end, away from the street, but except for them, the park was deserted. Cole slouched along behind us – keeping his distance, but clearly not letting his sister out of his sight. According to Olivia, Tam and Cole were the ones who hung out together, but Melanie was taking the lead with us.

We got to a bench and Melanie directed us to sit. She looked at my mom with interest. "Why do you care about Tam?"

My mom ignored the question. "Where is Tam's family? Have they gone to the police?"

Melanie shot her a look with a snort attached to it. "He doesn't have family. Just a dad who's a drunk. Me and Cole, we're his people."

Mom opened her mouth to speak, but I cut her off. "Like I told your brother, he's not the only one who's gone missing."

Melanie shifted her gaze to me. "The police act like he's a runaway."

"Look, we're trying to find the missing people. Olivia sent us to talk to you because she's really worried about Tam and she knows we can help. But we need to know whatever you can tell us about that day."

33

This girl had a way about her that wasn't exactly suspicious, but definitely wary. Both she and her brother stood like they were ready to bolt, but defiantly, as if running would be a choice, not a reaction. From our seat on the bench I could see Jeeves drive the Range Rover slowly by the park, and I realized he must be looking for us. I suddenly felt guilty for having sent him away.

Melanie considered me for a moment longer, then finally spoke. "The lady with the dog – she tried to get me and Cole to help her look too. She was actually pretty adamant about it when she called to us across the street right before the white van pulled up."

I stared at her. "Are you guys mixed?"

Cole finally spoke, and his tone was angry. "Race, or blood?"

I opened my mouth to try to pull my foot out of it, but Melanie got up angrily. "Why'd you have to go and ask that?" She stalked away from the bench, but I finally found my voice and stepped in front of Cole before he could follow her.

"I don't care about race. I'm mixed-blood. That's why I asked. And Tam is too, isn't he? Olivia said he was part-Seer. If he is actually mixed, it could be why he was taken. And if you guys are too, you could still be in danger."

Cole glared at me. "We're done here." He pushed past me and ran after his sister. Mom grabbed my hand so I couldn't follow. "Let them go, Saira. They're scared."

The black Range Rover cruised past again, and I waved to it. "Poor Jeeves has been circling the park, looking for us. Let's put him out of his misery."

I held her hand as we walked back to the street. I hadn't done that since I was a kid and it felt comforting and solid, like she had my back and I had hers. The Range Rover slowed to a stop and she got into the back seat first. I had my mouth open to apologize to Jeeves as I shut the door behind me, but the words died in my throat as a wave of Monger-gut hit me like a sledgehammer.

Seth Walters smiled at me from the passenger seat.

34

MONGER

"Lock the doors," Slick said calmly.

Before I could throw the door open again, Jeeves had hit the master lock and I was trapped.

"Child locks, please." Slick's voice was so casual it made my skin crawl. The click of the child-safety catch made it impossible for me to unlock my door, but worse, it meant Jeeves was doing what Slick wanted without even questioning it.

I tore my eyes away from Slick to glance at my mom, which felt vaguely like looking away from a snake. She was staring at him in a trance-like way, and I wanted to slap her awake - then I saw the ring.

Panic coursed through my veins like wildfire and I started banging on the window, half hoping I could break the glass. I remembered the last time my mom had been under the ring's influence – it was as if she'd been programmed like an automaton. Sanda had said there were rumors the ring could cause a kind of hypnosis that would make people believe and do whatever the wearer told them.

"There's no need for dramatics, Miss Elian. It's bulletproof glass, and you're quite safe in this car." His calm voice made me want to scream. I felt anything but safe.

Wait. I felt anything but safe.

He was telling me to feel safe, but I felt like life sucked more in this moment than possibly any other in a very long time. I looked over at my mom again. She had settled back in her seat and had a pleasant, placid look on her face. Jeeves was driving as if we were all out for a Sunday spin.

And I. Didn't. Feel. Safe.

Did that mean the ring wasn't working on me?

Why wouldn't it work on me?

I stared at Slick, and the smile tightened in the corners of his mouth. We were crossing the Thames on the Vauxhall Bridge in the kind of traffic it's easier to walk through, and when Jeeves finally turned left past the MI5 building, I knew where we were going.

I fought every protective instinct I had about what Slick and his ring had just done to my mom, and I turned away from her to stare out the window. I could tell Slick expected something different from me, but he wasn't going to get it. Not yet. Not until Mom and Jeeves were outside the range of the Monger ring.

The Range Rover finally glided to a stop and Slick spoke in a not-so-pleasant voice. "Get out."

"You first, and then you tell them to go home."

Slick's eyes narrowed fractionally. I guess I'd just busted myself in about a million different ways, but getting my mom and Jeeves to safety came first. I faced him grimly. "Just tell him to take her home as soon as I've left the car. Then shut the door and I'll get out."

"How do I know you won't run?"

I gave him a *don't be an idiot* look. "Because your goons followed us, because this is your 'hood, and because I'm sick of running from you. Just do it, Seth. You know the Clocker Head can't go missing."

He regarded me for a moment longer. "Unlock the doors," he told Jeeves, then he got out of the car and threw a hand signal to the black SUV I'd seen behind us. Before he closed the passenger door, Slick spoke to Jeeves again. "When Saira gets out of the car, take Lady Elian home. Saira went back in time to go find someone, and she's fine." He slammed the door and shot a look at me. "Now you."

I resisted touching my mom's hand when I looked at her. "Bye, Mom."

I did touch Jeeves' shoulder as I got out of the car. I gave it a squeeze like I was trying to wake him up, and he met my eyes for a bare second in the rear-view mirror as I slid out of the back door. When I'd closed it behind me the Range Rover pulled smoothly away.

Slick stood on the sidewalk like he was daring me to run, which I didn't. I may have ignored the line between bravery and stupidity at times, but this was not one of them. I thought I saw someone resembling Cole at the corner, out of breath. Technically, I guess we'd been stuck in traffic long enough that he could have followed us, and if *he* didn't do anything stupid, like get caught, there would be someone to report where I was. I drew Slick's eyes to me so he wouldn't notice Cole as I looked up at the building that housed his office. The arched windows of the second and third floors gave it the look of a strange monster that peered down at us balefully. Slick's grip on my upper arm was too hard, but I didn't say a word as he pulled me up to the front door, hit a button, glared up at a security camera, and when the lock buzzed open, he escorted me inside.

On my previous visit inside Slick's office building, Ringo and I had skipped the first floor and headed straight for the top. This time I was paying attention to every detail as we made our way to Slick's personal office. He gestured for me to sit across from his desk as if I was a client, and he closed the door behind me. I saw someone's shadow just outside the door and figured the goon squad had arrived.

I mentally ran down what Slick could possibly know about me. I was a Clocker, obviously, but I didn't think he'd ever seen me actually draw a spiral, so he probably thought I was like most Clockers who needed a pre-existing one in order to Clock. He knew I could run, which I'd done on Tower Bridge when I'd lost the

Monger goon he sent after me, and one of his guys had seen me as a Cougar at Elian Manor, but Archer said they'd kept me out of the guy's sight when I'd returned to my human form. I wasn't wearing the Shifter Bone right now because … a Cougar in London. Yeah, no. But at this moment, I had a very strong desire for my Cat's claws and Slick's face to meet up and have a party.

Slick was studying me as if I was something that baffled him. He looked a little like Daniel Craig from the James Bond movies in his expensive suit, and I thought he might be considered handsome if it weren't for all the ugliness in his eyes.

"Where's my son?" he asked.

Of everything I expected to come out of Seth Walters' mouth, that was only slightly less surprising than an apology and an offer for tea would have been. I fought down an instant, boiling anger, just so I didn't lose any tiny advantage I might have by saying something stupid.

"Dead," I said.

"No, he's not."

Wasn't Slick just full of surprises today? "How do you know?"

"I know."

The simple certainty with which he spoke sent a chill down my spine that had nothing to do with the Monger-gut I was currently wracked with in his presence.

"Where are all the Descendants you've taken?" Since he wasn't making sense, I decided to throw a non-sequitur at him for variety.

He smiled slowly. "Why don't we trade?"

Huh?

The slime in his voice practically coated the walls. "You get me what I want, and I'll give you your missing mixed-bloods."

"They *are* all mixed," I breathed.

He sneered. "They're abominations."

"We're *people*. Abominations are things that are hated and reviled. You know … like you."

Sass was clearly winning over don't-say-anything-stupid, and I could practically see Slick's temper build. He spoke through gritted teeth.

"Mixed-bloods are aberrations. Their skills are abnormal, they don't behave or respond like proper Descendants, and even their Families don't acknowledge them."

Something was starting to chime in my brain, but the hatred that was beginning to unfurl around the nausea in my guts obscured it. I tamped the hatred down firmly so it didn't take over.

"How'd you find them?" I managed to keep my tone almost totally even.

"When you stole my genealogy, we had to start from scratch. Modern birth certificates in the internet age are so much more helpful in determining parentage than old church records were, and frankly, anyone who opposed us with the Council was fair game. Of course, capturing mixed-bloods required a bit more brute force than it would with someone less abberant." He played with the dagger-shaped letter opener on his desk, the Monger ring winking at me like a malevolent eye.

"It's remarkable, really," he continued, "the amount of interbreeding that has occurred over the past hundred years. You people rut like bloody rabbits."

"Pot. Kettle." I said under my breath. My ability to be cautious had flown out the window with my patience, and as I stared at the ring, a lightbulb suddenly exploded in my brain. Slick said mixed-bloods were aberrant – that we didn't respond like proper Descendants. Respond? It was an odd enough word choice that I flung caution to the wind and tried something risky. "So, is every mixed-blood immune to the ring, or just me?"

Clearly, that was a mistake. I wasn't sure it was possible for Slick to get any scarier, but it happened. Right before my eyes. It was almost as if his Mongerness got bigger, and then rolled off him in sickening waves that filled the room like a noxious stench. I felt myself shrinking in my seat under his glare and had to anchor myself so I didn't run away screaming.

"We're done here." The way he said it made me seriously consider that he could take me out back and have me shot.

"You wanted something from me." I tried not to squeak in fear, but I wasn't sure I was successful.

"No, you're not ready to have that conversation. You need to understand the gravity of your situation before you realize how badly you want to work for me."

"Why do you want Tom? What could he possibly mean to you?"

Rage flashed in Slick's eyes. "Your petty Council politics will play right into my hands. And when it's time to shift the power to us, Tom will stand with me. His skills set him apart and make him someone to fear." Slick's grin was entirely too gleeful for my taste. "He has my blood."

"Which made him one of those *aberrations* you hate so much, and which you didn't mind spilling when you shot him!" I lashed back. Apparently, all my self-preservation instincts had fled too.

Slick's voice turned icy. "My grandfather once beat my father so badly when he was a child that my father vomited blood for a week. My father passed along the favor to his son. Tom knew my history. He knew the family tradition of blooding our children, and I believe he'd tell you he got off lightly to have only been shot in the arm."

"You don't know anything about Tom!"

"I know half his blood is mine!" he hissed. All of Slick's rage and venom suddenly put Archer's desire to find Tom in a new light. Half of Tom's blood came from the vicious man who sat in front of me, the same man who had finally succeeded in kidnapping me and who was the Monger Family enforcer. That blood now ran in the veins of a Vampire – essentially immortal and immeasurably strong, with Sight and Clocking skills. I couldn't imagine that Slick even knew about those skills, but if he ever got his hands on them …

Slick yelled at the goon outside the door, making me jump. "Watts!"

40

The door opened and an improbably tall Asian guy stepped into the room. Slick's voice was sharp and angry. "Cuff her hands behind her and take her to the museum."

I tried not to show him how very terrifying the words "cuff her" were to me, but he saw something on my face that made him smile. "Oh, little girl, if I really wanted to hobble you I could shoot out your kneecap or take off a foot. Try to run, and I will reconsider my leniency. For now I'll content myself with your eminent discomfort."

He waved a dismissive hand, and in a matter of seconds, my wrists were zip-tied behind my back and I was stumbling out of the office ahead of Watts. When the office door closed behind us I actually considered hurling myself headfirst down the stairs in hopes that I could summersault fast enough to get out the door before they caught me. With no hands, I couldn't hope to draw a spiral, and that escape hatch had been the ace in the hole that kept me calm in front of Slick.

A second goon, even bigger and meaner looking than Watts, met us at the bottom of the stairs. I dubbed him Beefcake, for the face that made a cow pie look good in comparison. He grabbed one arm, Watts took the other, and they frog-marched me to the back of one of those windowless white vans into which children disappear, never to be seen again. I hated those vans on principle.

The streetlights were conveniently out, and it was dark enough outside that I doubted I'd been seen by anyone when I was unceremoniously hurled inside the van. And when my ankles were zip-tied, and I was covered by a blanket that smelled like dog poop, I developed a gut-sink of epic proportions

It was well past tea time, and I assumed the Armans had gotten worried and called someone at Elian Manor. Connor knew where I'd gone, and he might check with Cole and Melanie, but whether Cole had actually managed to follow us across the bridge and would tell him, I didn't know.

Part of me wanted to just roll with this and see where they took me. Maybe "the museum" was where they were holding the other mixed-bloods they'd taken. Maybe someone there would have something sharp enough to cut through the zip tie and I could get us all out. And maybe the two huge guys in charge of my discomfort were sweet mama's boys who wouldn't hurt a fly, much less an eighteen-year-old girl, hog-tied like a pig for slaughter.

The van lurched as the screech of tires and a horrific smash of metal on metal filled my ears. One of the goons swore impressively as the van hit something that sent me crashing into the back of the seat. I heard the front doors fly open, and then the sound of something impacting with flesh.

I struggled to sit upright in the cargo area of the van, but the blanket had tangled around my head and shoulders, and panic made it hard to breathe.

A gunshot rang out – a very rare sound in a country where handguns were illegal – and then a voice I knew like my own called my name. "Saira!"

"Archer! I'm here!"

Sirens sounded in the distance. People were shouting, and suddenly the back doors of the van were thrown open, and sounds of wet gasps filled the space. The blanket was dragged off my head and then Archer collapsed next to me.

"No!" I couldn't reach him. My hands were still locked behind my back, the plastic zip tie cutting into my wrists as I tried to yank free. His eyes closed, and the wet-sounding breaths came from a gunshot wound in his chest. A fatal wound.

He was dying. "Archer! Stay with me." It wasn't just the chest wound though, it was everything. Every bloody gash, every trauma, every wound I'd ever seen him get bloomed on his body as it fought to close the hole in his chest. There was no blood left in his skin – it leaked out of his ribs, impaled on Wilder' sword, his stomach where a knife had gone in, his face, from his Tower fall, and even his neck where Wilder had torn into his skin to infect him with his plague.

I lost my ability to reason as I struggled to get to him, crying his name, tearing at the skin on my wrists to free them from the bonds.

Someone held my arms and I thrashed against them. The only thing I could see was Archer, dying in front of me. Tears and snot and screams flew from my face as I fought to get away from whoever held me back from him.

The zip tie was cut and I practically fell on his body with the force of my freedom. I could feel his heart beating. I could feel a rasping breath at my neck. But he didn't move, and he didn't open his eyes.

I didn't let go of him until a growling Bear voice pricked its way through the sounds of my sobbing. "Saira," said Mr. Shaw, quietly. "Let me take him."

I looked up at Mr. Shaw's worried face. "He can't go to a hospital," I whispered.

"I know," he said. "I've got this. But the police are coming. You'll need to give a statement. Can you do that without me?" Mr. Shaw was wrapping the stinking blanket around Archer's body as he spoke to me.

"It was Seth," I said, my voice oddly dull in my ears.

"I know. Archer talked to the kids."

I started to shake, and tears ran down my cheeks.

Mr. Shaw looked out the front window of the van. "I'm shocked he lives."

I followed his gaze and saw the crumpled remains of Archer's beautiful silver Aston Martin that had been t-boned by the van. Watts was slumped over the steering wheel, while Beefcake lay unmoving on the sidewalk.

Emergency vehicles with flashing lights mesmerized me as they came screaming down the block toward us.

A ragged sob caught in my throat, and Mr. Shaw kissed my hair. "I need to take him away from here," he whispered. I nodded, and he gathered Archer's blanket-wrapped body into his arms and climbed out of the van.

Mr. Shaw used the chaos of the vehicles to slip down a side street and out of sight, while I took a deep breath, choked past the lingering sob in my chest, and wrapped my bloody wrists around my knees to wait.

CONNECTIONS

Hours passed in a blur as I told and re-told my story to the police. Almost all of it was true, except for the parts that weren't. But it was easy enough to paint myself as yet another victim of the seemingly unrelated kidnappings, at least as far as Scotland Yard was concerned. I didn't even have to edit much of the conversation I'd had with Slick. Seth Walters was now a person of interest to the police, as was the unknown driver of the wrecked Aston Martin with false registration papers. I was going to miss that car.

The goon that survived – Watts – was in a coma, so he wasn't available to comment on where they'd been taking me. Slick's statement about "the museum" sent a bunch of police scurrying to call museum security at all the major ones in London, but no one had seen anything, and we were no closer to knowing where the mixed-bloods were being held. I left Melanie and Cole out of my recounting of the events. They had helped Archer find me.

My ankles were freed, and my wrists had been wrapped in gauze bandages by a paramedic, but I itched to unwrap them and put Mr. Shaw's green medicine on before the wounds closed up. Actually, I was just itching to get to Mr. Shaw. It had taken some concentration to answer the detectives' questions through the voice in my head that was screaming at me to make sure Archer was okay, but finally, they seemed satisfied they'd wrung every ounce of detail they could from me. Either that, or they were sick of Millicent and wanted us both gone.

Millicent Elian had come to my rescue. There was no other way to describe how she'd swept into the police station and parked herself by my side. She sold herself as my grandmother – responsible for me while my mother was ill. The look we shared on that statement told me she knew Mom had been tampered with, and they were dealing with it. My fears for my mother got tucked into the locked room in my brain where the voice screamed about Archer. It was almost a relief to shut the door on them both while I was being questioned.

We were escorted out by Police Constable Grant, a handsome black guy with a smooth voice and a very easy way about him. He held the door for Millicent, then shook my hand gently. His eyes widened slightly at the touch, as if he'd just sensed something about me, and he looked serious when he spoke. "If there's anything you need help with, even the things you didn't tell us – come find me."

It was my turn to be surprised, but I covered it with a nod. "Thank you."

I could feel his eyes on my back as we left the station, and I knew PC Grant understood that there may be things he didn't know, but not knowing a thing didn't make it any less real.

Millicent got behind the wheel of the Rolls that had been illegally parked in front of the police station but was completely without citation, which didn't shock me. I slid into the front seat next to her and leaned my head back with a bone-deep shudder.

"Are you injured beyond your wrists, Saira?"

I shook my head. "No. Just tired of keeping it together."

She looked over at me with something that looked suspiciously like tenderness and touched my arm gently. "You're safe now. You can let go."

Maybe it was kindness from Millicent, or maybe it was just the horrific events of the day draining out of me in the form of salt water, but I managed to cry almost the whole way back to Elian Manor.

When I could finally breathe without gasping, I thanked Millicent. She kept her eyes on the road as she turned down the long drive to the manor house.

"I believe that's the first time you've ever thanked me," she said softly.

I stared at her in the dim light from the dashboard and realized she was right. "Thank you for taking me in when Mom left me. Thank you for taking me to St. Brigid's, and for telling me truths that my mother hadn't." Her eyes had gotten moist and I took a deep breath. "And thank you for giving me and my friends a safe place to come home to."

"You're welcome," she said simply. She parked the Rolls outside the garage and turned to me. "Robert took your young man into the keep. We can move a bed in for you to stay with him if you'd like. I'll go check on your mother and Jeeves. Liz is with them in the library, and I'll have Sanda bring you food. Is there anything else that needs to be done?"

I was trying really hard not to let my expression show how stunned I was, and I deliberately softened my voice. "I need to talk to everyone about the things I learned from Seth Walters."

She nodded and gripped my hand tightly for a second. "We'll come as soon as we can."

I gripped her fingers back. "Thank you."

She gave me a quick smile and we got out of the car to go our separate ways in the manor. I was absurdly grateful for the swarm of canine love I was greeted with. It was one of the benefits of having Connor's family at Elian Manor – a pack of dogs happy to see me, no matter how crappy my day had been. I knelt down and gave Natasha, Connor's red dog, an extra hug before I opened the kitchen door. It was good to be home.

I headed straight for the keep, where the sight of Archer lying on a thin mattress on the big table nearly erased whatever peace I'd managed to find. His battered face now had yellow bruises and old scabs in place of the bloody, pulpy mess I'd seen a few hours before. And his chest rose and fell without the wet, sucking sound of a gunshot wound.

Ringo sat by his head sporting a bandaged arm and a worried expression as his eyes darted between Archer's sleeping face and my terrified one.

"You gave him blood?" I asked. He nodded mutely.

Mr. Shaw bustled into the keep behind me carrying a box of what looked like medical supplies. He stopped in his tracks as I turned to him, then dropped the box and held his arms open to me. Pure instinct had me rushing into them, and he held me as if it was more his need than mine that put me there.

"We've all been a little mad with worry for you," he said.

"I'm fine. Millicent rescued me."

He chuckled as he finally let me go. "I've never seen her move so fast in my life. I didn't even know she could drive a car, much less that she was any good at it, but she was in the Rolls and down the drive before I'd even finished telling them where I'd left you."

I looked over at Archer's sleeping form. "Thank you for bringing him back."

"I won't lie to you, Saira he was in rough shape. I've seen what you mean now about the old wounds resurfacing. To be frank, it makes me want to lock you both up in a tower and throw away the key, for all the danger you've been in."

I smirked a little at that. I knew how Archer had gotten hurt, because I'd been present for most of his injuries. But taken all together it looked like he played on freeways, dodging traffic for fun and sucking at it.

Mr. Shaw continued quietly. "There were enough injuries still repairing themselves that we could have tried the virus on him."

I looked sharply at him, my stomach suddenly full of razorblades.

He shook his head. "We didn't, though Ringo said Archer wants the cure."

Some of those razorblades flew out of my eyes at Ringo. His look back said he'd fight me if he had to, but he was too tired and worried to get up and start it.

I turned back to Mr. Shaw. "You've seen him at his weakest. Can you honestly tell me you're sure he'd survive something that turns off the only thing that has kept him alive through all those injuries? What if you turn it off and he has to survive every one of those injuries again? You know there's no way a normal human would live through that."

He looked at me for what felt like several lifetimes before he finally spoke again. "You're right. I have no idea the severity or scope of the injuries from which he would have to heal if we turned off the super-charged telomerase."

I waited for something more, some defense of his work, but although he opened his mouth to say something else, nothing came out. "Yeah, that's what I thought."

I went over to Archer's side and Ringo got up from his seat. He didn't look at me when he told Mr. Shaw to call him if Archer needed more blood. It hurt me that Ringo left without meeting my eyes, but it hurt me more that he would have been okay playing roulette with Archer's life. I looked up at Mr. Shaw. "You don't have to call him for blood. I can give whatever Archer needs."

He shook his head. "No, actually, you can't."

I stared at him. "I did before— in France."

"He can ingest your blood because it breaks down differently in his digestive tract, but he can't be transfused with it, which is what he needs. Despite the mutation, he's still a Seer, and your Clocker and Shifter blood doesn't mix."

"Are you sure? Because Wilder got Clocking skills from my mom's blood."

Mr. Shaw's voice turned hard. "Do you really want to find that out now? In his condition?"

"I don't know, it seems like you were thinking about injecting him with an untested viral cure *in his condition*." I should have bitten

49

back the words, but I was too tired, and the last of the fear-induced adrenaline had left me shaky.

But Mr. Shaw didn't see the bags under my eyes, or my trembling hands. He only heard the bitter words, and his eyes narrowed dangerously. "Saira, when I got Archer here he was unconscious and couldn't drink. Ringo was the one person in this house I could safely ask for enough transfused blood to keep him alive. Ringo jumped at the chance to help his friend, and you just treated him like he held a knife to Archer's throat. You accuse us of playing fast and loose with Archer's life, and yet somehow your love and care is worth more than any of ours? Grow up, Saira, you're not the only one with something to lose."

Mr. Shaw ignored my shocked expression and left the keep.

"Well, that was interesting."

I spun back to face Archer, who slowly cracked his eyelids.

"I pissed him off," I said as exhaustion coursed through me. I shouldn't have had any tears left to cry after the marathon session in the car, but apparently my eyeballs didn't get the memo. I sat, dully, and resisted touching him because he still looked so hurt. "And Ringo, and probably Connor by now too. The only person who isn't mad at me at the moment is – inexplicably – Millicent."

"He sounded more worried than angry. Much like a parent whose child just ran in front of a car."

I choked back a sob at his feeble attempt at a joke, and Archer cracked a tiny smile. The sight of it made my heart do backflips in my chest and I wiped my eyes messily. "How do you feel?"

"Like I got hit by a truck."

A fresh wave of slightly hysterical teary laughter hit for a second. "You did. Well, a van, actually. What were you thinking?" I smoothed the hair away from his forehead, and bits of dried blood flaked off with it.

"That I couldn't lose you."

"I would have Clocked out eventually."

"Your wrists were zip-tied behind you. There's no Clocking from the bottom of the Thames without hands."

He coughed, and then winced at the pain. I held my hand on his shoulder as if I could transfer healing through the bandage on his chest to the wound beneath. He looked around, and his voice was hoarse when he spoke again. "I feel like I'm somebody's offering to the Gods."

My bark of choked laughter made him smile again. "I'm sure it made sense at the time."

He looked at me through serious eyes. "I'm sorry."

"For what? Almost dying? I'm not sure I'm ready to forgive that yet." I was only joking a little bit.

"He took you, and there was nothing I could do to stop it."

I stared at him. "That's not on you!"

"I wasn't there." A weird anguish trembled in his voice.

"It was daytime. You couldn't be."

"Exactly." The word was dull and dead-sounding, and I wanted to shake some life into it.

"Archer, we've had this conversation before. I don't do stupid stuff during the day when you can't be there. This wasn't dangerous. I was with Mom and Jeeves and we were going to fricking tea!"

My voice broke and Archer looked instantly worried. "What did Walters do to them? Shaw called Cleary, and the minute I woke up he sent me to find you."

"The ring." I said. "He used the Monger ring on them. It was like they were both in a trance, and they did whatever he told them to do."

"He didn't use it on you?"

I shook my head. "I think he tried to, but it didn't work on me. I don't know why. He said something that made me wonder, so I asked him if it was just me or any mixed-blood and he got so angry—" Archer struggled to sit up. "Wait, what are you doing? You can't get up yet." I tried to push him back down to his makeshift bed, but he swung his legs over the side and sat, panting slightly, on the edge of the table.

"Help me to the sofa." His breath came harder, but it wasn't wet or bubbly-sounding, so short of pushing him back, I had no choice. I got my shoulder under his arm and helped him to the Victorian-style settee. He sat heavily, then arranged himself so there was room for me.

"Tell me everything."

So I did. He held my hand and looked into my eyes, and I shared every detail with him. And somehow the sharing of it took some of the weight away, like he was there to carry an end anytime it got too heavy for me to carry alone.

By the time I had finished the telling, I was curled next to Archer and the last thing I remembered was him stroking my hair and saying he loved me. I thought I heard the door open and Archer's voice rumble in his chest, but I was so deeply asleep it felt like dreams.

I snapped awake just before dawn, which I knew only because Archer told me he had to sleep.

"Are you better?" I asked.

"I will be when I see you tonight."

"Thank you."

I could feel him smile as he drifted off to sleep, and I carefully uncurled myself from his side and locked the door to the keep behind me.

BREAKING THE SPELL

I found Ringo in the library, up on a ladder, looking through old World War II books.

"He's sleeping," I said when I came in. I handed him up a cup of coffee with lots of fresh cream and sugar, and he took a satisfied sip.

"Peace offerin' or bribe?" He came down the ladder and sat on the edge of the table.

"Peace."

He nodded once. "Accepted."

"Thank you for giving him blood." I searched his face. He looked tired and pale, but otherwise unscathed from his donation.

He shrugged. "Ye do what needs doin'."

"Archer's right. We have to find Tom," I said.

Ringo's eyebrows arched up in surprise. "What changed yer mind?"

"Seth Walters wants him. He's willing to trade kidnapped mixed-bloods for him," I said.

He narrowed his eyes. "Ye wouldn't be tradin' Tom back to that monster."

"Clearly not. But what's so important about him that Slick would make that kind of deal? It seemed like he thought he could take over control of the Council if he had Tom with him, like they'd be afraid of Tom's power. And how does Slick know he's still alive anyway?"

Ringo looked thoughtful for a long moment as he sipped his coffee. "'E's got the mixed-bloods for sure, then?"

I ran down the same conversation I'd had with Archer the night before, and Ringo looked a little sick when I described the crumpled remains of the Aston Martin and the condition of Archer's body when he collapsed in the back of the van.

"It's good that Walters is on the run at the moment, but 'e should be banned from Council. And if it really was yer mixed blood that kept ye safe from that ring and its power to compel, then rescuin' those other mixed-bloods and bringin' them out of the woodwork is the key to leashin' the Mongers."

I stared at him. "That's it! That's why he's been taking mixed-bloods! They can't be controlled with the ring. This is huge, Ringo, because it means there's a way to stop the Mongers."

His eyebrows rose in surprise and he regarded me for a long moment. "It's an interestin' theory, but the only thing ye know for sure is that the ring didn't work on ye."

"But it makes sense, doesn't it? The Mongers want power and control. They get power when they can control the Families, but if mixed-bloods are unaffected by the ring, they can't be controlled."

He didn't look convinced. "What's to stop Walters from just killin' all 'is prisoners, if they are still prisoners? I mean that many mixed-bloods on the open market, and 'e'll 'ave problems tellin' anyone what to do."

"That would be mass murder."

Ringo scoffed and tossed his head at the World War II book on the table. "I've been readin' yer 'istory. Ye've 'eard of the frog in the water theory of war, right?"

"Throw a frog in a pot of boiling water and he jumps right out?" I said.

Ringo finished. "But put 'im in cold water and turn up the 'eat slowly, 'e'll stay in that pot until 'e dies."

"I know that's what Hitler did, but what does that have to do with the Mongers?"

"Ye ever 'eard of a little thing called the Mixed-Blood Moratorium? Or 'ow about the Death Edict for Vampires – technically, they're mixed too since ye 'ave to be a Descendent to be infected." He looked me straight in the eyes. "The 'eat's been being turned up for 'undreds of years. Killin' a whole slew o' mixed-bloods would just be bringin' the water to boil."

It was after dinner when we all finally met in the library. I had slept for a couple more hours, then spent a few hours working with my mom according to Liz's instructions. Speak slowly. Tell her what really happened. Don't get frustrated when she goes blank or doesn't remember.

I had been in medieval France when they brought my mom out of the Monger ring daze the first time, when she and Millicent had been hit with Slick's words in the Council meeting, and I had no idea it was so hard. Liz said that this time seemed worse, so the effects might be cumulative, and I couldn't imagine what it would feel like to have my will pre-empted like that. I thought we'd made some headway though, because her eyes cleared at one point and she suddenly realized it was me sitting in front of her.

"Saira! You're safe!"

"Yeah, Mom – I'm here," I said, grabbing her hand.

Then she lapsed back into her dreamy state. "Of course you're safe. He said you would be."

I left her room soon after that and Millicent took my place. She squeezed my hand briefly as she went into the bedroom, and I was ridiculously grateful for that touch.

Connor was already in the library, looking hollow-eyed and a little lost when I arrived.

"How's Jeeves?" I asked.

His eyes focused slowly, but he finally answered. "Did you know his first name is Mason? That's what my mum calls him when she sits in front of him, holds his hands, and tells him things that are true."

"What kind of things?" Liz had only just moved her family into Jeeves' flat above the garage during the summer, so it wasn't like she'd known him for very long.

"That she watches him work on the cars and she likes how strong his hands are. She notices all the nice things he does for us, but her favorites are the fresh flowers that magically appear in the kitchen window every week. And she loves that he's teaching me things – things a boy should learn from his fa—" Connor's voice broke and he cleared it wetly. "His father."

I caught his gaze in mine. "How do you feel about that?"

He held my eyes for a long moment before he finally spoke. "I want to shake him and make him wake up to her sitting in front of him. He needs to wake up, Saira. It's not fair—" he cleared his throat again. "It's not fair for Mum to finally find someone, just to have him disappear in front of her eyes."

"I got through to my mom for about a second. Has she been able to reach him at all?"

He shook his head. "I don't know, she hasn't told me. But he's not a Descendant. What if he doesn't come out of it?"

I couldn't answer that, and Ringo saved me from having to try when he came into the room holding a book open to a marked page. "I found the Monger ring!"

Both of us were by his side in a second. Ringo had been with me in Slick's office when we'd taken the genealogy, and he'd actually held the blood red gemstone ring in his hands for a second until I made him put it back. I didn't regret it, because that ring just *felt* nasty, but this wouldn't even be a conversation if I had let him nick it like he wanted to.

Ringo pointed to a drawing of a ring that instantly sent shivers down my spine. It was the same ring we'd seen in Slick's office, and the same one he was wearing when he snake-charmed my mom and Jeeves. Ringo read the description.

"It's called Le Sang du Christ, and it disappeared in 1842."

My limited French was enough to translate. "The Blood of Christ. That's graphic. Disappeared from where?"

"From the Vatican. The Blood of Christ has been in the papal records since about the ninth century."

I stared at Ringo. "The popes had the Monger ring?" It sounded blasphemous to even say it.

He shrugged. "It was part of the Vatican's collection until 1842."

"Do you think the popes actually wore it?" Connor looked horrified.

I snorted. "It might explain a lot — like maybe the Inquisition and the Crusades."

"*If* it's the same ring, how does knowing about it help anything?" Connor's voice was still incredulous.

Ringo answered him. "Because understandin' a thing that makes no sense might just give it edges to grab onto. And if the church 'ad it, they might know 'ow to fight it."

Connor scowled. "Bishop Cleary's Church of England. We don't know any bigwig Catholics."

Ringo and I shared a look, and I knew exactly what he was thinking. I grinned. "We do know a guy…"

Connor's face lost its scoffing grumpiness as he suddenly got it. "The Vampire from France?"

"Where did Bas say he'd be going next?" I asked the guys, but Archer answered from the doorway as he entered the room.

"From France he was continuing his Catholic immersion in England to learn English. But by the time of the Tudors he would have gone to Amsterdam. Why?" Archer's tone was casual and light, but he moved stiffly, like he was still in pain, and I rushed to his side. He kissed me lightly and accepted my help to the sofa.

"Because we need to ask him about the Blood of Christ," I said.

Archer made a wry face. "I'm not sure he ever actually drank that, but you can ask him."

I shook my head at him. "Seriously? You can pun, but you can't dodge bullets? Your self-preservation instincts are a little wonky, my friend." The air in the room felt so much lighter with him in it, and I tucked myself in next to him on the worn leather.

Ringo opened the book and showed Archer. "Le Sang du Christ is the Monger ring. This book describes it as one of the Vatican treasures that went missin' in 1842."

"You're sure it's the same ring?" Archer studied the drawing carefully.

"There's an inscription – just there." Ringo pointed to the inside of the band where two words – oravi and vici - were barely visible. "The ring I held in Walters' office had the words *veni, oravi, vici* engraved inside."

"I came, I spoke, I conquered." Archer said softly.

We all stared at him as the full weight of those three words hit us. I looked at Ringo. "You called it the power to compel. I think the words make it clear that the Monger ring gives the wearer the power to compel other people. And the Mongers have probably been using it for centuries." I shook my head in awed horror. "How many wars were started with that ring?"

The rest of the household filed into the library, and I welcomed the distraction from the thought of so much power in Monger hands. They must have just come from dinner because everyone was dressed in formal clothes, and even Jeeves had on a tuxedo. Archer struggled to his feet, but I knew better than to help him up. A second later, Connor followed his lead. I watched Connor's eyes dart between Jeeves and Liz. She sat at a table and then patted the seat next to her for him to join her. He complied with a vague smile that made my heart hurt. Mr. Shaw pulled a chair out for my mom, and Ringo stood to give Millicent his. I always loved seeing what Millicent wore to her formal dinners, and tonight's jewels didn't disappoint. She had on my favorite long gold chain with the emerald pendant that looked like it came off the shipwreck of a Spanish galleon, and a chunky gold ring set with a bloodstone intaglio and circled with diamonds. The striking jewels suited the severe lines of her satin evening gown, but not even the reflection of sparkly things could erase the worry in her eyes.

Millicent nodded regally to Archer. "You're looking well this evening, Mr. Devereux."

"Thank you, milady. You are stunning as usual." Somehow, Archer made courtly manners sound perfectly contemporary, and Millicent smiled at him. She looked at me and lifted the long gold chain with the emerald over her neck.

"Saira my dear. I've been meaning to give this to you. I'm sorry I missed your birthday." She held the necklace out for me to take from her hand. In my shock I got up and gave her a hug, which probably startled her as much as it startled me. She placed the chain over my head and the emerald fell to almost the same length as Elizabeth Tudor's black pearl did under my shirt. I stared at the pendant in my hand, then at her.

"It's so beautiful, but it's way too valuable for me to have—" I started to take it off again, but she stopped my hands.

"Nonsense. It is a thing. Lives are valuable. Things are just pretty to look at. Enjoy it, my dear. Eighteen is a time for joy."

Millicent's eyes actually sparkled as I kissed her quickly on the cheek. "Thank you."

My mom had a funny expression on her face when I sat down, as if she was concentrating really hard. "Bertram bought that emerald for Emily when she was pregnant with Tallulah—" Her eyes cleared as she looked at Millicent. "Your mother. He said it came from India and had belonged to a princess, so to a princess it would go." My mom looked relieved to have gotten the words out, but then confused at why everyone was staring at her, and she lapsed back into silence.

I looked at Millicent and whispered. "It should go to your family."

"You *are* my family," she whispered back.

"We interrupted something when we came in. What was this about the power to compel?" Mr. Shaw asked.

"We believe it is the power of the Monger's Family artifact – the ring. But Saira seems to be unaffected by it, which means perhaps the other mixed-blood Descendants are too." I was glad

Archer answered. I wasn't sure of my footing with Mr. Shaw after his outburst at me the night before. Archer handed Mr. Shaw Ringo's book. "The Monger ring has the red stone in it."

Mr. Shaw flipped the book over to see its title, then looked up in surprise. *The Treasures of the Vatican?*

Ringo responded. "It went missin' from Vatican City in 1842."

Mr. Shaw held the page open for my mom. "This is the ring that was on Seth Walters' hand when he lied to you. This is the ring that makes those lies sound like truths." My mom actually looked away, as if it was a picture of dead kittens or something. Liz held her hand out for the book.

"May I?" she said. Mr. Shaw handed it to his sister, and she studied the page for a long moment, then placed it in front of Jeeves.

"What do you see, Mason?"

He looked down at the page compliantly, shied away for a second, then seemed to force his eyes back to the page. Then he pointed to the Blood of Christ ring. "That was on his hand."

I held my breath, and I don't think I was the only one. "On whose hand, Mason?" Liz asked gently.

He closed his eyes, and Connor's face fell. But then he opened them again, and looked straight at Connor's mom. "On Walters' hand when he made me stop the car for Claire and Saira."

There was a collective sigh in the room, though Liz never let Jeeves' eyes leave hers. "What happened next, Mason?"

I thought she was deliberately using his name to keep him present. He winced for a second, but then his eyes cleared again. "I don't know," he said. "It's as though I were underwater with my eyes open, but anything I saw or heard was … distorted."

"Is it distorted now?" She asked him.

Jeeves touched Liz's face gently. "No. I see you very clearly."

The smile she gave him felt almost too private to witness, and there seemed to be hope lacing the tentative smile he returned. He finally turned his gaze to the rest of us, and when it landed on me, he looked relieved. "You're unharmed, Saira?"

I nodded. "Archer stopped them." I got up and went over to Liz. "Can I see the book again, please?" She handed it to me, and I took it back to my mother. "Mom, tell me what you see."

She shied away from the picture again, and I used the most firm, gentle, *mom*-voice I could find in my arsenal. "It can't hurt you now, Mom. It's just a drawing in a book. It has no power here."

She looked back at the page, but just couldn't keep her eyes focused on the ring. They kept sliding away as if it was just too much to bear. "I can't … Saira." She said, with effort. But it didn't sound like she was saying my name, more like she was talking about me.

"I'm right here, Mom. The ring has no power over me, and Seth knows it. I think it's why he's been after me. I'm a threat to him when he uses that ring, because I can't be compelled by it."

Her eyes drifted up to mine, and after a moment they seemed to focus. "You're immune?"

"Apparently." I smiled. "You don't have to worry about the ring getting me, Mom. I'm fine."

Her eyes cleared even more, and Mr. Shaw took her hand. "We're all here, Claire. Are you with us, or do you still feel as though you're underwater?" He shot a quick glance at Jeeves, who nodded. Yes, he was still with us. My mom took a deep, shuddering breath and then looked around the room, focusing on each face as she went. "Where's Logan?"

A Voice from the Past

Liz looked at my mom oddly. "Logan's back at the flat. Why?"

My mom seemed to try to concentrate. "I don't know."

I didn't like that, and neither did anyone else. "Think, Mom. Did Seth mention his name?" The thought that Slick might even think about Connor's little brother made me nauseous.

She finally shook her head. "It's gone." She looked at me with clear eyes. "I can't remember."

"But you're back, aren't you?" I didn't have to ask because I could see it in her eyes.

She looked up at Mr. Shaw, and he squeezed her hand. "Yes, I think I am."

Liz turned to Jeeves and was about to speak, but he was already rising to his feet. "I'll just go to the flat." She gave him a grateful smile. "Thank you," she whispered. Then she spoke to her brother. "That still took longer than I like, but at least we know how to break the ring's effects."

Millicent shuddered. "It's not an experience I wish on anyone, much less twice." She focused on my mom. "Are you well, Claire?"

"I don't like the memory gaps, but yes, I am well, thank you."

I stood and addressed the room. "A couple of things came out of yesterday's drama that we need to talk about." I knew Jeeves would get the rundown from Liz later, and I figured we'd have to tell the Armans and Ms. Simpson too. But the group in the library was sort of the core of my adopted family, so I told them everything that Ringo, Archer, and I had been discussing about Tom and about the missing mixed-bloods.

We all agreed that it was even more vital than ever that we find the mixed-bloods as soon as possible. No one trusted Seth Walters, and everyone assumed he'd be in stealth mode now that he'd been tagged as a person of interest by the police. That could work to our advantage because maybe he'd stay so low that he couldn't do anything to the people he held captive. My mom and Mr. Shaw decided to bring Ms. Simpson up to speed so maybe they could all go to Ms. Rothchild and confront her about her brother-in-law.

"Hey, speaking of Mongers at school, how come Raven usually goes by Walters and Patrick is always Rothchild? They're full siblings, right?" I asked.

My mom answered. "Monger leadership comes down the male line. As Raven's father is a Walters, she uses his last name most of the time, but when Patrick was born, Markham Rothchild insisted he take his mother's last name, probably because he intends to stay alive long enough to pass the leadership directly to his grandson."

Mr. Shaw spoke as if he suddenly remembered. "I do believe the Rothchild children have been withdrawn from St. Brigid's."

Liz Edwards stared at her brother. "That's odd. I would think the Mongers would want to keep all of their children in place at the school, if for no other reason than to gather information."

"You mean spies?" I asked. "But for what? It's not like St. Brigid's is a hotbed of political activity."

"For two reasons, Saira," Archer said. I was startled he would weigh in on the turn this conversation had taken. "One, revolutions generally start with the young, educated people. If there were going to be a revolution in Descendant politics, one place to sow the seeds would be among the students of St. Brigid's. And two, the power players of the current Descendant Council are all connected with the school. The Armans, your mum, Shaw, Ms. Rothchild, and even Miss Simpson – all have strong voices in the Council. Removing the young Rothchilds from St. Brigid's would indicate

63

either fear or confidence on the part of the Mongers, and I, for one, would like to know why they did it."

"There's a third reason it's an odd choice to pull the Monger children," my mom said.

"What's that?" I asked.

"When the school was originally built, it was fortified with certain defenses. If one were serious about seizing power among Immortal Descendants, taking St. Brigid's would be a logical step."

Liz looked worried. "It's one thing to imagine the Mongers using their ring to control individuals, but quite another to think they would take the school."

My mom nodded. "If I hadn't been victim to the Mongers' power I would feel that way too."

Archer added, "There are too many things swirling around Seth Walters to ignore. Why does he want Saira to bring Tom to him? What is his plan with Tom, and with the ring? And then there are the mixed-blood Descendants. To take over forty people who have been hiding from the Council anyway appears to me as though someone is playing a very long game. Unfortunately, whatever the game is, they're also playing it quite close to the chest."

"Do you think Raven knows anything?" I asked. "She and her uncle seem pretty tight, but she's only eighteen."

"So are you," said Connor, with a look on his face that screamed *duh*.

"Good point."

Archer's eyebrow went up with an *I may have a plan* expression. "Doesn't she fence?"

I shrugged. "Yeah, I think so."

"You've become quite accomplished with blades. Perhaps we should find out where she trains?"

Connor piped up. "There's a fencing gym in Brentwood the Rothchilds go to. Patrick was bragging about how many competitions Raven wins there."

I shook my head. "She'd never willingly talk to me."

Ringo spoke up. "I can get 'er to talk."

All eyes turned to him, but it was me who spoke. "You're going to take up fencing to meet Raven Walters? She'll have a blade in her hand. It's a little like learning to swim to get cozy with sharks." I didn't like it, but I didn't know how to put the brakes on it either.

Archer spoke to Ringo. "I can work with you on your skills tonight."

I looked around the room. "Does anyone not think it's even a little dangerous for a guy from Victorian London to be trying to meet the granddaughter of the Monger Head? Why are you all okay with this?"

Mr. Shaw sighed. "Information is everything. If there's one thing I've learned from Mongers it's that he who holds the information holds the key to power. There's too much we don't know, and if there's any information Raven Rothchild does have, Ringo is one of the few people in this world I'd expect to be able to get it."

Ringo rolled his eyes at me. He must have picked up the habit from Connor, and I was going to have to break him of it. "Ye think I can't blend in with the bad element? Or maybe ye don't trust my learnin' of this time?"

"Or how about I like you too much to send you into the viper pit?" I snarled back.

He waggled his eyebrows at me. "Question is, who's the viper?"

The meeting broke up, and I hugged my mom good night before Mr. Shaw escorted her out. I didn't miss his approving glance at my arm linked through Archer's, and I hoped my teacher and I were okay again.

Whatever it was that had prompted my mom to ask about Logan had put everyone on edge, especially since Logan was part daredevil, and therefore had a diminished self-preservation instinct. Something I'd been accused of on more than one occasion.

Archer, Ringo, and I met in the great hall. Archer had gotten his fencing gear from the keep, where he stored his not-insignificant collection of weapons. He was still weaker than usual, so he demonstrated the proper fencing techniques, then had us square off against each other. Ringo was quicker than I was, but all the sword practice I'd gotten in over the summer showed, and I surprised him a couple of times with moves meant more for a longsword than a fencing foil.

Archer stopped us. "Fencing came out of the gentlemen's code of conduct from the eighteenth century as a way to settle a score. It's much more about the gamesmanship of scoring against an opponent rather than drawing blood."

I snorted. "Sorry, I must've lost my copy of the gentleman's handbook."

Ringo smirked. "Left it with mine, I'd guess."

Archer scowled to cover his own smile. "While I generally applaud your defensive instincts, you'll need to shift your mindset from warrior to sportsman to compete with modern fencers. Fencing is not a martial art like the longsword is."

He stepped in to show Ringo some of the finer points of scoring against an opponent, and I took the chance to study Archer as he moved. He was undeniably graceful, but it was a prowling grace, underlined with pure strength. Even when he pulled his punches, he was still stronger than any of the rest of us. I made a mental note to ask Mr. Shaw about how the strength and speed enhancements that seemed to come with his porphyria mutation might be affected *if* he chose to go ahead with the cure. It was a line of thinking that made me mentally cringe, and I dove back into the physical business of fencing with Ringo.

When Ringo was pronounced reasonably proficient, Archer and I followed him upstairs to the east wing library he and Connor had turned into a game room for themselves. I hadn't spent a lot of time in the east wing since I broke out of the guest bedroom Millicent had tried to lock me into, but I got the same bone-deep comfort from the books in that library as I had done when I first came to Elian Manor. I started poking around the contemporary books while Ringo and Archer got down to the online business of figuring out how to get Ringo into Raven's fencing gym.

Underground London caught my eye immediately, and I curled up on a sofa to flip through it. I had just gotten to a chapter about the ghost stations of the London Underground when Sanda knocked softly on the door before she entered the room.

"Sir, there's a telephone call for you. Mr. Singh, from the Tower." She said.

Archer looked up in surprise. As far as I knew, Archer hadn't spoken to Ravindra Singh, my former boss at the Tower of London and his comrade in code-breaking during World War II, since before we went to France. He went to the extension on the desk and hit the speaker button.

"Professor Singh, how can I help you?"

Sanda backed out of the room and closed the door quietly behind her. Ringo and I listened silently as his clipped English voice echoed over the speaker. "Mr. Devereux, I'm very sorry for the late hour. I have an odd situation with which you may be able to assist me."

"I'll do what I can, of course."

"Ah, excellent. I appreciate it very much. I say, did your grandfather happen to leave any papers with you from his time at Bletchley Park?"

Archer's eyes locked on mine as he spoke. "It's possible, Professor. Could you perhaps be more specific?"

Ravi paused for a long moment before he finally said, "I'd prefer to do so in person, if I may. Perhaps you could come to my office?"

"I can be there in an hour. Would that suit you?"

He sounded relieved. "Oh yes, that would suit me very well, thank you."

Archer looked concerned. "I'd like to bring Saira with me if that's acceptable."

"Yes, of course. I trust both of your discretion in this rather ... sensitive case. Thank you, Mr. Devereux. I'll leave your names with the guards."

"Perhaps you'd rather leave Bishop Cleary's name rather than our own?"

Ravi sounded pleased. "Ah yes, a capital idea. Thank you, Mr. Devereux. Indeed, I'll be expecting Mr. and Ms. Cleary to arrive in about an hour. Until then."

Archer hung up the phone and looked thoughtful. "That was odd. Documents from Bletchley? We were never allowed to leave the grounds with anything – no exceptions – and he knows that as well as I do."

"But do you have anything from your time there?" I asked.

"Only memories." I might have imagined something wistful-sounding in Archer's voice, and I decided I'd very much like to know more about his time at England's famous World War II code-breaking compound.

Archer went off to put away the fencing gear, and Ringo and I continued on to the kitchen to grab whatever leftovers we could find from the formal dinner we'd skipped. The cook had left a pot of beef stew in the Aga cooker, so it was still warm. She didn't like it when we avoided the dining room, and I was perfectly capable of preparing food for us, so it was her professional pride that finally drove her to leave us food. No one else was going to cook in her kitchen if she could help it.

We talked about the mechanical and electronic things Ringo had been tinkering with, and the things he imagined he could make. He was fascinated by metals and loved the symmetry of electricity. The stories depicted in the video games he played with Connor were equally intriguing to him, and I could see I needed to introduce him to more of my favorite fantasy authors. He tended to spend all of his time with history books these days.

"What do you know about Bletchley Park?" I asked him as we ate.

Ringo shrugged. "What Archer's told us, mostly. They only started writin' about it in the 1970s after Bletchley was declassified. They were crackin' German Enigma codes by 'and until that Oxford guy ... Turing, I think it was, and 'is team built the bombe to do it for them. The code-breakin' machine did in hours what it took the men months to do."

"Ravi and I worked on a machine called Colossus, which had been designed by Tommy Flowers to do the same thing, except on the Lorenz cipher rather than Enigma," Archer said as he entered the kitchen. He sat down beside me and inhaled deeply. "Ah, beef stew with mushrooms, sage, and wine."

"Want some?" I teased, expecting him to shudder. Instead, he looked away from my bowl to Ringo, who was just beginning to speak. It was an odd reaction and left me a little unsettled.

"What's the difference between Enigma and Lorenz?" said Ringo.

"The Enigma machine was an electro-magnetic encryption machine used by the Germans. It was based in the Morse code, 26-character alphabet. It had five to eight rotors, with the army and air force using five, and the navy using six, seven, or eight." Archer had put on his teaching voice, which always reminded me of happy times in Ringo's flat before Archer had been infected by Wilder.

"More rotors equals better security?" I asked.

Archer nodded. "But Enigma had a fundamental flaw – a letter could never be encoded as itself, which is ultimately how it was broken. The Lorenz machine was commissioned for German high command and used the International Teleprinter Code, in which each letter of the alphabet is represented by a series of five electrical impulses. It also utilized twelve rotors and was only finally broken when a German message of four thousand characters was sent twice without changing the settings. We didn't capture an actual Lorenz machine until after the war, whereas the Poles had captured Enigma before the war began."

Ringo was captivated. "They built a decodin' machine based on encodin' *theory*? That's fantastic!"

Archer enjoyed his enthusiasm. "Yes. They used the encryption theory of Lorenz to design the decryption machine, called Tunney. But in order to decode any message, they first had to determine the day's settings, which was why my machine, Colossus, was built. It could read paper tape at five thousand characters a second, and the wheels that turned the paper went thirty miles an hour. It was a practical electronic digital processing machine. I understand they've rebuilt one from some old plans and some old memories. It's at the museum of computing at the Bletchley Park complex. I haven't been, of course, but it's an hour by train. You could go explore."

Ringo grinned. "You know I will."

Archer checked the slim gold watch I'd given him. "We should go."

I stood up and cleared our bowls. "London Bridge, or closer?"

"He's left names at the front gate, so we should use it. London Bridge is close enough. It'll be good to run." Archer said.

Ringo pushed me out of the way at the sink. "I'll wash. Ye two go. But come find me when ye're back. I'll be in the lab tinkerin' with machines." He grinned at us, and I blew him a kiss as we left the kitchen.

OLD SECRETS

We were both dressed for free running in dark clothes and good boots, and it had been too long since I'd run through London just for the joy of running. I was so tempted to scale an outer wall of the Tower of London complex where I'd worked for a month, but Archer was right, we were expected at the front gate.

A few minutes later we were sitting across from Ravi in his office. He must have been past ninety now, and was physically frail, but as mentally sharp as they come. A copy of the Armada Portrait hung above his desk, and I gave Elizabeth Tudor a nod of greeting. Her famous six-strand black pearls were currently on display in the Jewel House at the Tower and had already drawn thousands of visitors. My hand went absently to the black pearl pendant Elizabeth had given me which lay hidden under my t-shirt. It had been joined tonight by Millicent's emerald, and I thought I was in danger of looking lumpy in ways that had nothing to do with my negligibly-endowed chest.

Ravi had hugged me and told me he still hoped I'd come back to work with him at the Tower. I assured him it was my dream job, and as soon as I finished school, I'd come begging for work.

Then he finally got down to the business he had summoned Archer about. "As you know, your grandfather and I worked together in H Block maintaining the two Mark I Colossus machines that were housed there. The Wrens essentially ran the machines, but we both had engineering backgrounds and were trained by Max Neumann to make repairs."

"Wrens, as in birds?" I asked.

Ravi smiled. "Wrens were the nickname given the Women's Royal Navy Service, into the service of which so many of England's brightest young women were pressed. The Wrens who operated Colossus were chosen as much for their height as for their intelligence, as the machines were very tall and complex. You, my dear, would have made a spectacular Wren."

Archer looked entirely amused at that idea and I almost stuck my tongue out at him, but fortunately for my dignity, Ravi continued.

"We rarely saw the messages that were decoded, of course. The Colossus machines were built to determine that day's settings for the Tunney—"

Archer answered my look of confusion. "It's what w— they called the machine they'd designed to decode the Lorenz cipher." I heard his near-slip, but it seemed Ravi hadn't. Then again, Ravi still thought he was talking to his good friend's grandson.

"Indeed," Ravi said. "Each one of the decoded messages from Tunney was sent directly to the mansion, where the military commanders worked. In fact, in all the time I worked in H Block, I think I only ever saw one decoded message from Tunney, in a stack I'd just given Stella to run to the mansion. I started to read it before I even realized what I was doing, though it was in German, so I didn't understand more than a few words. The ones I recognized however, have stayed with me. Kunst. Schatz. London."

Archer stared at him and translated automatically. "Art. Treasure. London."

Ravi nodded gravely. "Over the years I did wonder what that message meant, but it was near the end of the war, and messages were coming in from every listening station around Britain. One message couldn't occupy more than a couple of minutes of my time. Or so I thought."

Ravi reached into his desk and pulled out a manila envelope. It had been hand-addressed to him, a fact that was remarkable enough in this day of computer-printed labels to get my attention. He shook out a torn piece of paper that was attached to a hole-punched strip of paper that looked a little like a ticker tape and handed it to Archer. "The Bletchley Park Trust discovered a small room hidden behind a fireplace in the mansion's library."

Archer's expression didn't change, but the muscle at his jaw jumped as he clenched his teeth. "Did they, indeed?"

Ravi nodded. "More remarkably, a bedroll lay against one wall, and a half-burnt candle sat in a brass holder next to it on the floor. All indications were that someone had been living there, can you imagine?" Ravi sounded horrified. "When they unwrapped the bedroll, these scraps of paper fell out."

Archer took the papers gingerly in his hands. The ticker tape was torn, and the scrap of paper attached to it was typewritten in German. "June 4, 1944. Entrance from Holborn. Flammable art treasure. Extra care. Werwolf is London native, T. Landers. Mission set for Ju—" He looked at me. "It cuts off."

Ravi held his hand out for the papers. "Odd enough that the decoded message was attached to the teleprinter tape, but odder still is this." He turned the ticker tape over and handed it back to Archer. "Ravi. Find this tape. –A"

I stared at Archer, sure that my expression was giving a whole novel away. Archer was expressionless, and Ravi seemed to have eyes only for the scrap of paper.

"It's your grandfather's handwriting, Archer. I can't imagine what he could have been doing in a hidden room behind a fireplace at Bletchley Park with a piece of paper we weren't allowed to have."

My eyes jumped to Ravi. "You think he was a spy."

Ravi sighed deeply. "I know my friend was not a spy. The good people at the Bletchley Park Trust may have other thoughts on the matter, but as far as I know, they haven't brought MI5 into this. It took very little research to discover I was the only Ravi to have worked at the mansion, and they brought the puzzle to me first. Now I have brought it to you."

Archer spoke quietly. "May I keep the paper to compare against anything I might find?"

Ravi winced. "I'm very sorry. I promised to return the original to the people at the trust."

"Here. Photograph it." I handed Archer the iPhone my mom had given me as a birthday present. I didn't have that many people to call, so I didn't carry it very often. The camera feature was the one I used the most.

When Archer had finished, Ravi tucked the scraps of paper back into the envelope. "I haven't returned to the Park since the war ended, but I find I now wish to see this hidden room. I fear I may be too old for the train travel, however. The bustle of the stations is more than I can handle these days."

Archer reached a hand out to touch Ravi's arm. "I'll tell you what. If you can arrange an after-hours visit for us, I'll be very happy to drive you to Buckinghamshire and push your wheelchair myself."

The idea seemed to delight Ravi. "That would be quite extraordinary, young man. I'll see what I can do."

We left his office soon after that and made it back to Elian Manor before midnight. Clocking into the walled garden put us in direct line-of-sight of the laboratory, and it was clear from the yellow glow of lights that Ringo was still up working. Archer took my hand and we walked in silence toward the lab.

Just before I opened the door, Archer turned me to face him. "I don't remember writing that note," he said quietly.

I exhaled deeply, dreading the implications of my next words. "Maybe because you haven't yet."

When we arrived at the Elian Manor lab, Mr. Shaw and Connor were back at work on the viral delivery system for the Vampire cure, and Ringo was deeply engrossed in dissecting the motherboard of a computer. Our tale of Archer's note to Ravi

74

surprised them all, and the content of that note became the primary subject of discussion.

"Are we going with the assumption that 'London native T. Landers' is Tom?" I asked.

"Given that Tom Landers is a fairly common name, and he has access to all of history, it *is* a huge assumption to make," said Mr. Shaw. He looked pointedly at Archer. "However, the fact that you know Tom, and you wrote the note narrows the odds considerably."

"Ringo found anecdotal evidence that may point to Tom's presence in World War II as well." Archer said thoughtfully.

Mr. Shaw considered Archer for a long moment before addressing him. "What do you know about the Werwölfe?" He pronounced it with a German accent, which made it sound like *Vervolf-a.*

"You're joking, right? Tom might be a lot of things at this point, but he couldn't be a werewolf too. He'd be dead." Connor said. He'd been bitten by one, and we'd gotten an education in them when his infection had to be burned out by one of Mr. Shaw's chemical concoctions.

Archer shook his head. "Not the mutant kind, spelled w-e-r-e. Hitler's Werwölfe, spelled w-e-r, were a group of young men who had come through the Hitler Youth program and were hand-picked near the end of the war to become terrorists. Hitler feared he was losing, you see, and his plan, unrealistic though it may have been, was to have Werwolves throughout the occupied territories setting off explosions and causing enough destruction that perhaps the people would rise up against the Allies. His hope was that in the mayhem, his high command would be able to regain their foothold in Europe."

"But they clearly lost the war. What happened to the Werwolves?" I asked.

"Poor leadership and not enough resources, apparently. No one really knows why the terrorism plans fell apart."

"Did they ever pull anything off in London?" Ringo asked from his seat in the far corner.

"Nothing of which I'm aware." Archer sounded grim.

"What does 'entrance from Holborn' mean?" I asked.

"Holborn Underground station is up near the British Museum. Could that be it?" Connor asked.

Archer suddenly jumped up and began pacing. "There was a rumor during the war that many of the treasures of the British Museum were moved out of the galleries and stored in one of the Underground stations to protect them from the bombing raids."

I breathed quietly. "Art treasures." I looked up at Archer. "Which station?"

"I don't know. As I said, it was just a rumor."

"That's all been declassified now, I'm sure," said Mr. Shaw. "I have a friend at the Home office I can call tomorrow."

"If you don't mind me asking, why are we looking into a seventy-year-old mystery about something that didn't happen?" asked Connor.

"Because Archer doesn't remember writing that note, yet here it is. And he didn't remember being infected by Wilder until my interference caused it. In our whacked-out world, just because a thing didn't happen doesn't mean it won't."

Connor rubbed his temples as if the whole notion of time travel hurt, which to be honest, it sort of did, and then he nodded. "Good point." He looked at Archer. "And if it is Tom Landers leading some sort of art heist for a group of Hitler Youth, after you find him and stop him, you're going to want that cure, right?"

The grim expression had hit Archer's eyes. "Right."

DIFFERENCES

Archer was in a prowling mood when he left the manor, so I just kissed him and let him go. Those moods had been few and far between since we got back from France, but I could feel this one coming on a mile away. Ever since Slick had taken me, Archer had been extra hard on himself for things he had no control over. That, of course, was not a conversation I could have with him in this mood.

There was no note the next morning when I woke up, so I assumed he had gone to sleep in the keep as usual. I grabbed coffee and a muffin from the breakfast room sideboard and went back upstairs. There was a dormer window on the third floor that was easier for roof access when my hands were full, and I dropped down next to Ringo to have my breakfast with a view.

"How long have you been up?" I asked him after a sip of coffee.

"A while. Archer and I 'ad a talk before 'e went down for the day."

That surprised me. "About what?"

He sipped his own coffee, loaded with cream and sugar, in silence. I knew better than to prod Ringo. He'd tell me whatever he was going to tell me, but he'd tell me less if I poked at him. Finally, he took a breath and spoke. "We were discussin' women." My eyebrows shot up, but I wisely, and with some difficulty, refrained from comment. He continued. "Ye're very different from men."

"We can do anything men can do." I didn't usually get defensive about equal rights because I'd grown up with a strong, capable mom who did the job of two parents. But every time I had Clocked backward, I'd either had to dress like a man to get by or put up with attitudes from natives that I was weaker because of my gender.

He gave me a strange look. "I didn't say anythin' about doin', did I? People can do what they can do – some are stronger, some are faster, some are more limber. Bein' a man or a woman doesn't come into the doin' of a thing. Except babies, of course. But that's just nature."

He let his eyes travel out over the vista. "We were talkin' about the way we think. The way a man sees 'is job in the world, or in 'is family."

"How is it different than the way a woman does? I don't think I did my job at the museum any differently than the guy interns did."

He shook his head. "Yer back to the doin' of things." He sighed as though he was saying it badly.

"Don't try to give me context, just tell me what you talked about." I tried to sound more patient than I was. Ringo's mouth quirked in half a smile.

"We talked about the future. Our futures, actually. About what defines us as men."

"What defines you?" I asked. "Isn't that something you decide – who you're going to be?"

Ringo turned to look at me. "It's not just who we decide to be. It's who the world sees when they look at us. Do they respect us? Do we respect ourselves? Are we doin' somethin' that matters, or are we just doin' a job? Are we doin' enough to provide a life for the ones we're responsible for, and are they proud of us for doin' it?" He exhaled. "That's how men think."

I thought about saying it wasn't different from how women think, but then I really considered what he had said. If that's the way men thought about the world, shouldn't I, as a partner to a man, want to be provided for, cared for, and protected so that he could feel all those things? But I was totally capable of doing all of that for myself and did so regularly. "Was it a theoretical conversation or a practical one?"

He grimaced. "A little of both." The silence after that statement stretched between us until I realized that was all I was getting on that subject. It wasn't a confidence booster for sure.

"You put a lot of pressure on yourselves," I finally said.

He scoffed. "Yeah. Ye could say that."

We climbed back into the dormer window and went downstairs, lost in our own thoughts. Just before he went down the hall toward the east wing, he turned back to me. "I'm not sure 'ow well either of us really knows 'Is Lordship. 'E's 'ad a big life, with three lifetimes of memories to guide 'im and keep 'im company."

I tried not to think about how big Archer's life had been before me, because that path led to insecurity, which hung out and drank tea with pointless things like jealousy on a regular basis. Ringo called out to me as I turned toward my room. "I'm goin' to Raven's fencin' school today. Do ye want to join me?"

Confronting Raven sounded far more entertaining than spending too much time alone in my head. "Come and get me when you go," I said.

I could hear Ringo chuckle as he walked away down the hall.

Instead of going to my room, I went to my mom's bedroom and knocked. She wasn't there, but her gardening hat was gone from its usual place on her dresser, so I slipped out to the balcony of her room and used the drainpipes to climb down, just to stay in practice. I found my mom in the walled garden that had always been hers. Remarkably, she wasn't alone. Millicent worked nearby, pulling up dead plants and replacing them with winter bulbs. I must have sounded as surprised as I felt, because they both smiled when I said good morning.

"Would you like your mother to yourself?" Millicent asked, sitting back on her heels to look up at me.

I dropped down next to them and started pulling dandelions to cover my shock. My mom tossed me a pair of gloves. "Here. Save your hands."

I pulled the gloves on and met Millicent's eyes. "I don't want to bore you with my stupid stuff."

"Your *stuff* isn't stupid, Saira. And if it's acceptable to you, I'd be honored to be a part of one of your mother/daughter conversations."

I don't know what possessed me to tease her. "You're kind of freaking me out, Millicent. I'm not sure what to do with all this … kindness." Maybe I was testing to see if this transformation in Millicent was real or if my imagination had gone into overdrive and was conjuring kindness out of thin air.

I didn't expect her response though, and it was perfect. She scoffed. "Yes, well, you've been *freaking me out* since the day you arrived. So perhaps we're finally even?"

We all burst into laughter and then settled into an easy working rhythm as we tended to the garden.

My mom spoke first. "You looked like a woman with a mission when you came in here, Saira."

"I just had a weird conversation with Ringo." I took a breath. "It was about the differences between men and women. He says men think differently than us."

"This is certainly true," she said.

"And always has been," added Millicent.

My mom smiled. "Was this about Archer?"

"Yes. No. I don't know." I sighed dramatically. "They talked about stuff, but Ringo wouldn't be specific, and I got insecure because now I assume it was about me. But mostly, the conversation made me wonder how we can ever want the same thing if the things he needs to feel good at aren't things I need him to do for me?"

My mom looked thoughtful for a moment before she spoke. "It used to be simpler."

I fought mightily against rolling my eyes. "You mean in the old days, when women knew their place?"

She laughed. "There were so many things wrong with Victorian ideas of what a woman was *allowed* to do, but none of us ever questioned what a man's role was in our lives. We needed them, they needed us, and our mutual need made for uncomplicated ideas of who we were to each other. Since the beginning of time, a woman who bore children had to be protected from danger, and it became hardwired into a man's DNA to do so."

She sat back and wiped a lock of hair back from her face. It sounded like she had given this topic a lot of thought. "Somehow, especially in America, the idea of equality between the genders shifted into *sameness*. It's a shift that has caused quite a bit of confusion in relationships because it's difficult to find mutual need if everyone is equal *and the same*. It's in our differences that we can seek the things that complement us and be the things that support our loved ones."

Millicent spoke quietly. "There was a gentleman once – Sean Mulroy – just after the war. He had been a soldier, a pilot, and he came to the manor looking for work. My parents were still alive then, and I was young, but not so young that I shouldn't have been married."

She sighed – something I'd never heard Millicent do – and then continued. "His family was Irish, which, even in those days, was considered only a step above tinkers. But worse than that to my father, he might have had mixed blood. There were Irish Clockers left in those days, and Sean certainly seemed to know a bit about our Family. But I also had the sense he could See things before they happened; he was always moving things out of the way before they were knocked over or smashed. He never confirmed his heritage, of course, beyond his Irishness, and my father hired him to work in the field, despite the fact that he had a Trinity College education and had been a hero in the war. There were so many people looking for work at that time and very few people with means to pay them, which meant that any paying job was like gold, and many of the laborers were far more educated than the jobs demanded."

Millicent absently picked a piece of lavender and brushed the flower against her cheek. It made her seem young and wistful, and I could suddenly see the twenty-eight year old version of herself, with long, lustrous hair, a wide, smiling mouth, and crystal blue eyes that missed nothing.

Her voice was even quieter when she continued. "He always seemed to find me whenever I stepped outside the manor, and I made up excuses to cross his path several times a day. It became a dance between us. A glance, a smile, some clever comment to make him laugh. I once twisted my ankle trying to climb a tree for a perfect apple, and when he found me struggling to make my way home, he wrapped my ankle in his own shirt so carefully and so tenderly, I felt as though I were made of glass. After that he always brought whatever fruit he could forage from the fields around the manor – always with a posy of wild lavender."

Millicent had a faraway smile on her face as she twirled the stalk of lavender. "My mother encouraged me – perhaps she recognized that I was already becoming set in my ways and therefore unlikely to marry. But my father could only see the possibility of his mixed blood, his Irishness, and his lack of title. It was he who planted the idea in my head that my field-working ex-pilot would never be able to support me in the manner a woman of my station would be expected to maintain. He impressed upon me that as the last Elian, I would be Family Head after my mother, and no man whose title or worth was less than mine would ever accept my position of power."

My mother sucked in a breath. She'd never heard this story before either. Millicent's voice caught on her next words. "So I set a test for him. I told him I could only marry a man who had made something of himself, a man with more ambition than bringing me wildflowers."

My mom exhaled softly. "Oh, Millicent."

"It was cruel, and so unjust. The hurt in his eyes cut slashes across my heart as he looked away, bowed his head, and said he'd trouble me no more." Millicent took a deep, shaky breath and caught my eyes. "I had wounded his pride, you see. I let him believe that there was nothing I needed from him that he could give. I was wrong though. So wrong. What I didn't know then was that without someone to care for the woman, all the status and titles in the world couldn't replace the need for another's arms to comfort me when the weight of responsibility became too heavy to bear alone."

Millicent's words came out in a whisper. "Even as the words left my mouth, I knew I'd made a mistake." Her eyes hadn't left mine. "So don't ever believe, like I did, that you don't need care. It may seem unnecessary or even superfluous because you're strong and capable, but I promise you, its absence would leave a hole in your life that no amount of self-reliance can fill."

Tears pooled in my eyes, and I realized that words couldn't take away the pain that Millicent had lived with for more than half a century. So instead I kissed her cheek. "Thank you for that," I whispered.

Millicent wiped at her own eyes and laughed a little at the fact that my mom had just done the same. "I've never told anyone that story. It feels a little … lighter to let some of it go."

She stood and brushed off her trousers. "So, I gather the reason this has come up now is that your young man is struggling with your kidnapping and his inability to stop it?"

I let out a frustrated breath. "Maybe that's at the root of it, but he *did* stop it. He put his body in the way and then got shot for his trouble, and here I am – not trapped somewhere with a group of the mixed-bloods we're trying to find."

Millicent looked hard at me. "You wanted to be taken to them, didn't you?"

My mom's eyes were locked on me when I blurted. "I don't know. Maybe?"

Mom gasped, but Millicent didn't blink. "You thought you'd be able to Clock them out, a few at a time, right under the Mongers' noses." There was no question in her tone, and I finally nodded.

"Bob said they had tied your hands behind your back," Mom said. I nodded. "And you thought they would cut the ties once they had dumped you, even though Seth Walters knows you're a Clocker?"

"He doesn't know that I can draw my own spirals."

"He's not stupid, Saira," Millicent said. "All he would have had to do was threaten to kill everyone he'd taken if you so much as set foot out of his sight, and you would have been as trapped as they all are. He'll have cameras on them – he'd be a fool not to – and you were his prized prisoner. How easily he could have made you do things against your will – all he would have had to do was hold a gun to one child's head." She spoke the words in such a reasonable, straightforward tone there was nothing I could push back against. She was right, and she saw in my eyes that I knew it, so she went in for the kill.

"There's a part of you that resents Archer for having ridden in on his white horse to rescue you, because you felt very certain you could rescue yourself – and about forty people with you." Her eyes were boring into mine, and despite every instinct I had that said *run*, I didn't look away. "Here's the truth, Saira. He didn't ride in to rescue you because you needed him to. He believes in your strength, he knows your skills, he *trusts* you. No, Archer put himself in the way of a bullet because it's what *he* needed to do. And, whether you accept it or not, you needed him to do it too."

"Not pulling punches today, are you, Millicent?" I tried for a joking tone, but I wasn't joking.

She smirked. "It's not in my nature." That smirk was so out of character for the stately matriarch of the Elian Family that I couldn't help smiling in spite of the brutal truths she'd just laid on me.

"Well, thank you. I'll get over the bruises, but consider the lesson learned."

"Really?" She peered closely at me. I nodded, and then she gave me a proper smile. "Good. There's one other thing I'll say before I've hit my quota for advice for the year. The only difference between men and women is *everything*, and that's what keeps things so interesting."

THE FOIL

Ringo found me in the garage watching Jeeves teach Connor how to change the oil in the Rolls. I had no doubt Connor could have described the process step-by-step from what he'd read in a book, or seen in a tutorial, but it was really good to see him make his hands do what his brain knew was right.

"Jeeves, could ye take me and Saira into town?" Ringo said.

Jeeves looked up in surprise. "Have you cleared it with the Ladies Elian?"

"We will," I said. "And I can Clock us home. I just haven't seen the fencing gym where we're going." Clocking as a mode of transportation felt like cheating, but I wasn't really so confident about vehicular return trips at the moment. Jeeves must have sensed my thoughts because he considered for a moment before answering.

"I'll take you in the Rolls." He looked me straight in the eyes. "There are no automatic door locks in the Rolls."

Relief washed over me. Jeeves understood my fear about being locked into another car by a driver under the influence of the Monger ring, and he didn't take it personally. "I can't imagine Walters would come out here – not while he's in hiding."

Jeeves nodded. "My feelings as well. And despite the threat, I strongly believe that none of us can afford to become prisoners in this house."

In a way, Jeeves was overcoming his own fears too. In light of my recent conversations about a man's need to care for the people he was responsible for, I guessed it had been really hard on Jeeves to have that instinct subverted by the Monger ring.

I turned to Ringo. "I'll just get some things and meet you back here after I talk to Mom."

He nodded. "The bag of gear's outside. I'll wait 'ere." Ringo crouched down next to Connor and they immediately started talking *car* to each other. I ran back into the manor and up to my room.

The daggers Archer had given me were tucked away in my dresser drawer. I slipped them into special leg holsters that fit under my jeans, and I instantly felt safer and more dangerous. It was similar to the way I felt when Archer had my back, and the thought of his satisfied expression if he ever heard me say that out loud made me smile.

Finding my mom took a bit longer than I expected. She and Mr. Shaw were together in his lab having what looked like a fairly intense conversation, which they broke off when I came in the door.

I looked at them oddly. "What's up?"

My mom seemed unsettled. "In light of what happened yesterday, the Armans want us – the Council – to unite against the Rothchild family and oust Markham from his place as Monger Family Head. They've called a special Descendant Council meeting to vote on it."

I stared at her. "Oh crap. Mom, don't go."

Mr. Shaw growled. "That's what I told her too."

Possible scenarios were swirling around in my brain. "What if Markham has the Monger ring now that Seth Walters has gone underground. He could compel all of you to dance a jig and there would be nothing you could do to stop him."

"But if I don't go, Camille won't have the numbers to carry the day. Removal of a Family Head must be unanimous, plus there has to be another Monger ready to step in with at least sixty percent Family approval."

I shuddered. "I don't even want to know six Mongers, much less find the sixty percent to vote some new bad guy in."

My mom sighed. "Mongers aren't evil masterminds, Saira. Nothing is as black and white as that."

"I don't actually know any good Rothchilds, so my empirical evidence says otherwise."

She shook her head. "In any case, there's a process to removing a Family Head, but that begins with a Council vote."

"I don't think I'll feel good about anything the Council does until there are mixed-bloods in the room." Both of them stared at me suddenly. "What?" I asked.

Mom looked at Mr. Shaw with wide eyes. "Do you think it would work?"

"What would work?" I had obviously said something momentous, and I hated not knowing what it was.

Mr. Shaw answered my mom. "It would have to be timed with a vote to remove the moratorium. Otherwise we'd never get the Families to approve the new Heads."

"What are you guys talking about?" I raised my voice to get their attention, and it finally seemed to work. My mom turned to me with the beginnings of a smile.

"You have to become the Clocker Head."

"Wait, what? No. No, I'm not Head material. You're the Head. I don't do politics." If I could have backpedaled out of the room, I would have.

She explained. "We'd have to replace all three non-Monger Heads with mixed-bloods, and then fill the Council room with them as well. Then we could vote anything through and the Mongers couldn't compel us otherwise."

A feeling of dread flooded through me, because I knew it was actually a decent plan. "I hate your plan, and I can see a million things you'd have to do first, like find the missing mixed-bloods and get them out. And here's something to chew on while you consider your Council coup: why isn't Death represented at Council? If you're doing away with the moratorium against mixed-bloods why not do the same for Vampires?"

My mom looked at me for a long moment, and I wondered if she was actually hanging on to the old prejudice, despite knowing Archer. She finally spoke. "I believe Ringo's analogy of the frog in boiling water works in this instance too. Let's get mixed-bloods on the Council first. Once they are recognized and fear of their unique skills diminishes, integration should be relatively painless, particularly as you're all loved Family members already. I'm afraid the Vampires have known less love and much more fear, at least in the last five hundred years. That will take more effort and patience to undo."

"But you'll try? Eventually, I mean. After the immediate threat of the Mongers is neutralized, and when no one is 'mixed-blood,' we're all just Family?"

My mom touched my face gently. "Yes, we'll try."

I hadn't even considered the idea of Archer being able to step out openly among Descendants, and I thought back to how easily Bas, the Vampire student of world religions, had hung out with the Shifter priest at the fifteenth century French church. He seemed unfazed to be a Vampire, though he did miss the Shifter skills that were no longer dominant in him.

I turned my attention back to my mom. "So, what about this Council meeting? I'll go for you if I have to, but I'm still on their hit list."

"You're not going either," Mr. Shaw growled.

I smiled at him, but with a light warning in my tone. "Careful. You start telling Elian women what we can and can't do, we get a little stubborn."

"Oh, it's a conversation we've had. It's just his inner caveman holding his club and looking around for people to bop on the head." My mom's tone of voice held a wink, and I realized she dealt with exactly the same male need to protect as I did. I barely contained the smirk.

"Mom, I know you'll do what you feel you need to do, and if you do go to the meeting and the ring comes out, you can stick your fingers in your ears, or get one of the MacKenzie boys to tackle the Monger wearing it so you can Clock yourself out of there. Whatever support you need from me, I'll be very happy to give you."

My mom breathed out a happy sigh. "That was exactly what I needed to hear, Saira. Thank you. I believe I'll call Camille and see what sort of diplomacy I can accomplish on the phone."

"Sounds like a plan." I stood to leave.

She looked at me questioningly. "You seem to be going somewhere."

I knew this was going to hit every one of their protective instincts, so I deliberately kept my tone as calm and casual as possible. "After the conversation we had about Mongers last night, Ringo got himself into Raven's fencing class this afternoon. She's never seen Ringo before, so he's going to try to work some of his Ringo charm on her. I'm not wild about him going on his own, so obviously, I'd have to stay out of Raven's sight. We Googled the building, and we have a plan for that. Remember, I can Clock home at the first sign of a threat." I hoped the expression on my face was one of earnest trustworthiness, or, at a minimum, responsible adultness.

Mr. Shaw's jaw was clenched tightly, but he didn't say anything. He just looked at my mom for her reaction. "I can't say I love the idea, Saira, because as capable and grown up as I know you are, you're still my daughter, and my instinct to keep you safe is deeply ingrained." We shared an understanding smile at those words. "But I trust you to know what you need to do and to do it carefully. I assume Archer knows of this plan?"

I nodded, hiding my relief. "He's kind of the one who suggested it, but they don't have night classes, or he'd go. He trusts me to be Ringo's invisible safety net, and we can always call you guys if we need back-up."

Mom sighed. "Have Jeeves take you so he knows exactly where you are."

"I've already asked him. He said he'd bring the Rolls."

She grimaced. "I hate that he feels he needs to consider which car is safest."

"We're all going to be dealing with the aftermath of that attack for a long time, I'd imagine." Mr. Shaw sounded gruff and unhappy.

I nodded. "I'm going to be a lousy taxi passenger for a while, I think. Anywhere but the front seat of a moving vehicle is going to be tough for me."

He pulled me in for a quick one-armed hug, then kissed the top of my head. "Be careful, take your mobile, and let us know when you return."

I shot them both a grin as I headed toward the door. "I will."

Ringo met me back at the garage, the bag of fencing gear in one hand and his eyebrows raised in question. "I told them where we're going."

He nodded. "Good. I was going to 'ate if I'd 'ad to disobey yer ma."

I laughed. "No wonder she loves you so much. You're like a dream son."

Ringo's face lost all trace of humor. "It's been a long time since I was a son."

The seriousness in his tone made my heart hurt for him. He bent to mess with the string on his bag and didn't meet my eyes, so I touched his arm. "Come on, let's get Jeeves and go."

I sat up in the front seat next to Jeeves, and he dropped us off one block behind the building that housed Raven's fencing gym.

"If you'd rather not use your own mode of return transportation, you both have my mobile number. Please call me when you want to leave and I'll meet you back here with the Rolls," said Jeeves.

"Thanks. We'll probably be an hour or two, but come and get us early if the Armans get to Elian before we call."

Jeeves nodded seriously. "Yes, Ma'am."

I smiled at him. "I'm not nearly fancy enough to be a ma'am."

"I disagree. You are quite suited to the honorific." Jeeves gave me a slight smile in return as we got out of the Range Rover. Ringo and I immediately slipped down the side alley and watched Jeeves drive away without incident, then we headed toward the back of the gym. Just as we'd seen on Google Earth, the fire escape extended all the way to the ground floor, and the back of the building was without windows. I checked the clock on my phone.

"You have ten minutes to get changed for the session. I'll see you in an hour." Ringo must have been able to see the worry in my eyes because he tossed his chin at me to get my attention.

"I'm not the one in danger here, no matter how good 'er fencin' skills are, so quit lookin' like I'm goin' off to war." He laughed at the face I made. "No, strike that. I'm goin' off to make friends with War, or maybe just kick 'er arse."

"Have fun storming the castle." I leapt up to the fire escape ladder and began my ascent, laughing at the look of bewilderment on Ringo's face. Clearly there needed to be a screening of *The Princess Bride* in his future.

It took me a bit to get settled at the edge of the big skylight that looked down on the main practice floor, and a few minutes later, Ringo entered the room holding his helmet and foil. He went over to talk to a young woman I thought was one of the students, and I realized suddenly that I hadn't ever shown him a picture of Raven.

"No, not her," I muttered under my breath, but ten seconds later I understood that she was actually the coach when she gestured to a young guy I recognized as Patrick Rothchild, Raven's brother, to come out and face off against Ringo.

I wasn't actually that high above them on the roof, and if anyone had bothered to look up they would have seen my unsmiling face staring down at them. But people never looked up, so I was feeling pretty invisible, at least until something cast a shadow on the floor and I realized it came from behind me. I pulled back from the skylight and spun to find myself face to face with the biggest eagle I'd ever seen. Its piercing golden eyes regarded me steadily from about four feet away, and the fear that clenched my heart relaxed.

"A Philippine Eagle, huh? Does your mom know you're out?"

Logan tilted the bird's head in a gesture that could either mean "of course," or "are you kidding?"

I didn't think he would Shift back to human form since that would put a naked boy out in public, so I settled back into my original position. "Stay back far enough so you don't cast a shadow on the floor below us." It was actually kind of nice to have the company, so I continued talking.

"Ringo's going up against Patrick Rothchild right now – I guess so the coach can assess him. She's the young, pretty one with long brown hair." I pointed to the young woman who watched Ringo and the Spawn dance around each other. I'd seen Ringo battle with a sword in France and he was pretty lethal, but the Spawn was a dirty fighter, and I didn't trust him.

"We call Patrick 'the Spawn' because he's Ms. Rothchild's kid. He's also Raven's younger brother, and she was my roommate when I first got to St. Brigid's. Everyone calls her the Crow behind her back, probably because as a bird species, crows are right up there with pigeons in the rats-with-wings category. She's over there, the blonde, tossing her hair while she pretends not to watch." I pointed to Raven, standing in an arrogant pose off to one side, and looked to see if the Eagle was following along. His golden eyes whirled with the intensity of his gaze, and I envied his ability to Shift into something with eyesight like an eagle.

Ringo made an aggressive move and scored against the Spawn, who instantly hurled his foil and threw down his helmet before he stormed off the floor. "Spoiled Monger brat," I said as much to myself as to the Eagle.

Raven casually pushed off the wall she'd been holding up and donned her helmet. She approached Ringo with every ounce of her arrogance wrapped up in easy grace. I pretty much loathed her anyway, but her obvious athleticism just added fuel to that fire.

She nodded once to Ringo, then got into ready mode. Since I wasn't a fencer, I could only think in terms I knew, and Ringo's ready mode didn't have nearly the same elegance Raven's did.

They were about the same height, but their skills were very different. Ringo wasn't necessarily outmatched in the skills department, but he was definitely outclassed. Everything Raven did with the fencing foil screamed technique and training, while Ringo's moves were pure offense and defense. He was battling, she was practically dancing. It was actually pretty spectacular to watch, except for the despising her part.

She scored on him twice in quick succession, but then he got in a sneaky hit to her stomach and it pissed her off. "Look, she's suddenly paying attention." It didn't seem weird at all that I was speaking to a giant Philippine Eagle, or that he seemed to follow everything I said.

"He's fought with a double bladed sword before, so there's more slash than jab in his motion. She keeps having to duck away instead of dance." I watched him score another hit to her vest, and I could practically see the steam rise off her. It was really hard to tell if beating her at this would make her more or less likely to talk to him. At the rate he was going, I thought he might be lucky to make it off the floor without a knife to his throat.

The coach finally clapped her hands to stop the match, and Ringo waited until Raven's foil was completely down before he lowered his. He was definitely still in warrior stance though, and I thought that when Raven pulled off her helmet, her glance at him was a little wary.

The coach moved Ringo's body into a couple of positions and had Raven demonstrate the correct counterattack. Then the coach called to Patrick, who was standing with a group of guys against a wall. She pointed to some other foils that looked heavier and longer mounted in racks above a tall wardrobe and indicated a ladder on the other side of the room. Patrick crossed his arms in front of himsef aggressively and stood his ground.

The Eagle's wings fluttered, and I looked back at Ringo in time to see him set down his foil and helmet and take off sprinting across the floor. He leapt off a pommel horse, hit a high bar, and did a double flip around to get the height to land, seated, on top of the cabinet. He retrieved the foils, tossed them down to the Spawn, who had to quickly uncross his arms to catch them or be hit in the head, and then Ringo hopped down to stick a perfect landing. He casually strolled over and took the foils from a very startled Spawn.

"Oh, bravo," I breathed before I turned my attention to Raven. Ringo's freerunning show had startled and impressed her, and there was an interesting look of respect and thoughtfulness on her face. The coach clapped Ringo on the back with a huge grin, then took the larger foils from him and demonstrated some complicated moves.

Some other students walked into the gym and I realized the lesson must be over. The coach shook Ringo's hand and seemed to indicate he should come back. Then Ringo shook Raven's hand with one of his charming smiles, instead of the cheeky ones I usually got, said a couple of words while he packed up his fencing gear, and strolled out of the room.

I turned to Logan's Eagle. "Alright, dude. Time to fly home. Thanks for hanging out with me though. If you see my mom, could you let her know we're heading home soon?"

The Eagle tilted his head at me in that way that either meant "sure" or "I'll conveniently forget the minute someone puts a snack in front of me," then he took off in a great flap of his enormous wings. Apparently Philippine eagles really were the largest eagles on the planet.

I texted Jeeves that we were ready to be picked up, and I was just getting to my feet when I looked down and froze. Cole Thomas had just entered the gym. I dropped back down to my knees, and pressed my face to the glass to make sure I was actually seeing what I thought I saw. The big, dark-skinned guy, built like

Adam, moved in that slouchy way some guys do when they pretend nothing matters. He crossed the room to where Raven was still putting her gear away, and when she looked up and saw him, one of those big "oh yay, you're here!" grins crossed her face before she threw her arms around him.

Okay, wow.

TRACKED

No part of this situation looked good for the presumably mixed-blood friend of a kidnapped boy. Kissing the niece of the bad guy who orchestrated the kidnappings was at worst, traitorous and at best, evidence of dangerously bad taste in human beings.

Cole was smiling at Raven as she said something to him, and the whole scene was so surreal I felt like a cartoon character trying to rub an illusion out of my eyes. I backed away from the skylight and climbed down the fire escape. When I hit the ground, Ringo was already in the alley waiting for me with his gear bag slung over one shoulder. He had an easy smile on his face.

"Well, that was interestin'," he said.

I grimaced. "You could say that."

He looked surprised. "She wasn't all nasty, ye know. I managed to impress 'er enough that she agreed to spar with me again."

We started walking toward the street where Jeeves would hopefully pick us up in a few minutes. But then a voice behind us yelled, "Hey, new kid!"

I realized my mistake as soon as I turned, because the voice belonged to Patrick Rothchild, and I'd just busted Ringo by association. "Oh, poop," I muttered under my breath.

"Ye and yer excrement talk." Ringo hadn't turned and was half-laughing at me as he ignored the Spawn and kept walking. I fell into step next to him, and it clearly pissed Patrick off to be ignored.

"New kid! I'm talking to you! You hang out with trash like her, you're going to get sent to the same dump." Patrick wasn't especially big, and he was only about fifteen years old, but he was as mean as a snake and always traveled in a pack of dangerous boys. I could sense about three of them behind us with Patrick – all Mongers if my spidey senses were working properly. We were about ten yards from the street, but I wouldn't give the Spawn the satisfaction of seeing me run.

Suddenly, a white van with a smashed front end screeched to a halt on the street in front of us, effectively closing the end of the alley. The side door slammed open, and a couple of big Mongers tumbled out. I recognized one of them from Slick's office building, and my confidence instantly liquefied. Ringo tensed beside me, and I could feel him making the same decision I was making. Forward into the white, windowless kidnapper van was clearly the wrong choice. Backward past four teenage hoodlums held more options for success, but they could still potentially slow us down enough for the adult Mongers to get their hands on us. So, up it was.

I was very happy we both had the ability to see in three dimensions, because the dumpster was exactly the right height from which to leap for the barred window with a big enough ledge to stand on. From there it was another uncomplicated jump to the rusty fire escape ladder and up to the roof. Ringo flung his fencing bag at the Spawn's crew since they were closest to us, and we were both up and on top of the building before the first Monger made it onto the dumpster.

"Back toward the gym." Ringo urged. The flat rooftop of the commercial building we were on abutted the gym roof, and as far as I was concerned, anything that took us away from the windowless van was the right direction.

I could hear the Mongers yelling at the Spawn's crew to follow us, and a few moments later the screech of tires told us they were on the move. The gap between buildings was only a few feet, so it was an easy jump to the gym roof, and just as I was about to make it, my phone rang.

Ringo practically screeched to a halt and pointed to my pocket. "Answer it. Could be Jeeves." We were both breathing hard, and he scanned the buildings around us for our best escape plan.

"Saira, I'm here. Where are you?" It was Jeeves.

"On the roof. Mongers found us."

"Can you make it back to our pick-up spot?"

"I don't know, what are you driving?" I didn't like being suspicious, but it was my default reaction at the moment.

"The Rolls."

I hesitated. "Why?"

There was no hesitation in Jeeves voice. "No door locks."

That was the confirmation I needed to hear. "We'll try."

"Keep me on the line and call directions if you need me to move."

"Right. Thanks."

I tucked the phone back in my pocket as Ringo pointed to a building next to the gym. "No fire escape in back, so there must be a way down the front. They'll have to go around to catch us."

The jump to that rooftop was only about five feet, but it was slightly higher than the one we were on. I nodded. "Okay. I'm going off the ledge." The ledge at the edge of the gym rooftop was about two feet higher than the roof, and would give me the elevation to make it. I took a breath, then took off at a dead sprint. I hit the ledge with just the right stride length, and launched off. If I undershot I'd need my hands, but I managed to catch the edge with my toes and land on my feet. Ringo landed right beside me.

"Made it," I told Jeeves in my pocket.

"Now down," said Ringo. I paused to look for the white van but didn't see it on the street below us. Ringo was already headed down the fire escape ladder, which ended at the second floor. It was a fairly simple jump across two balconies to the top of an electrical box and then down to the street.

My phone was in hand a second later. "Jeeves, we're next door to the front of the gym."

"On my way," I heard faintly as I tucked the phone back in my pocket.

Just then, the double doors to the gym opened and Raven and Cole came out laughing about something. Her fencing bag was over his shoulder, and she looked ... happy.

Until she saw me.

Raven's eyes flicked between me and Ringo, then narrowed dangerously.

But I wasn't watching her. My gaze was locked on Cole's shocked expression. Was it because I had seen him with Raven, or something more nefarious?

"What are *you* doing here?" Raven practically spat the words.

The big Rolls Royce screeched around the corner as brazenly as an elegant old lady with balls of steel can do, and sped to a halt right beside us. A quick glance showed me Jeeves was alone, and Ringo was already opening the back door.

"You mean, why am I not your uncle's prisoner? I don't know, ask him." I shot Cole a wary look before slamming the door behind us. Jeeves sped away before I was even properly seated, and I had a serious appreciation for seatbelts a moment later when he took a corner like he was driving a getaway car.

In a sense, I guessed he was.

"Thank you," I said to him, my eyeballs glued to the view behind us. Raven stared after us as we drove away, and a moment later, her brother ran out of the alley just as we rounded the corner.

My voice echoed strangely, and I realized the call was still connected and I'd been on speakerphone. I hung up and my voice sounded normal again, at least as normal as one can sound when gasping for breath like a guppy out of water.

Jeeves looked grim. I could only see his eyes in the rearview mirror, and I realized I was in the backseat again. In the grand scheme of things-that-sucked, my backseat PTSD was minor in comparison to the windowless van that I kept seeing whenever I shut my eyes.

"Monger goons with a van," was all I managed to say out loud.

Ringo filled the rest in for me. "Raven's brother didn't care for the way I made him look the idiot. 'E came after me, saw Saira, and must've made a call."

I shook my head. "No, they were there too fast. They knew exactly where we were. It's something else." I thought back to my brief time in the back of the Mongers' van when they'd zip-tied my ankles. I suddenly kicked at my boots like they were on fire. When the one was off I picked it up gingerly and ran my fingers across the soles.

There, like a small black tack, was a thing stuck into the rubber just inside the heel where I would never have seen it if I hadn't been looking. "A tracking device." I dropped the boot like it burnt my hands, and Ringo picked it up thoughtfully.

"So small?" He examined it closely. "They set this when they 'ad ye, I expect?"

I nodded, trying to keep the revulsion of having been tracked from turning into vomit. "Get rid of it," I whispered.

Ringo looked at Jeeves. "Clearly they know we're goin' back to the manor, so losin' it now just confirms she found it. I say we 'ang on to it a bit longer and maybe figure a way to use it against them?"

Jeeves nodded slowly. "I agree."

I shuddered. The knowledge that Mongers had known every move I made in my boots was chilling enough, but this tracking device seemed especially designed to stick into the rubber sole. It was just so … premeditated. I mentally added shoes to the list that included back seats and white vans. It would be inconvenient, but I'd deal.

When we arrived at Elian Manor a few minutes later, I bolted from the car and ran to the house in my socks. Ringo followed me in carrying my boots, which he left by the kitchen door. I had already poured us both a cup of tea and was clutching the steaming mug in both hands in an attempt to keep them from shaking.

Ringo's voice was quiet and calm. "Which part gets ye most? The trackin', the findin', or the chasin'?"

I took a deep breath, trying to steady my thoughts. "The premeditation. They knew I'd run, and they planted the tracker to keep me on a leash."

"Maybe 'e wanted ye to run, so ye'd bring Tom back with ye and 'e could take 'im when ye landed." I shuddered violently and Ringo put a hand on my arm. "It's time for some new boots, eh?"

I gave him a feeble smile. "They were new."

He gave me a bigger one back. "And they'll fit me perfectly."

I almost barked a laugh, but it got hung up on the sob that was stuck in my throat. "For a minute, until you grow again."

Ringo's expression got serious again. "Mongers don't seem to be causin' ye trouble here at the manor anymore, so the tracker can stay 'ere. Leave it with me and I'll figure somethin' nasty to do with it. Somethin' that gets 'em where they live."

I nodded, very grateful that he was my friend. "Archer's going to be so delighted to hear about this when he wakes up," I grumbled.

Ringo shrugged. "'E'll beat 'imself up for a bit and add it to the list of ways 'e's failin' ye. And then ye'll feel 'orrible for makin' 'im feel bad, even though it wasn't yer fault. And finally, ye'll kiss and make up, and we'll get on with the business of figurin' this whole thing out."

I stared at him. "That sounds terrible."

"It does, doesn't it? Glad I'm not the one in love with ye." He shuddered dramatically and just managed to dodge the wooden spoon I threw at his head.

 VISIONS

There was a message from Professor Singh that he had gotten permission from an old friend for us to tour Bletchley Park after hours, and if we would be so kind as to pick him up at the Tower, he would work late until we got there. He had never questioned Archer's schedule, and I figured he must think Archer had a busy job during the day.

I took a long bath but still couldn't bring myself to wear any of my shoes, so when Connor found me in the east wing library, I was curled up on a couch in my socks. He dropped a shoebox next to me.

"Here. Mum sent them for you."

I looked up from my *London Underground* book in surprise, then opened the box. Inside was a gorgeous pair of oxblood leather boots. "They were to be my Christmas present, but she'd been questioning oxblood as a choice for me, so she'll get me black instead." I could almost hear the shudder in Connor's voice.

"They're gorgeous."

He rolled his eyes. "They're boots. Boots are not gorgeous. Boots are functional and, ideally, comfortable. What these also are is free from tracking devices. Mum pulled them out of the Christmas cupboard as soon as Jeeves told us what happened. I didn't even know Mum had a Christmas cupboard here. We knew about the one at home ages ago, of course."

I looked up from admiring the boots at his tone. "Do you miss home?"

He thought about it for a long moment. "I miss the memories of my dad at home, and I miss Mum's kitchen. The dogs are here though, and I like working with Uncle Bob in the lab. And it's been a long time since I've seen Mum laugh as much as she does since we moved into Jeeves' flat." He nodded at the boots. "Try them on."

"Are you sure you don't mind?"

Connor made a face. "Even the name oxblood is wrong, never mind the color. Mum doesn't need to be experimenting with my wardrobe."

I laughed and tried them on. They fit perfectly, despite the three-year age difference between us. I looked at Connor critically. "Your feet have grown."

He shrugged. "It happens. Now, tell me about Cole. Ringo said he was with the Crow at the fencing gym."

I described how Raven had greeted Cole and that they'd definitely looked like they were a couple when we saw them on the street. And I told him my fears about Cole's allegiance if he was hanging out with the Monger Head's granddaughter.

"Maybe it's the other way around and Raven's luring Cole and his sister in so the Mongers can capture the two that got away." Connor said.

I sighed and rubbed my eyes. "Where are the Seers when you need them?"

"On their way over. That was another thing I was sent to tell you. Adam and Ava are coming for tea. Mrs. Arman called to say we could have them for two hours."

I stared at him. "She didn't actually say that."

"No, but there is definitely a time limit on their visit. She and your mum were very short with each other on the phone, and it didn't seem like a social call."

I wondered if my mom had told Camille that she wouldn't be going to the Council meeting, and if so, how Camille was feeling about my Family in general. I shoved Family politics to the far corners of my brain and just let myself be excited to see the twins – they'd been away in France with their parents for weeks.

I tucked the laces into the tops of my new boots and stood up to go. "I love these boots, and I'll be the one buying your Christmas pair. Maybe I can find something in green or purple."

"Because oxblood isn't wrong enough," he deadpanned as we left the room.

Connor's dogs had joined the pack of the gardener's dogs, and the swirling mass was happily greeting Adam and Ava as they stepped out of a Range Rover. The Armans' driver nodded to Jeeves familiarly, and once Ava had scooped a dog into her arms, she waded through the rest of the pack to give me a kiss on each cheek in the French way.

"I missed you! I actually had to threaten Maman that if she didn't let us come and see you in person, I would tell the Shifter heirs which one of them their father had chosen to Head the clans after him."

I laughed and hugged Ava. "I missed you too. How was Paris?"

"Hot. Beautiful. The usual." She gave me a measured look. "We traveled south for a couple of days and stayed in Château Landon. Did you know the abbey is now a rest home?"

I thought about the gorgeous abbey that looked like it had been carved into the mountain where we had met Bas, the Vampire priest. "Did you see the spiral in the painting of the Shifter tree?" I asked.

Ava shook her head. "They've covered it with some sort of cheap plywood that they wallpapered over. Maman believes it's still there, though, underneath the trappings of institutional décor."

That abbey had been such a beautiful building; I hoped none of the artistry of it had been destroyed. Granted, the last time I'd been there was in 1429, so the chances it was intact weren't good. I wondered how Vampires like Bas and Archer could stand it when places – and people – they'd loved decayed and died.

Adam scooped me into his arms for a big hug, and then squeezed the breath out of me with another one. "That one's from Alex. She sends her love."

"Where is she?"

He beamed proudly. "She got into a choreography workshop at the Paris Opera School of Ballet. She'll be there three months."

"Oh wow! That's fantastic. I didn't know she was dancing seriously again."

"She said I wasn't the only thing she loved that she had broken up with."

I linked my arm through his and we all entered the manor. Most of the dogs stayed outside, but Connor's dog, Natasha, and Rocky, the little Jack Russell terrier in Ava's arms, came upstairs with us. Ringo was there working at a table by the window. He had the little clip and magnifying glass set-up I'd seen people use with circuit boards, and he was taking the tracking device apart with tiny tweezers.

"What's that?" Adam was hovering over his shoulder in an instant.

"Mongers stuck a tracking device to the sole of my shoe." I spat the words out of my mouth like a bad taste.

Ava shot a look at Adam. "I told you."

"What? What did you See?" As unnerving as their Seer abilities were, Ava and Adam were usually pretty forthcoming about things that affected their friends.

Ava sighed and dropped on the couch next to Connor. I had to move books off the chair, but since most of them were my books, I couldn't really complain. Ava looked over at Adam for help, but he just shrugged. "They're your visions, not mine," he said.

"I've been having really strange flashes of Sight for the past couple of days." Ava's normally cheerful voice had an edge to it that didn't sound like her. "The closest things I can compare them to are the visions that reflect in the Seer cuff."

106

I stared at her. "You mean like all the possible futures at once?"

"Maybe. I don't know. They seem really disjointed and at odds with each other, like they couldn't possibly all come true."

"Tell me what you've seen," I said.

She took a deep breath. "I saw you and Ringo running on rooftops." She included Ringo in her gaze. "I saw a white van, and I saw you both being shoved into it."

"That last part didn't happen." I had trouble keeping the tremor out of my voice at the thought of the van.

"Right, but it could have," said Connor.

I shot him a look that said, "no way," and he shot me one right back that said "way."

Ava inhaled again. "People. Underground, I think. Alex's cousin Daisy is there. Her family is so worried they've actually come out to my parents about her being mixed. She's Shifter and Seer, and the family put signs up all around Russell Square where she was last seen …" Ava's voice faded.

"Ava?" I looked at her with concern. This was information we could use to find people, but Ava had gone unfocused. She shook herself, and her eyes found mine again. "Where'd you go?" I asked.

"Back there. Underground. I keep seeing a boy I don't know. And he sees me too."

Adam stared at his sister. "He sees you having visions about him?"

She looked confused. "I think so. He tries to talk to me, but I can't understand what he says."

"That's not a Seer thing. We don't interact with other people in our visions." Adam was clearly shocked.

"You also didn't think you could change things you'd Seen, so maybe you don't actually know *everything* there is to know about your skills?" I could have pulled the punch, but Adam could take it, and I wanted to get back to Ava's vision. "What does the boy look like?" I asked.

Ava didn't hesitate. "He's our age, tan, like he spends time outside, and he has green hair."

Adam snorted. His skepticism rolled off him in waves. "He's a leprechaun."

She gave him a dirty look. "No. He reminds me a little of Ringo, only with eyes that always laugh, even when he's serious. And his hair's *dyed* green and sticks up everywhere, but not like he uses hair gel or anything. It just does."

"Definitely a leprechaun," smirked Adam.

Ringo spoke quietly. "Charlie says they're the size of small children, with a nasty laugh and razor teeth. So I don't think Ava's lad is a leprechaun."

That got everyone's attention, and Ava gave Ringo a quick, thankful smile. My chest constricted at the quietness in Ringo's voice. He missed Charlie, the girl who would know what a leprechaun looked like because she could see creatures most people couldn't. I knew Ringo combed history books looking for any mention of her. Valerie Grayson took Charlie back to 1554 to train her to become a lady and run a household. Not that she needed the training, but she had loved Valerie like a mother, and after Valerie's only son, Henry died, there was room in Valerie's heart for a surrogate daughter.

"Anyway, he Sees me, and he keeps trying to tell me something that I don't get." Ava screwed up her face in concentration and let her eyes unfocus, but then finally sighed. "No. It's something out of the line of my Sight."

Ava turned to Connor. "I've Seen your little brother in the same underground place, but he's laughing, like it's fun."

Connor's face drained of color, but he didn't let his expression change. "You know for sure it's Logan?"

Ava looked Connor squarely in the eyes and nodded. "He keeps Shifting animals. He can do that, can't he." It wasn't a question, and Connor nodded silently, looking sick.

"No one knows that," I breathed.

"People know. My mother and I have both Seen him Shift in full view of others from different Families. If they don't know it yet, they will."

"What else have you Seen?" Connor's voice was tight.

"I've Seen dark times, where Mongers rule us all with iron fists. I've seen people die …" she looked directly at me. "And I've seen them walk in daylight."

I couldn't breathe, and I went to the window. The view from the east wing was of the woods, and I could almost picture myself running among the trees as hard and as fast as I could go. Great, I'd resorted to imaginary escapism, but at least I didn't actually give in to my impulse to run. Social awkwardness aside, I needed to hear everything Ava could tell me about her visions.

"You've seen him die?" I said to the window as much as to Ava. I traced the line of a raindrop against the glass. The weather in England could always be counted on to add to a somber mood.

"Yes," she answered. "And I've also seen him live. That's why I said my visions seem impossible."

She didn't know about the cure. She didn't know Archer might have to be hurt to the point that his body started shutting down in order to introduce the virus that could cure him.

She didn't know that trying to live might kill him.

I kept my back to the room so I didn't have to see Ringo's or Connor's faces. "What else?"

Ava hesitated so long I thought she hadn't heard me. "Except for the van and running on the rooftops, you're not in any of my visions, Saira."

I tried for a scoff, but it might have come out more like a sob. "Am I ever?"

"Almost always since just before we met," she whispered.

I turned to face her and plastered a shiny fake smile on my face. "I've been replaced by a leprechaun, I guess."

Ringo's voice was solemn as he spoke to Ava. "Ye can't see into the past, right?"

She nodded. "Not unless I was going to be there."

He looked at me. "Right, then. Ye'll be goin' back. It's why ye're not in 'er visions."

"Then why is Archer in them?"

Ava turned her eyes to me. "Because he doesn't go with you?"

I looked desperately at each one of them in turn and said with every ounce of conviction I could muster. "He always goes with me. He promised to go where I go."

Ava nodded. "Of course he would." She said words meant to soothe the panic that was growing in my chest, but I knew that underneath them was the same fear that spiked in the eyes of everyone in that room – the only reason I would ever Clock anywhere without Archer was that he would die.

Adam came over and wrapped an arm around my shoulders. "You've said it yourself, Saira. Our Sight is just about possibilities, and Ava's visions are contradictory anyway. You definitely don't need to be time traveling just to get out of my sister's visions. She almost never has them about me, and we're practically the same person."

I took a deep, shaky breath and pulled some snark out of the region of my oxblood boots. "Except for all those things that are different." I stepped back from his well-meaning comfort. It wasn't helping my ability to breathe. "I totally suck as a friend right now, but I really need to go run."

Ringo and Connor immediately stood up. "Cat or human?" Asked Connor.

"Me."

He gave me a look full of scorn. "They're both you."

"Not Cat, then." I was already headed toward the door, but Ava grabbed me as I passed her. She pulled me in for a quick hug.

"The good guys always win, remember?"

Ringo threw his head at Connor. "I'll go. We'll be back when she remembers she's only 'uman."

Adam tried for levity, but I heard the concern in his tone. "Good luck with that."

I gave a half-hearted smile and was already sprinting when I hit the hallway. Ringo was right behind me.

I needed pure freerunning. No talking, no thinking, no straightest-line-between-two-places parkour. I needed to push my body past what I was comfortable doing; past what was easy. The flip off the end of the banister might have given Ringo the hint, or maybe it was the shoulder roll when I hit the ground, but there was no question about my intent once we got to the woods. I was up the stone wall with one handhold, and then did a front flip off the other side to continue the sprint where there were more natural obstacles. I wasn't usually this showy when I ran, but it made me work harder at staying whole, and I wasn't really running to run away. I was home. Elian Manor was my home, and it was filled with my people. I ran to dull the white noise of "what if" and "maybe." I ran to shift my brain into survival mode, where the "what ifs" had no power, and the only things that mattered were good footing and strong holds.

Ringo understood it because he took the lead and pushed me way past my comfort zone. He climbed like there were suction cups on his feet, just to double-flip back down to the ground. He caught me when I stumbled and pushed me when I faltered. He was me without fear, and when we were a mile away from the manor I finally felt the breath loosen up in my chest.

We free-climbed a big boulder and finally stopped moving when we were both on top. The view of the farm and woodland was so peaceful and beautiful in the golden light of magic hour, it gave me breath rather than stealing it away.

"I miss 'er." Ringo was talking to himself as much as to me. I didn't expect him to be the first one to break the silence, but his words didn't surprise me.

I nodded. "Me too."

He looked at me. "I worry though. She's findin' 'erself back there, and I'm learnin' everything of this time. If we do meet again, will we even find our way back to common ground? We 'ad it in our flat for a time – both 'idin' out, both from the street, both 'avin' survived somethin' 'orrific—" His voice trailed off and his gaze went back out to the view in front of us. "I already feel different than I was when I loved 'er. I don't even know where or when I'll fit, much less if I'll fit 'er."

I turned to face him. "Ringo, I've never met anyone who can fit any time or place better than you can. You could be a Neanderthal hunter or a Renaissance nobleman, and you'd wear it as if you were born to it. And for what it's worth, I think that knowing who you are, and having confidence in yourself is the access to finding common ground with anyone."

He met my gaze and seemed to really consider my words. "I suppose you're right. What she and I 'ave is common background, a thing only a 'andful of people in the world might 'ave. But give a man some tools and a will, and 'e can build a bridge to any ground and make it common."

I linked my arm through his. "Whoever you love is absolutely lucky to be loved by you, and whether it's Charlie or someone you can't even imagine yet, your love will be an epic one."

Ringo smirked a little. "An epic love. I like that."

I shrugged. "Everyone should be the star of their own life, and some people choose big lives to star in. You're always going to be one of those people."

Ringo stood and helped me to my feet. "Says the pot to the kettle. Are ye done feelin' sorry for yerself yet?"

I sighed dramatically. "I'm too lazy to dance at my pity party for long."

"Good. Because yer goin' to need yer wits about ye to learn what I'm goin' to teach ye."

I grinned at the challenge in his face. "Bring it!"

We worked on a backflip combo for an hour, and by the time the sun had set, I was exhausted, in pain, and totally happy. I tried not to feel too guilty about having basically run out on my Seer friends, but their visions were more than I had the fortitude to deal with.

112

It was a straight parkour run back to the manor, and by unspoken agreement we stopped at the kitchen for bowls of stew to bring with us to the library.

Archer was already there with my mom and Mr. Shaw. One look at the sweaty glow on our faces and he held a hand out to me with a smile. "Good run?"

I nodded and kissed him softly. "Necessary."

Archer held me close and studied my face. His voice was meant for my ears only. "You look so … alive. You're beautiful." He kissed me again, quickly, then let me go. "Eat. We need to leave to pick up Ravi."

I dropped into my favorite armchair and spooned bites of the Moroccan chicken and olive stew into my mouth while Mr. Shaw continued his conversation with Archer.

"How did you know about the hidden room at Bletchley?"

"I built the damn thing."

Mr. Shaw's eyebrows rose. "You built it?"

Archer nodded as though he realized how ridiculous that sounded. "When I first met her, Saira warned me about both world wars. I spent the Great War running intelligence operations, and when the second war broke out, it was clear that codebreaking would be the key to England's survival. When Bletchley was chosen as the headquarters for the codebreakers, I made sure I was on the night crew doing the retrofitting before they moved everyone in. By that time I was an accomplished forger and was able to create identities for the people I needed to be, and the government's need for secrecy guaranteed that none of the original builders came back to identify me when I returned to the park as an engineer."

Mr. Shaw stared at Archer. "That seems awfully fortuitous."

Archer's expression was wry. "Occasionally, I am still a Seer."

The look on Mr. Shaw's face was odd and I couldn't read it. "Most people, when faced with the inevitability of war, would find a safe place to ride it out."

"That is not my nature." There was a placid calmness to Archer's tone, and I thought about how easily he had accepted my own inclination to go headfirst into things that needed fixing. Of course he did, because it's what he'd been doing his whole life.

I set my bowl down and looked over at Ringo, who was also done. "Shall we?" I started to rise, but was practically blown backward by Ava's entrance into the library. It was like she arrived on a whirlwind that slammed the door open and dropped her in the middle of the room. Adam and Connor were on her heels.

Ava looked straight at me. "You have to get ready. You're going to war."

GOING TO WAR

It was one of those announcements that would be greeted either by pin-drop silence or utter chaos. In this case, it was both. The complete absence of sound happened when all the breath was sucked out of the room, and lasted just until the first "no" left someone's brain through their mouth. It might have been mine. It wasn't even what I really wanted to say, but since I'd eliminated the more colorful expletives from my vocabulary, it was all I could grab onto in the mass of denials spinning through my head.

Ava was still focused on me, and I realized that both Adam and Connor were pale and tense-looking next to her.

"What did you See?" I managed to squeak out.

"I Saw it too," said Adam.

That didn't make me feel better. Because one Arman vision wasn't bad enough? In fact, that they were still at Elian Manor was entirely upsetting, because whatever the Arman twins had Seen was important enough to defy their mother's time limit on their visit. And no one defied Camille Arman.

Ava's voice was low and urgent, and everyone else halted their various denials to listen to her. "You're leaving from Bletchley Park tonight. You—" she swiveled her eyes to include Ringo in her gaze. "—and you."

"Wait—" Archer started to speak, but Ava held up her hand to stop him.

"You can't go. We need you here to rescue the Mongers' captives."

"Why do I need to leave tonight from Bletchley?" This time I was the one who cut Archer's protest off before it could begin. He looked frustrated.

"Because it's where you're going, and you have to direct your Clocking to a very specific time, so you can't mess around with location."

"Saira's not going without me." Archer's tone was low and fierce.

Ava gazed directly at him, as if she needed to tattoo her words on his brain. "She won't be without you, Archer. You're already there."

Another stunned silence blanketed the room, and a wave of relief washed over me. Archer couldn't go with me because he was already there, *not because he was dead.* But right on the heels of relief was a whirlpool of trepidation about too many things to contemplate. Ringo was the one who finally broke the silence when he moved toward the door. "I'm off to find Sanda. We'll be needin' the right kit." His voice was entirely conversational, and it sounded odd in a room full of shocked expressions. He turned to me before he left. "Are ye going as a man or a woman this time, Saira?"

My eyes were locked on Archer's horrified ones, and somehow I was able to get the words out. "As myself."

Ringo sighed. "So, a pain in my arse, then. Right. Any idea the exact season and year, Ava?"

Ava's eyes hadn't left mine. "Season, no. You have to figure that out. But the year is 1944."

Whatever color was left in Archer's face fled, and he finally tore his eyes away from mine to turn to Ava. "How do you know that?"

"It's in the notebook your professor friend brings. And it's because of Tom."

Ringo slipped out of the library muttering to himself about clothes and weapons, and my eyes followed him just so I didn't have to deal with whatever was going through Archer's head.

"I'm going with you." Mr. Shaw's sudden statement to me made me jump.

Ava shot him a stern look that reminded me of something from her mother's arsenal. "No, Mr. Shaw, you need to be here. You're the one person standing between Logan and Connor and the Mongers who know they can be used against Saira."

My eyes found Connor's across the room. He looked as sick as I felt, but he gave me a feeble smile anyway.

My mom spoke in that tone of voice she used when she was being all badass Clocker Head. "Ava, have you discussed these visions with your mother or Jane Simpson?"

"Ms. Simpson knows. She's had every vision I've ever had since I first went to St. Brigid's."

That was startling news, and I could see it register on everyone's faces.

"And your mother?" My mom wasn't letting up, even though the revelation of a Seer secret had rocked her a little.

"She'll hear it better from Ms. Simpson than from her daughter." The calm confidence with which Ava spoke made my mom's eyes widen.

"You've been tag-teaming her for years, haven't you?"

Adam spoke quietly. "We prefer to call it information flow management."

I could see respect for both Adam and Ava bloom in my mom's eyes. She'd always liked them, but I thought she finally saw them as competent, politically inclined Descendants.

Archer held his hand out to me. "I need to talk to you," he said quietly.

We slipped out of the library as Mom and Mr. Shaw continued their conversation about Family business. I gave Connor's hand a squeeze as I went past him, and the look in his eyes was equal parts worried and grateful.

Archer pulled me into a sitting room lit only by wall sconces that cast interesting shadows from the decorative plasterwork on the walls. He sat me down on a gilt chair and brought another one closer so he could take my hands. His expression was serious.

"We were working with the SOE in 1944, and I spent a lot of time in France with one of their agents who was running the French resistance fighters at the time."

I met the worry in his eyes with confusion. "What's the SOE, and why are you so serious?"

"The Special Operations Executive was formed by the British government to run espionage, sabotage, and reconnaissance in occupied Europe. Some of them trained in codebreaking at Bletchley Park, and I got to know Nancy when she was there." Archer's expression was wary, and it sent red flags waving in front of my eyes.

"Who is Nancy?"

"She was the agent I worked with in France."

"Why are you telling me this, Archer?"

"Things were different during the war. I just didn't want you to be surprised when you see me then."

I tried to say the words I was thinking, but they wouldn't go past my rapidly constricting throat. Why tell me about Nancy? What was she to you? Those words got hung up in my brain where I could see them floating in the air like unexploded bombs.

Ringo knocked at the open door, and I was suddenly very glad for the interruption. His eyes met mine. "We're ready," he said quietly.

I let go of Archer's hands and stood up. "Okay, let me just run up to my room. I'll be right back." My voice was working again – kind of. Ringo looked at Archer oddly, as if to ask what he'd done to me, but I rushed out of the room and was down the hall before I could hear them say anything.

My room was quiet and peaceful, but the silence was doing nothing to calm my pounding heart.

118

What had Archer said before, when we sat on the roof and talked about marriage and sleeping together? That no matter what else had happened in his life, he had only ever loved me. Did that mean something else *had* happened. Something with Nancy, maybe?

I shuddered and turned my brain to the business of packing for war. What does someone bring to a war? Weapons, of course. I slipped the daggers Archer had given me out of their case and strapped them to my ankles. My new oxblood boots probably weren't WWII regulation, but too bad - they were awesome and I wasn't leaving them behind. The Shifter bone, because being a Cougar could be useful if I needed stealth … or teeth. A tin of green medicine and a mini Maglite, because I didn't travel anywhere without either one. And clean underwear. Leopard print thongs with tiny pink bows, because they were the most unlikely undergarments for war ever invented.

And because Archer knew someone named Nancy.

I was making stuff up – I knew I was making stuff up. Archer hadn't said anything about Nancy other than she was an SOE agent and he worked with her in France. But the fact that he pulled me out of the library to sit me down and tell me about her freaked me out. Why did I need to know that? What was he preparing me for?

I shoved my meager supplies into a leather satchel I'd swiped from Archer a few months before, grabbed a black Sharpie from my art supply drawer, and closed my bedroom door behind me.

Sanda met me in the hall. She was carrying a silver tray with a note on it, like something out of *Downton Abbey*, and her expression was unreadable as she held it out to me.

"What's this?" I picked the letter up off the tray.

"There's a young woman in the front parlor. She says she'd like to see you alone."

That got my attention. I slit open the envelope and pulled out a handwritten card on thick Italian paper. It read *I need to talk to you.* ~Raven

The shock must have been obvious in my eyes when I looked at Sanda. "Seriously?"

Sanda's words were casual. "Do you know, Miss Millicent used to receive male callers in the front parlor when she was young. Her parents could sit in the back parlor and feel very confident that she was being chaperoned."

In other words, someone in the back parlor can hear every word that's said in the front one.

I said solemnly, "I think I left a book in the back parlor that I might need. Could you ask Archer if he would get it for me?"

She spoke with an equally serious tone. "Of course, Miss."

She led the way downstairs, but I beat her to the bottom on the bannister. I didn't get even a glimmer of disapproval. Just a clucking sound and, "Well, if I knew you were going to do that I could have saved myself the trouble of cleaning it."

I forgot to wipe the smile off my face when I entered the front parlor, a room I rarely used because it was full of spindly-legged furniture and lots of porcelain. It was one of the few rooms in this enormous house that made me feel too big.

Raven, with her perfectly petite frame, and her perfectly made-up face, perfectly suited the gilt and silk Louis XVI chair she rose from when I came in. The smile died on my lips when the Monger-gut hit – always the pleasant side-effect of being in the same room with Raven's Family.

"How do you know Cole?" Raven's tone was somewhere between an accusation and a demand, and it was exactly what I needed to give me back my confidence in the face of her perfection.

"Hello, Raven. So nice of you to drop by." I didn't get close to her. The thought of another tracker being implanted on me made me shudder.

She ignored the pleasant smile on my face, which was forced anyway, and asked again. "Cole said you were a friend of Melanie's, but I want to know what he's not saying."

Fascinating. What was Cole's game? I watched her in silence while I decided how to answer, and my eyes dropped to her feet when she finally shifted uncomfortably. "Nice boots." I actually meant it. They were boots I would wear if I had to dress fancy and still look like I could kick butt.

"Thanks." She said automatically. My eyes shot back up to her face. That's what she had done. She wore her boots like armor because she was scared. It made me decide to tell her the truth and let her deal with it however she was going to.

"Cole and Melanie are friends with one of the kids your uncle kidnapped a couple of weeks ago." I could see the protest rise and stopped it before it could leave her mouth. "Right after I left them, your uncle tried to take me."

"You're lying." She really believed that.

"No, I'm not. Seth Walters has kidnapped over forty people. I thought Cole might have informed him where I was the day he grabbed me, but he also helped my friends find me, so now I don't know what to think, especially since he seems to be friends with you."

Raven shook her head. "Cole doesn't know Uncle Seth."

"That's probably a good thing, considering he and Melanie barely avoided the same fate as their friend."

The sneer was back in her voice. "You're not making any sense. On one hand you wondered if Cole was working with Uncle Seth, and on the other, you say he was supposed to be kidnapped by him? Pick one, although they both sound ridiculous."

"Okay, I'll pick the second one, but only because Cole's probably a mixed-blood, which puts him on your uncle's hit list."

She scoffed angrily. "Cole's not—" her voice trailed off uncertainly.

Oh … poop. She hadn't suspected, and I might have just outed Cole and Melanie to a Monger. I didn't like the guilt that prickled at my stomach and I tried to backpedal. "I don't actually know for sure. It's just that everyone else he's kidnapped is …" I trailed off lamely.

Raven's eyes finally met mine again, and this time, hers were inexplicably filled with fear. "Who else knows?"

I stared at her. "About Cole? I have no idea who knows. And it's really only a guess."

"No one can." She whispered. She was genuinely terrified.

I didn't like the fear in her eyes. "Raven, what have you heard about Seth's plans?"

She shook her head and picked up her purse to leave. Then she turned to face me, pushing the fear away and pulling on a cloak of arrogance. "Stay away from my uncle."

"I didn't ask him to kidnap me." I didn't like the defensiveness in my tone.

"He hates you, Saira. He blames you for … everything."

She swept past me and out the door of the room. I ran to the door and called after her. "Why aren't you going back to school?"

She turned angrily. "So we can't be held as leverage."

A moment later she was gone, and finally the Monger-gut left too. Guilt still pricked at my stomach for having outed Cole to her, though, and not even Archer's voice next to my ear when he found me in the hall could erase it.

"Are you alright?" He murmured.

"Leverage?" I asked.

"In war, treacherous people assume their opponents to be equally so."

I exhaled the sigh that had been squeezing my chest. "I don't like that I ratted Cole out to her."

He touched my shoulder. "Well, let's see what she does with it."

I wished he would have said *its okay*, or *you did the right thing*, but it wasn't okay, and we both knew it. So I shoved the guilt down around my knees, pulled up my own confidence, and squared my shoulders.

"Let's do this."

BLETCHLEY PARK

After some very emphatic hugs and lots of last minute advice from pretty much everyone, Archer, Ringo, and I left Elian Manor with Jeeves to get Professor Singh at the Tower of London and take him to Bletchley Park.

The minute Ravi was in the Range Rover, he pulled a small book from his coat pocket. "I found my journal from the war." Archer took it from him and carefully opened the bookmarked page and read from crackling paper, yellow with age.

He read, "June, 1944. Devereux working SOE. Going on wolf hunt. Colossus lonely without him." Archer looked up at Ravi. "A wolf hunt? I don't remember—" He caught himself in time and finished the sentence. "—my grandfather having mentioned anything about this."

What he meant was he didn't remember having worked on this, because it wouldn't happen until I could get back there to tell him about Tom's involvement with Hitler's Werwolves.

Ravi's voice was strong even as his hand shook when Archer handed the journal back to him. "Frankly, I don't remember having written it. At my age, however, I'm lucky to remember if I've taken my medicine today."

"But I bet if I asked you something about Tudor England you could still write a dissertation on it." I genuinely admired my former boss, and it bothered me that he felt like he was slipping.

Ravi smiled. "Thank you, my dear. I daresay you might be right."

We chatted about the various marriage proposals Elizabeth Tudor had received throughout her reign, and the likelihood she would have married Robert Dudley if he hadn't already been married to Amy Robsart at seventeen, and worse, if Mrs. Dudley hadn't mysteriously died from a fall down some stairs in 1560. Dudley's infidelity with Elizabeth in the Tower reminded me of my unfinished conversation with Archer about Nancy, and I had a hard time holding Archer's gaze when his eyes searched mine during a diatribe by Professor Singh on sixteenth century morals. A discussion about morals was the last thing I needed to be engaging in at that moment.

The guard at the gate to Bletchley Park waved us through when Professor Singh gave his name, and I could sense a change in Archer's mood when we drove onto the grounds.

"My friend is meeting us at the mansion so we can see for ourselves this room they've found behind the library wall." Ravi looked up at Archer as he helped him from the car and into a wheelchair we'd brought with us. "It's a pity your grandfather isn't here. He'd remember Miss Stella O'Brian with the same fondness I do. She was a Wren, you see, and worked with us on Colossus for much of the war. He would have enjoyed this."

I caught Archer's smile, hidden in the darkness of the car park. He winked at me as he started pushing Ravi's wheelchair up the long drive to the mansion. "Oh, I'm certain of it."

Ringo and I fell into step behind Archer and Ravi. Ringo slung an oiled canvas rucksack over one shoulder that I hoped was full of anything Sanda could find to help us blend into 1944. Even better if there was money or some sort of luxury goods we could trade if we needed to. I carried my own leather bag, and although Archer hadn't said anything, I knew it bothered him that we had the bags with us.

The Bletchley Park mansion loomed up to the right of the drive in a mish-mash of architectural styles. The Tudor-Jacobean red brick was jumbled up with Victorian gables and crenellated parapets in something that looked as if a factory and a wedding cake had a baby mansion and named it Bletchley. It was so ugly it was beautiful, and I couldn't take my eyes off it.

"Bleedin' 'ell," Ringo whispered under his breath.

There was a smile in Archer's voice. "At a certain point in gaudy architecture, it becomes necessary to embrace the mayhem, as Herbert Leon did when he turned the original brick country house into this gothic confection."

He rang the bell and then stepped back behind the wheelchair. The door opened, and a woman I could only describe as stately stepped forward and kissed Ravi on each cheek.

"Ravindra Singh, you finally came to visit me."

He was clearly moved by her gracious welcome, and the smile on his face was infectious. He looked back at us. "Saira, Ringo, Archer, I'd like you to meet Stella O'Brian, the most efficient and intuitive codebreaker I ever had the pleasure to work with."

The smile on her face fairly glowed as she glanced up at us – until her eyes found Archer's. "But you ..." Her voice trailed off in a whisper that matched the shocked expression on her face. Ravi spoke jovially, as if seeing ghosts were the most natural thing in the world.

"It's remarkable, isn't it? The resemblance to his grandfather? Of course, it helps that he's named after him as well."

She hadn't taken her eyes off Archer, and he held his hand out to her in greeting. "It's lovely to see you, Miss O'Brian." His voice was warm and genuinely happy, and the shock in her expression shifted to something so welcoming, I could see a flash of the beauty she had been when she was young.

"Oh Archer, it's so good to see you." I looked sharply at her. Stella O'Brian's words may have been neutral, but everything in her tone of voice said she knew he was the same Archer Devereux from all those years ago. She smiled vaguely at me, then she tucked her arm into Archer's, and he pushed Ravi's wheelchair into the mansion.

125

Through her small talk with Ravi, I gathered that Stella had come back to Bletchley Park last year as a resource to the preservationists and a part-time docent. She loved to answer questions about her work at the mansion, especially because people had been forbidden for so long from speaking about their part in the codebreaking efforts of the British government.

She hadn't let go of Archer's arm, and I could see that despite her upright posture and regal bearing, she actually needed the support. She had to be over ninety years old, after all, and I didn't begrudge her his attention, even though I could feel the clock ticking on my time with him. If Ava was right, and we were leaving from Bletchley Park tonight, I had maybe another hour here.

I thought about the Archer I'd find in the past – fifty years older than the one I'd first fallen in love with. *This* was my Archer now. This man who had survived Bishop Wilder and Joan of Arc with me, who knew my flaws and loved me anyway, who knew I liked black coffee more than tea, reading more than watching TV, and running more than almost anything except being with him. He knew I was a Cougar, and still he put me on a pedestal and made me feel like the most beautiful girl in the world.

The Archer in 1944 didn't know any of that, and suddenly I wanted to clutch Archer's hand and beg him to come with me. Ringo must have sensed I was about to do something rash because he sidled up to me and spoke in a low voice. "She knows."

I looked over to where Archer, Ravi, and Stella stood at the arched entrance to a grand, wood-paneled room I assumed was the library, and saw how she couldn't take her eyes off his face. She looked pensive when she thought no one was looking, and broke into a happy smile whenever his eyes met hers. She must have felt my gaze on her because she looked over at us with a contented smile.

And then Stella did something I recognized. Her eyes went a little glassy and unfocused, then she twitched, and when they refocused on my face, they went wide with recognition. "She's a Seer," I whispered back to Ringo.

Stella detached herself from Archer and Ravi with an apologetic smile and carefully made her way across the room to us. "You're Saira," she said. Despite our earlier introduction, it seemed like something for which she needed confirmation. I nodded yes, and her expression settled as if a question had been answered.

"He talked about you, you know."

I kept my tone carefully neutral, trying very hard not to betray the emotional sinkhole that had suddenly opened up beneath me. "Do you remember me?"

She gave me a slow smile. "Not yet. But I wouldn't, would I? You haven't gone yet."

"Is there anyone I should know when I go back? Anyone to watch out for?" Was I hoping for information about the Nancy Archer had mentioned? Maybe, but I didn't get it from Stella.

"Commander Marks was a Monger …"

"I'll be avoiding him," I said quickly.

She smiled. "He wasn't so bad. Lots of us were Seers, but just like anything else, we didn't discuss it. The SOE sent some Shifters to train with us, but they never stayed long and didn't much care for the regular staff. Archer was friendly with some though, he would know."

Nancy was SOE. Was she one of the Shifters Archer was friendly with?

Stella's eyes wandered back to where he waited with Ravi. "I suppose I should show you the hidden room. You'll want to take note of it, as I believe it's the place from which you'll depart." She included Ringo in her gaze, and then went forward to rejoin Archer. He clasped her arm in his and she leaned on him for support as they moved into the library.

"Do ye think she knows what 'e is?" Ringo asked quietly as we fell into step behind them.

"If she does, she doesn't care."

I felt a wave of insecurity about all the things I didn't know about Archer's past wash over me, and I wanted him to brush off self-doubt that itched on my skin, but I also knew that unless I could reach all the itchy places myself, the doubt would start burrowing in and making me its home. My mental metaphors were starting to gross me out, and I hurried to catch up to the others as Stella showed Ravi the catch, hidden in the woodwork, behind the fireplace.

"I'd 'ave found that in thirty seconds," Ringo whispered under his breath at my shoulder.

"The workers discovered this when they pulled the paneling off to restore the wood. It was so well-hidden that it was only the seam of the door that gave it away." Stella spoke with authority, and I thought she probably intimidated most people.

"Okay, maybe not." Ringo looked impressed with the mechanics of the hidden latch, and when Stella pushed it in, a small seam opened up between the panels.

"Voilà." Stella placed her palm on the panel and leaned into it. The door moved effortlessly, opening inward to a pitch-black space behind the wall. "I believe you'll need to walk in, Ravi. There isn't room for the chair."

Ravi moved slowly, but he could still walk, and Archer helped him to his feet. Stella pulled a small flashlight from her pocket and clicked it on before stepping into the void. Archer looked at me with a brief wince and a smile before he escorted Ravi in after her.

Ringo stopped to check out the latch mechanism and whistled his appreciation. "Another skill to add to the list of things to learn from 'im."

I slipped past him and into the space behind the wall. My night vision adjusted instantly to the gloom, but without Stella's flashlight, I would have been blind in the pitch black. A bedroll rested against one wall, and a stool sat next to it. There were three hooks on the wall, and one of them still held a wooden hanger. I pictured Archer's current wardrobe and realized he must have been living a very spartan lifestyle while he was here.

"Inside the bedroll is where we found the scraps of paper with your name on them, Ravi." Stella's voice was hushed, as if the room were still a secret. All I could think about was how lonely this existence must have been for Archer, and even though the alternative was more than I could handle, the single bedroll made me unbearably sad for him.

I suddenly had to get out of the tiny space, and I strode past Ringo without looking at him, trying very hard to hold the tears back. I made it out of the library before they came, and had to lean against the arched wall to stay upright as silent sobs wracked my body.

It was like he had lived in a cell – in a kind of solitary confinement that wasn't even living. He would have dressed in the dark, constantly hoping the library was clear every evening when he escaped. Everything in secret, everything hidden, and totally alone in the knowledge of who he really was.

And yet Archer had talked about me. As though somehow the smallest time we had spent together in 1888 made such an impression that I could still be real for him fifty years later.

His arms wrapped around me from behind and I turned and flung myself into him. He stroked my hair and murmured soothing sounds until the tears had calmed down enough for me to breathe without gasping. "I'm sorry," I whispered into his neck.

I swiped the wet streaks from his skin when I stepped back from him, then pulled the hem of my t-shirt up to wipe my face. His hands went around my bare waist, and his touch made my breath catch. "Why are you sorry? What's this about?" Archer wiped a lingering tear from my cheek as his eyes searched mine. I mentally debated the risks of sounding like the idiot I'd been if I spilled it all.

And because being an idiot wasn't the worst thing that could happen, I gave him the short version of my fear about the cure, my jealousy about whatever life he'd had before me, and my sadness at the solitude he must have known for so many years. I was about to Clock without him, to a version of him I didn't know, and I was pretty much a walking emotional disaster. The word-vomit-fest took less than five minutes, and I'd managed to at least get the tears and snot under control by the time the others came out of the library.

Ravi was back in his wheelchair looking tired after the few minutes spent on his feet. Stella, on the other hand, looked like the visit had invigorated her. She saw my face and gave me an understanding smile.

"Would you boys like to see the Colossus they've reconstructed in the H block? It's the National Museum of Computing now, of course, but you may still recognize the building, and you'll certainly recognize the machine."

Ravi's energy sparked at the idea. "Oh yes! I'd heard they built it using plans drawn from memory."

Archer's arm tightened around me as we followed them out. Ringo had taken over the job of pushing Ravi's wheelchair and managed to provide support to Stella as well. I knew it was selfish of me to have Archer by my side, but I needed just another minute or two until my knees didn't threaten to buckle with every step.

"The British government ordered all but two of the Colossus machines destroyed after the war. They didn't want the rest of Europe to realize they'd broken the Lorenz cipher," Archer explained. "The Russians were still using Lorenz, and I believe we continued to break their codes until about 1960, when it was finally revealed to them that we had Colossus. At that point the last two machines were broken up, and, as I understand it, thrown down coal holes. Consequently, the world didn't realize until recently that the English were at the forefront in computing. Credit has always gone to the Americans for their ENIAC innovations."

"That's what you guys get for having so many secrets," I smirked.

"It seems the Americans may have been the ones to let slip to the Russians that we'd broken their code," Archer shot back.

Oh. Touché.

Ravi and Stella carried on the conversation with memories of working on the Colossus machines, and Archer held me back a step so we could speak privately.

130

"I had fallen deeply in love with you in 1888, but then you were gone, and I had a new life to navigate. The first years passed quickly enough as I still lived in a world with which I was familiar. Watching my father's decline was difficult, of course, and it was perhaps fortunate that I hadn't made friends at Kings College from which to have to hide myself, but for the most part I tried to pretend I wasn't a monster and dreamt about the time we could be together again."

I held my breath, not even bothering to protest the 'monster' comment. I could feel the "but" part of the conversation coming.

"And then England went to war. You had warned me, of course, but no amount of foreknowledge could have prepared me for the sheer human devastation. It was in the Great War that I accepted that my monstrousness couldn't hold a candle to what I'd seen others do, and it was worse than you can ever imagine at the front lines. The term 'shell shock' was coined during that war, and so many, many had it. But emotional injuries were considered weak, concussive brain injuries hadn't been studied yet, and unstable, damaged men were sent back to the front lines." Archer's voice trailed off, and he looked away from me as he spoke. I sensed he was with his memories more than with me.

When he continued, he spoke directly to me. "Twenty-one years later, when Britain entered World War II, a new crop of young men volunteered for the madness, believing their patriotic duty could be served in a few months. Their shell-shocked fathers and I knew better, and I was determined to stay off the front lines of that war. I needed very much to continue to believe in the goodness of humanity, because war is terrifying. And terrified people make choices they'd never make if the circumstances were different."

There was something he wasn't telling me, and I'd never heard such hesitancy from him before. He was staring into the distance again, unfocused and not present.

"Archer? What is it," I said quietly.

This time his eyes didn't return to mine. "I thought it could continue where we'd left off. I thought I could find you and marry you and live the life I'd dreamed of, because I'd left the war behind me where it couldn't touch you. But I should have known it would catch up to me. Monsters always get theirs in the end."

The resignation in his voice scared me. "What are you talking about? I don't understand."

He inhaled shakily. "There was someone. Someone important to me."

And … there it was. I clamped down on muscles that threatened to shake and made my expression as passive and neutral as I could manage.

Archer stumbled on, deliberately not looking at me. "There was a mission in France. The intensity of surviving overcame … my control … everything."

"You slept with someone. That's what you're saying?"

He closed his eyes as if wincing at the words. "The memory is a blur."

It was the wince that got me. I usually only got nauseous around Mongers, but nausea suddenly wrapped its fist around my stomach and twisted. My heart pounded and I flushed with heat, but I forced my voice into something normal. "Was it Nancy?"

Archer hesitated. "I truly can't say. She was dynamic and fascinating, and I did go to France with her, but so much of that time is missing from my memory."

My voice dulled. "You don't remember."

His eyes had locked onto mine, as if they begged for my understanding. "It may be the shell shock … from the Great War. Even now, anything explosive makes my mind just … blank for a moment. I lose my bearing and feel as though I'm underwater, as though sound and movement go into slow motion."

I couldn't even process what he was saying. It was too much information, and every bit of it sucked. "So, you've basically had PTSD for a hundred years?"

"A form of it, I'm sure. Memory loss is a typical symptom of what they began to call battle fatigue."

"But wouldn't your virus have healed it?"

He gave me an odd look. "Only part of the damage was physical, and psychiatric help doesn't keep my hours."

The fist in my stomach twisted tighter.

Archer stopped walking. "Why is my shell shock the focus of your inquiry? I would have thought you'd want to know …" His voice trailed off, and I thought I'd never seen Archer at such a loss for words.

"That I'd want to know about your lover?"

He winced. Good. I was cringing inside at the term, the thought, and everything about the idea.

"I really don't, Archer. I get why you told me. Running into the two of you getting cozy together would be phenomenally awkward, and more than a little bit painful, but I really wish I didn't have to know. I mean, it was like, seventy years ago, and you hadn't seen me in more than fifty years. Rationally, it doesn't make sense for me to even care."

"But do you?" he asked quietly.

Finally, he was meeting my eyes again. I exhaled. "Yeah, I care."

"I'm sorry, Saira. As I said, I know it happened, though I don't have any of the details. But I thought you should know, so maybe you won't hate me when you return."

Ringo, Ravi, and Stella were waiting for us at the entrance to a long, cement block building. I took Archer's hand and threaded my fingers through his. "I couldn't hate you."

I could feel the tension begin to seep out of him. "Thank you."

"But don't do it again," I said. "You're mine."

He gripped my hand tightly. "Yes, I am."

COLOSSUS

Ringo held the door for us, and Archer went to push Ravi's wheelchair. Ringo whispered to me as I passed him. "Are ye alright?"

I smiled a little too brightly. "I'm fine."

"Liar." His eyes searched mine for a brief moment, but he didn't press the issue. It wasn't my story to tell, and dissecting my feelings at that moment was about as appealing as dissecting the formaldehyde squid eyeball that squirted eye juice at me in fifth grade.

The first room we entered was set up for visitors to see the history of the Tunney machine, including a listening station where the encoded messages would have been received and instantly translated into teletype tape by Wrens. It was a really well done exhibit that looked like the Wrens had just stepped out for a cup of tea.

The next room held a giant machine covered with valves and wires that was nearly as tall as the ceiling and practically filled the room. I couldn't even imagine how all the parts worked together to find the code key from hundreds of millions of possibilities, and even though the cell phone in my pocket was a technological giant in comparison, this machine could give anything an inferiority complex.

"We used to dry our laundry on top of it." Stella's voice was quiet in the room, and I turned to find her watching me. She was

134

smiling. "The girls in the other huts were jealous that our woolen stockings would dry in time to wear home, while theirs were always still damp from the walk to work. It was one of the perks of working with Colossus. The other perk was working with those two men." She nodded toward the other room where I could still hear Ravi expounding on the life of a Colossus engineer.

"What was he like then? Archer, I mean."

Stella had moved next to me at the railing and was looking at Colossus as she spoke. "He was very serious, as if he knew that the work we were doing here meant life or death. It did, of course, but we didn't know that at the time. It wasn't until the Bletchley Park archives were declassified that the statistics began to come out. Your President Eisenhower credited our work as having shortened the war by two years. And certainly, we were instrumental in the success of the D-Day landings in 1944."

I gasped at the realization that I'd forgotten something so important. "When was D-Day?"

"June 6th. Wrens were absolutely glued to the teletype machines translating the enormous number of messages that came through from German high command. It was around that time that Archer was sent to France with the SOE mission to help the French resistance fighters to stop the 2nd SS Panzer Division from getting to Normandy. There were no men available to replace him, so Ravi promoted me to help him keep the beast running."

June 6th. A day when all English eyes would be focused across the channel at Normandy. Tom would know the date. Could his mission in London be planned around the Allied D-Day invasion? It seemed too horrible to contemplate. No matter how disillusioned Tom had become, I didn't think he would actually betray his country.

"There was a note attached to a piece of tape, like the stuff that ran through Colossus. They found it in the bedroll in the hidden room, and it was addressed to Ravi. Did you see that?"

Stella's eyes widened and she shook her head. "I didn't. One of the curators asked me about Ravi, and of course I told them his full name, but I didn't know why. What was the note?"

I showed her the photo on my phone.

She seemed startled. "June 4th, 1944. The day I got engaged. It was just before Archer left for France."

"Ravi remembers having seen this message when it came out of Tunny. He said you took it up to the mansion."

"I often did take messages up to Colonel Marks. But I never read them."

"The torn tape is only part of the message, and Archer wanted Ravi to find the other piece."

"Those tapes were always tearing, and this piece of tape isn't actually the message itself. It's the teletype transcription of the encoded message. It was run through Colossus purely for the purposes of determining that day's code settings."

"Which means what?"

"It means that this piece of tape is from an encoded message which can't be decoded without the settings from June 4th, 1944. And as all the records from Colossus were burned right after the war, it is now just a torn relic of an extinct codebreaking process."

And there it was.

That was the reason I had to go back in time. Ava and Adam had Seen me go, but until that moment, I hadn't really accepted that there was a compelling reason to. Not really. But unlocking the rest of the encoded message about the mission in London could only happen with the decoding key from that day, so in one fell swoop I had motive to go and a date to focus on. June 4th, 1944.

Stella was studying me, and I realized I was going to need her help when I went back. "So, who'd you marry?"

She gave me a sly smile. "Colonel Marks."

I gaped at her. "The Monger?"

"Of course I didn't advertise the fact that I was Family. My mother had been very private about her gifts. Not even my father knew, and James' parents had been killed in the Blitz."

"Did you have any children?" I tried not to let my shock show, but Stella's expression began to shutter and I quickly added. "I'm mixed, by the way, and I wasn't raised with Family prejudices. I'm just curious."

She seemed to assess me before she answered. "Our son lives in Portsmouth, and my grandchildren and great-grandchildren are scattered around Britain."

I had a sudden thought. "Are they all accounted for?"

Her assessing look turned hard. "Why?"

"Because mixed-bloods have been disappearing around London. A Monger named Seth Walters is responsible for the kidnappings, and we've been working to find them."

Her expression shifted to concern immediately. "My family is safe."

"And no one knows about them?"

"We lived in Australia after the war. Our son didn't go to St. Brigid's, and neither did his children. My grandson married a Seer, but her family never met James and assumes I'm the only true Descendant in Nolan's family."

"Good. I'm sorry if my questions made you uncomfortable."

Her smile didn't reach her eyes, but I didn't think it was because of me. "When James and I fell in love, the world was at war and the prejudices against mixing seemed so unimportant. James would have been appalled, as I am, at the prejudice that remains."

Archer pushed Ravi's wheelchair into the Colossus room, and I thought Stella was glad for the interruption. She went to Ravi's side and pulled a stool around so she could sit next to him to talk. Archer came up behind me and touched the small of my back lightly.

"Is everything okay?"

I turned to face him. "The note you left for Ravi was from June 4th, 1944. I think I need to get there on the third so I can tell you to look for the decoded message."

His eyes narrowed. He wasn't happy about this trip, and honestly, neither was I. I tried to diffuse the tension with practicality. "Where should I find you?"

The expression on his face was unreadable. "If you arrive at night, I'll be here. If it's daytime, I'll be in my room behind the library wall."

I winced. "I should probably plan to Clock in your cupboard then, since there would have been a whole shift working with you here. Hopefully you're not too jumpy about strangers in your space."

He leaned in and smelled my skin. "I'll know it's you."

"Fifty years later?" I said incredulously.

"I'll always know you." The whisper of his breath in my ear made me tremble. I leaned my head back onto his shoulder and he held me like that for a year, or maybe just a minute, tattooing my skin with his heartbeat.

"I think Ravi may have overdone it." Stella spoke to us as she held his hand in hers, and surreptitiously checked his pulse. Archer and I raced to his side.

Ravi cracked an eye open and glared at her. "I'm not dying, just tired. A quick nap will do wonders."

Archer smiled at him and stood to navigate the chair out of the Colossus room. "Let's get you back to the car."

Ravi finally allowed Stella's hand to slip from his. "Thank you, my dear. It's been far too long, and yet you remain as lovely as the day I met you."

Stella leaned over and kissed him on the cheek. "Ravindra Singh, you always could charm the gold from a leprechaun."

Archer wheeled him out and Stella held her arm out to me. "Come, my dear. I put on a good show, but I'm as exhausted as he is. Walk me to my car?"

I took her arm and we navigated our way out of H Block, shutting off lights and locking doors behind us. Ringo emerged from the darkness outside as we made our way back to the mansion.

"Where have you been?" My voice was just above a whisper. The Bletchley Park grounds at night seemed to require stealth and quiet, as though its secrets were still being kept.

"Reconnaissance," he whispered back.

"We're leaving soon," I said quietly.

I could see his silent nod in the dark, and Stella squeezed my arm. "When you see me again, please tell me to trust my Sight. Even when it shows me impossible things." I could hear the smile in her voice. "And tell me James really did like butter, he just gave me his ration coupons for it every week because he knew how much I loved it."

"Will it shock you to know I'm a Clocker when I meet you then?"

She shook her head. "Oh no. One of my grandmother's dearest friends was a Clocker, and she often told me stories of the places they dreamed of seeing together when they were girls."

I laughed. "I promise, it's not as glamorous as it sounds. Did your grandmother ever get to Clock with her friend?"

"No, sadly. Her friend suddenly became heir to the position of Clocker Family Head, and they grew apart as responsibilities changed."

I stared at her. "Was her friend Emily Elian?"

Stella sounded surprised. "Yes, I believe she was."

"Emily was my aunt." That announcement was met with stunned silence. "I'll introduce you to her granddaughter when I get back, if you like."

"I ... I'd like that very much." She hesitated a long moment. "You said you were of mixed blood. Is your mix one of Time and ... Death?"

I stared at her. "Death? No. Time and Nature. My mom Clocked forward to have me. She's native to the Victorian era."

"Oh, I see. I'm sorry, I thought ..." It wasn't that she sounded relieved, exactly, because it seemed like she knew what Archer was. But maybe the idea of two Vampires in such close proximity was unsettling.

It actually unsettled me. Not the idea of being around Vampires, but the idea that I could be one.

It would solve a lot of problems.

And create about a million more.

I realized I hadn't answered Stella, and she must have thought she offended me because she apologized. I told her there was no need to apologize, but I was only partly engaged in the conversation while my mind was spinning with all the possible ramifications of adding Death to the mix.

"No." Ringo whispered to me. I jumped, because it sounded like he was answering the question I'd just mentally asked myself. Could I become a Vampire so Archer didn't have to risk the cure? "No," he said again. His tone of voice was like he was trying to shake some sense into me.

I climbed off of my mental merry-go-round long enough to say goodbye to Stella. She held my hands in hers, wished me luck, and said she looked forward to the memories she'd have of meeting me in 1944. I told her I would invite her to tea with Millicent when I returned. She cupped Ringo's cheek in her hand and looked sternly at him. "Don't get caught, my dear."

Before either of us had a chance to comment on that cryptic statement, Archer jogged over. "Ravi's already asleep and will likely stay that way long enough for me to get him home without his noticing that you didn't return with us," he said. He bent to kiss Stella on both cheeks, she asked him to come visit her again, and she got in her car and drove away.

"She's lovely," I said to Archer as he waved to her one last time.

"She always has been."

"She married a Monger."

He shrugged. "James Marks was a decent fellow, as colonels went. He certainly loved her enough to make up for any deficits in his heritage."

"How'd he feel about you?"

"If he knew what I am, he never let on, and considering the hours Stella worked with us, he was actually quite civil."

"Are ye goin' to tell 'im what ye were just thinkin', Saira?" Ringo's voice was quiet and held none of the teasing tone ours had.

"I wasn't really—"

"Yes, ye were. Tell 'im." Ringo's tone didn't allow for wiggle room.

Archer was waiting expectantly. I sighed. "Stella asked if I was a mix of Time and Death, and it made me wonder—"

"No." The quiet certainty in Archer's voice was exactly the kind of tone that made me bristle and immediately want to do exactly what I'd been denied.

My eyes narrowed at him. "No? Just like that? You haven't even heard what I was going to say."

His eyes narrowed right back at me. "You wondered if you were turned, would that alleviate any desire I have to attempt Shaw's cure? Because if your hours were suddenly in line with mine, perhaps I wouldn't need to see the sun again or feel it warming my skin. And if you were essentially immortal, perhaps I could let go of my unreasonable and inconvenient need to keep you safe. Is that a fair approximation of your thoughts?"

It was, but I'd rather have walked barefoot over hot coals than admit that out loud. I glared at him. "It made me *wonder*—" I had to think fast to come up with something plausible that didn't let him be right. "It made me wonder if *Tom* still had his Sight and would See me coming. He obviously still has use of the Clocking skills he got from Wilder, and that made me wonder how good your Clocking skills might be, since you had some of my blood." I put my hands on my hips and dared either of them to contradict me.

Ringo's eyes laughed at my obvious re-direction, and he turned to Archer and said in a perfectly calm and reasonable voice, "Good point. 'Ave ye tried to Clock on yer own?"

"Obviously not. I have no interest in going anywhere Saira isn't. I did try to draw a spiral once. That went nowhere." Archer had schooled his own tone of voice to match Ringo's casual one, and I forgot to be so mad.

"You did?"

Archer nodded.

"Do you want to try tracing one of my spirals?"

"No, but as much as I hate to admit it, it's time you did. I need to get Ravi back home to his flat, and now that it's clear when and where you should arrive, additional delay just makes it that much longer before you return."

We had started to make our way back up to the mansion when Archer grabbed my hand suddenly, and pulled me around to face him while Ringo walked ahead. "I'm not kidding though, Saira. I won't turn you, and another Vampire would likely kill you." His eyes burned fiercely. "The way you feel about my desire to attempt Shaw's cure is the way I feel about this. If it were something I believed you truly wanted for yourself, I might understand it. But to even consider something so … life-altering, as a means of avoidance – that, I can't abide."

All the air went out of my defiance and my shoulders slumped. Archer pulled me into his arms for a quick, tight hug before we continued walking. "In a perfect world, you're back before I wake up tonight, and then we go find the missing mixed-bloods together."

My voice was a whisper. "If Tom finds me and we can leave 1944, I *will* be back before you wake up tonight."

He sighed. "Finding Tom that quickly is about as likely as my perfect world scenario." He kissed my forehead and we got to the mansion just in time for Ringo to open the front door from the inside. I didn't even ask how he'd gotten in. That would be like asking the sun how it set that day.

We slipped through the dark mansion to the library, and Archer opened the secret door in the fireplace wall. "I'll be needin' the plans for that door when we get back," said Ringo.

Archer smiled. "Ask me in 1944. It'll be a lot fresher in my memory then."

142

Ringo pulled a mini Maglite from his satchel, then tossed me the other bag he had somehow stashed in the secret room. He aimed it at the white plaster wall, then pulled out a piece of white chalk. I thought that was pretty brilliant and I told him so. The spiral would be nearly invisible when we left. "Milady," he said as he handed it to me.

I threw my arms around Archer and held him tightly. My heart was pounding so hard I could feel it in Archer's chest, and I inhaled the warm, spicy scent of his skin. "I love you," I whispered in his ear.

"Come home to me," he whispered in mine.

Tom – Limoges, France – June, 1944

They were beating the kid again.

Karl was taking it because standing up to the bullies was a sure way to get stabbed in his bunk. I was halfway down the stairs on my way back to the planning room, away from the grunts the tough guys made as they punched the kid in all the places the bruises wouldn't show, when I heard it.

The whimper.

If Karl had kept his mouth shut, if he'd taken the beating like a man, I could have left them to it. They were Bestien – beasts – all of them, and they'd made their little Nazi beds with perfect corners and blankets you could bounce a mark off of. They'd drunk the Kool-Aid and swallowed their Aryan master race bollocks hook, line, and sinker. And when they turned on each other like sharks, I didn't get in their way. Let them take each other out. It would save me the trouble.

But the whimper had come from a piece of humanity that somehow survived the brainwashing. It was weakness in a world where the weak were exterminated, and suddenly it was the only thing worth a damn in the whole place.

I turned and went back up the stairs.

"Hört sofort auf!" My German was good enough to communicate with the bullies, but the tone of my voice would have sufficed on its own. "Stop it. Right now."

144

They froze and stared at me. The smaller, weasel-faced sniper had been about to punch the kid in the kidney, and he braved a question. "Why?"

"Because I said so." I was already bored and regretting my brief, altruistic impulse.

The sniper dropped his arm and shared a look with his fellow Bestien. There were five of them, because of course five on one was sporting, and I could almost hear them wondering if they could take me.

I smiled.

They left.

I was that terrifying.

A reputation can be a useful thing in war, and mine was becoming the sort from which legends are made. At first it was just playing the odds – Germany was going to lose this war, so if I threw in my lot with them, somewhere along the way a bomb or a tank would take me out. I was counting on that.

At first, they weren't sure what to do with me, an apparently traitorous Englishman. They tried to shoot me as a spy a few times, which didn't work, obviously. Then, when they realized my skills might be handy, they put me to use, though they kept me pretty far away from any of the senior Nazi officials, because, well … I'm hard to explain. Then the Crimea happened.

The regular German army was taking its cannon fodder to Russia, and since I preferred to kill Russians rather than Englishmen, I signed up. I also knew the Russians were going to wipe the floor with the Germans, so naturally, that's where I wanted to go. The Germans' view of me changed the night I cut through a swath of the Red Army with a sword. A Soviet officer intended to run me through and I was tired of smelling like my own blood, so I took his ceremonial blade from him and added his to the mix instead. His comrades started shooting, and that pissed me off because … more blood, so I removed them, one by one. In the end, I stood alone in the middle of a Soviet command camp, surrounded by the bodies I'd hacked to pieces, and covered in …

yes, blood. The smell of it sickened me, even as I craved it. My reputation as a killer to be feared was born.

It wasn't really how I'd planned things, but since then I'd made it work to my advantage. I got myself attached to the Werwölfe, who got the jobs no one else wanted because the body count on both sides was always so high.

But they were bullies. I didn't care about them, and the way Karl was looking at me, like I was his personal savior, made me want to kill the bastard myself.

I was no one's savior.

"Thank you." He had to clear his throat of weakness to make his voice work.

I glared at him. "They'll be back. You should go."

He looked stricken. "I can't leave the Werwölfe. My mother would cry if I dishonored my family."

I shrugged. "She'll cry when they beat you to death, too."

I left him there, on top of the tower of a commandeered estate just outside Limoges where the Werwölfe had come to quell recent resistance activity from the French terrorists known as the Maquis. My boots were silent on the stone steps, and my entrance into the study startled Diekmann, the SS Sturmbahnführer in command of our small terrorist unit. He wasn't afraid of me, which made him dangerous, and he carefully schooled his expression to betray nothing. I didn't like him – I didn't like any of them, and Diekmann was most likely insane – but he was also meticulous, thorough, and he left nothing to chance.

"Take Karl off my team," I said in German.

"No. He's a useful navigator. You need him." Diekmann studied a map of the villages around Limoges as he spoke so he didn't have to meet my eyes. "You are also fluent in French, are you not?"

I stared at him. "Yes," I said carefully.

"You speak it without accent."

"I speak it with a French accent. What's your point?"

Diekmann ground his teeth together. "SS Brigadeführer Lammerding has requested that the Werwölfe infiltrate the local resistance so that we may discover their weapons caches. They have been entirely too active in this area recently, and Lammerding suspects a bigger plot."

I stared at him. "You can do with the rest of them what you like. I'm only here in France waiting for the quickest way to London."

Diekmann faced me properly, and there was madness in his eyes. I actually wondered if he would attack me, and part of me wouldn't have minded. "You do not have a say in the matter, Werwolf. Did you not wonder why Berlin would send you to England via France? This mission is your first priority. The English mission was merely the carrot they dangled to get you here."

I glared at Diekmann. "They don't intend to go forward with London?"

He waved a dismissive hand. "Of course they do, but they don't need you to do it. Your interest in the London mission is obviously personal. We've decided to exploit that." His gaze turned sharp. "Find the Maquis weapons, or you will be removed from the English mission."

I growled furiously. "Remove me and the mission will collapse."

Surprisingly, he growled back. "Locate the resistance headquarters, slay some terrorists, and I'll send Karl home."

Bastard.

Finally, I grit my teeth. "Send him home now. Oskar and Johann will kill him while I'm gone."

"Get me French weapons information and I'll put him on a train myself. Until then, I'll send Oskar and Johann into the woods to hunt. God knows we could use the fresh meat."

Those two were trained snipers, so it was logical to send them out for food. If I was lucky, maybe they'd manage to get themselves murdered by the French terrorists so I wouldn't have to do it. "When does my transport leave for London?"

"You're set to depart on June 12th." Diekmann could sense he was gaining ground with me.

"The inside man is expecting me?" After the Crimea, the Werwölfe had recruited me for the mission in London. But the inside man was the reason I took the job.

"He's expecting an English art broker, which means, yes, he's expecting you." Diekmann's tone was dismissive.

"The man's a thief. What makes you think a man who betrays one country won't betray another?" I allowed contempt to lace my voice.

Diekmann snorted, no doubt thinking it was ironic to hear that from an Englishman in the German army, then he ground out the words. "George Walters contacted us regarding this gift to the Führer, and he will be paid very well for his services. Additionally, we have his wife and his brother in our custody."

"That presupposes he cares about their well-being," I said.

Diekmann scoffed. "Only a monster would willfully cause the death of his family."

What he didn't know was that George Walters *was* a monster.

George Walters was my great-grandfather.

BLETCHLEY PARK – JUNE, 1944

Never mind the Clocking, I almost puked from disorientation. It was pitch black in the hidden library room, and Ringo's clutch on my arm was the only thing that proved I wasn't trapped in the nothingness of *between*.

"Is 'e 'ere?" Ringo struggled to keep his voice low.

I quickly stifled my relief at the sound of his voice. A tiny, niggling part of my brain had wondered if he would actually make it to 1944 with me, or if he would be kicked through to a date he didn't already occupy. It begged the question of why Ringo wasn't already here, considering it was still within a natural lifespan, but it wasn't a question I wanted to ask, and certainly not out loud.

But since I could barely find my voice anyway, I had to whisper. "I don't think he's here. I didn't focus on the time, only the date. So it's probably the same time as it was when we left."

"After midnight, then. Right. Can ye sense any Mongers in the library beyond the wall?"

I'd been getting better at sending my spidey sense, as Archer called it, out beyond me. It was actually more like my Cougar sensing predators in her vicinity, because it was particularly effective with Mongers, but I could often sense regular people too.

"No Mongers."

"That's somethin', at least."

Ringo set his satchel down against the wall and I did the same. Before we left Archer, we had handed over everything that didn't

149

fit 1944, including my phone, which would have been dead in about eight hours anyway. I kept a Maglite and my daggers, and then changed into the wartime clothes Ringo and Sanda had scrounged from the closets at Elian Manor. Archer had admired the wool wide-legged trousers and suit jacket I wore, and I had to admit, I felt a little like Katherine Hepburn in the outfit. Apparently, women in Britain had taken to wearing their husbands' clothes to work because of rationing, and to save their dresses for special occasions, so according to Archer, my preference for practical clothes would finally blend into the period.

"I'm goin' out to find my own place. Are ye stayin' in, or will ye go find 'im?"

"You're not going to sleep here?"

I couldn't miss the scowl in his voice. "I wouldn't take kindly to another man where my woman slept, and I've no idea 'ow long it's been since 'e's seen me. I'm not willin' to risk it, thank ye very much."

Ringo slid his hand along the wall until he found the hidden latch. He flipped it and then waited a breath before allowing the door to open a crack. The library beyond was dark, but the moonlight shining in was like daylight in comparison to the pitch-blackness of the tiny room hidden behind the fireplace wall. There were desks set up near the windows, and I realized that any room without curtains would be dark because of the general blackout restrictions throughout England that were put in place during the Blitz. That's why Archer had managed to hide his secret room's existence – no one worked in the library at night.

I followed Ringo out and he closed the door behind us.

"I'll walk ye to H Block," Ringo whispered in my ear.

I nodded, and we slipped out of the library and down the hall to the front door. The front of the mansion had the biggest windows, so it seemed safe to expect it to remain unused at night. The air outside was crisp and remarkably silent, and we walked quickly down the drive toward the blocks. They were also dark and silent, but we could see that those windows had blackout drapes, and the occasional seam of light spoke of night shifts working inside.

Ringo checked the war-era watch on his wrist. "A tenner says they'll be breakin' for tea in five minutes."

"Then we better be in H Block by then." Four minutes later we had made it to the outer door.

Ringo put an arm out to stop me from entering. "Wait. Tuck back against the wall for a minute. Let's let 'em leave first."

As if by some alarm bell we couldn't hear, the doors to various blocks opened at once, and Wrens emerged chattering in whispered voices to each other like wind rustling through trees. Then, a minute after that, the men emerged. Some wore suits, and some wore khaki pants with their shirtsleeves rolled up. Their voices were low but carried further on the night air, and from their conversation, I gathered these were the engineers and mathematicians.

My heartbeat slammed in my throat, and I realized I was terrified to see Archer.

Ringo gripped my hand for an instant and whispered in my ear. "Go on. 'E didn't come out."

"Come with me?" Nerves made my voice shake.

"I'll be behind ye for back-up, but ye can do this just fine."

I took a deep breath, then stepped around the open door and almost ran into a girl about my age and nearly my height just pulling on a uniform jacket as she ran out.

"Oh, I'm so sorry. I didn't see you there." She said a little breathlessly.

Her voice hit me like a jolt, and I grinned at her. "Hi, Stella."

I slipped in past her and caught a glimpse of her startled look as I turned the corner into the Colossus room.

The massive machine was making a humming, clacking noise that wasn't unpleasant, just rhythmic, and it was definitely putting off heat. It was at least ten degrees hotter in that room than it had been outside, and I took off my jacket without thinking.

There was a man kneeling behind Colossus, and the movement must have caught his eye because he stood suddenly, and I stepped backwards, startled.

"Saira?" His voice sounded like shock and surprise and hope and wonder all wrapped up in a whisper I could barely hear over the clack and hum of Colossus.

I managed a smile somehow, despite my nerves, and was surprised to find my voice actually worked. "Hi, Archer."

He looked different. The same, but somehow less … himself. Until he smiled.

"My God, it's really you." He was already moving toward me, and my own body was in motion before I could think the command. But he didn't fling his arms around me like I expected, and my arms were already held wide when he stopped right in front of me. I dropped them self-consciously as he searched my face with his eyes.

"You're here," he whispered. His eyes brimmed with tears, which to my complete shock, rolled down his face. He didn't even seem to notice.

I nodded and reached up to wipe a tear off his cheek. He held my palm to his face and closed his eyes. His hand trembled, and I whispered, "Hey, it's okay. I'm here."

His smile was back, and it was so heartbreakingly beautiful I wanted to cry. Then his eyes shifted, and he suddenly saw Ringo behind me. They widened in surprise. "Ringo? Is that you?"

I turned to find Ringo grinning at Archer. "Ye think I'd let 'er come see ye without me?"

The surprise was replaced with pure joy as Archer strode to Ringo and threw his arms around him. It was the hug I'd expected. "God, man! It's been a half a century since I've seen you like this. It's so good to see you!"

Ringo hugged him back. "You too, my friend."

Archer stepped back from him and his eyes locked on mine again. "So I did find you."

"You knew you would. I told you that you would."

152

He looked at me with something like longing. "There are times I wonder if it was all just a dream. But then I remember the things you told me," he waved his hand around the room, "and I trust that you are real."

I touched his face again. I couldn't help myself. "I am real."

Someone cleared their throat behind me, and I spun around to find a young Indian man standing next to Colossus. I was about to say hello to Ravi when Ringo poked me. He shook his head sharply when I turned to glare at him.

Archer reached for my hand. "Ravindra Singh, this is my … this is Saira." Despite the hesitation, his tone was proud.

Ravi's expression, initially suspicious, became something friendly and warm. He stepped forward to take my hand. "Miss Saira. It is a pleasure to finally meet you." He bent to kiss the back of it, and his smile was bright and genuine.

"Thank you, Mr. Singh, it's a pleasure to meet you, too."

"Oh, please call me Ravi. It is what my friends call me, and I would be honored if you would as well."

Archer introduced Ringo to Ravi as his brother, and I could see the pride shine in Ringo's eyes. Despite their physical differences – Archer was dark-haired with blue eyes and refined features, and Ringo had sandy blond hair, green eyes, and an impishness that would probably still light up the old-man-face he would eventually wear – they both held themselves with calm confidence, and they moved with a similar athletic grace. They really could be mistaken for brothers, and I knew it was how they thought of each other.

"I'll go for tea, Ravi," Archer said. "Can I bring you anything?"

Ravi shook his head and gave me another smile before returning to his work. Archer ushered us out and spoke in low tones. "I have a private place to talk."

"Your secret room. It's where we came in," I said quietly.

He looked startled for about half a second, then smiled again. "Hearing you say that makes me absurdly happy. It just confirms that we've been together in your time."

"Still are. You'd be here with me if you weren't here already."

Something clouded in his expression, but he didn't say anything else until we had all slipped into the hidden room inside the mansion. "As you've no doubt assessed, the public rooms at the front of the mansion are unused from sundown to sunrise. With rationing being what it is these days, the big blackout drapes originally made for these windows were cut up long ago to cover the windows in the huts. That's where the important work is being done."

He lit the stub of a candle on a stool next to his bed, and I dropped down to sit cross-legged on his bedroll. I patted the spot next to me. "Sit. I can't think with both of you looming over me, and I'm too tired to stand anymore."

Archer hesitated for a brief moment before he finally sat. Ringo squatted with his back to the door and his arms around his knees.

"As you say, my future self would be here with you if I weren't already here. That takes this visit out of the realm of a social call. So, how can I help you?" Archer's voice had a clipped, formal edge to it that hadn't been there when he first saw us.

Ringo was silent, obviously waiting for me to take the lead. So I bit my tongue against all the lame protests his tone inspired and ran down the bare facts about the message they'd be receiving tomorrow.

Archer's gaze didn't waver. "So, I'm to look for a message about an Englishman named Landers leading a Werwolf incursion into London, decode it, and pass it along to you." Again, his tone spoke volumes more than his words did.

I sighed. He was clearly annoyed, and I was too tired to disarm it. "There's a huge amount of back story to it, but I'm afraid to tell you most of it because whatever you know now could affect the future when it actually happens. And I'm feeling pretty useless at

154

the moment because I haven't slept in way too many hours. Can I just lie here for a minute and figure out what's safe to tell you?"

The hard edges around his eyes softened a little as he stood and offered me his bedroll. "Of course. I'll leave my shift early so perhaps we can have a chance to talk before I go down for the day."

"I'd like that." I smiled up at him. The tenderness was back in his eyes, but I couldn't shake the feeling that I was on eggshells with this Archer. Then he looked at Ringo, and the tenderness was gone again.

"I only have the one blanket, but I can find a small rug for you if you'd like." Archer's voice was carefully neutral, and Ringo responded with a smirk. He wasn't letting Archer put up any formality walls with him.

"Ye'll remember yer lady talks in 'er sleep. If I'm to get any rest, I'll need to find a cupboard for myself and meet ye back in yer 'ut at sundown if it's just the same to ye."

My eyes were drifting closed, but I could hear the smile in Archer's voice. "Yes, she does talk in her sleep, doesn't she. Come, I'll point you in the direction of a private cupboard that could work."

I was asleep before they'd even closed the door.

"Archer?" I whispered into the darkness.

"Shhh, stay asleep," he whispered back.

I reached for him, and I *was* still mostly asleep. I found him sitting on the edge of the bedroll, and I pulled myself into his lap before I gave it a second thought. When he tensed, I realized my mistake and struggled to sit up. This wasn't my Archer, who held me close without hesitation, and who had slept wrapped around me as often as we could find time to be alone. I didn't know this man, not really. Not yet. And fifty years was a long time ago for him.

"What time is it?" I asked.

"Nearly dawn."

"Then you should lie down. I'll sit."

He hesitated. "Would you being lying next to me in your time?" His whisper was so tentative it was almost silent.

"Yes."

I could hear the catch in his breath when he spoke again. "Then we'll share the bed."

"Only if you shove all your Victorian judgments about my morals down around your ankles." I tried to keep my whisper lighthearted, but I meant it.

"I don't think—"

"Yes you do. But we haven't done more than sleep – actually sleep – together. Even seventy years from now you have the crazy idea that we have to be married for anything to happen."

"We should be married," he said quietly.

"*There's* the Victorian in you. That's the one I'm talking about." It's hard to scoff a whisper, but I pulled it off.

"No. I mean we *should* be married. I should have married you fifty years ago." His whisper dropped again. "I wanted to."

Instead of yelling *What is it with you and marriage?* like I wanted to, I remembered that this Archer and I had never had that conversation. So I took a deep breath and said simply, "I'm too young."

"And I'm too old." His voice sounded sad. "And the world is at war. And people are dying. And you are not in your time. But among all the uncertainties in the world, of one thing I am most certain. You are the reason I have the strength to go on. Since we first met, every path I've chosen has been with you imagined by my side, with the hope that someday we would walk a single path together, find a place that is ours together."

I couldn't find the right words to respond, and Archer reached for my hand to pull me close to his side. In this position, I knew I'd be able to sleep again, and I settled back into him. "I'm sorry," he said. "I've had far too much time to dwell on my feelings for you, and you barely know me. I find I'm jealous of myself – of all the time and experience with you I will have. Forgive my intensity."

My chest was tight and I couldn't breathe properly, but the warm, spicy scent of his skin was like my home and I felt myself begin to relax. "It's okay. You've done it before."

"I have?" He sounded slightly less intense, and I thought he might be relaxing into me, too.

"Yeah, I had just come back from my first time in 1888 and your older self dropped a whole bunch of intense emotions on me. God, I should have names for all of you. Victorian Archer, Modern Archer. What should I call you?"

I could hear the smile in his voice. "If I have my way, you'll call me husband."

I did eventually fall back to sleep, despite the *husband* word that made me itch, and finally woke when Archer lit his small lantern at dusk. He looked just like himself, and a little like Cary Grant. I, on the other hand, felt like a giant vacuum had sucked all the moisture out of my eyes, and rats had taken up residence in my hair. I sat up, rubbed my face, and struggled to finger-comb the tangles out. My hair was still at bob length, which made it somewhat easier, but Archer picked up a comb and turned my back to him so he could work through the knots. His touch was so gentle, I felt myself melting into him. Fingers running through my hair was my kryptonite, and Archer chuckled.

"You're like a cat getting her fur stroked. I almost expect to hear a purr."

"Mmm, this is me, purring." I sat up suddenly and turned to face him. "Oh, right. You should know. I can Shift into a Cougar, but I have to be wearing the Shifter family artifact – this bone – to do it." I pulled the leather cord out from under my shirt and showed him the ancient carved bone.

Archer's eyes widened in surprise, and not, I hoped, disgust. "How does it feel, to Shift?"

Okay, not disgust, but I wasn't sure why I was even worried about that. Maybe because my Archer and I had already been through so much together by the time he learned about my feline nature, and this one only had a week in Ringo's loft in 1888 to go on. "At first I hated it because I couldn't control my Cat. But I've been working with Connor and Mr. Shaw, and they've been teaching me how to be a boss."

"Shaw is your teacher?"

"Right. Descended from my father's brother."

Archer nodded thoughtfully. "And Connor is ...?"

"A friend. Of both of ours. He came with us to France ..." I sighed. "Okay, here's the thing. Once we have the message, the plan is for us – me and Ringo – to go deal with whatever there is to deal with on our own." His mouth was already opening to protest, but I cut him off. "Honestly though, I have the feeling the two of us won't be enough. But if you come with us, trying to protect you from information you shouldn't know yet feels like sending you into battle with an unloaded gun."

He regarded me steadily. "You once told me my memories about you weren't clear until you had set them in motion, so why shouldn't it work that way now? If, as you say, I've already done these things without proper foreknowledge, you telling me now is only going to clarify the memories of you telling me about them for my future self. At the time we did the things, I didn't *know* yet."

I narrowed my eyes. "You think it'll be the same thing?"

"I don't see why not. Temporal rules seem to have held so far."

"Easy for you to say. You didn't see the split."

"The split?" He looked confused and horrified at the same time.

So I told him. Or at least I gave him the bullet-point version of Wilder escaping Tudor England with Tom, then turning Tom into a Vampire and Clocking back to an alternate timeline that Henry Grayson had created by capturing Joan of Arc. We didn't have time for a lot of detail, but the broad strokes were pretty mind-blowing all by themselves.

"And the mixed-blood boy who is now a Vampire is the one you believe to be working with the Werwolves?"

"According to the scrap of message you left for Ravi, it seems pretty likely."

He thought for a moment, then held his hand out and lifted me to my feet. "Come. There's someone I'd like you to meet. She might have information about the Werwolves we could use. And," he checked the watch on his wrist, "I can still catch Colonel Marks before he heads off for the night."

"You know he's a Monger, right?" I quickly whipped off the blouse I'd been wearing and grabbed a clean t-shirt from my bag. I was wearing a cami underneath, so I didn't even think twice about what Archer might think, but despite the fact that even his Victorian self had seen me in less, he still turned around uncomfortably as he answered me.

"Colonel Marks is a good man, but more importantly he is *my* commanding officer." The tension in his shoulders was evident, even with his back turned to me.

I sighed at Archer's discomfort. I couldn't help it. There literally was no room for modesty in the cramped hidey-hole he'd made for himself behind the walls. But, since his back was already turned, I quickly slipped off my trousers and took advantage of still having clean underwear in my bag. The whole quick-change took less than a minute, but Archer's expression was pained when I told him I was ready. I pulled my jacket on over the t-shirt and buttoned it up as we slipped out of the room.

We made our way out of the mansion, but turned away from the main block of huts. Archer led me to a nondescript building set apart from the rest of the outbuildings on the grounds. The door opened and a pretty Wren came out, followed by her even prettier friend. I didn't think I imagined the way their eyes sparkled when they saw Archer. The first one said, "Hello, Captain Devereux." She was like a little bird with a bright, chirpy voice.

"Where have you been hiding, Archer? We've missed you." The other bird's voice was neither bright, nor chirpy, and I thought I'd never heard a sultrier-sounding bird in my life.

I looked at his expression, which was friendly and open. Could he not see the calculation in their eyes?

"Have a nice evening, ladies," he said with an even smile.

He held the door to what was clearly a bar open for me. I kept my voice deliberately light. "Popular, aren't you?"

He winced very slightly. "If the work weren't so damned important, I wouldn't live so … publicly."

Oh. Nothing like a cold dash of perspective. Archer entered the dimly lit space, hazy with cigarette smoke, and looked around. The scratchy sound of vinyl playing big band tunes came from the corner, where some couples were swing dancing. A few people called greetings to Archer, and he waved perfunctorily, but his eyes didn't stop searching.

I was so glad it was illegal to smoke indoors in most twenty-first century places. The only good thing the smoke did was cover the smell of so many people together in one windowless building. Although, after having been in the fifteenth and sixteenth centuries with courtiers and warriors sweating in heavy woolen clothes that probably never got washed, wartime Britain smelled pretty civilized.

Archer seemed to find whoever he was looking for and took my hand to weave through the tables. I noticed the eyeballs on us, and wondered if it was him, or me, or the fact that he was holding my hand that got so much attention.

We stopped in front of a table in the corner, sort of the "holding court" spot with a prime see-and-be-seen factor. Three handsome soldiers flanked one small brunette, and it was clear who the leader of this pack was. She was older than me, maybe thirty, with wavy dark hair in a style that looked like it had to be set with pins every night, full lips, and bright green eyes. Her eyes danced merrily when she spotted Archer, and she held a hand up to the guy on her right who was trying to talk to her.

"Hold it, love. Devereux's got something to say."

Her voice was throaty, tinged with an Australian accent, and sounded sophisticated coming from such a tiny woman. The smile she bestowed on Archer was as if the sun rose and set on him. I knew the feeling, but I didn't appreciate anyone else knowing it.

He bent down and gave her an affectionate two-cheek-kiss greeting. "I'd like you to meet Saira. She needs to pick your brain about the Werwolves while I talk to Marks. Saira, this is Nancy Wake."

Nancy Wake. Nancy. A sinkhole opened up in my stomach. This vivacious woman with glittering eyes and a smile that could melt an iceberg – this was Nancy. Had it happened yet? Was it still to come? I hadn't defined *it* yet in my mind, mostly because I didn't want to look, but I suddenly felt like the little kid peeking through fingers at the scary parts.

I squared my shoulders and held out my hand to shake Nancy's. She regarded me for an eternity, or maybe just a heartbeat, and then turned the full wattage of her smile on me and shook my hand. "Shove off, boys. The lady and I need to talk." Nancy didn't look at the soldiers she'd just dismissed, and they dutifully stood up and grabbed their drinks. Nancy directed me to a seat, then caught Archer's eye.

"Tell Marks I need you with me in France. The drop leaves tomorrow night."

I stared at Archer, practically daring him to tell her where she could put that idea, but he just laughed. "You know I'd follow you to the ends of the earth, Mouse, but not without Saira."

He would? And ... Mouse?

Nancy gave me another appraising look, then dismissed Archer. "Well, tell him anyway. We'll see what we have to work with."

Archer touched my shoulder lightly. "Come find me in the hut afterward?"

I nodded with more confidence than I felt. "Sure."

His smile was a private one, just for me, and then he turned and wove his way back through the crowd and was gone.

Nancy caught the bartender's eye and held up two fingers. I was about to protest, but she cut me off. "If you don't want it, I'll have it, so don't spoil my fun."

"Wouldn't dream of it," I muttered under my breath.

Nancy's gaze locked onto me again, and I had the sense of being a bug under a microscope. Then she smiled. "I appreciate the compliment, love. He happens to be one of the few men I respect around here, but I know when a man's available, and that one isn't." Her gaze sharpened. "But you would know that, wouldn't you." It wasn't a question, so I didn't answer it.

"What can you tell me about Hitler's Werwolves?"

Two glasses of amber liquid were delivered by a young guy in a military uniform. Nancy gave him her glittering smile. "You're new. Buy me a drink later and tell me about yourself."

The young soldier looked flustered, but nodded enthusiastically and then tripped over a chair in his embarrassment. Nancy turned a serious gaze back to me.

"A group of them have been using my Maquis as target practice in Limoges."

"What are your Maquis?"

Nancy looked at me oddly. "You're young, but is it possible you've been living under a rock?"

"It's possible." I looked her straight in the eye, and slowly, she smiled.

"The Maquis were born out of the French resistance to the Vichy puppets. *My* Maquis are trained guerrilla fighters, working mostly in the free region of France."

Guerrilla fighters brought to mind the old eighties movie *Red Dawn*, with the kids in the Colorado mountains fighting the Russians who had invaded the US. It was a great movie, even though almost all the heroes died, including the leader. I hoped the comparison didn't bode ominously.

"We're specifically looking for an Englishman who may have joined up with the Werwolves."

Nancy's expression thundered instantly, and she spat on the floor in a distinctly French move I would have expected more from a coarse farmer than a petite Australian beauty. "The Nazi bastards have been hinting at English and American spies infiltrating our pilot escape network, and I heard rumors of a particularly deadly one in France. If that's your man and he's in my district, I'll need a description immediately."

I considered her for a moment. This woman clearly had a network of people. If there was any chance Tom was in Limoges, she might find him.

"I haven't seen him in a couple of months, but he's my age, a little shorter than me, slender, with dark hair, dark eyes, and a little bit of a gypsy look to him."

Nancy snorted. "You've just described half the men in France."

"He also speaks fluent French."

Her eyes narrowed dangerously. "He's in France for sure, then. I'll need everything you have on him. An Englishman cannot be allowed to run with those wolves."

Secret Message

I bumped into Stella outside H Block after I left Nancy Wake at the bar. She seemed to be waiting for someone, and I guessed it was me by the way she took my arm.

"You're Saira, right? Archer talks about you when we push him, but it's like pulling teeth to get him to admit anything about his personal life."

She waited expectantly, as if daring me to confirm or deny. I just smiled. "It's nice to finally meet you, Stella."

"There, that's another thing. How did you know my name last night? I know Archer doesn't talk about any of us. He takes his confidentiality agreement very seriously."

"You're right. I haven't spoken to Archer about you."

"Then how?" She watched me expectantly.

"I believe your grandmother was friends with my aunt." I needed to talk to Archer because although the Stella I knew was absolutely lovely, I really didn't know anything about this young woman who was engaged to a Monger.

Her eyes widened dramatically, and I wondered if I'd just given something away. "I haven't Seen you before," she whispered.

"I only just got here."

"That's not what I meant." Her voice was very tentative.

"I know." I had an impulse to reassure her, so I took her hand and squeezed it. "By the way, Colonel Marks loves butter, he's just saving all of his for you."

164

Her breath caught in her throat, and she gasped as I continued. "And trust your instincts. They're good ones." I squeezed her hand again to try to erase the shock in her expression. "Come on, I'm guessing Archer and Ravi have messages to send up to your colonel."

Ringo was inside the hut watching the Colossus machine with rapt fascination. The clattering was a constant noise in the background, which reminded me of the rhythmic sound of a train. He looked up with a grin. "Did you ever see somethin' more perfectly elementary? It's completely brilliant, and it explains the fundamentals of computin' better than anythin' the modern machines with their amazin' processin' speeds can do."

Archer was adjusting something at the top of Colossus and had just noticed my entrance. His smile was instantaneous, but I returned it tentatively, still unsure about my own confidence in the face of whatever Nancy might mean to him.

Just then, Ravi entered with a stack of messages. His eyes lit on Stella with relief. "There you are. Can you just nip up to the colonel and slip them into his box? They're the last from today's code."

Archer hopped down from the stepladder just as Stella accepted the stack. His sudden movement startled her and she dropped a couple of the slips. Ravi and Archer immediately bent to help Stella gather the papers. Her hand seemed to hover over one for a moment while she did a momentary glassy-eyed stare, and I saw her surreptitiously push it toward Archer's hand as she gathered the rest into a pile. Archer slipped the message into his pocket as Stella reorganized the stack of papers.

Archer asked casually, "Where did this batch of messages come from?"

"German high command in Paris." Ravi said. "The Paris messages all come through the listening posts the SOE has with the Maquis all around France. Most originate from the Hotel Majestic."

"Hotel Majestic? Sounds like a hotel at Disneyland," I mumbled under my breath. Ravi must have caught the words because he looked at me strangely and clarified.

"It's the Paris home of the German high command."

"Right." I cleared my throat. "Of course."

Ravi handed the messages back to Stella. "Colonel Marks gets the honor of digging into the mysteries of Hitler and his lackeys. Run these up, if you would, Stella? And perhaps take your break for tea while you're there?" His smile was the only indication he knew she would spend her tea break with Colonel Marks.

When Stella had gone, Archer caught my eye and then included Ringo in his gaze. "Ravi, if you don't mind, I think I'll take a quick break as well."

This time Ravi's smiling eyes found me. "Of course, old chap. I'll babysit the beast while you're gone. Take all the time you need."

Archer led us outside and we headed toward the pub, which surprised me. "We're not going back to your room?"

"It's fine for whispering, but there's not enough light to read by," Archer said.

"And the pub is a good place to read a message you're not supposed to have?"

"No one expects you to discuss secrets in plain sight."

I sighed. "Just like no one ever looks up." My eyes had been scanning the landscape around us, and as we passed the mansion, I thought I saw a curtain flutter in an upper-floor window.

"Who works upstairs?" I whispered.

"Colonel Marks. I imagine we'll need to go there next."

Archer opened the pub door and ushered us inside. It was a little less crowded than it had been before, but Nancy still held court at her table by the back wall, and Archer waved to her across the room. Her bright smile back to him made me grumpy like it was Monday morning and there was no coffee. Archer settled us into a table near the door and went to the bar for drinks. I worked very hard not to watch as Nancy waved him over and he knelt down to talk to her. And I definitely tried not to see him touch her hand as he stood up to return to the bar. He came back with bubbly water for me and pints for himself and Ringo, but no explanation of his exchange with Nancy. Ringo caught my eye and must have seen the green in them because he gave me a quizzical look. Jealousy had always been something I pitied in other people because it just seemed so effortful. I wasn't committed to being one of those people, so I took a breath, let it go, and smiled.

Ringo's glance went to Nancy's table as he sipped his drink while Archer pulled the slip of paper from his pocket to read. Archer's expression darkened, and he held the paper out to me. I shook my head. "I can speak it well enough, but you're fluent."

"Right." The message went back into his pocket. Archer wrapped both hands around his pint glass and stared into it, deep in thought.

"Um, dying a little here." I prompted.

He seemed to shake himself and looked up at both of us. "Sorry. It's the same message you described to me. It appears the Werwolves have a target in England, accessed by Holborn station up near Russell Square. Or, if they're using explosives, something above-ground. The mission is being led by an Englishman called T. Landers, and has been planned for June 12th."

The date had been the missing element, and I exhaled sharply. "That's after D-Day."

Archer's eyes narrowed and his voice dropped. "Be very careful, Saira. What occurs to you as known history is still very top secret information now."

I flushed, embarrassed at my carelessness. But I also usually traveled with my Archer, who knew the same things I did, plus about a ton more.

Ringo spoke quietly. "Then find us a new place to talk, because censorin' Saira's not the way to figure this thing out."

Archer looked abashed. "You're right, of course. Forgive me. I've spent so much time surviving I sometimes forget how to live. Perhaps it's time for Ravi's tea break after all. The clatter of Colossus should cover our conversation there."

Nancy watched us leave the bar, but no one else seemed to have noticed our presence in the room. Ringo whispered in my ear. "Last one's a rotten egg," then took off running. I was behind him a breath later, not caring that we were unauthorized guests on a wartime military installation. I didn't even look back to see if Archer had followed us on Ringo's route that took us up and over a garden wall, across the roof of the shed, up a tree to dodge the sentries who were just changing shifts, and down the roof of one of the huts. We dropped in front of H Block and had already caught our breath by the time Archer rounded the corner. I half expected scolding from him, or at least a disapproving expression, but instead he wore a big, delighted grin.

"My God, I've missed you two." Archer's whispered voice could have been a shout for how much joy was in it. "You're magnificent!" The words were meant for both of us, but his gaze settled on me in a way that made me flush with pleasure.

Archer went in first to relieve Ravi for his tea break, and we hid behind the door until he had gone. "Thanks," I whispered to Ringo.

He shrugged his shoulders. "Just 'cause she watches 'im doesn't mean 'e sees 'er," he said.

"It's dumb, I know. I'll let it go."

"Do that," he said as we slipped back inside the Colossus codebreaking hut.

Archer was studying a map of London that had the Underground stations marked. I stood next to him and pointed to the British Museum. "Apparently, they used … or are using at least one Underground station to house some of the treasures of the British Museum while the threat of bombing exists. Mr. Shaw was trying to find out which ones, with the assumption being that they're accessible from Holborn," I said, pitching my voice low enough not to carry over the clatter of Colossus.

"That would likely be Aldwych, and perhaps one or two others. I can get a message up to the Home Office through Nancy's contacts at the SOE. We should be able to ascertain the stations and who manages them within a day or two. But that's only a small part of this mystery." Archer's gaze had shifted to the map of Europe.

"Why is Tom Landers involved?" I asked, trying to prompt him to put his thought process on loudspeaker.

He sighed. "That too, of course." He studied the message again. "I was actually wondering why this would be sent to the 2nd SS Panzer Division?

"The 2nd is in Toulouse right now, and their business is my business. What do you know about them?" Nancy entered the room with a raised eyebrow, her gaze locked on Archer's.

"Nothing specific. There's a message directed to them about our English Werwolf."

She regarded him steadily before she spoke. "My boys confirmed that a Werwolf unit landed in Limoges a few days ago. They intercepted a message to their commander, but it was in code."

"Can you get it to me? I'm told we're good with code around here," Archer said.

I loved the polite snark in his tone, and it made it easier to just roll with Nancy's presence. "Have they seen the Werwolves?" I asked.

She nodded. "We have spies throughout the Limousin area."

"How do they know it's the Werwolves?" Ringo asked. Nancy suddenly realized he was there, and her gaze sharpened, even as her voice turned to honey. "Devereux, darling, don't tell me you actually managed to smuggle *two* PONTIs into Bletchley."

Archer smiled benignly at Nancy. "My mistake. Nancy, may I introduce a person of great importance to me. This is Ringo."

She made a show of studying him head to foot. "One name?" Her eyebrow rose suggestively. "You haven't earned a surname yet, is that it?"

Ringo smiled disarmingly. "Nah, just too important for one."

169

Nancy laughed out loud, and it was a charmingly genuine sound. "Well, Ringo, have you ever seen the wolf trap symbol with which the Werwolves decorate their armbands?"

Ringo shook his head, so Nancy continued. "It's based on the ancient Viking rune called a Wolfsangel. It looks like a backward Z, lying on its side, with a slash mark through the middle."

She took the pencil out of Archer's hand with familiar ease that made me clench my teeth. She drew the symbol on a scrap of paper with all parallel lines. "This is the Werwolf rune. That's what the new group in Limoges wears on their armbands."

Archer exhaled and looked at her. "Can you get us to Limoges, Nancy?"

"All three of you?" She asked in surprise.

I nodded, and then gave her a piercing look. "We're the only ones who can identify the Englishman, and like you said, an English spy anywhere near your pilot escape network is a very bad idea."

She studied me, then looked at Archer, and a slow grin spread across her face. "Apparently they aren't PONTIs, are they?" She swept toward the door. "We leave tomorrow night."

When Nancy was gone, I turned to Archer. "PONTIs?"

He shook his head with a chuckle. "People of No Tactical Importance."

Ringo and I slipped back to Archer's hideout while Archer invented an excuse to cut out of work early.

"What do you think of Nancy?" I tried to keep my whispered voice casual, but I knew Ringo too well to think he'd be fooled.

"She's got the stones of a bloke, for sure, and brash as anythin'. I don't think she suffers fools, and she admires Archer for 'is brains, and probably 'is looks too. But if she fancies 'im, it's not returned, least not in any way that counts. Why are ye worried, Saira? It's not as if 'e 'as eyes for anyone but ye."

I shrugged. "Just something he said before we came."

The secret door slid open and Archer entered with a plate of sandwiches in one hand and an extra lantern in the other. He handed the plate off to Ringo and closed the door behind him. "I didn't think I could carry two bowls of soup, but the canteen has chicken and potato if you want to take your chances."

I took a ham sandwich from the plate. "This is perfect, thank you." Archer didn't eat regular food, and yet he was the one who remembered to feed us. "The Germans don't know that you've broken their code, right?" I had been wondering whether there was any chance the information was planted, but it seemed Archer had already thought of that.

"Most of our work right now is to make sure the disinformation we've placed about Operation Overlord is effective. So far it seems to be working, which means Colossus is still unknown." Operation Overlord was code for D-Day, and Archer wasn't holding back secret information from us, which was treason if anyone overheard him.

I looked Archer in the eye. "As long as time stays intact, Operation Overlord will work. But that's why Tom is such a wild card. He could seriously wreak havoc on the time stream if he wanted to. But even though he seems to be working for the Germans, I can't imagine he would want England to lose the war." I said this with confidence I was pretty sure I actually felt.

Archer looked thoughtful. "I don't know Tom, so I can't begin to understand his motives. In my experience though, the only reasons a man would betray his country are financial or personal."

"There are a million better ways to get money than going to work with the enemy," I said vehemently.

"Indeed there are." Archer sounded grim. "I had means, and have had ample opportunity to invest my family's money to ensure its longevity."

"I don't see money as something that would motivate Tom, not given what he's been through. So what personal reason could there be for him to be here, now, on the German side of this war?"

Archer's expression was serious. "So it's true that Wilder's ingestion of your mother's blood resulted in Clocking skills which he then passed on to Tom when he turned him?"

I nodded. "We know Tom can Clock, but I don't believe he has quite my skill. It's true he managed to kill Wilder twice on two different timelines in medieval France, but I don't think he can make portals like I can."

"He went to the trouble to kill Wilder twice?" Archer asked. "Such hatred is concerning. But Wilder isn't in 1944, so that couldn't be the source of a personal vendetta. Who else does Tom hate with such fervor?" Archer's eyes flicked between both Ringo's and mine.

"'Imself," Ringo said, finally.

THE MAQUIS

We met Nancy at the Cranfield Aerodrome, which was about ten minutes by car from Bletchley Park. It was a harrowing trip on dark country roads, and I was very glad for such good night vision. Nancy handed Archer a set of papers, then looked all three of us over with a critical eye.

"Your shoes are too good. They'll give you away as agents if Gerry or the collaborators lay eyes on you."

"One good rainstorm and a stomp in the mud will change that," said Ringo

"You sound like an old Cockney I used to buy chips from before the war," Nancy scoffed.

"Maybe I am an old Cockney, and I'm just better at disguise than any of you SOE types." Nancy stared at Ringo, and then burst out laughing. She actually had a fairly infectious laugh, which, when combined with her magic smile, made her somewhat irresistible. She looked at Archer and jabbed her thumb in Ringo's direction. "I like this one, Devereux."

I had to bite back the snarky comment that threatened, and Ringo caught my eye with a wink. Archer distributed the paperwork Nancy had given us, and I saw that I had a hastily forged identity card with a picture that looked vaguely like me, and the name Hélène Klene.

"Keep the English-speaking to a minimum." Nancy's gaze took in both Ringo and I, and we nodded. Ringo showed me his card, with a photo of a scruffy-haired kid that actually looked a lot like the street urchin he had been when I first met him. "Louis Houle," I read out loud. I looked at him with a grin. "It suits you."

Archer showed me his card, which actually did have his picture on it, with the name Alexandre Devère. He looked much rougher in the photo than he did standing in front of me. "You had this ready to go before we got here, didn't you?"

"I've helped Nancy organize several of the Maquis networks around Auvergne and Limoges, and this trip we plan to disrupt as many German forces as possible."

"So it's pretty fortuitous that the Werwolves might be operating in the same area, huh?" I spoke to Nancy with an edge in my voice.

She shrugged. "The only difference is two more passengers. Unless you're idiots, and then I'll have to cut you loose or shoot you myself."

I opened my mouth to share my ungenerous thoughts about her tone, but snapped it shut when a tall man in a military uniform stepped out of the aerodrome building and strode toward us.

Archer stood up a little straighter beside me, and even Nancy directed her not inconsiderable focus his way. The man was in his late twenties and handsome in a square-jawed James Garner way.

"Colonel Marks, I didn't expect to see you here tonight." I thought Nancy purred, and I might have been offended for Stella's sake if I hadn't known how things turned out.

My Monger-gut kicked in, but I pushed it down. According to both Stella and Archer, Marks was a good guy. His eyes found Archer's first. "You're ready, Devereux?"

Archer nodded smartly. "Yes, sir."

"The latest batch of messages you chaps decoded contain several from Paris about the increased reprisals against Maquis groups and the civilian population." Colonel Marks was speaking to Archer, but Nancy interrupted.

"Which means our missions against Gerry are working."

He turned his gaze to her. "We expect the 2nd SS Panzer Division to be called up from Toulouse to the Normandy coast in short order. It should be a four-day trip for them, but if those fifteen thousand troops arrive there before we're ready for them, they could make the difference in our ability to gain an Allied foothold in Europe."

"We'll harass the hell out of them, sir." Nancy said quietly.

"See that you do, Mrs. Fiocca."

I didn't have time to process that little tidbit of information because Colonel Marks' eyes were suddenly locked on me, even as it was clear he was still speaking to Nancy and Archer.

"Normally, I'd have to approve every bit of cargo that goes with you, as you're using military transport. However, I'm assured that there are extenuating circumstances in this case, and that certain ... events will play out in such a way that I should ignore the unauthorized cargo and allow the mission to proceed."

I couldn't have torn my eyes away from Colonel Marks' gaze, even if his gaze had let go of mine. The Monger-gut was still whirling, but my own instinct for predators wasn't pinging, so I made an instant decision.

"A member of my Family, and, incidentally, yours, has gone rogue, sir. If we can stop him before he returns to English soil, we will."

Colonel Marks' eyes widened slightly as he understood my emphasis on the word *Family*.

"Your Family being ..." He waited for me to finish the sentence.

"Anachronistic, sir."

The startled expression he wore might have been because he realized I wasn't from this time, or because Clockers were just that rare. I knew Millicent was still a young woman, and her parents were both alive, but I didn't know of any others that Colonel Marks would be aware of.

"Good luck, then, Miss." He nodded to me, and then inclined his head to Ringo before spinning on his heel and walking back toward his waiting car.

"Well, that was interesting. I didn't know you and the handsome colonel were related." Nancy's tone sounded speculative, and despite my desire to snap the words, I laced them with sweetness instead.

"Well, Mrs. Fiocca, it would seem there *are* things you don't know."

Ringo smirked at me as we grabbed our satchels and flung them over our shoulders. The airplane we approached was parked facing down the runway, and there was an open door near the tail. The pilot was finishing an inspection and looked up with a grin. "Ready to fly, are you?"

He spoke in an Irish accent with the accompanying Irish smile in his voice. The pilot was in his mid-thirties, black-haired, fair-skinned and had twinkling green eyes. His face held an easy grin as he shook hands all around. "I'm Sean Mulroy, and I'll be your tour guide tonight."

His name sounded familiar, and I struggled to remember if I'd read it in a history book or something. He helped Nancy into the back of the plane, then Archer handed her our bags and followed her inside. I was next, and when Sean's large warm hand engulfed mine, something in my touch startled him. "Oh, right, then. Up you go, Miss … Elian, is it?"

I stared at him. "Do you know my Family?"

His easy grin was back. "I know of them, of course. Might even have been related to them at a time. And then, o' course, I'm Irish. We know things."

Irish pilot. Possible mixed-blood. Familiar name. I took a chance. "Well, after the war, if you ever do run into the Elians, they have a daughter named Millicent you might like to meet."

His eyes brightened. "Is that so?"

"The manor's in Ingatestone, but you should know, she can be a bit prickly that one, and her father won't trust your intentions.

176

Millicent and I are a lot alike, actually. We think we can do everything on our own, but we actually need someone strong enough to stand at our back, even when we push them away. Just something to think about if you ever do meet her."

"Interesting advice, Miss Elian. I'll bear it in mind."

I gripped his hand tightly and almost gave him a hug, but managed to catch myself just in time. "It's really nice to meet you, Sean Mulroy. I hope to see you again."

He looked a little dazed as he handed me up into the belly of the plane, and Ringo whispered behind me, "Meddlin'?"

I looked him straight in the eyes and gave him the raised eyebrow. "Maybe."

Ringo grinned back. "Thought so."

The interior of the plane had seven seats and was like being inside the ribcage of a whale shark. Nancy was already strapped into hers, and Archer helped me into a seat next to him, while Ringo chose one behind us. "Normally we'd parachute in, but we'll have to take our chances with a landing in the free zone." Nancy's tone was back to being friendly, and I found it hard to stay annoyed with her.

"Thanks. I'm a little rusty on my parachuting skills."

She grinned. "I thought as much. Mulroy's the best VIP transporter there is, though. He'll get us in, and get himself out before Gerry even realizes they've got visitors."

There were bags already loaded into the cargo area of the plane and Nancy caught my glance. "Guns, explosives, money. All the things that keep life interesting, don't you think?"

I looked at Archer's face and could see his jaw clench. He wasn't such a fan of the killing toys either, I was glad to see.

Sean yelled back to us to put on our headsets so he could talk to us during the flight, and once the engines had started I also realized they were the only ear protection we'd get. There was no such thing as insulation in this airplane.

I turned around to find Ringo staring around in rapt fascination. He'd never flown before, so his experience was one of marvel and delight, whereas mine was a little more of the oh-God-I-hope-this-thing-makes-it variety.

Our flight across the channel was just over an hour, according to Sean's commentary, and then another hour overland to the airfield at Limoges. I estimated it was probably just after midnight when we started to land, and it looked like the whole town was dark. Archer must have read my thoughts because he spoke into the headset quietly. "Maquisards will come with lights when they hear the plane."

"And there they are," said Sean. "When we stop, be prepared to jump out. I have about five minutes on the ground before they come looking for me, and I'd like to live to fight another day, if you please."

I braced for a landing I couldn't see, and Archer gripped my hand tightly as we bumped lightly on the runway. Sean was a better pilot in his little plane than most commercial airline pilots I'd ever flown with, and I was out of my harness and out of the plane as soon as the door was thrown open.

Nancy used hand signals to direct two Maquisards to empty the cargo area of bags, and when the door was fixed back into place, the two taps on its metal body to let Sean know he was clear was the only sound I heard.

A minute later, Sean Mulroy's little plane was down the runway and had taken off, its engines already fading into the distance.

The four of us followed the Maquisards into the woods just off the runway, and it wasn't until we were a couple hundred yards away from the airport that anyone dared to speak.

Nancy issued rapid-fire orders to the men in French, and Archer translated for us under his breath. "We're going to Gaspard's headquarters at a farmhouse outside of town."

"Are you going to be able to find a protected place to sleep?" I whispered back.

Archer smiled grimly. "Fortunately, the Maquis keep hours like I do. I'll be fine."

178

About an hour later, I was very glad for my too-new boots after a hike that would have turned ankles and caused blisters in anything else. I could sense several Mongers around the farmhouse when we finally arrived, and I told Archer as much.

"Seems logical the Maquis would attract them," he whispered. "There's a lot of anger in this country about the German occupation."

"Just watch your back. There's more than a couple," I murmured.

Ringo and I sat in the kitchen of the big stone farmhouse sipping hot mint tea and staying out of sight of the group of young men and a couple of women who lounged against the walls of the big sitting room. We could hear them, though, and easily picked out Nancy's and Archer's voices as they conferred with a skinny guy they called Gaspard and two of his lieutenants at the table in the center of the room. They consulted maps and argued the about locations for setting explosives. Even with my limited French, it was clear Nancy and Archer were the plan-makers, and they used the Maquis as consultants. What was the population of this town? Was the map correct about that bridge? And who could be counted on to help ... or hurt their missions?

Occasionally, one of the men would shuffle into the kitchen for water, or to scrounge a piece of bread. One or two of the older men smiled at us in a hospitable way. The younger men seemed suspicious and hard, and their initial reaction to our presence was always a scowl. My predator instincts were starting to shift into high gear, and I could practically see Ringo's street-edges sharpen in a way I hadn't seen since I first met him in London.

I didn't know what their lives had been like for the past four years since the Germans had occupied France, but it seemed like everyone carried a layer of anger, sometimes just below the surface of their skin, and sometimes it was hard and thick, like armor. Bodies were lean and strong, and spoke of too much running and hiding, and not enough sleep or food.

We had walked among soldiers before, but these people were different. Archer came into the kitchen after a pair of scowling guys, probably in their early twenties, with flinty, fifty-year-old eyes, had passed through the room. He read the tension in Ringo instantly, and then looked to me for an explanation.

"Nothing happened."

"Then why does he look like he wants to tear them limb from limb?" Archer nodded at Ringo, who had shifted his gaze back down to the mug he gripped as if it was the only thing keeping his fists from flying.

"They spat, that's all."

"And called her Putain," Ringo grumbled.

"I've been called worse."

Archer looked at me. "Why are you downplaying it?"

"Because they're like feral wolverines, and the idea of one of you taking them on over some imagined slight against me makes me want to throw up. I just want to go someplace where no one can knife us when we sleep and close my eyes for a minute without worrying we won't wake up."

Archer looked at Ringo's fists clenched around his mug and he nodded. "Let's go."

We left the farmhouse by the kitchen door without telling anyone we were going, and I was absurdly happy Archer didn't feel the need to say anything to Nancy.

Archer led us into the woods, and within about ten minutes, I no longer felt the random Monger-gut I'd been having since we landed among the Maquis. We emerged into a small clearing on the edge of a much bigger one, and I realized we were on the outskirts of a village.

"Where are we?" I whispered. There was just enough light from the moon that the moss growing on the low stone walls looked like bloodstains.

"Oradour-sur-Glane. My father's gamekeeper came from this village. This is his great-granddaughter's farm." Archer led us to a stone barn just outside an old farmhouse and put his finger to his lips as he carefully opened the big wooden door just enough to slip inside.

When the door was closed behind us, I chanced another whisper. "Does she know you?"

He nodded and pulled open the door to an empty animal stall. Against the back wall, carefully concealed, was the edge of a trap door in the floor. Archer pulled it open and indicated Ringo should go first. "It's about five feet down," he whispered, and Ringo dropped straight down. I wasn't a fan of blind drops, so I did use the ladder, and Archer was right behind me as he closed the trap door over our heads.

"Another priest hole?" I whispered in the dark. It reminded me of the hidden cellar where we had found young Pancho, the twelve-year-old brother of Thomas Wyatt, hiding from the Queen's Guard. Archer lit a candle stub and a small room was illuminated. There were blankets stacked in one corner, and a crate with a lantern on it stashed behind the ladder.

Archer smiled. "Something like that. These are tough times, and I imagine this hiding spot has been used more than once since the war began. Francoise DuLac showed me this place when we were children. The current owner of the farm, Marianne, knows I've come once or twice in the past few years."

"What does she know about you?" I was curious how he explained himself to other people through the years.

Archer piled some blankets together for us and tossed some others to Ringo. "She knows our families have been friends for several generations and that the scholarship I set up for the girls of the DuLac family is putting her daughter through school in England."

"Just the girls?" I wasn't sure what surprised me more, that he'd set up a scholarship, or that it was for the girls.

"Francoise was my best friend as a child, until I went to school and her father sent her home to France. He thought an education would be wasted on a woman and refused to allow her to attend even the primary school in this village. So, when Francoise had her own daughter, I made sure there was a fund in place for her to send little Dominique to school. That fund has continued, and can only be accessed by the DuLac women for their daughters."

"Is Marianne part of the Maquis?" I quickly ran a toothbrush over my teeth. The little hidden room was actually reasonably warm for being underground, and I thought I might even be able to sleep without my boots on.

Archer shook his head. "Her husband is in a German prisoner of war camp, and her son is still young. She grows enough food to feed them and some of her neighbors too, and otherwise, she keeps her head down and stays out of the Germans' sights."

"I didn't know you had such strong ties to France." I stretched out on the blanket and used my satchel for a pillow.

Archer sat down on the blanket and looked at me oddly. "I haven't spoken about the DuLacs to you?"

I shook my head. "I remember a hunting story you told me once about your father, but otherwise, no."

He sank into thoughtful silence, and I suddenly realized why. I reached a hand out and held his. "We've talked about the important things. If they had died tragically, you would have told me."

Ringo lay on his blanket with his eyes closed and an arm thrown across his head. "She's right. Ye would 'ave said somethin'."

Archer finally nodded, then blew out the candle. It was pitch black in the underground room, and I felt Archer put something near my satchel. "A fresh candle and matches, for when you wake."

"Thanks," I whispered. Then I felt Archer tug at the laces on my boots. "What are you doing?"

"You're safe here, and I'll keep you warm," he answered, as he pulled my boots off, laid down next to me, and pulled a blanket up to cover us. I laced my fingers through his and fell deeply asleep.

182

Oradour-sur-Glane

Archer left the barn at sunset to see how things fared with Marianne DuLac and her son. He was back twenty minutes later with an invitation for us to join them for dinner.

We were careful to stay to the shadows as we made our way into the ancient farmhouse. As with every farm I'd ever entered, the door opened right to the kitchen, where a fire burned cheerily in the hearth and a pot of soup bubbled away in a big cast iron pot hanging above it.

A young woman, not older than Nancy, stood at the sink basin peeling winter beets. Her fingers and the knife were stained a deep, dark red that looked too much like blood for comfort. The room smelled so good and was so bright and welcoming after the angry vibe of the Maquis safe house, I shrugged off the sense of foreboding and stepped inside.

"Marianne, I'd like you to meet my friends, Hélène and Louis," Archer said in French. Marianne's face lit into a lovely smile and she wiped her hands clean on her apron.

She held her hand out to shake ours, and told us in French how welcome we were in her home. Both Ringo and I smiled graciously but said nothing, and I realized Archer had introduced us by our aliases in order to protect Marianne from the information that there were more foreigners in her neighborhood than just himself.

When neither of us spoke, Marianne merely switched to more non-verbal cues to invite us to sit. She and Archer carried on a rapid-fire conversation in French, which Archer didn't translate, and I looked around for something I could do to help. There were carrots to be peeled, and after a couple of hand gestures, I settled in to work at the big kitchen table with a paring knife.

I was zoning out on the lyrically guttural sounds of French when a bang sounded at the door, and all three of us were out of our seats in an instant. Marianne said something to Archer with the next bang. When something dropped outside, Ringo's posture relaxed and he went to the door to open it.

A young boy stood in the doorway with an armful of chopped wood. He looked shocked to see Ringo and sheepish at having dropped several pieces. Ringo snatched the wood from his arms before more could fall, and the boy smiled gratefully at him.

Archer introduced us to the boy, whose name was Marcel. Marianne's son was not more than about seven or eight years old. He clopped inside on worn, wooden-soled shoes, which looked remarkably out of place on a child. He was too thin for any growing boy, and pale in a way that spoke more of fear than of a life spent indoors.

Ringo gave him a grin and indicated that Marcel should show him where to stack the wood. Within a few minutes Ringo and the little dark-haired boy had stacked a very professional-looking pile near the hearth.

Marianne pulled the heavy pot out of the fireplace, and I jumped up to help her serve five bowls of steaming vegetable soup. Marcel and Ringo washed their hands, and then we sat at Marianne's heavy wooden table to eat. Marianne and Marcel immediately bowed their heads in prayer, and even I sent a quick thank you to the universe for the moments of peace this meal represented.

My attention wandered around the room while Archer and Marianne talked. Heavy timber beams held the ceiling and framed the waxed plaster walls. The ceiling was higher than Tudor era rooms I'd been in, so I guessed it was probably built in the 1700s. There were faded patches on the walls where it looked like paintings had hung, and I wondered if they had been hidden, stolen, or sold for food. We ate with simple pewter spoons, yet the ladle Marianne had served the soup with was silver that had been allowed to tarnish, maybe to hide its quality from casual thieves.

The soup was excellent, full of root vegetables and wild mushrooms, but the bread was coarse, and Marianne kept apologizing for it, especially since Archer had claimed a prior meal as the reason he wasn't eating. She had wanted to open a bottle of wine for us, but he quickly assured her that none of us drank it, so she should save it for a special occasion. I had the sense that the four years of war in France had affected the DuLacs, and probably everyone else, badly. Marianne's garden was growing, and she had the woods to forage for firewood, mushrooms, and probably meat, but things like wine, refined flour for bread, and leather for shoes were scarce and expensive.

When the table had been cleared, Ringo brought a chocolate bar out of his bag and slid it across the table to Marcel. The little boy's eyes lit up with so much surprised joy I felt tears prickle. He looked to his mother for permission to open it, and after her quick, grateful smile at Ringo, she told Marcel he could. Marcel took a big bite of the chocolate. The expression of pure bliss on his face brightened the whole room.

Marianne and Archer continued their conversation, and from the bits and pieces I understood, it seemed that they discussed German soldiers in Limoges. I knew from my own reading that France had been divided in Hitler's agreement with the Vichy government in 1940. The Vichy was to keep the middle and south of France, and German forces would control the north, including Paris. Then, in 1942, Germany invaded the south anyway, and Marshall Phillipe Petain became a puppet leader. Consequently, free France was a hotbed of Maquis - the very angry sons and brothers of men who had been sacrificed by the Vichy in their feeble attempt to keep the Germans at bay. The best that history said about the Vichy was that they'd kept France from being fully occupied. The worst was that they were collaborators, anti-Semites, and more culpable than even the Nazis in rounding up and deporting their countrymen.

Marianne wouldn't let any of us help clean up after dinner, and she sent us away with some bread, cheese, and a jug of water. Marcel solemnly shook all our hands and said very formal goodbyes to us as we left the farm house. He gave Ringo a shy smile though, which Ringo returned with a quick rough hug.

When we were back in the barn, Archer finally spoke to us in English again.

"Marianne offered us a room in her house, which I turned down. She said her farm has not been bothered by either the Germans or the Maquis, so I told her we'd be very happy to stay in her barn. This way we can make use of the cellar room as necessary."

Ringo shrugged. "Sounds good to me." He looked around the big stone barn that had farm equipment housed against one side and empty animal stalls on the other. Bales of old hay stood against the back wall and he pointed at them. "Anyone mind if I make some beds?"

"I'll help," I said, and together we unbound a bale and pulled the straw into two of the stalls. Archer went to get water from the pump in the garden, and with the addition of a couple of blankets from the cellar room, Ringo and I had fashioned a decent double bed in one stall and a comfortable twin bed next door. We left the rest of the straw bale in the stall with the trap door, just in case we ever had to cover the traces of our occupancy there. We decided our personal bags would either be on us or in the cellar room hidden from view.

Everything about our stay at the DuLac farm had to be secret, and none of us felt very good about putting Marianne and Marcel at risk. But we needed a secure base from which to search for Tom and his Werwolves. We all agreed that the Maquis were useful for France but shouldn't be trusted for our much smaller mission.

Ringo was shifting the last of the hay from where it had been stacked. "Well, 'ello. What's this?" He reached down and pulled out a bow. The wood was old and worn, but the string was still tight when he twanged it. He handed it to me and dug around under the loose hay until he found a simple cloth quiver with five arrows in it. The arrowheads were all hand-hammered metal, and the feathers in the shafts were still intact. I handed the bow back to him, and Ringo nocked an arrow and let it fly across the barn. The arrow struck the far wall with a thunk that left the shaft vibrating, and we stared at each other in surprise.

"This is fantastic," he said a little breathlessly.

"When did you learn to shoot a bow and arrow?" My eyes narrowed at him, and he grinned.

"Ye were out learnin' to be a Shifter. I 'ad to find somethin' besides electricity and chemistry to learn. Somethin' useful."

There were so many ways to respond to that statement, I just went with the question that struck me first. "Okay, maybe a better question is, who taught you archery?"

Ringo grinned. "Millicent, of course."

The hinge on my jaw broke and I stared at him in shock. "You're joking."

He shook his head. "As if I'd joke about anythin' 'avin' to do with Millicent Elian. I'd sooner drink spoiled milk from a yeasty codpiece than face 'er wrath about anythin' misspoken."

"A yeasty codpiece? That's … vivid." I shuddered and tried to school my expression, but he could see the laughter that threatened.

Ringo looked pleased with himself as he shouldered the quiver and bow. He turned as Archer came in with two buckets of water. "Do ye know these woods?"

Archer nodded. "Deer, fox, hare, pheasant."

"Are ye goin' out, or can I hunt?"

Archer seemed startled that his feeding habits would be discussed so casually, and he shot me a slightly mortified look. I had forgotten how uncomfortable my modern Archer had been admitting to the sustenance needs of a Vampire. So, I shrugged to show him my lack of concern, and then bent over my satchel to dig out a linen cloth.

"I'm happy to go with you for company, but I have no need to go for myself," Archer finally said, only a little awkwardly.

"I've a mind to do a little scourin' of the woods for yer wolves. If I 'appen upon any deer while I'm out, well, that wouldn't be unwelcome in the 'ouse, I reckon." Ringo threw us a jaunty wave and left the barn.

Archer laughed quietly as the door closed behind Ringo. "God, I've missed him."

I nodded at one of the full buckets. "Any chance I can use some of that for a sponge bath?"

"That's why I brought it. I could use one too."

I quickly stripped off my wool jacket and the cotton shirt Ringo had found for me in the bowels of Elian Manor's 1940s closets, and dipped the cloth in the cold water. It wasn't a bath or a shower, but it would do.

"You know, if I had a police box to Clock in, I would definitely make sure it had a shower ..." My words faded away as I turned to find Archer stripped to the waist, scrubbing at himself with a wet washcloth.

He looked up and caught me staring. There was a moment of pure motionlessness from both of us. I tried to speak, and then had to clear my throat to do it properly. "I don't often ... see you," I faltered. The words sounded lame and I tried again. "I'm pretty used to naked Shifters. They don't really think about it, and it's no big deal. But you don't ..." I faltered again. "You're always dressed."

"Does this bother you?" His voice was low, almost quiet, and his eyes never left mine as my gaze trailed over strong shoulders, lean hips with those V lines that defied explanation, and an improbable washboard in between.

Was he kidding? *Is he kidding?* My Cougar surged just below the surface of my skin, and I flushed with the heat of her, and maybe the heat of him.

Stop it, I snarled at my Cat. Her presence unsettled me.

"It ... affects me." I inhaled, which was a mistake because my Cat was so close to the surface and the heady warm spice scent that was Archer filled my senses.

"Really." A statement, not a question. Spoken in quiet tones reserved for darkness and a shared bed.

"My Cat is too close. She wants me to Shift."

Archer's eyes dropped to the Shifter Bone that dipped into my camisole. "Show me."

My Cat surged up, called by the heat that suddenly flushed through me. I closed my eyes and locked my skin in place. After a long moment I opened them again. Archer's gaze was dark and direct, and I felt gripped by it. I wanted more than his eyes on me.

I stepped out of my trousers and lifted my camisole over my head. A chill in the barn was the only thing that kept me from igniting.

And then I Shifted.

I knew the air around me rippled and shimmered, and I felt my Cat become herself. Become *my*self. And with every languid stretch of her muscles, I knew I still had control.

Archer gasped quietly. "My God, you're exquisite."

I went to him then, wearing the confidence of my Cat like a silky heat. His fingers trailed through my fur, weaving through the tawny strands with gentle strength. His touch startled a rumble from deep in my chest, and I realized I'd purred.

Archer dropped to his knees in front of me and looked into my Cat's eyes. "It's still you. Your eyes are still yours." His voice was reverent and laced with awe. I ducked my head under his hand and he stroked the length of my body, feeling muscle and sinew relax under my Cougar skin.

It was the most luxurious thing I'd ever felt, and my chest rumbled with reflexive purring. I nuzzled his neck and inhaled the scent of him as my heart pounded in my Cat's chest.

The luxury of being petted had become something primal, and I pulled myself away from my Cat's instincts.

189

I wanted him for me, not for her.

So I Shifted back.

His hands were still on me, on my naked skin when I returned to my human form. He didn't flinch, and neither of us moved. Archer's eyes still held mine until finally, he closed them and seemed to find his self-control. I could feel him pull back, so I removed myself from his hands and quietly pulled on my clothes.

Archer's eyes finally opened again when I was dressed, and he seemed shaken. I waited for him to speak, but he took my hand in silence and led me to the straw bed I had made for us.

My heart was slamming against my ribs, and I tried not to let him feel my trembling. He laid us both down and then turned me away from him so that he could wrap around me like a cloak. I waited for some movement, some indication of what would happen, but Archer just held me, wrapped in his arms, as if he would never let me go.

Eventually the butterflies quieted and the trembling stopped. And when I woke up, he was gone.

Archer – Present Day

The hollowness since she'd left was crushing.

I'd felt like a shark the past few days, always moving so I didn't have time to feel her absence.

When I woke with a vivid memory of the night in Marianne's barn when I'd left her sleeping, I was furious at myself – at the man I'd been then. I was consumed with jealousy that she was with him – with *me*. It was utterly irrational and arguably insane to be jealous *of myself*.

Saira's habit of running had become my own, and I'd found it was generally an effective means of avoiding the company of the well-meaning and wonderful family with which she had surrounded herself. I'd been least successful at shaking the young Shifters since coming to stay at Elian Manor, and they had been methodically eroding my will to be alone.

I returned from my rooftop prowl, having been kept company by a large Philippine Eagle, to find Adam Arman in the library with his sister, Ava. Sanda had set tea things for three, and I raised my eyebrows. "Expecting someone?"

"Hoping to find you, actually." Arman looked me right in the eyes. There was defiance in his gaze, as if he dared me to challenge him. I permitted myself a small smile at Sanda's observance of propriety in setting a tea cup for me despite the fact I hadn't used one in over a century. In fact, the last cup of tea I'd ever had was from a chipped green mug in Ringo's flat. I shook my head to clear the image of Saira, so beautiful in that flat on the last day of my life as a normal man, and focused my thoughts on the present.

"If it's a social visit, I warn you, I've been better company." I sat at my favorite library table and swiveled the captain's chair away from the view of my own hollow-eyed gaze in a mirror over Arman's left shoulder. Ava's expression was entirely too sympathetic for my temper, so thankfully it was her brother who spoke.

"Our parents are playing a very political game, and their focus at the moment is the Descendant Council. Despite Lady Elian's appeal to wait until there's a suitable replacement for Rothchild if they remove him by force, they continue to insist that the vote be held at the next Council meeting. With Shaw and the Ladies Elian so clearly at odds with our parents' plan, we can't go to them for help."

"For help with what?" I studied the young man, who always seemed so comfortable in his own skin. It was a trait that had taken me several decades to learn, and I admired him for it.

"There is a war coming between the Immortals," said Ava, "and the mixed-blood Descendants are in the biggest danger."

My eyes narrowed. "Don't you mean between the Immortal Descendants?"

Ava's gaze never left mine. "I mean what I said."

The ramifications of her statement were staggering. The original Immortals hadn't appeared among the Descendant Families for centuries, maybe even millennia. Whatever Ava had Seen was far bigger than Family squabbles about who the current Monger Head was.

I studied them for a long moment, until the silence in the room became deafening. Whatever the Immortals were planning had nothing to do with me, so that couldn't be what inspired the Arman twins to visit. "Why come to me?"

Arman glared at me. "We need to find the mixed-bloods, and you're sitting here twiddling your thumbs. I want to know what you're waiting for."

"What makes you think I've been waiting?" In fact, I'd been prowling around London museums nearly every night looking for signs of Seth Walters and his Mongers. I inhaled and deliberately changed my tone. "Information. That's what I'm lacking. What do you have?"

That question, and perhaps my less defensive tone of voice, seemed to unlock the tension that had coursed through the twins since they had walked in the door. Arman almost sighed in relief. "We figured out who the leprechaun is that Ava's been Seeing."

I raised an eyebrow at Ava and she smiled. "He spelled out his name on a wall. It's Tam."

"Olivia's friend?"

"The one who was with Cole and Melanie when he was taken, yeah." Arman nodded.

"Did none of them think to mention he has green hair?" I scoffed. I was clearly still in a mood, and Arman had put himself directly in my way. "Where are they being held?" I was ignoring, for the moment, the remarkable fact that Ava and this Tam could communicate through her Sight.

"I asked him, of course." Ava's voice smiled as brightly as her face did, while undeniable wisdom danced in her eyes. "They're in an Underground station. He doesn't know which one, but I Saw the train carriage where they sleep."

Connor spoke as he entered the library. "Must be a ghost station." Young Logan was right behind him, excitement writ large on his face. Connor turned to him. "Upstairs in the game room is the *Underground London* book Saira's always poking through. Grab that?"

Logan shot him a look of *you're not the boss of me*, but then exploded into the shape of a Hummingbird and was gone. Connor rolled his eyes. "And ... now he'll be naked for the rest of the night."

That got a laugh from the twins. I'd grown very fond of the Edwards brothers, and the young one's ability to wind up his elder sibling reminded me of the way Ringo poked at Saira – always subtle, but right in the places that mattered.

Connor turned to me. "By the way, Uncle Bob said his Home Office contact told him about two ghost stations where they hid art from the British Museum during the bombings in World War II: Aldwych and the British Museum station."

"There is no British Museum station. To get to the museum you get off at Holborn or Tottenham Court Road." Arman sounded so sure of himself. "And why was he asking about that?"

I realized the twins had likely not heard about the contents of my note to Ravi, so I quickly filled them in on the details of what we knew, just before Logan entered the library swimming in a shirt and shorts I'd seen Ringo wear, and holding a book open to read as he walked. He was talented in more than just the ways of Shifting, obviously. "There *is* a British Museum station," he announced, "but it's been closed since 1933."

"There are a lot more ghost stations than those two around London, though." Arman said.

"But Aldwych and British Museum are closest to Russell Square, which is where Daisy was spotted the night she disappeared." Connor reminded him.

"Notwithstanding the proximity to Holborn station, does it seem odd to anyone else that we're collapsing the Werwolf mission of 1944 with the missing mixed-bloods of today?" There shouldn't be a link, and if anyone else had suggested it, I would have thought they were indulging in fanciful coincidence. But somehow, I felt there was a connection. I'd directed the question to Connor. Aside from Ringo, with his encyclopedic knowledge of anything he'd ever read, Connor was one of the most logical people I'd ever encountered.

"Tom is the link," he said simply.

Arman stared at Connor. "Why?"

Connor shrugged. "I don't know why. But Tom's the link. He's mixed, and Walters – his biological father – was willing to trade mixed-bloods for him. And now Tom's messing around there in 1944? The two things are definitely linked."

Ava spoke quietly to me. "What do you See, Archer."

I growled in frustration. "I don't See anything. But there's something …" I focused on Connor. "Run down everything Saira told us about Walters when he had her in his office."

Connor recited, nearly word for word the conversation Saira had had with everyone after her ordeal. I stared at my feet as Connor spoke, my eyes tracing the pattern of the Turkish rug under them. Then something he said clicked and I looked up.

"What did Walters say about shooting Tom?"

Connor took a breath and repeated his last words. "Walters said Tom knew why he'd done it. He talked about the men in his family blooding their children – about how his grandfather had beaten his dad so badly he vomited blood for a week."

That was it. That was the thing that clicked. "Who is Seth Walters' grandfather and where was he in 1944?" I asked.

Connor dropped to a computer and began typing furiously. If Ringo had been here he would have found the answer in one of the books high up on the shelves he'd already scouted. The difference between the young men fascinated me.

While we waited for Connor to complete his search, Arman caught my eye and spoke quietly. "Do we leave this to Shaw and the adults on the Council?"

My gaze was steady. "Believe it or not, Arman, I *am* the ranking adult."

Connor piped up with a cheeky tone. "The adultest adult. Better at adulting than anyone I know."

Arman's eyes widened fractionally. "Right."

Connor smirked at Arman's surprise. "A hundred and fifty years, more or less, will do that to a bloke."

"What have you found on Walters?" I scowled at Connor, but he was focused on the computer and missed it.

"Hang on …" He read through the page and then clicked a link, read some more. "Seth Walters' father was Francis Walters, born in 1945 to George and Lydia Walters."

"Where was George Walters in 1944?" I asked.

Connor looked up at me with genuine surprise on his face. "He was in London, the head of private security for Ronan Rothchild."

"Why do you look so surprised?" I asked Connor.

He scanned the page he was reading for confirmation. "Markham Rothchild's father, Ronan, sat on the board at the British Museum."

"There's the link," Arman breathed.

"Tenuous," I agreed. "But yes, it's there."

"It should come as no surprise that George Walters was a bad guy." Connor's fingers flew over the keyboard as he did another search. "He spent several years in prison after the war for assault, was accused of some very shady business practices, and then in the 1960s he was arrested for knifing a business rival to death."

I drummed my fingers on the table, furiously putting the pieces together as I knew Saira would have. She'd have gotten there faster though, which I realized when the last piece fit into place. "The Grandfather Paradox."

Connor knew what I was talking about immediately and was already nodding. The others waited for me to explain. "The Grandfather Paradox is a time travel conundrum. What if a man traveled back in time and accidentally killed his grandfather before he could meet his grandmother? How, then, could the man have been born to travel back in time?"

"I don't understand," Arman said, frustrated.

Connor interrupted with the impatience of one used to being the smartest in the room. "If Tom kills George before Francis is born, then Seth Walters can never be born."

Arman's eyes narrowed as he saw the ramifications. "But if Seth isn't born, then Tom can't be."

"Which may be the point." I said, rubbing my temples. "Nonetheless, all of this presupposes Tom *would* actually go to such massive lengths to encounter his great-grandfather during a mission designed to steal treasures from the British Museum. I think we can agree it's an enormous supposition to make."

That statement seemed to suck all the enthusiasm out of the room, which Arman fought with frustration. "We're still not closer to figuring out where the missing mixed-bloods are being held, though."

"Sure we are." Logan's voice piped up from the sofa where he'd retreated with Saira's book. He turned it around to show us a full-page black and white photograph of a stripped out Underground station. Ava gasped.

"That's it. Except there's a train standing on one of the tracks. That's the place Tam showed me."

"What is that, Logan?" I moved closer to him to see.

"Some urban explorers wrote about visiting all the ghost stations in the 1980s. The British Museum station is the hardest one to get to because they took down the street entrance in 1973."

"What do you mean, took it down?" I asked.

"They literally knocked the building down and put something else in its place. So now, the only way in is through the Underground tunnels," Logan finished proudly.

"The Mongers are using *live* tunnels to bring the mixed-bloods in?" Connor sounded disbelieving, as older brothers will, but Logan stood firm.

"Why not? The trains don't run at night, and maybe the British Transport Police are Mongers too? It's not like they're moving a mass of people. One or two at a time can slip past the Station CCTVs with no problem. I've done it loads of times."

I grimaced. "Of course you have."

Arman got up and started pacing. "So, when are we going?"

My first instinct was to tell him there was no "we" in this. I would be going alone. But if we found the missing mixed-bloods, someone would need to go to the police, especially if there were

Monger guards to deal with. Arman was eighteen, athletic, and from a good family, so his credibility with Scotland Yard wouldn't be questioned. And he'd probably try to follow me anyway.

But because opposing Arman was second nature, I addressed Ava. "Can you try to contact Tam again?"

"I can try. The visions don't always come like that, but if he's thinking about me, we might link up."

"If you do, please try to confirm they're in the British Museum station, and let him know we're coming."

Arman was just barely keeping his frustration in check, but relaxed just a fraction when I finally turned to him. "Buy as many headlamps as you can, and we'll bring them to the mixed-bloods. I'd prefer to have the police lead them out, but if we have to do it ourselves, they should be prepared." Adam nodded and I turned to Connor. "Find out the Central Line schedule, see if there's an actual map of the tunnels. If you can determine schematics of the stations closest to the British Museum, that would be useful as well."

And because young Logan looked so hopeful, I added. "Whatever information you can find about how the urban explorers got to the British Museum station will save me from stumbling around dark tunnels like a fool, and would be appreciated." His enthusiastic nod made Ava giggle.

I looked around the room. They were all so very young, and yet their sense of responsibility and willingness to *do something* was more advanced than that of many adults I'd known.

I focused on Connor and Logan. "Tell your mum what we're doing, and I'll do the same with Jeeves."

"What about my uncle and the Ladies Elian?" Connor asked.

I turned to Ava. "When is the Council meeting?"

"My mother has called a special session for two days from now, at seven p.m. She has insisted that all Family Heads and their heirs be present." Ava had a crisp, authoritative way about her when speaking about business that enhanced, rather than contradicted, her ethereal loveliness.

"She needs the numbers to try to remove Rothchild," added Arman.

I returned my gaze to the young brothers. "No one can say anything to your uncle or to the Ladies Elian. If they decide to go to that Council meeting, and if the Monger ring is used on them, we can't take the risk they'd tell the Mongers what we're up to." I included the twins in my statement, and Arman looked grim.

"Walters won't be at the meeting. It's too dangerous for him to be out in public right now," he said.

"I hope you're right," I said, "but with all the Family Heads otherwise occupied, he may decide it's a perfect time to eliminate his mixed-blood problem. I'll stay at Bishop Cleary's tomorrow. Meet me there at sundown in two nights with whatever exploration supplies the Edwards boys think we need."

Logan's face betrayed his excitement at being included in the planning, and I hoped it was enough to preclude a desire to participate in the rescue attempt. I had the sense that an outright "no, you can't come" would guarantee that he'd find a way to join us.

I turned to Ava. "I presume you'll be going to the Council meeting as well?" She nodded. "You've seen what the ring looks like. Study the Monger hands, Rothchild and his daughter in particular. If that ring appears, get out, and get a message to Jeeves. If Claire and Millicent are there, he will be waiting in the car, and he'll know how to proceed from there."

"I will," she said solemnly. Then she touched my arm with a careful hand. The sudden shock of a vision clouded my head, and her fingers gripped me, hard, as she Saw it too.

Darkness. A tunnel. Danger from all sides – the live rails, Mongers with guns, rats who watched with glittering eyes from the shadows. Then the ghost station, where a hulking train lurked in the darkness, filled with people afraid to sleep too deeply. There was fear, and some anger, in the shadows.

A gunshot. And then panic – people running, following Arman's call. More shots fired, and a dull metal thud as a stray bullet hit something metallic, something old.

Then a deep rumble. Not a train. The earth itself.

Ava gasped and pulled back as though my arm had burned her hand. She stared into my eyes with a wild look. "It's too dangerous …"

My heart was still pounding as the vision finally faded. It left a lingering fear in its wake – fear not for my own safety, but rather a deep, abiding fear of leaving Saira alone.

I could sense Ava pulling back, making a different plan, and there was hopelessness in her expression. I touched her sleeve, careful not to encounter bare skin again. "I have to do this, Ava. There's no other way."

Her whispered voice trembled as she searched my eyes. "You can't."

"You know I do."

Tears filled her eyes and she shook her head. "Saira will know."

"What will she know," I asked Ava gently.

"That you knew you'd die, and you went anyway."

THE WOODS

Ringo came back just after sunrise with two rabbits and a pheasant to clean. I took the pheasant because I knew chickens and could deal with the feathers and blood, and because gutting a rabbit was more hardcore than I knew how to be at the moment.

He raised an eyebrow but said nothing about Archer's absence. Maybe he thought Archer was down below in the cellar. For that matter, maybe he was. I wasn't going to chase him down though. My ego and confidence had taken a hit, and I was too busy ignoring the prickling of indignation, guilt, and insecurity that had made me slightly nauseous when I'd woken up alone.

After we'd cleaned ourselves up from the bloody work, Ringo handed me the skinned and gutted meat. "Take these to Marianne, would ye? There are some chanterelles in my bag as well for 'er." He collapsed on his bed and peeked an eye up at me from the shadows of his stall. "I didn't see signs the Germans 'ad been about, and the Maquis are likely down for the day, so ye should be alright if ye go out."

I hoisted his bag on my shoulder. "Sleep tight."

"What does that mean?" His eyes were already closing.

"It's a thing moms say when they're tucking you in."

"Well, it sounds 'orrible, like ye'll not move and wake up stiff as anythin'."

"The follow-up to it is 'don't let the bedbugs bite,' because that doesn't give kids nightmares."

He chuckled sleepily at the irony in my tone. "No bedbugs when ye sleep on the ground. The rats get 'em."

I shuddered. "Right up there with yeasty codpiece. Thanks for that."

He was still chuckling when I left the barn.

A layer of mist hung over the garden, and it gave the place an eerie feeling of silence – a suppression of sound rather than the absence of it. As if the land itself was holding its breath, waiting for the war to come and spoil it.

The kitchen door of the house opened, and Marianne stepped outside with a basket over one arm, and a beautiful embroidered shawl wrapped around her shoulders. She didn't seem surprised to see me, and was delighted with the meat I held out to her. "From Louis," I said softly in French.

She spoke rapidly as she led me inside to the sink, where I laid the meat and washed my hands before digging the chanterelle mushrooms from Ringo's pack. More rapid French as she happily took them from me and began preparing a marinade of lemon, olive oil, and rosemary. I helped chop the rosemary as Marianne made very quick work cutting the rabbits into pieces, which she dropped into the bowl with the marinade, then covered with a heavy plate. The pheasant was prepared for roasting, and then everything was taken down the stairs to the cellar, which was nearly as cool as a refrigerator. I noticed the gaps in her food shelves and realized that Marianne and Marcel were living a farmer's version of hand-to-mouth.

We went outside again to find the mist had burned off, and dew on the leaves sparkled in the sunlight. Marianne gestured that I should follow her into the garden, where we spent a very pleasant hour picking lettuce, spinach, early radishes, strawberries, gooseberries, and currants. The little bits of medieval French I'd learned on the river made the sign language intelligible during discussions of simple recipes and gardening techniques, and when Marianne indicated that I should accompany her on a walk, I readily understood.

I asked her, through hand gestures and my limited French, whether it was safe for her to be seen with me, and her answer was a scowl and a tug on my arm as she opened the garden gate. I did a quick appearance assessment, and the phrase 'what's the worst that could happen' played like a perseverant chant through my brain. But I was there to find the Werwolves, and going to the village in broad daylight sounded safer than sneaking around at night ever would, especially with the lurking Maquis to contend with after dark.

Oradour-sur-Glane looked like something from a postcard of French country life. The dirt road ambled past stone farmhouses and gave way to cobblestone streets that wound around small shops with second-floor apartments. We passed several large barns attached to smaller buildings overlooked by a lovely old stone church that sat up on a hill. The town square was at the center of the market district, sort of like a fairground, and several people were out with baskets over their arms, either buying or selling edible things.

A dour-faced woman walked past us as we entered the town square. She was leading a group of about ten rowdy village children in a resolute march. At the end of the line I spotted Marcel walking quietly alone, and Marianne left my side to give her son a kiss on the cheek before he was led back to school. Marcel threw me a quick wave before they rounded the corner, and I thought he looked especially small against the big personalities of his classmates.

Marianne explained to me, in simple language, that the village school was hard for her boy because he was so quiet. I asked if there was another school for him. Marianne hesitated, then whispered the words in French so quietly under her breath I barely heard them.

"For Jews."

The fear that laced her tone told me everything about the culture in this country that had been occupied by Germany for the past four years. As Nancy Wake had so blithely pointed out, Tom, with his dark gypsy coloring, looked like most of the French people she worked with. Coincidentally, most of the Jewish people in Europe did too. Which meant anyone with the slightest anti-Semite inclination could point at almost any Frenchman or woman and raise suspicion about them, just on looks alone. Even Marianne, with her soft black hair and sun-browned skin, was a candidate for ethnic investigation if she crossed the wrong person. It was a chilling thought to carry as we entered the village square.

Marianne led the way to a short, round woman wearing a crisp white apron, whose basket was similar to the ones we both carried. She reminded me of a mother goose in the way she clucked over the vegetables Marianne held out for her inspection, and then proudly showed off her own fresh cheeses. When the trade of goat cheese for radishes and spinach had been made, Mother Goose clucked quietly to Marianne about various people scattered around the town square, her eyes lighting on each person before beginning another round of gossip.

Marianne didn't contribute to the conversation except to nod or murmur the occasional 'hmm,' and only as Mother Goose was winding down did Marianne's eyes finally flick to me. I'd been standing back, out of the line of her sight, but with the carefully guarded expression in Marianne's eyes I took another step into the shadows of the barn behind me. Cool air hit my back, and I turned to find myself in the open doorway of a working garage. An old Citroën sedan teetered on jacks, and a pair of legs stuck out from underneath the heavy steel car.

The legs bent and kicked the mechanic out from under the fender. I almost stepped back outside, but realized I was more afraid of being noticed by Mother Goose than by the person who had just stood up to retrieve a wrench from the work table.

Especially as she seemed to have more to hide than I did.

Her hair was cut very short like a boy's, and there were tracks of grease smeared up her arms and across one cheek. From a distance I would have thought she was a lanky teenage boy, but I had done my own masquerading, and I knew to look beyond the coveralls and boots, the chipped and dirty nails, and the short, scruffy hair. She was close to my age and, like me, had no obvious curves, but her cheeks looked soft, even over the razor-sharp cheekbones, and she didn't have a man's Adam's apple.

She reached for a wrench and then spotted me, frozen in place just inside the door. "Puis-je vous aider?" Her voice was husky, and I wondered if it was naturally that way, or if she put it on like the red bandana she pulled from her pocket to wipe off her hands.

I backed toward the door. "Sorry," I muttered in English before I could catch myself. Crap.

Her eyes widened fractionally in surprise, and I waited for them to narrow. They didn't, but her voice dropped to a whisper. "Do you need help?" She said in accented English. It didn't sound like she was asking as mechanic to customer.

I shook my head quickly. "I'm sorry to intrude."

I continued backing out of the garage, because being English or American in occupied France was not good for anyone's health.

The mechanic nodded, but didn't take her eyes off me. Right before I stepped back out to the town square she gave me a quick smile and lifted her hand slightly in what could have been a wave.

Fascinating.

I blinked in the bright sunlight after the cool darkness of the garage, and it took a moment to spot Marianne and her basket a few meters away from where Mother Goose had corralled some other victim. The gossipy woman looked up at me and her eyes narrowed slightly as she tried to place me. The companion said something to her, and I slipped behind a post and back into the shadows of the building to avoid further scrutiny. I caught up to Marianne as she finished her trade of delicate, leafy lettuce for a small basket of eggs, and I realized there'd been no chickens at Marianne's farm. It was an odd fact in a time when resources were scarce and self-reliance in food production could be the difference between starving and surviving this war.

Marianne traded my full basket for hers, and we continued walking around the square. She greeted people she knew and made another trade for a wax paper-wrapped block of what looked like butter. Marianne was done after that, and as we walked past the garage on our way out, I tapped her arm and gestured inside. "Une fille?" I asked quietly.

Marianne nodded. "Rachel."

It wasn't until we'd gone past the church again that I used my quiet mix of French and pantomime to get more of Rachel's story from Marianne. It seemed that Rachel's father owned the garage and was the main mechanic in town. He had been taken to the camps with the first wave of internments. Rachel had cut her hair then and became Raoul. Even the worst of the village informants knew that if they turned her in as a Jew, the village would be left without its last mechanic.

We turned left off the road back to Marianne's farm, and she indicated the vegetables she still had in her basket. She had another trade to make, I guessed, and I followed her down the dirt lane and over the rise of a small hill. It hadn't looked like anything from the main road, and I was surprised to see a vineyard tucked away in an area that wasn't really known for its wine production.

The leaves were just showing green on the twisted vines that managed to look neglected even as they teased their spring colors. The lane ended at a stand of trees where an old stone farmhouse stood sheltered from the sun. There were two windowless outbuildings, which I assumed were for wine production, but everything had an air of shabbiness, as if the vines grew out of stubbornness and the buildings stood only because they were too well-built to fall down.

And then I heard the singing.

It sounded like children, more than just a couple, with voices that blended together in beautiful harmony. The sound came from one of the outbuildings of the otherwise deserted farm.

Marianne smiled at my surprise as she led me to the farmhouse. She didn't knock or enter, she just took whatever vegetables she hadn't traded out of her basket and arranged them carefully in a box next to the front door. My eyes kept stealing to the outbuilding where the voices danced and wove a tune I didn't recognize, with words sung in a language that didn't sound like French to my ear.

"The Jewish school," Marianne whispered in French.

Oh wow. No wonder she wished Marcel could come here every day. I supposed that people would notice if she took him out of the village school, and they'd both be in danger if it was known he came here.

The song ended and Marianne sighed, then picked up her empty basket and we turned to go back up the lane. When we were out of earshot of any farm, I asked about the school and she tried to explain it to me.

I gathered that the winemaker had died before the war began and left the place to the church in the village, but most of the villagers had forgotten it even existed. When the Germans began to round up the village Jews, they began with the adults. By the time they came for the children, most of them had disappeared. It was presumed they had gone to live with relatives in some other region, and to be fair to the French villagers, Marianne said no one really looked too hard for them.

"So the children live there? Who cares for them?" I asked Marianne.

"The priest hides them until it's safe to move them, and he stays with them several nights a week. Many of us from the village secretly help to feed them."

I knew there would be meat in the box on the front doorstep of the vineyard house tomorrow morning after I told Archer and Ringo about this place. Somehow, I didn't think Nancy's resistance fighters were doing too much feeding and caring for the people they were trying to "save."

When we got back to Marianne's farm, she waved me away from helping her in the house. Ringo was still passed out in the barn, and I stubbornly resisted the urge to look for Archer in the barn cellar – mostly because I didn't want to know if he wasn't there.

My brain was still spinning on the Jewish kids, hidden away in a forgotten winery, and the knowledge that the Werwolves were out there plotting something destructive in this region. It made me antsy, like my thoughts were making my skin feel too tight, and I needed to run to loosen everything up. It was risky to run during daylight hours, but I hoped the forest would hide me from curious eyes.

I didn't wake Ringo, and I didn't leave a note. But I did tell Marianne I was going into the woods. She admonished me to be careful, like any mother would, and I nodded solemnly and promised to be back in an hour. It was more than I would have promised just about anyone else, but I thought Marianne had enough to worry about without me adding to her list.

I tucked my wide pant legs inside my long socks, which looked entirely ridiculous, but I didn't have a mirror and wasn't planning to run into the forest fashion police. The woods behind Marianne's farmhouse seemed to stretch for several kilometers providing the border for most of the town, so I headed in the opposite direction of Nancy's Maquis headquarters and moved as deeply into the trees as I could.

My sense of direction had always been good, but because there were no street signs or billboards to mark my way, I did take the time to stack a small cairn at every change of trajectory. Within about ten minutes of log-hurdles and tree-climbs with back-flip dismounts, I was breathing hard. And twenty minutes into the forest, I came to a rocky waterfall in a tiny spring where the pool at the bottom was perfectly clear and just deep enough to plunge my hands into and splash my face with the cold water.

The sound of the waterfall made the tightness in my chest open up, and when I'd stopped gasping from the run, I discovered I could actually breathe again without feeling like I needed to climb out of my skin. I wasn't sure how much forest was left before the land was cleared for farms again, and the tree above me was perfectly built for scaling, so after a long, satisfying drink from the spring, I leapt off a boulder and hit the lowest branch.

I was in a giant ash tree that had just gotten its spring foliage, so I had to go pretty high before I could see enough to get my bearings. I had run a lot farther than I thought – either that or the strip of forest was narrower than it seemed – because a road wound around the leading edge of the trees about a kilometer away from my tree. I shifted in my perch to get a better view and startled a kestrel off an upper branch. It flew off toward the road and passed over something that glinted metallically in the sun. It looked like some sort of vehicle that had pulled off the road and parked among the low brush.

And then I saw motion in the woods, leading away from the vehicle and headed toward my tree.

Crap.

I considered carving a spiral into the upper trunk of the ash and Clocking myself away, but a: that could be catastrophically stupid if I ended up twenty feet in the air at my destination, and b: I hadn't drawn myself a spiral at Marianne's farm or anywhere else in France during this time period. A rookie mistake, I realized, because now I had no automatic escape route.

My second thought was to jump down and run for it. But even though that was probably my best option from a safety standpoint, I wasn't willing to cut bait just yet. I wanted to see who was coming.

I could hear men's voices, but not what they were saying, and as I settled back against the tree for stability and comfort, I was able to make out two people. They weren't exactly in stealth mode, but they did move carefully, and I got the sense that they'd had some training – which meant they were likely either hunters or killers.

When they were close enough for me to actually understand their speech, I also caught my first glimpse of a military uniform, and I realized I could understand most of what they said because my high school language training was automatically translating the German into English in my head. Killers, then.

According to Nancy, this area was part of the free zone, which meant these guy weren't supposed to be here.

"It's as good a place as any to get away from the radio chatter." It came out in a grunt, as if he was speaking from a toilet. I thought Grunty might have been the big one in the lead.

I shifted again, very slowly and carefully, until I could see Grunty clearly enough to memorize his uniform. He wore basic olive drab combat fatigues with the same round green helmet I'd seen in every war movie. There were a couple of patches sewn on one shoulder though, and I searched for identifying features.

The other guy threw off his pack and dropped to his knees in front of my waterfall to splash his face. I was irrationally annoyed when he spit into my spring.

"Now they'll think they need the pig-dog to clear the way." Loogie's voice was thin and whiny, and fine tendrils of Mongerness wafted up to wrap around my gut. Pig-dog was one of those insults that sounded so much nastier in German, especially since *Schweinehund* was almost always pronounced with a leer.

It didn't surprise me that Loogie was a Monger, just like it didn't surprise me that I'd felt so many Mongers among the French Maquis. But being only a few feet from a German Monger armed with what looked like a sniper rifle sitting under my tree in occupied France wasn't an ideal scenario in which to find myself. Since I operated under the assumption that they tend not to give sniper rifles to guys who suck at shooting, I made myself relax into my aerie perch and wait them out.

"We can't kill him. Karl's like a little weiner-dog, always on the lookout at his back. And the place the *Schweinehund* sleeps is like a damn fortress." Grunty said.

"We'll lure him out. Or stir up the French pigs to do it for us." Loogie pulled out a huge knife and began whittling a stick as he sat back against my tree. If he looked up, he'd see me high above him. I didn't like it, but I couldn't move.

Grunty threw a rock into the spring with a curse. "We trained to make trouble, not to go hunting to feed men too lazy to steal what they need."

Loogie hawked up a big wad of phlegm and spit into my spring again. Ew. "Maybe I should climb a big tree and start sniping actual *Schweine*, what do you think?" Loogie tapped the trunk of my tree with the butt of his rifle, and I closed my eyes. The little girl that believed in invisibility cloaks took over for a second, even as fear surged like ice up to the surface of my skin.

"Sounds like good fun, but instead we should go hunting Maquis. The rat said they emerge at nightfall, and with the 2nd Division on the move, they'll be out for sure. The roads around Limoges have some nice cover for sniping." Grunty sounded excited at the prospect, and I very badly wanted to know who "the rat" was.

Loogie wiped his face with a rag and got to his feet. "*Ja*, let's do it. Maybe we can pick off a few French pigs, and who knows, if the *Schweinehund* gets lucky and actually infiltrates, we can pick him off too."

Grunty picked up his rucksack as Loogie shouldered the sniper rifle. Of course he had to spit one last time into my spring, and I just barely held back from throwing a stick at him. As they trudged off through the woods toward their vehicle, I suddenly knew what I had to do.

Slowly and carefully, I pulled off my jacket, then my boots, and I stashed them securely in the crook of the tree. Then, when the two men were out of sight of my tree, I quickly shed the rest of my clothes and stuffed them up against the trunk.

My hand went to the Shifter bone around my neck, I closed my eyes, and allowed *her* to surge up.

I felt the shimmer of a thousand pinpricks as my body became the Cougar, and I could feel her stretch languorously in my mind. *Are we stalking, or can I hunt?* she said, with the edge of a purr in her tone. *Stalking*, I told her firmly. I was absolutely not interested in bloodshed if I could possibly help it.

211

The drop to the forest floor was easy and felt a little like flying. The stink of sweaty wool uniforms and unwashed bodies hung in the air around where the German soldiers had sat, and I sneezed the stench out of my Cougar's very sensitive nose. I took off at a silent sprint through the forest, following the scent trail that was about as subtle as if it had been painted neon pink.

I practically skidded to a stop just outside the clearing where their vehicle was parked. The soldiers were already seated inside with the engine running, and just as Grunty drove away, I finally caught a glimpse of the insignia on his uniform. The ends of the sideways Z jagged with the sinister angles of Hitler's Werwolves.

The boxy tank-like jeep picked up speed down the dirt road, and I ran along the edges of the forest behind it until I was out of forest to hide in. They were far enough ahead of me that I knew I'd soon lose their scent if I continued, and the likelihood of being spotted was too high, even in the dusky light of early evening.

I reluctantly turned around to make my way back to the tree that loomed over my spring. My Cougar was strangely silent in my head as I loped through the woods at a steady pace, and I felt quite comfortable in my animal form. My Cougar was stronger than my human body was, with more endurance, and my senses were more automatically in tune with the sights and smells of the forest around me.

Which was why my heartbeat quickened as I approached my tree. *Mine*, my Cougar said firmly. The scent of him in the air marked his presence as well as if I'd already seen him.

I leapt to the top of a boulder, from which I could finally see down to my spring.

There was Archer.

And oh boy, did he look pissed.

STAKE OUT

I startled Archer with my jump to the rock, and smug satisfaction helped calm the instinct that had sent the hair on my Cougar's spine straight up when I saw the expression on his face. An instant later he recognized me, and it was like his whole body sighed in relief.

My clothes fell from the sky, and then Ringo jumped down out of the ash tree holding my boots and looking, if possible, more angry even than Archer had.

"Ye couldn't wait to go lookin' fer trouble, could ye?" Ringo spat. I'd never seen him so fierce, and I hesitated up on my rock. It seemed safer in my animal skin, maybe because I knew it was the only way I could outrun him.

Archer hadn't taken his eyes off me, but he spoke to Ringo behind him. "She'll have an explanation." His voice sounded reasonable, and not at all as disappointed as I thought he'd be.

"Ah, she always does." Ringo was still spitting mad, and he turned his back. "Go ahead – Shift so ye can explain."

I'd never seen Ringo act like this – usually he was an ally, or at least a neutral party when Archer got angry at me for being reckless. Archer gave me a small, wry smile, then turned his back too.

My clothes had fallen between Archer and Ringo, which Archer realized only when I jumped down off the rock and walked around in front of him to Shift back to my human form. His eyes widened suddenly, and he turned his back to me again, but not before he got the full show, and I was perversely delighted to make him uncomfortable.

I did throw my clothes on quickly though, because the sun had gone down and there was already a chill in the air. I'd barely gotten my feet in my boots when Ringo turned to glare at me.

"So? Did ye lie to Marianne or lose track of time?'" he growled.

"Neither. And since when are you my keeper? Did you follow me here?" I threw my best glare back at him.

"Ye left a trail a mile wide, and when ye didn't come back in an hour like ye told Marianne ye would, of course we came to find ye."

I fought the urge to stick my tongue out at him, because I'm not twelve. I wanted to though, so I bent to tie my shoe and said nothing instead.

"Who was wittlin' 'ere?" Ringo kicked at the wood shavings Loogie had left under the tree.

I looked up at him defiantly. "A German soldier – Werwolf, if I had to guess, based on the Wolfsangel rune."

Archer exhaled sharply behind me. "In case the date has escaped you, Operation Overlord has gone into effect." He knelt down to brush a leaf off my jacket, then sat beside me on the ground. "Tell us."

The only thing I could detect in his voice was concern, and it siphoned a little of my defiance away. Ringo was still standing, arms crossed, a few feet away, so I ignored him and spoke to Archer.

I told him about walking in town with Marianne, about Mother Goose, and meeting Rachel, the girl mechanic. I told him about the village priest who made Jewish kids disappear, the villagers who turned in their neighbors, and the children singing at the old winery. I gave him the kind of details I would have saved up to tell my modern Archer, who always wanted to hear full retellings of conversations, and words that painted a picture of the experience. And I spoke to empty my head of all the things that I

214

struggled with about being in this time, and this place, in these circumstances.

And when I finally got to the part about the German soldiers and the spitting and the grunting and the horrors of their conversation, Ringo had moved closer and squatted down to watch my face, and every bit of Archer's attention was tuned to me. I could feel their interest sharpen and hear their breath catch at the part when Loogie tapped my tree with the butt of his rifle. I had a storyteller's audience, and I felt them take ownership of my experience as they invested themselves and made it their own. I had followed the plot, unfolded suspense, and shared my own emotional journey as if Archer and Ringo had been right beside me. I allowed no stinginess in my words, and even as I felt myself beginning to unburden, I could see my truths settle in and become a part of them.

"I'd 'ave done the same, I s'pose." Ringo nodded to himself as if that was that.

My gaze had been caught by Ringo's words, but then my eyes slid to Archer for his reaction. He was watching me thoughtfully when he spoke.

"When you didn't return, Marianne became frantic. She woke Ringo with her worry that perhaps Madame Bouchard – the one you call Mother Goose – had raised suspicion about your identity and had you detained. He woke me when he confirmed the signs that you'd gone into the woods, and with every cairn we found, I feared there wouldn't be another."

My chest constricted at the thought of Marianne's worry, but Archer's calm, quiet voice was somehow at odds with his words. "And here, where it was clear you hadn't been alone, I was moments away from donning the armor and grabbing the sword to ride into the fray to rescue you."

I smiled a little at the image. "Find a white horse and you're good to go."

A twinkle in his eye was the only thing that knocked some of the dust off his dry tone. "The Prince of Darkness rides a bold, black steed. I hardly fit the Prince Valiant archetype, which is, perhaps, my point. I was set to rescue you, willing to throw regard for safety, secrecy, and good sense straight out the window in my quest to be your savior. And then there you were, perfectly unharmed and entirely capable of minding yourself."

Something went *clunk* in my brain – that thing that Millicent had said about the differences between men and women. I spun toward Ringo.

"Is that why you were so mad? Because you were all set to rescue me and I didn't need it?"

Ringo looked uncharacteristically grumpy. "Ye don't usually need it, so that wasn't a surprise. I s'pose I was afraid."

I waited for the sentence to go on, but it didn't. "Afraid of what?" I finally asked.

He shrugged. "Just afraid." He held my gaze. "Most of my time with ye 'as been spent in the past, with knives and swords and the odd pistol bein' aimed in yer general direction. We both know stayin' whole is just a matter of bein' faster and smarter than yer opponent – and ye always 'ave been that."

He sighed and waved his hand around him in a generally inclusive gesture. "But 'ere – now – in this war, everyone 'as a gun. And that's not even the thing ye 'ave to be most afraid of."

I stared at him. "I'm not in danger of being run down by a tank, Ringo."

He made a face at me, which helped diminish little of the worry that was lining his eyes. "It's the turncoats and traitors and scared people just tryin' to survive ye 'ave to fear. Fast and smart can only keep ye so safe from them when they set their sights on ye."

I sat back and tried to choose the words that mattered. I included both of them in my gaze. "I get it. I get the fear, and I have those same fears for both of you. But you should know that I got really defensive when I saw how angry you both looked, and my first instinct was to run."

"I'm sorry 'bout that, Saira." Ringo said. He looked straight into my eyes when he spoke. "I can't say it won't 'appen again, but ye've said it yerself, I've chosen my family, and ye two are it."

I gave Ringo a grateful smile as Archer reached for my hand. "I'm sorry," he said quietly.

I shrugged. "It's not the first time you've been angry at me for taking risks, and it won't be the last."

He studied me for a moment. "Is my protectiveness of you very stifling in your time?"

Ringo smirked, and I almost answered too fast. But then I saw the tension around Archer's mouth, and I thought I should be fair.

"Yes, but I think I do the same thing to you, so we're pretty even. You did have to mellow out a little at the Tower of London, but we worked it out."

Archer looked startled, and I thought dropping our Tudor-era adventures into the conversation probably wasn't the best idea. But he surprised me. "Why would you need to protect me? I'm immortal."

I shot Ringo a glance, and he shrugged as if to say 'you're on your own.'

I stood up and held my hand out to Archer. He took it and got to his feet with the kind of grace I'd never been able to manage. "That's a long story, and as much as I'd love to hang out in the woods with you guys all night, I'm bummed to say we should probably go find Nancy and her gang of cutthroats before the snipers start picking them off."

Archer gave me a smirk worthy of his modern self. "You can talk while you run, can't you?"

Ringo barked a laugh that earned him a glare from me, and I smiled with thorny sweetness. "Lead the way."

Archer laughed and we took off through the woods at a decent pace. As we ran, I told him about the old wounds that had begun blooming on him every time he got hurt, and about Connor and Mr. Shaw's theory about the mutation of his telomeres. It prompted a whole conversation, led by Ringo, about the science of genetics. I was impressed at Ringo's ability to break things down into digestible pieces and at the sheer amount of knowledge he had picked up from his listening post in the greenhouse lab.

Archer was clearly fascinated with the genetics of Immortal Descendancy, and I was so engrossed in Ringo's explanation that I forgot to anticipate what came next.

We had intersected the road far beyond the town and dropped our pace to a stealthy walk so as not to attract unwanted attention. I missed the significance of the look Ringo shot me until Archer asked him, "Your friends are doing such precise work in their laboratory. Is it merely research, or do they work toward an end?"

The outline of a building materialized in the misty night, and the prickling edges of Mongerness reached out from the shadows. I whispered, "We're here."

Archer's voice was pitched low. "You didn't answer my question."

I stopped to face him. "They're working on a cure for you – a virus that neutralizes the mutation. But they think you have to be badly injured for the virus to work, and they don't know if it would reset your telomere response to normal *after* healing the wounds, or if you'd die from the wounds themselves." I thought I had managed to deliver the information without the emotional breakdown that laced its fingers around my heart every time the subject came up.

"The unknowns are somewhat concerning." Archer's delivery was so deadpan I almost barked a laugh, but caught the sound just in time.

"You think?" I avoided Ringo's eyes and kept mine locked on Archer. He touched my face gently and might have kissed me, if it hadn't been for the Monger who materialized behind us.

Ringo and I both stiffened, but Archer spoke sharply to him in French before taking my hand to continue walking. The Maquisard moved quietly ahead, and I assumed he'd been told to inform Nancy that we were there.

Ringo walked a little apart from us, and his silence had weight to it, as if it was a heavy thing instead of an absent one. Just before we walked into Gaspard's farmhouse, I hung back and let Archer go in first. I touched Ringo's sleeve. "What?" I whispered.

He didn't pretend not to know what I was asking, and his eyes met mine directly. "You're settin' 'im up."

That earned a double-take. "How?"

"If 'e agrees with ye that the cure is too dangerous, ye'll take that back to Archer and use it against 'im."

"Use it against him? I don't even get that."

"Really? Ye don't think 'e'd wonder if ye wouldn't just come back to this time and choose this version of 'imself?"

I stared at Ringo in shock. "They're all Archer."

He raised an eyebrow. "All?"

I tried to explain, even though I knew I was tap-dancing in a minefield. "The student we first met, this one, and mine."

"So, only the one from yer time belongs to ye, eh?"

I glared at him in exasperation. "I don't get it, Ringo. What do you want me to say?"

His eyes held mine for a moment before he looked away. "I don't know. It's not my business, anyway." He nodded at the door. "Go on in. Ye 'ave things to tell them."

I debated staying there and making him work through whatever weirdness was crawling around his brain, but I really didn't want to know. There are some things it's just better to leave unsaid, and I was already feeling prickles of guilt about his comment. If the Archer from my time was the only one that belonged to me, then any comfort or connection I made with this Archer was in the realm of cheating … on him … with himself. I closed my eyes with a shudder, then squared my shoulders to step inside the farmhouse. My relationship sinkholes had no place in a room full of Mongers and Nancy Wake.

Archer shot me a quizzical look when we entered the main room, where Nancy and Gaspard were studying a map and several other young men were doing whatever small tasks they could busy themselves with. There were rifles being cleaned, knives sharpened, and satchels emptied and re-packed. It was the kind of work people created so they could stay in a room and listen in.

Archer and Nancy stood next to each other, and the height difference between them was noticeable. He was at least ten inches taller than she was, and I had the thought that she was too short for him.

Not to mention, too married for him.

Not that I had a lot of room to talk though considering how murky my own situation was when it came to Archer. I mentally flipped Ringo off for having planted the seeds of doubt and discomfort in my head. Was this Archer, in 1944, a different man than the one I was with in my present? Then again, the Archer I'd first fallen in love with had been the young student in 1888, and this Archer was closer in time to him than the one waiting for me in London. For that matter, according to the rules of time travel, the reason he was waiting in London for me instead of being here was that he couldn't be where he already was. That fact alone supported the idea that Archer was just Archer, no matter *when* I was with him.

My mental voice *hmmphed* as if to say, *so there,* and I started to feel a little split-personality-ish for talking to myself. This philosophical morality talk could wait. We had snipers to find.

Archer continued his conversation with Nancy and Gaspard in French, and I could tell they were trying to figure out the most likely spots for a sniper to lay in wait. I instinctively moved to Archer's side to see the map. Gaspard stiffened and made a move to grab the map off the table, but Nancy snapped at him. "Arrêt!"

She turned to me. "So, love, let's see what you bring to the table, shall we? The goods on the snipers are yours. Pretend you're one of those rat bastards and tell me where they went."

I was surprised that she gave me that respect, and I looked at Archer. "Point to the approximate location of my tree."

His finger dropped on a spot in the forest just south of Oradour-sur-Glane, and I studied the landscape around it. There was the creek I'd followed, and the spot the soldiers had pulled their vehicle off the road. I traced the direction they'd taken when they left, studying the small hamlets dotting the route to Limoges.

"Where are we now?" I asked Nancy. Gaspard practically growled as he stormed away from the table, muttering unflattering things probably having to do with animals and body parts.

Nancy scoffed at the concern on my face. "Don't worry about him, love. My first night here he tried to convince some of the Maquis to cut my throat and steal my money."

"What happened?"

She laughed and said cheerily. "I got them drunk, then told them I was the only one who knew all the drops, all the codes, and where the liquor was stashed. If they listened to that one," she indicated Gaspard, still glowering in a corner, "they'd get none of it." She blew him a kiss across the room, and his scowl darkened. "Gaspard never did get over the fact I'm still here drinking with his boys."

She directed my attention to another spot on the map. "But now we have sniper problems to keep us busy. We're here now, and these were last night's targets." She pointed at two bridges.

I placed mental dots on each of the places on the map, then scanned the roads surrounding them. There were two other bridges nearby, one of which was outside a village and surrounded by farmland, and the other was a train trestle bridge that crossed a river. I pointed to the train bridge.

"There."

"Why?" she asked with interest.

"You said your mission is to slow down a panzer division that's trying to get to Normandy. If it was me, I'd take out anything that runs north/south, especially trains. Blowing a bridge seems like a pretty efficient way to do that."

Nancy studied me. "It is. The charges were set earlier today and we plan to blow tonight's train."

I stared at her. "Why the train? Why not just the tracks?"

"Because Gerry has a habit of commandeering our trains."

"But wouldn't a train be full of people?"

"Most likely." She didn't back down, and I held her gaze.

"That's a lot of people." I was pretty sure it wouldn't just be soldiers on that train. My temper was rising, and there were a whole bunch of words I'd been biting back that were just waiting for the floodgates to lift.

"There will be reprisals," Archer said.

"I'll work them to our advantage," she said with a shrug.

That did it. The shrug. Like she couldn't be bothered with trivialities. I stared at her, my eyes narrowing. "You'll work reprisals to your advantage? Correct me if I'm wrong, but reprisals are not just restricted to the eye-for-an-eye routine. You take out a bridge, they'll take out a school, isn't that how it works?"

Nancy studied me, her expression hardening. "You find the English infiltrator, and leave the rest of the war to me."

Archer met my eyes and then tried to redirect the conversation. "Where is the main body of the 2nd SS Panzer Division right now?" he asked Nancy.

She shifted her gaze back to the map, studiously avoiding my glare. "A couple of days south of Limoges, assuming we can keep up the pressure. We've been taking out the advance groups as they enter the Limousin region, and so far they haven't been able to organize themselves into anything bigger than a small battalion."

Nancy tapped the location of the train bridge. "I'm sending scouts to look for signs of the snipers around my charges."

"We'll go with them," I said sharply. It felt like all the eyes in the room swiveled to me, even though it was probably only Nancy, Archer, and Ringo who stared. "You said to find the English spy, right? Well, he's Werwolf and so are the snipers. I need them alive so we can find the rest of their group."

"Snipers can be eight hundred to a thousand meters away from their targets, Saira." Archer was not thrilled with my suggestion.

Nancy's eyes narrowed. "Listen to Devereux. Stay here and out of the way, because I promise you, when I find those snipers, I'm taking them out."

I glared right back at Nancy. "You're going to have to shoot me first, then. I need to follow the Werwolves back to their base, which I can't do if they're dead. All we have to do is scare them away and they'll run, and then you'll get to blow up your train full of people as planned."

The look Nancy directed at me was all sharp edges as she grabbed my arm and pulled me out of the room. She surprised me so much I forgot to resist until we were in a bedroom at the back of the house and she had kicked the door shut in Archer's face.

"She'll be fine, Devereux," she said as it slammed. "Watch the door."

I wrenched my arm out of her surprisingly strong grip. "Seriously? You didn't need to grab me." I'd had time to work up to this level of mad. Pretty much since I'd known Nancy, I'd been working up to it, and I wasn't letting it go easily, no matter how much she yelled at me.

She laughed at me like I was an annoying, naïve child. "I must've left my manners in Marseilles where the Gestapo tortured my husband to death."

Just like that, my indignation burst like a balloon, and I felt, in the pit of my stomach, what it would be like if it were me talking about Archer. Nancy must have seen the pain in my face because the edges she wore like armor softened a little.

She sat on the bed and I leaned against the dresser. She looked tired, and about ten years older than she was. "It's hard to be so strong, you know, love?"

I didn't say anything. Her question didn't seem to need an answer, and she finally met my eyes. "I was in Marseilles in 1940 when the Germans invaded. I got busy making life hell for them right away, and my husband's money protected us for a while, but when I joined up with the resistance to get people out of France, they finally figured out who I was. We were mostly just getting

English pilots over the mountains into Spain, but they couldn't catch me, and it made them angry. The White Mouse, the Gestapo called me, because I slipped through their traps every time." Nancy's expression was more grimace than smile. "I used to dust a little powder on, have a drink, and walk right past their checkpoints with a pretty smile, daring them to search me. God, what a flirtatious little bastard I was."

She leaned back against the headboard and studied me. "I left Marseilles in 1943. They were getting too close and I thought if I was gone, they'd leave Henri alone. It took me six tries to cross the Pyrenees into Spain, and I had no idea they'd already brought him in for questioning. They thought he knew where I was, see?" Her gaze drifted to the far wall, but she was staring at nothing in particular. "The Germans tortured him for three months before he died."

The words trailed off, and finally she took a breath and re-focused on me. "Do you know, I never broke down. Not even when they did capture me, then let me go when a friend lied for me, or when I rode a bicycle five hundred kilometers to replace codes my operator had been forced to destroy, or when I had to kill an SS sentry during a raid so he wouldn't raise the alarm. I've always been the strong one, even when I found out about Henri."

She pulled a small gold band out of her pocket and slipped it on her ring finger, holding her hand up to admire the wedding ring. "Henri took care of me. He protected me so I could protect all the other people who needed me. He *fueled* my strength with his own."

She stroked the ring gently, lost in thought, then finally slipped it off her finger and put it back in her pocket. "I pretend he's still alive, you know, still waiting for me to come home. Because frankly love, without someone like him, someone strong and capable for me to lean on, I'm almost all used up."

I waited for the punchline, something to explain why she had shared so much with me – a stranger.

She exhaled and jerked her head toward the door. "They don't know about Henri. They don't know I pretend he'll be there when this is done. They don't know anything that would loosen my grip or call my leadership into question."

She stood up and straightened the buttons on her blouse. "There's room for both of us, Elian, but don't challenge my authority in front of the Maquis. Behind closed doors is fine, but not in front of men who expect a woman to be weak. In this world, neither of us can afford that."

I finally found the strength in my voice to speak. "I'm sorry for your loss, Nancy. Actually, those words don't even begin to cover how deeply sorry I am."

Her eyes held mine, and then she nodded once as if to say, *it's done*. But I wasn't done yet.

"You're right, I'm just here for the Englishman, and you're the one who's been fighting the war. And yeah, it might be stupid to care about keeping two jerks alive just for the information they have. But finding the spy will *save lives*. You may not care so much about one guy when you're planning to blow up a whole train, but isn't that the point of this whole thing? Some of those train passengers might not be soldiers, and might not even be German. If you're not protecting those people – the ones living their lives, just trying to survive this war – then what are you all fighting for?"

She held my gaze for a long time without a word before she finally opened the door. Archer stood outside wearing a worried expression as he searched my face.

"I don't envy you, Devereux." Nancy pushed past him down the hall of the farmhouse.

"Is everything okay?" he asked me quietly.

"I don't know."

We had reached the main room where Ringo waited for us. He shot me a raised eyebrow and a quick smile. I sent the same thing back to him.

Nancy stopped and turned to me. "You can come tonight. And I'll try not to kill your snipers on purpose."

That startled me, but I kept the surprise off my face and composed myself enough to ask, "Do we go in a vehicle or on foot?"

Something in her tone had shifted. The intensity was gone and had been replaced with her characteristic ease and confidence. The switch unsettled me with its speed, but if she could let it go, I could too.

"We travel by bicycle. You do ride, don't you?" She wore the hint of a teasing smile.

I had a sudden mental snapshot of the old banana-seat bicycle my mom found in a thrift store when I was about six. She tied a piece of plastic onto the right handlebar to teach me my left from my right, then ran alongside me, holding the seat while I got my balance. I didn't even know she had let go when I finally got it, and for a long time after that, I used to picture those handlebars in order to choose the right direction.

"Yes, I ride." I didn't miss Ringo's tension though. "But it's been a long time. Can I have ten minutes on a bike to practice?"

Nancy said something to one of the young Maquis fighters and he indicated I should follow him. I caught Ringo's eye and he left the room with me. Archer might have gone with us, but Nancy called out to him from the map table. "Devereux, I need you." He winced just enough to make me smile, then joined her at the table.

The young Maquis wheeled an old-fashioned bicycle out of a shed and brought it to me with a smirk. I thanked him in French and he stood, arms crossed, waiting to see me make a fool of myself. So I shot him my best arched-eyebrow glare and he finally got the hint that I didn't want an audience.

Ringo and I walked around to the back of the barn with the bicycle, and he murmured under his breath, "Tell me about Nancy."

"She's pretty badass," I murmured back, "but I'm still not sure I like her."

"Yeah, sometimes ye badass people are 'ard to like."

He got an elbow to the ribs for that one, and when we turned the corner I whispered to him. "You've never ridden a bicycle, I take it?"

"Ye'd be right at that."

"Okay. I'll show you." I got on the bike and did a quick pedal around the yard. The frame was made of solid steel and it felt like a beach cruiser with skinny tires and an uncomfortably hard leather seat. The only brake was a single hand grip, so stopping was sketchy, but putting my feet down helped.

"I'll hold on until you get your balance," I said quietly. Ringo nodded and got on, and for about fifteen feet I walked next to him, holding the seat like my mom had done for me.

"Okay, let go," he murmured, and only wobbled a little when I did. He bit his lip in concentration as he pedaled, but within one lap around the yard, the intensity had been replaced by a grin that lit up the night.

Archer found us there about ten minutes later, and immediately caught on to what had just happened. He stood next to me and said quietly, "He didn't know how to ride?"

"He does now," I said proudly. We watched Ringo do a figure eight maneuver around a barrel and then come to a running stop in front of us. His face was flushed with pleasure.

"Well, why didn't ye tell me ridin' was such fun?"

"Wait until you try a mountain bike."

The look of astonishment on his face was awesome. "There's one of these built for mountains?"

Archer grinned at his enthusiasm, but his smile slipped when he turned to me. "Nancy and two of her men are ready to leave. If we are going with them, we need to get moving."

I suddenly felt woefully unprepared to face the two snipers I'd hidden from just a few hours before. The only thing I had with me were my daggers, which I wore in small nylon and Velcro holsters strapped to my calves, because I didn't like guns and wouldn't have taken one if it were offered. I didn't think Ringo was armed, although he could have been packing a sonic screwdriver for all I knew. And Archer certainly didn't need the pistol he carried tucked into the back of his waistband. It was probably more for show than because he'd actually use it. People might have wondered why a guy would go around unarmed in a war.

Nancy's bicycle had a basket on the front, and she saw my questioning glance into it. "Supplies," she said cryptically. Two other bikes were parked there waiting for us, and the two men with Nancy gave us twin looks of boredom as we mounted up. The basket had made me think of Toto's prison on Miss Gulch's bicycle in *The Wizard of Oz*, so the taller guy became Tin Man, and the short, skinny one became Scarecrow. They must have understood English because Nancy didn't bother to speak French as she gave us quick directions. According to my gut, neither of the two Maquis with us seemed to be Mongers, so at least they had that going for them.

The quiet clatter of pedals was the only noise on the road as we cycled past the fields of the occasional farm. The night was moonless, which would work to our advantage when we got in range of hiding snipers, but wasn't great in unfamiliar landscape. Nancy knew her way though, and we followed behind her like ducklings.

After about twenty minutes, Nancy pulled her bicycle over to the side of the road, and we all coasted to a stop near her. She spoke quietly to her Maquis, and they pulled their bikes off the road and melted into the woods in about a minute. Then she turned to the three of us.

"The bridge is about a kilometer ahead. My men will fan out to approach from either side, so I suggest we stay here, on the north side."

Ringo and I both looked up at the same time. In our experience, no one else ever did, so up we would go to scout. There was a tall tree about twenty feet away from us, and another one about twice that distance away on the other side of the road. I looked at him. "Right tree or left?"

"You should take left. It looks an easier climb," he smirked

"None of your sass, Mister. You owe me for the riding lesson."

He grinned at me, then turned to Nancy. "Do ye 'ave binoculars among yer *supplies*?"

I was surprised he thought to ask. His reading about technology must have been pretty extensive. Nancy raised an eyebrow at his emphasis on her supplies but handed over a compact pair. "I take it you're planning to scout?" she asked.

Ringo nodded. "Seems a smart thing to do." He slung the binoculars around his neck as she moved away to give the Maquis her instructions. I was about to protest, but he cut me off. "Ye 'ave cat eyes. Ye don't need these."

He was right, of course. My own vision was sharper than most, and if I really needed cat eyes, I could Shift and borrow my Cougar's long-distance vision. It wasn't a bad idea for scouting in general, and I tucked it away for consideration.

Ringo took off for the far tree, and I sent Archer a quick smile before I scrambled up the closer one. It was fairly densely-branched and easy enough to climb, but there were only a couple of spots that gave me a good view of the valley ahead. I was about twenty feet off the ground when I finally laid myself out along a nearly horizontal limb and settled in to scan the forest.

I could see the train trestle bridge in the distance. If I ran it, I could probably get there in about ten minutes, and faster still on a bicycle. When I twisted around to see what was behind my tree, I could see the dark outlines of Archer and Nancy by the side of the road. She was using hand gestures to show him where her guys had gone, and I could just make them out as they lurked through the forest toward the bridge.

I studied the horizon for the high points where the snipers might be hiding. Several of the trees just north of the bridge looked promising. The southern ones were tall, but the topography of the valley put them lower than the bridge. The train the Maquis intended to blow would be coming from the south, which might also argue for the northern trees. I thought if I were going to set charges on a bridge, I'd set them on the northern side so more of the train was already on it before it exploded and collapsed. It was a little scary that I was trying to think like a terrorist, and scarier still that it seemed so easy to do.

I focused my attention on a stand of trees about halfway between the one I was in and the bridge. It's where I would have set up camp if I'd wanted to keep an eye on the northern approach to the trestle. I couldn't see real detail in the trees, and the branches were fairly thick, so I doubted I'd even be able to see in daylight.

But then a tiny pinprick of light flared about two-thirds of the way up the farthest tree, and I realized what they said was absolutely true. Smoking could kill a person.

After memorizing the terrain between my tree and the snipers', I scrambled back down my tree and sprinted back over to where Archer and Nancy waited. Ringo ran up right behind me. "You saw that?" he asked a little breathlessly.

I nodded and spoke to Archer. "There's a stand of tall trees, maybe half a kilometer from here, with a clear shot of the north side of the bridge. They're in that."

"How do you know?" I couldn't tell if Nancy believed me.

"Saw a lighter spark."

She nodded like she'd expected it. "It's why I quit smoking myself. The smokers were always the first ones hit in the trenches during the Great War."

Not to mention the cancer, I almost said, but just caught myself in time.

"We should split up and approach from either side," Nancy continued. "Archer and I have the firepower, so we'll take the lead." She held up her hand to halt my protest before it could form. "We won't actively aim to kill, but I'd like to get them out of those trees, and even better if they run." I nodded, and she continued. "You two follow us in case they do make a break for it. If I had to guess, I'd say they have a vehicle stashed somewhere in the woods near the road up ahead. If they run, be ready to cut 'em off."

Archer looked like he was about to protest Nancy's arrangement, but I was already nodding. "Sure. That sounds fine. Ringo and I are both climbers, so we can keep an eye on them from whatever tall trees we come across."

Archer's expression darkened. I thought the protectiveness thing must be kicking in again for him to be annoyed, although Nancy seemed pleased enough with the arrangement. She started off through the brush, but Archer hung back.

"What? I'll be fine." I dared him to challenge my ability to stay safe, but instead he grabbed me by the shoulders and gave me a rough kiss. I gasped against his mouth, and he broke away and glared at me for a second before following Nancy through the brush.

I stared after him, then turned to Ringo. "What the hell was that?"

Ringo shrugged. "Probably jealous. Might 'ave a little fear and concern mixed in for good measure, but 'e's mostly just green-eyed."

"About what?" Nothing Ringo said made sense to my brain.

"About us. 'E thinks ye chose me." Then Ringo nodded to my clothes. "Ye goin' to lose those?"

My mouth definitely dropped open. Had everyone around me suddenly gone insane?

"Excuse me?"

Ringo's eyes widened, and then he doubled over. My first thought was that he'd somehow just been shot, until I realized his shoulders were shaking with laughter. "What's so funny?"

"Ye thought I meant we ..." He pointed back and forth between us. "I meant ye should lose the clothes so ye can Shift and go as the Cat."

Oh. My face flamed and the twelve-year-old in me wanted to punch him. So I tried for poise instead. "Right. That's what I was thinking. Can you carry my stuff, or will I need to stash it near the bikes?"

Ringo was still snickering to himself. "I can carry it." He graciously turned his back to me, and it took me about twenty seconds to strip down and pile everything, including my daggers, onto my boots. I tucked my underwear into the pocket of my trousers – he didn't need to be messing with those.

The Shifts were getting easier, especially the practical ones that weren't driven by emotion. My Cougar and I said hello to each other, and I prowled around scenting things while Ringo tucked my stuff into something he could wear slung over his shoulder.

"Try not to get shot, will ye?" He still had a smirk in his voice, so I butted into his knees and made him stumble. My Cat didn't care about poise. I took off at a full sprint and Ringo cursed under his breath. I knew it wasn't for the hit, but for the fact that I was so much faster than him in this form.

It was exhilarating to run in Cougar form. My night vision was pretty spectacular, and I was able to keep to the shadows, even on the moonless night. I slowed to a fast slink to give Ringo a chance to catch me, and even at the much slower human ninja pace, we still made great time.

I scented Archer and Nancy ahead of us and leapt into the branches of a big oak to see what I could of the terrain. Ringo waited at the bottom, and I thought, with some satisfaction, that he sounded a little winded.

The snipers' nest was just ahead of us, and Archer and Nancy were sticking close to a line of underbrush that hid them from the view of anyone in the upper branches. Nancy had taken the lead, and I snickered as she walked through a spiderweb and did the get-it-off dance to knock it away from her face. Their position was a good one for invisibility, except, I realized with the equivalent of a mental scream, the snipers weren't both in the tall trees. One of them, Grunty from the size of him, was positioned at the base of the tree in which his comrade was perched.

And Grunty had just seen Nancy's spiderweb dance.

FIRE-FIGHT

He was utterly silent as he hoisted his rifle to his shoulder and looked for the source of the motion. The silence was a good thing, because at least Loogie might still be unaware of them, but Grunty would find them in about ten seconds if he had a night vision scope. It was technology Ringo had assured me the German army had begun to use, and who better to have scopes than snipers?

I growled with as much menace as I could throw into my Cougar's voice and leapt out of the tree. Ringo dove out of my way as I barreled through the brush, straight toward the tree where Grunty stood. I pushed every muscle I had into a full sprint because I was about to have two sniper scopes trained directly on me. I just hoped Archer would figure out that he needed to get himself and Nancy out of sight.

The first bullet came from above and hit the ground about five feet behind me. That meant Grunty couldn't see me yet, but Loogie had me in his sights, though his judgement of my speed was off. Right, well, he wouldn't make the same mistake twice.

I shifted direction suddenly, lunging to my left just as another bullet hurtled down from above. He was still a tad slow, though his judgement was getting better.

But I was smarter.

I leapt up the trunk of a tree, ran along an arterial branch, and jumped across the open space to the next tree. Loogie hadn't been expecting that, and only shot into the first tree long after I had already left its branches. I didn't know where Ringo was, but I hoped he was staying out of sight. Archer and Nancy were still in danger if Grunty decided the human threat was bigger than the feline one, so I zig-zagged out in the open a couple of times, just so Loogie would let loose a volley of shots and keep Grunty's attention on me.

One of those shots actually came from the side where Archer and Nancy had taken cover. It went wide and high, so I hoped Archer had gotten a good hit in on Nancy when he realized she was aiming at the Cougar. The side shots stopped after that, so I guessed he had.

The overhead cover was thinning, and there were only a couple more places I could see to dodge the bullets that now fired from both sniper weapons. I altered my speed and direction with each step, but dirt clods and rocks were hitting me as bullets ricocheted off the ground. A big boulder loomed ahead, and I darted behind it, just as a Grunty shot split the hairs on my tail.

I crouched behind the boulder, confident that neither shooter could hit me if they held their positions. But Grunty was on the ground, and if he took about twenty steps away from that tree, he'd have me back in his sights.

My heart pounded beneath my Cougar skin and my breath came in shallow pants.

It was a good run, she said. I was a little surprised until I realized her tone was one of agreement rather than praise. We'd done it together, minds and body working in concert, instinct and thought combining to keep us intact.

I ran down a mental list of my escape options, none of which were particularly comforting. I thought Archer knew where I'd ducked out, so hopefully he and Nancy would be able to come up with something distracting enough to give me a chance to run.

Shifting back to human was an option if I had any hope at all that a naked girl in the woods would distract the snipers. I thought it was just as likely that Loogie would shoot me *because* I was a naked girl in the woods.

The shots had stopped, but with my predator sense, I could hear the crackling of footsteps on dirt. I tensed, ready to spring either at Grunty or away from him, depending on which side of the boulder he came around. I wasn't ready for the sound of an impact, or for Grunty's sudden appearance on the right side of the rock – face down in the dirt. I leapt away and almost reversed direction to attack when I saw a figure appear where Grunty should have been standing.

"Saira. It's me!" Ringo's fierce whisper broke through my Cougar's fight instinct. Just in time too, because he had to leap behind the boulder to avoid the shot from Loogie's rifle over our heads. He put a hand out to my neck, and I realized we were both trembling, most likely from adrenaline, though terror wouldn't have been unreasonable.

Another shot clipped the edge of the boulder and sent bits of granite flying at us. One of them must have clipped Ringo's cheek because I could smell blood on him that hadn't been there before.

He dropped to his stomach and slithered forward toward the form of Grunty, still sprawled on the ground at the base of the rock. Blood dripped down from Grunty's scalp, and I thought he might have hit his head on the rock when Ringo pushed him from behind.

Ringo reached a tentative hand forward and gripped a piece of leather. Slowly and carefully, he pulled the strap until he had Grunty's sniper rifle in his hands. The hands were still shaking, but Ringo's grip was firm as he slithered backward away from the edge of the boulder.

He finally sat up and leaned back against the rock. There were tears in his eyes as he pulled the rifle into a shooting position. But the rifle was too long and it trembled too much in his hands. He switched his grip to use the rifle like a club if he had to, then wiped his nose and finally looked into my Cougar's eyes. He burst out in an embarrassed chuckle and rubbed the tears away fiercely.

I sat next to him with my back against the boulder and leaned into him. His hands didn't leave the rifle except to wipe away snot and tears, but I could feel the adrenaline shake slip away and sensed his composure returning. I didn't think Ringo would ever tell me why the tears came, and I probably wouldn't ask him.

Grunty was still breathing, but I wasn't sure he would regain consciousness. That left one treed sniper. I wanted him to run, but not until we were close enough to the road to be able to intercept and follow. And now that he knew where we were, he could just keep a line of sight on our rock and wait. There was nothing ideal about this scenario – nothing at all.

Ringo and I had Grunty's sniper rifle, so if we had to, one of us might be able to take a shot into the trees to scare him out. It was hardly ideal because of the fire we would draw to our barely protective rock, and I knew our best bet to get out of this alive and intact was to run. I was faster than Ringo, and could draw Loogie's fire away from the rock so he could escape. It might be the only way to get back out to the road in time to follow Loogie when he inevitably ran.

I got my Cougar body into a crouch so Ringo could read my body language. He looked at me for about half a second, then shook his head. "No, ye can't be another distraction to the sniper. We run together or not at all," he whispered fiercely.

I lifted my lip to show him teeth. *I'm meaner than you,* I said to him in my head. *I'm faster, and I can take his fire so you can run.* Ringo looked at my expression and matched it with a fierce one of his own.

"Fine, if you do that, I'm not running. I'll stay here and shoot until one of us runs out of bullets. Ye will not get shot for me."

I growled at him and would probably have bitten, except for the explosion.

BOOM!

We barely even had time to think before we leapt forward and bolted. I took the lead because Ringo paused a half-second to sling the sniper rifle over his shoulder, but then he was right behind me. The night sky was on fire with orange and red and gold, and I realized the Maquis must have blown the bridge. It was about the only thing that could have distracted Loogie enough for us to escape, and despite my prickly conscience about the train that could have been on it, I was absurdly relieved.

I suddenly ducked behind a big oleander bush, and a moment later, Ringo was next to me. I Shifted, in a shimmer of colors, and didn't even register the surprise on Ringo's face until I had time to think again.

"Clothes," I said, thrusting out my hand. He took my clothing bundle off his back and re-adjusted the sniper rifle to fit the extra space while I got dressed.

"Their truck will be stashed someplace close." My whispered voice came in gasps, and Ringo was nodding his agreement.

He jerked his head to our left. "The bridge is blown, so 'e'll 'ave to go past us to get back to Limoges. We'll do better on our bicycles than on foot."

"If he goes back for Grunty, we might have time to get them." I shoved my feet into my boots and quickly did up the laces.

Ringo made an indiscernible face. "Not sure there's anythin' to go back for."

I looked at him sharply. "He was still breathing when we left."

"'E was bleedin' and 'e wasn't movin', neither of which is promisin'."

Now I had an idea what the tears had been about, but we were already burning up precious seconds, so I just said, "I say we go for the bikes, and maybe Archer and Nancy will stake out Grunty."

He nodded sharply and hauled me to my feet. "I'm leadin' this time."

Ringo didn't once look back to see if I was still with him, which I took as a compliment. He just knew I'd be there. I kept anticipating the zing of sniper fire whizzing through the air, but the woods were silent around us except for the pounding of our boots on the dirt.

A few minutes later we were back at the road where we'd left our bicycles. We propped them up just behind a bush by the road so they'd be ready to ride at a moment's notice, and then we settled down into the gully to wait for Loogie's vehicle to drive by. I was struck by how very silent the night had gotten. The explosion seemed to have distracted the crickets from their chirping, and even our breathing had gone quiet.

"Thank you," I said quietly.

Ringo looked at me a long moment before he spoke. "I'm not goin' back to 'Is Lordship without ye."

My breath caught in my chest. There were so many motives for why we did what we did, and I probably had ten of them for running my Cougar out into the open to draw the snipers' fire away from Archer and Nancy. It actually didn't surprise me that one of Ringo's motives would be to make sure I got back safely to present-day Archer. But until he said that, I hadn't quite realized that he was still holding onto the idea of two different Archers, which meant every time Ringo saw me hold Archer's hand or get kissed by him, a part of him might think I was cheating on his friend.

We were lying on our stomachs with our heads toward the road, and I rolled over onto my back and nudged him to do the same. He did, fitting his arms behind his head as he looked up at the sky, now streaked with dark gray smoke. I laid my head on his shoulder and folded my fingers together across my stomach.

"You know what I was thinking about earlier tonight?" I said to the sky.

"No idea," Ringo answered.

"Time travel rules."

He made a non-committal sound in his throat. An owl swooped overhead noiselessly. The silence was becoming unnerving, and I felt like it needed to be filled with good things.

"Archer couldn't go where he already was, right? That's why he didn't come with us."

"Right. I know." Ringo was quiet a moment before he continued. "But it's different knowin' a thing in yer 'ead, and knowin' it in yer 'eart."

"What makes your heart feel differently?"

Ringo sighed deeply, and I thought I could almost hear the tension in his chest. "Yer Archer trusts me. 'E trusts me to be yer friend and to take care of ye. 'E doesn't wonder if ye'd ever choose me, because 'e's so sure of what ye are to each other."

I opened my mouth to protest, or say something, or maybe just catch flies, but Ringo's scoff cut me off. "Ye remember when we first got 'ere, to this time? I wouldn't stay in 'is secret library room with ye? Yer Archer's the one who told me to step carefully around 'imself. This war was 'ard on 'im, and there are still 'oles in 'is memory."

I nodded. "Yeah, he told me about the PTSD."

"The thing 'e called shell shock? It wasn't just about the fightin' though. 'E also told me about Marianne and Marcel."

"He did? Why wouldn't he have told me?"

"Because he didn't remember what 'appened to them. It's one of the gaps, and 'e feels damaged for not knowin'."

My voice came out in a whisper. "Didn't he try to find them after it was over?"

"Saira, 'e wasn't the same then ... now, I guess. Whatever 'appened in this war changed 'im."

"He said he went to live in the cellar at St. Brigid's after the war."

"Seems a lonely existence for a man who broke secret codes at Bletchley Park and worked with the French resistance, don't ye think?"

"You think he was hiding?"

"Yeah, I think maybe 'e was."

It made sense, what Ringo said. Archer had given me only the broadest strokes about his time in World War II, and what he had told me had seemed fraught with ... I didn't know, maybe guilt? Well, whatever had happened to him in this time was my problem now. I faced Ringo, propping my head up on my elbow.

"It's not a reason to hold them as separate people. If anything, it's our chance to maybe help him heal whatever it was that happened here." I considered my words. "Think about it as preemptive friendship. Worst case, we'll know the truth of this time for him and maybe understand him better in our own time. Best case, we might actually be able to take away some of his burden."

Ringo had turned his head to regard me but stayed on his back, and eventually his eyes went back to the stars above us. He finally nodded. "Right. Ye're right. We're not just 'ere to find Tom, we're 'ere with Archer."

"It's a chance to know a part of him we could only otherwise take his word for, and maybe bring back his memories in the process."

"Right." Ringo sighed as if the conversation had exhausted him.

I leaned over and kissed his cheek. "Thank you for saving my life."

He smirked, and my heart smiled. My Ringo was back. "Who else could watch a Cougar's back? A Wolf wouldn't be caught dead, and a Bear ... too important. Only me."

I poked him in the ribs. "Yup. Only you."

ARCHER – PRESENT DAY

It was utterly irrational to feel this way, and yet entirely reasonable at the same time. I hated Ringo with one breath and loved him with the next.

My memories from the war were becoming clearer with each day Saira and Ringo were gone, and I was startled to realize how very much she had impacted that period in my history. For so long I had assumed that the missing pieces were the result of wartime trauma and of choosing to forget. It was unsettling to know the memories had never fully been there in the first place.

I woke to an overwhelming sense of envy. I had always known Saira's connection with Ringo was unique and remarkable, as my own connection with her had been since the beginning. Yet the memories of France that were becoming clear were laced with a sense that I had invaded something private between them; that I was the interloper, and they played the central role.

My thoughts were full of these contradictory emotions as I sought out the greenhouse laboratory, a beacon of light in the darkness, as a moth would seek a flame. Shaw was working alone, as no doubt Connor had been called into the garage flat for the night. I had instructed the brothers to tell their mother about the things they'd been doing to help us prepare for the tunnels, but I doubted that conversation had happened yet. I had a letter for Liz Edwards in case Connor and Logan decided it was, as Saira would say, easier to ask forgiveness than permission, and it would be dropped off with more than enough time to make sure they'd be well and properly grounded when I descended into the tunnels.

Shaw looked up at the sound of the door closing, but his expression was blank for the second it took to register who I was.

"I'm interrupting," I said, preparing to turn and go.

"So?" Shaw's tone was gruff, and it was a forcible reminder of the Bear he became.

"So, you look as though you're on the verge of curing cancer or ending world hunger. In my experience, it's best not to interrupt things like that," I responded dryly.

He smirked at that and ran his hands through his ginger mane. "You, of all people, are welcome to interrupt this." Shaw stepped away from his microscope, which had left a pressure ridge around his eyes. "I believe I've eliminated as many variables as I can control in a lab. The only further tests that can be run on the telomerase inhibitor are practical."

I leaned back against the desk as casually as one can when one needs to support one's shaky legs. "The cure is ready."

Shaw shook his head grimly. "I don't believe I can say it's ready with the degree of certainty I'd like, however, it's as ready as I can make it."

I stared at him. "What's next?"

"I believe that's up to you."

"You said before, I would have to sustain some sort of massive injury in order to overload my own system so it didn't attack the virus."

He nodded solemnly. "That is true."

I exhaled sharply. "It's what Saira is afraid of."

"I can't say I blame her," he said in a tone I could only describe as gentle.

I looked at the work table in front of him. "In what form would the cure be administered?"

Shaw picked up a small plastic syringe. "This. The carrier virus is blood-borne, therefore, direct injection into a vein will be most effective."

"Do you, by chance, have a cap for that needle?"

Shaw scowled. "Of course I do." His gaze rested on me a long moment before he spoke. "You want to carry a loaded syringe with you."

"Two of them, if I may."

"One for you. and one for Tom?"

I smiled, though without any real humor behind it. "One never really knows when one might encounter a mortally wounded Vampire."

Shaw looked entirely thoughtful as he pulled two plastic syringes out of their wrappers, then brought a rubber-capped vial out of the locked cabinet behind him. I was mesmerized by the syringe-filling process, and fascinated that something as enormous as life or death could be contained in a vessel so small. When both syringes were filled and capped, he wrapped them up in a foot-long strip of silk and handed them to me. "You can use the silk to tie off an arm, or it can be a bandage in a pinch."

My smile was slightly more genuine at that. Shaw's preparedness was something Saira had always admired about him, and I could see that it had rubbed off on Ringo as well.

I didn't really think through my next words before I said them. "I'm beginning to remember things."

Shaw stopped the workspace fussing he'd been doing and fixed his gaze on me. "About the time that Saira and Ringo are in now?"

I nodded, silently debating the wisdom of continuing. It had been a very long time since I'd sought anyone's opinion but Saira's. "I find I'm struggling with residual anger. Some of it is at myself, for the things she is experiencing with me now, and some of it is directed toward Ringo."

I could tell that surprised him, but he merely waited for me to continue and said nothing.

"I know it's irrational to feel this way about a young man I consider my brother, and yet I believe it is the reaction of my younger self to the trust she has in him and the ease with which they relate to each other."

Shaw considered for a long moment before speaking. "It seems to me it was your younger self who felt threatened by Ringo."

"You speak of it in the past, and yet I feel as if it is happening right now."

"It may be happening now, but it is your past, and the younger man you were did not have the benefit of all of your experiences with Saira and Ringo. It is you who is enriched by this time they're spending with you in the past. The man they know there is less complete than the one you are now."

I sighed in frustration, and then shocked myself with painful honesty. "Perhaps that's my concern. The man they know there isn't … whole. What if Saira decides I'm not enough for her after spending time with that version of myself?"

He arched an eyebrow at me. "Did you forget how young and naïve you were when she originally fell in love with you? I believe there was a time you were concerned that you had become too sophisticated and world-wise."

I scoffed at myself. He was right. "When do we believe we're enough for the people who love us?"

His gaze was direct and unflinching. "When are we enough for ourselves?"

HUNTING

The sound of low voices carried on a sudden breeze, and Ringo and I sat up warily. It was another minute before the voices could be heard again, and then we relaxed. It was Nancy speaking quietly in English, which meant she was walking with Archer.

Archer must have already heard us, but our presence startled Nancy when they came into view.

"Oh! It's you!"

Archer strode over to us, his eyes scanning first me, then Ringo, looking for injuries I guessed. "You're well?" he said quietly.

We both nodded. His voice softened to a whisper. "Thank you."

He meant thank you for distracting the sniper. I smiled. "Thanks for not letting me get shot."

I meant by Nancy, who was tucking various things back into her bicycle basket. "You had your men set off the explosives?" I asked her.

She grimaced. "It was early, but given the circumstances with the snipers it couldn't be helped."

"Thank you. It gave us the cover we needed to get out of there."

Nancy's eyes were caught by the sniper rifle on Ringo's back. She held her hand out for it. "Mind if I have a look at that?" Ringo handed it over and she studied it, and then him, with grudging admiration. "So, you got this off the big one, then? Devereux said it was you who took him down, but I didn't believe him. Then again, I thought I saw a lion in the woods, so maybe I don't know everything." She held the rifle out to him to take back, but he shook his head.

"You don't want it?" she asked, surprised.

"I don't much care for a weapon that'll get me executed just for 'avin' it."

She slung it over her own shoulder. "Only if they catch you."

"That's not comfortin'," Ringo said solemnly. "Did ye truss yer man up for questionin'?"

Nancy shook her head. "Dead."

I looked at Ringo. His expression was grim, but Archer caught the exchange and clarified. "Shot. The sniper from the tree shot him before he ran."

Relief and disgust warred for dominance in me. Relief won.

"We thought if we waited 'ere, we'd catch 'im on the drive out." Ringo said to Archer.

"Apparently, he hid his vehicle in a field just beyond the stand of trees. We had discounted it as a hiding place because one would have to cross a stream from there in order to get out." Archer sounded annoyed with himself, and I spoke up with a realization that I could have anticipated the stream-crossing maneuver.

"Except those kind of cars were, I mean *are* amphibious. Put the plugs in the bottom and they float." I knew this because a VW Thing was the slightly less ugly stepchild of its World War II predecessor, which was what the snipers drove. My mom had once borrowed a bright orange convertible Thing from our surfer neighbor when we lived in Venice Beach a lifetime ago.

Ringo looked up in interest, but Archer had already shifted gears. "You were right about them being Werwolves. The dead one wore their insignia on his shoulder." His tone was serious.

Nancy sounded angry. "If there is indeed an Englishman working with this lot, I'm going to string him up myself."

I had no intention of letting Nancy anywhere near Tom Landers, not that she'd get very far with her threat if she did find him. "Were there any clues on the body about where they might be staying?"

She scoffed. "Nothing. But I'd bet boots to buttons they're quartered in Limoges waiting for the 2nd Panzer Division to come in. You can be sure my men will be scouring the city at daybreak."

I didn't bother to tell her that if Tom was hiding in Limoges with the Werwolves, he'd be down during the day. She might find his team, but he'd have made sure he was safe from casual eyes.

At this time of night it would be foolish for us to try to get to Limoges, mostly because Archer would have to go down in a couple of hours, and we didn't have any guarantee of a safe place to bunker. I turned to Archer and Ringo and kept my voice casual.

"Guys, I'm done for the night. Would you see me back so I can get some rest?"

Nancy looked a little suspicious. "I'd have thought you'd want to head the search party for your Englishman."

I smiled faintly. "I'm exhausted and would probably get myself captured if I stumbled around Limoges in this state. I guess I'm just going to have to trust that if you find him, you'll let me talk to him before you string him up."

Her eyes narrowed speculatively, but she nodded. "Do you need a place to sleep?"

I shook my head. "No thanks, I'm good."

"Well, if you're staying in any of the villages around here, watch yourself. They're full of Vichy sympathizers without the sense to know they're playing for the wrong team." Her tone was dismissive, but I could hear the warning underneath. I wasn't sure who I was more nervous about though, the Vichy French or her Maquis, many of whom had struck me as armed thugs masquerading behind a noble cause.

"Are any of the villages safe-havens for Maquis?" I asked as innocently as I knew how to.

She shrugged. "My people are in every village and town in Limousin. We've spread our resources around in order to become malaria-carrying mosquitos, buzzing around German ears and driving them to such distraction they don't even realize they're already dying."

Right, which meant there were definitely Maquis around Marianne's village.

We said our goodbyes to Nancy when her saboteurs returned for their bikes, and as we pedaled away with a promise to return the bicycles the next night, I realized Nancy no longer intimidated me like she had when we first met. She was a person who believed passionately in her cause, which wasn't really too different from me, and I admired her commitment to it, even though I disagreed with some of her tactics.

I had also let go of the idea that she was a threat to me with Archer. Whatever it was that had happened in my Archer's past wasn't happening with Nancy now, and despite the emotional tangle I'd been trying to unravel about my feelings for him in this time, that particular thread was more like spider silk than a thick strand of wooly yarn.

We'd been riding in silence for a while when Ringo suddenly held up an arm to stop us. Remarkably, none of our brakes squeaked, and we were able to halt with comparative stealth. Ringo tipped his bike to the ground quietly, then slipped forward into the woods. Archer and I followed right behind him without question.

There was a small clearing just ahead, and a young buck stood in it, remarkably oblivious to our presence. Ringo must have spotted him from the road as he headed this way, and whatever breeze there was came from the direction of the deer, so he hadn't scented us yet.

Ringo shared a silent communication with Archer that he should be the one to go around to the back side of the glen so we could surround the deer. "Ye might still smell o' cat," he whispered in response to my raised eyebrow. Archer disappeared into the shadows while Ringo and I spread out on our side of the deer. Using hand signals, Ringo told me we'd drive the deer toward Archer, and since Archer had the only firearm among us, it made sense he would be the one to make the kill.

I didn't stop to think about what we were doing, probably because this was food in a time when people were starving. But I'd never actually hunted a deer before, and my heart was pounding when Ringo motioned to me to take out my daggers. I didn't want to be the one to actually kill the animal, no matter how pragmatic I was being about our need for meat.

We circled around in complete silence, with every ounce of my focus on foot placement and controlling my breath. I was about ten feet from the buck, close enough to see the brown-red of his coat, when his head shot up and he stared around him with huge, terrified eyes. His nostrils flared as he swiveled his head in the direction Archer had gone, and I suddenly realized I might have to be the one to take him down if he bolted in this direction.

Ringo must have realized that too, because he threw a rock that landed in front of me, just as he stepped forward into view. The simultaneous sound and movement drove the buck straight toward Archer, and a moment later the crash of something big going down could be heard through the woods. Notably absent, however, was a gunshot, and a sick feeling coursed through me.

I ran toward the sound, hoping it was the deer that had gone down and not Archer. Ringo got there first, and I saw him turn as if to protect me. But then he stopped himself, and in a fluid motion, he stepped aside.

The buck was down, and his legs twitched with a final convulsion before going still. Archer was bent over him, and it looked like he was holding the buck's head as it died. A hunting knife was clenched in his hand, its blade black with the deer's blood.

Ringo took a step back and made the nearly silent "chhhttt" sound he used to get my attention. His eyes were locked on mine like he was using his mental powers to make me retreat. I thought I'd been pretty stoic about gutting and cleaning the pheasant he'd hunted, so I didn't understand why he was trying to will me away.

Until I realized Archer wasn't just holding the buck as it died. He was drinking its blood from the gash at its neck.

Ugh. Nausea roiled in my stomach and fear surged through me. The instinct to run very fast and very far away hit at the same moment as a single word pounded my brain.

Vampire.

I stumbled backwards gracelessly, and the sound made Archer look up.

There was blood on his chin, and an intent expression on his face.

There was hunger, and fear, and embarrassment in his eyes.

There weren't fangs protruding from his mouth and his eyes weren't glowing yellow with malevolence. He wasn't a creature, he was a man taking the only sustenance that gave him nourishment.

And I was his girlfriend.

The fear began to drain out of me as I watched him struggle with the knowledge that I had now seen him feed. His eyes searched my face for a long moment before he finally bent his head to continue drinking the blood that had been coursing from the gash in the buck's throat. It was like he didn't want to see my terror or my disgust. He didn't want to watch me turn and flee, so he turned back to do the thing that would cause me to run.

Except I didn't.

Ringo watched me with interest as I crouched down and sat on my haunches to wait for Archer to finish. After a moment, Ringo did the same, and we sat in silence, not watching Archer eat, nor looking at anything in particular.

My Cougar rose up with interest at the scent of the fresh kill that drifted on the breeze. I let her come up enough to say one word to her – *Archer* – before I felt her give the feline equivalent of a nod and then drift back down to her resting place inside my bones. It was an odd feeling – this acceptance – both of Archer and of my own nature, and I sort of sat there marveling at it for a moment. I still didn't think I'd be letting my Cat hunt anytime soon, but at least the thought didn't repel me anymore.

I looked up to find Archer standing a couple of feet away from me as if he was afraid to come any closer. His face had been wiped of blood, though I could still see some on his collar where it had dripped when he saw me watching him.

I got to my feet. "Should we butcher it here or take the whole carcass back to Marianne's?"

Archer flinched, like he expected something much worse to come out of my mouth and had braced for it. Ringo rose smoothly and brushed himself off. "I say we do the cuttin' 'ere. That way we can divide the meat three ways and pack it in the hide."

Archer stepped forward and looked us both in the eyes. "I'm sorry you had to see that." His voice was so tentative it made my heart hurt.

"How long had it been since you'd eaten?" I held his gaze.

"Not so long that I couldn't control myself. But sometimes opportunity overrides will, and I knew if I ate now, I'd need less later."

"When does the control get 'ard?" Ringo asked. His tone was as straightforward as mine had been. We were letting Archer know it was okay to talk about, and he seemed to relax a little.

"I try to hunt every three days or so to keep the craving under control." Archer took a deep breath and I thought I heard a shudder in it. "In December, 1940, I was in London on the night of the worst air raid that city has seen. I hadn't eaten in four days, and in fact, had been at the train station to leave London for Epping Wood so I could hunt."

He paused, and I thought he must have been reliving it in his mind, because the shudder was back and there was an edge of desperation in his voice. "When the sirens blew, there was a mass exodus to the Underground station, and I couldn't escape the tide of people without raising suspicion. So down I went, and I spent the worst night of my life, surrounded by hundreds of people filled with the blood my body craved. It was as though I were an addict in an opium den with no money to buy. An older man near me was bleeding from a cut on his hand, and I literally shook with the effort not to leap on him as I got up and moved to the far end of the tunnel."

251

"Is it a craving or a compulsion?" I asked.

Archer met my eyes and then looked away. "A compulsion. No matter how much you persist in believing me harmless, this isn't just a 'condition,' Saira, it is a beast that must be fed to stay dormant, otherwise it rears up and takes control."

"Kind of like my Cougar, then?" I kept my voice carefully neutral, but his eyes snapped to mine.

"You don't have to kill to feed the beast."

I shrugged. "You probably don't either."

"Yeah, ye're just bein' a drama queen," Ringo said lightly.

We both stared at him, and I burst out laughing. "Where'd you hear that?"

Ringo cocked an eyebrow with a grin. "Millicent."

My mouth dropped open. "No you didn't!"

He laughed and wagged his eyebrows up and down, and suddenly the mood of the conversation shifted. "Come on, ye lot. Time to get to work."

He pulled a Bowie knife out of his boot that looked like something a hunter would wear and held it up as a dare. Archer scoffed and pulled his own knife to compare blade size. So of course, I rolled my eyes at both of them and drew my daggers out and brandished them with ninja sound effects. Because that's how badass I was with my daggers. The laughter that erupted was the perfect antidote to the business ahead of us.

Cleaning and butchering the buck was actually far less bloody business than it would have been if Archer hadn't fed from it. Of course, Ringo had to comment on the fact, but Archer took it in stride. He seemed more relaxed than I'd ever seen him about the whole drinking blood thing, and it made me wonder if he would remember this in his future and let go of all the shame he had about me knowing he had to eat.

Ringo was a very efficient butcher, and Archer had done a lot of field dressing of his father's kills when he was young, so I followed their lead, and we soon had three, big, well-packed bundles of venison to bring back.

I told the guys I wanted to stop by the old winery to bring some meat for the Jewish kids who lived there. Archer looked thoughtful.

"I suppose it could be considered kosher. Deer have cloven hooves, and the animal was completely bled before being butchered," he said wryly.

I hadn't even thought about what might need to be done to make the meat kosher, but since I didn't know the rules, all we could do was tell someone what we'd done – minus the part about Archer drinking the blood, of course – and let them decide.

The baskets on the front of our bicycles were useful for carrying our bundles of meat, and within about ten minutes we were walking the bikes down the long dirt drive toward the old winery.

"I didn't know this place existed," Archer whispered as we crested the hill. The winery spread out in the small valley in front of us, and a light was on in the farmhouse.

"Apparently most of the village has forgotten it too," I whispered back.

The night was actually louder than it seemed the closer we got to the farmhouse. Crickets chirped and trilled, and a pair of barn owls called back and forth to each other across the property. It made me feel slightly better about climbing the back steps to what I assumed was the kitchen door, almost as if it wasn't unreasonable to think someone might be awake in the hours before dawn.

Rather than leaving the meat outside, I knocked quietly on the door. The crickets instantly stilled, and I could feel Archer and Ringo step in place behind me. My confidence slipped the longer it took, and I almost put the meat down and backed away, when finally the door opened.

And so did my mouth.

"Bas?"

BAS

The twelfth-century Moorish Vampire who stood in the kitchen doorway looked as shocked to see me as I was to see him. His clothing was casual, his shirt open at the neck, and his trousers were old, but well-made. He wore his hair cropped shorter than it had been in 1429, and without facial hair, he looked younger than he had then. Considering that his skin hadn't seen the sun in more than eight hundred years, his appearance could pass for vaguely Spanish or Basque, which, given Hitler's prejudices against blacks, among others, meant he had a better than average chance of surviving the camp round-ups.

"Saira." His voice rolled warmly in accented English, and I remembered he had been going to spend time in Tudor England after Elizabeth brought Protestants under her protection. He clasped me in both hands and brought me forward for a three-cheek-kiss greeting. Then he saw Ringo behind me, and looked confused at first. "Ringo, was it?" He held out his hand, then when Ringo went to shake it, brought him in for the same three-cheek kiss. I had felt Archer stiffen at my greeting, and then with Ringo's obvious familiarity, he seemed less sure.

When Bas turned the full wattage of his smile to Archer, the uncertainty became full-blown confusion. "Archer, my friend. It has been far too long." Archer got the same greeting as we did, and graciously submitted, though Bas could instantly feel his reluctance and pulled back.

254

Bas still held Archer's shoulders as he studied his face. "It is you, but not you. What has happened?" When Archer didn't immediately answer, I did – but I directed my response to Archer.

"This is Bas. We met him in 1429 at Château Landon when we were on our way to Orléans to find Joan. He is a mixed-blood Descendant too, of Nature … and Death." I tried not to hesitate between the two Family distinctions, but I knew my voice betrayed me. Then I turned to Bas.

"This is Archer, my Archer, but he has no memory of having met you. He is from this time, and wasn't on the trip to France with us … before."

Bas nodded, still studying Archer's face. "I see. I am sorry to have been so familiar with your woman, given that you do not know me and know my friendship to be true. Please accept my apologies."

If Archer was startled by Bas' heartfelt apology, he gave no indication. Instead he smiled and held out his hand to shake. "I apologize that I'm not yet the man you know. I look forward to making your acquaintance." Time travel conversations were definitely a ten on the scale from one to weird.

A huge grin lit up the Moor's face and he shook Archer's hand enthusiastically. He stepped back and gestured us inside the house. "Come, my friends, tell me your tales and I'll tell mine. Let us begin this acquaintance that we be strangers no more."

It was hard not to be infected by Bas' enthusiasm, especially as he clapped the guys on the shoulders and led us all into a warm kitchen full of the scents of cooking. I looked at Bas in surprise. "Why are you cooking? You don't eat food."

"Ah, I don't, but the little ones do, and they like my food better than the food Sister Agnes makes when she cares for them." He leaned forward and dropped his voice as if he was revealing a great secret. "I use better spices."

Then he spotted the packages of meat. "Ah, what is this? You've brought the children gifts?"

I explained how we'd hunted and cleaned the deer, and Bas nodded thoughtfully. "I think God would approve in the spirit of the laws, whether or not the letter has been upheld. These are interesting times, and God's grace is found in the generosity of strangers."

He accepted the meat and immediately took it downstairs to the cold cellar where it would keep for another day or two before it had to be cooked. All three of us used the time to wash our hands in the old porcelain sink, and then Ringo started lifting the lids of pots and inhaling the delicious scents of the meal cooking on Bas' stove, while I quietly filled Archer in on our fifteenth-century meeting with the Moorish priest. At least I thought he was still a priest, considering Marianne's story about who was rescuing all the Jewish children and bringing them here. Archer seemed particularly intrigued by Bas' commitment to studying a different world religion every century, and it was a reminder to me of Archer's own ecclesiastical studies in 1888.

When Bas returned, he washed his hands, then scooped out two bowls of stew from the pot on the stove and placed them in front of Ringo and me. "Eat," he said in a warm, deep voice.

I thought about being noble and declining so the kids would have more, but my belly was empty and I was getting a little light-headed from exhaustion. I thought I could probably do more to help keep the kids fed if I fed myself, so after a quick look at Ringo to make sure he was eating, I dug in.

The stew was delicious, full of complex spices that tasted like I imagined a Moroccan spice store would smell. Bas watched us inhale his stew for a moment, then turned to Archer.

"How have you come to be in France?"

It seemed Archer had decided to trust Bas – maybe because of our history, or because of his relationship to God, or maybe just because of the way Bas had greeted him. He didn't even hesitate to fill Bas in on his mission to help Nancy plan the targets for the Maquis disruptions of the 2nd SS Panzer Division's progress to

Normandy, and on his own work as a Bletchley Park codebreaker for the English.

Bas' experience as a man of various churches had likely placed him at the center of several of the great wars through history, and he seemed to instantly grasp the significance of everything Archer revealed. They discussed the Maquis' plans for a few minutes, but he seemed most intrigued by the English secrecy around their codebreaking activities. "It's a good long-term plan. This war won't last forever, and if their enemies do not realize their codes have been broken, England retains the upper hand in diplomatic relations."

I picked up my empty bowl and went to the sink to wash it. "That's exactly what happened. The Russians didn't find out until the 1960s that their Lorenz code had been broken."

I didn't really think about what I'd said until after the words were out, but the silence behind me betrayed my thoughtlessness. I spun to face the guys with a gasp. "I'm so sorry! I know better than to talk about my history like it's yours."

Archer's tone was gentle. "And usually for you, I would know the same history as you do."

Bas fixed his gaze on me. "I assume there is some anomaly that prevents the Archer I met in Château Landon from being here now? And how is it that you two are in this time and place?"

I explained about the rule of time travel that prevents a person from being in the same time as himself, and then all three of us brought him up to speed about the possible cure for vampirism, our search for Tom Landers, and the possibility that he could be working with Hitler's Werwolves.

Bas asked a few questions for clarification, but mostly he just listened and absorbed what we told him. He sat back in his chair and steepled his fingers in front of his chin in a way that reminded me of our friend Bishop Cleary. I almost looked at Archer for a private grin at the resemblance, then realized I was, yet again, having a memory that this Archer didn't share.

"Do you intend to take this cure, Archer?" Bas spoke directly to Archer, and his question surprised me. Of all the things we'd said, that was the first thing he focused on.

"I don't believe it is my choice to make yet." Archer's eyes didn't waver from Bas', and I could see Ringo's eyes move back and forth between them like a tennis ball in a match.

"Is it not? This is now the first you've heard of the possibility of a cure, and the things that are happening now will become part of your history when you are the man who can make that decision. Therefore, it seems to me that you do have a say – in this moment – about whether you will take that cure."

"I wouldn't take it now, if that's what you mean."

"Why not?" Bas leaned forward with keen interest.

"Because whether it worked or not, I would die before I could be with Saira in her own time."

Bas smiled. "This is becoming a philosophical discussion of which I very much approve. What if, after you took the cure, Saira were to take you from this time and bring you forward with her to her own time. If, as you say, you would be dead of natural causes anyway, it should be possible, no? Then, you could live out a natural, human life with Saira in her time."

I interrupted whatever Archer had been about to say. "It wouldn't work like that. If I took Archer out of his natural time, he would stop aging. Yes, he would potentially be human – if he survived the cure, which has a huge question mark attached – but he would essentially be immortal until he came back to what would have been his natural lifetime."

"Yer ma does it," said Ringo. I wasn't sure what point he was arguing, but for that matter, I wasn't sure what point I was arguing either.

Bas' eyebrows rose questioningly, so I told him about my mother being out of time and her visits back to the nineteenth century every two years just to keep aging properly.

"So, it could potentially be done," he said finally.

I narrowed my eyes, not sure where he was going with this. "Theoretically. Why?"

Bas turned back to Archer. "If you removed the obstacle of a life without Saira from your choice, would you make the decision to become mortal again?"

"Yes." His answer came so quickly and so resolutely that my stomach clenched. Ringo shot me a told-you-so look, but I purposely ignored him and kept my eyes on Archer.

"Why?" Bas asked the question that rang in my ears.

Archer took a breath, started to speak, then cleared his throat and took another one. His gaze remained on Bas when he finally spoke. "There is something that happens when you know that life is finite: a desire for greatness, for whatever fleeting moments of brilliance you can leave in the world after you're gone. And whether the end of your life is five years away or fifty, the fact that you just don't know is a great motivator for not waiting to begin that thing that could potentially be your legacy. Whether it's a work of art, or a scientific breakthrough, a good deed, or a child, leaving something of yourself for others to experience and remember is sometimes the greatest excuse to live a life that's more than just crossing the distance between birth and death."

We all stared at Archer with varying degrees of surprise and respect. I had never heard him talk about leaving something behind, maybe because for him, there was no "behind." He finally met my eyes again, and they seemed to search mine for my reaction. I smiled at him after a moment because it took effort to make my face do anything while my brain was spinning so fast.

He seemed to take comfort in that smile.

Bas finally broke the silence. "I would not take the cure."

Once again, the space filled with the silence of surprise. I was the first one to find my voice. "Why not?"

"It is a similar answer to Archer's, but from another side. I, too, am interested in this idea of a legacy. I am here now, despite your warnings about this war, Saira, because I cannot stand by and do nothing as people find unthinkable ways to destroy each other. I admit that I began my studies of God so many centuries ago for the purely selfish reason that I wanted to discover why He had allowed this thing to happen to me. Why He had put me in that alley in the medina with the man who stole my blood and infected my body with this scourge. But I found no answers to my personal question there, because I no longer believe God *does* anything."

Bas looked at the expressions on our faces and must have seen varying degrees of shock. "In many times, that statement would result in my very painful death by fire, and I shall tell you of my near death at the stake another time." He smiled mischievously, and I suddenly realized how very young he must have been when he was turned. Certainly less than thirty, but given how few people even saw adulthood in the twelfth century, maybe he was closer to twenty-five.

"Yeah, I want that story," said Ringo, and Bas winked at him. "It's a good one. But to my point. I have come to believe, through my studies, that it is not God who *does* things – good or evil, right or wrong, careless or thoughtful – it is men. Perhaps God was the creator, or perhaps God is the encompassment of generosity and love, and as such, acts as a beacon by which men can see the paths they choose."

He got up and began pacing the kitchen, his tall and well-built presence filling the space with more than just his frame. I could see that he would be an inspiring spiritual leader in whatever faith he practiced. "I have lived more than eight hundred years, and I have been able to touch many, many people's lives with the idea that the doing of deeds comes naturally from who one *is*. First, one must *be* love and generosity in order that the doing of loving and generous things becomes as natural as taking breath."

Yeah, the man was a born spiritual leader. I could practically hear the "Amen, brother" declarations from the rafters.

When Bas returned to his seat at the table, his face still glowed with the passion of his words. Archer leaned forward to speak.

"You have found your calling, then, and it seems to give fuel to your deeds in a way that has sustained you through the centuries.

It also seems to be a solitary calling – one that can be self-generated, rather than one that needs the goals and desires of another to fuel it. I believe that may be the difference between us, Bas."

Bas looked intrigued, and he cocked his head like a bird. I remembered he had been a Shifter Eagle before he was turned, and it was the first time I'd seen a sign of it in him. "Explain," he said.

Archer turned to me. "I have been alone in my life more years than I've spent days with you, and yet in all that time that I have only answered to my own calling, never have I been more truly called to … greatness, than when I'm with you." He turned his attention back to Bas. "So, while I do see very clearly the idea that who we choose to *be* informs our actions, for me, this does not exist in a vacuum. The choices I make about who I *am* have the greatest meaning, and come from the most selfless place, when they are inspired by my love for her."

His words made my chest feel like it was filled with warm, fuzzy light, except then my brain started whispering, and the whisper grew to a shout, until finally I spoke, just to stop the noise in my head. I used careful, controlled words in a neutral tone in hopes that I could make sense of the thoughts pinging around my brain. "Archer, I can't be your reason for being."

He arched an eyebrow, but I continued quickly. "It's too much responsibility for one person to have over another. Some days I can barely make a decision for myself and have confidence it's the right one. I don't think I'm strong enough to be responsible for anyone else's choices too."

Archer's voice was gentle as he took my hands in his to make his point. "Saira, my choices are my own every time. None of them are your responsibility. This is not the thing I'm talking about though."

Ringo watched us both thoughtfully, and Bas got up to put a kettle onto the stove. Archer continued in a voice meant only for me. "Who you are, what you stand for, how you relate to the world around you inspires me. I find myself choosing paths that are right and good and generous because I believe they're the ones you would choose, and I find greatness in myself because I aspire to be a man worthy to stand by your side."

He could see me about to protest again, so he continued quickly. "That's not to say I have always made the right choice. There was a dark time just after the Great War when any choice at all was more than I could bear, so I hid, and I felt sorry for myself, and I chose no greatness at all. There have been times in my life when I hated – myself, Wilder, what I've become – but nothing in that hatred gave me the same feelings of worth, or of *rightness*, that choosing greatness does. Yes, I can choose to be great whether or not you are with me, but I don't have to think about choosing greatness when I'm with you. I just do it."

Oh.

Well.

In that case …

My brain went silent and all the protests left me in a whoosh. I was just working up something worthy to say when Ringo's voice cut through my careful word-crafting.

"Ladies and Gents, I believe it's time to go. At least two of you are about to turn into pumpkins." He stood to go, and I looked outside to see just the beginnings of pink in the sky.

"I do have safe lodgings here, if you'd like, as well as at the church in town if you ever find yourself caught out." Bas turned off the stove just as the kettle boiled, and poured the heated water into a tub in the sink. He then added some cold water and moved a washcloth and a sliver of soap to the counter next to it.

Archer looked at both of us for a reaction, but when we didn't give him one, he answered the question. "We'll be fine tonight, but I appreciate the offer very much. If I may ask a question?"

Bas had begun lathering the soap in his hands. "Of course."

"How are you able to be a nocturnal priest?"

He lathered the soap and rubbed it over his fairly impressive jaw. Bas the Moor was a striking man. His size alone or the timbre of his voice would be enough to turn women's … or men's heads.

262

Add to that the sheer magnetism of the man when he spoke passionately, and he was nearly irresistible.

"I have pre-dawn services and sundown mass. We're a community of farmers, you see, so changing the church's hours to suit theirs only made sense." The mischievous smile was back as he lifted the washcloth to his face. "Forgive me for grooming in front of you. I need to be at church for the early risers."

There was a quick, single knock on the door. Three of us stiffened instinctively, Bas did not. "Come," he said.

The door creaked open carefully and a young face appeared. It was Rachel, the mechanic's daughter I'd seen at her garage near the village square. She looked warily at the people gathered in Bas' kitchen, but when her eyes found mine, they widened in surprise.

Bas smiled at her. "Rachel, these are my friends. They've brought venison for the children. If you need some, please help yourself."

She answered him quickly in French, then gave us all a quick look before she ducked back out of the room. I didn't even think to wonder that he had spoken to her in English. When the door had closed behind her, he said to us, "She stays with the children while I am at church until Sister Agnes can come."

"You're the one who rescued them, right?" I asked Bas as we were taking our leave.

His expression turned solemn. "As I said, I could no more stand by and do nothing than I could deny the existence of God. This place is where I was needed, so here I came."

Impulsively, I reached up and kissed the cheek he had just cleaned. "It's really good to see you, Bas."

He gave us all a warm smile. "It is wonderful to be among friends."

We left the farmhouse in the silence of contemplation, which lingered even when we'd returned to Marianne's farm. Archer took the last bundle of venison inside to her cellar while Ringo and I hid the bikes. We met in the barn over the bucket of water. Ringo's wash was fairly cursory – more of a face and teeth kind of thing. Archer and I were more thorough, though less so than the previous night when we'd been alone.

Finally, when Ringo had gone to his bed of rushes, and we had snuggled down into ours, I turned to Archer and whispered, "Don't choose things just because you think I'd want them. If you want something, no matter how I might feel about it, please choose it."

Archer kissed my forehead and then tucked me into his chest. He didn't say the words my Archer would have said, so I did it for him. "I love you," I whispered.

The tightening of his arms was the only clue that he'd heard me.

DREAMS

The church was filled with people. Women carried babies in their arms while small children clung to their skirts. A young woman pleaded with a soldier at the door. He held his rifle in both hands and stared straight ahead as if he couldn't see her or hear her cries.

Bas stood at the altar in his priest's robes, directing women with prams to safe places against the walls. Saira was gathering little boys around her and quietly leading them to the door behind the altar in the south transept which Bas had shown us was the way to his sleeping crypt. She was careful to avoid the eyes of the soldiers who were filing into the nave, and kept her motions small so they didn't attract attention.

I was the only other man in the church besides Bas, and he'd given me a set of ecclesiastical robes with which to masquerade myself. I was helping some of the young women with babies slip behind the altar to hide in the space between it and the wall. There were fifteen soldiers in the church now, all of them grim-faced and silent as they held their rifles at the ready. They wore the uniforms of the German SS, and they had the dead eyes of boys who have seen things that men should never know.

A young Frenchman slipped in through a side door that a girl had unlocked. I was about to gesture that he should leave – according to a young mother, all the men in the village had been rounded up and taken to the town square, and he could be shot for being here – but then he threw something. I watched the bottle move as if in slow motion, saw the rag hanging out, saw the fire spin with the bottle's trajectory. And then it exploded.

Gunshots from the soldiers' rifles filled the air. Children screamed and ran out of the nave to the north and south transepts trying to escape the deadly gunfire. My eyes locked with Saira's as she screamed my name, and then I heard the shot that hit my chest. I felt it bury itself with a burst of heat and pain in my lungs. A rib broke and another bullet tore into my heart. I fell backwards, into the fire that still burned on the church floor.

"No!" I cried, even as I gasped at the realization that I'd been asleep. I'd been dreaming.

I wasn't shot. The hot fire of a bullet hadn't torn a hole in my heart.

My heart.

My heart?

I looked over at Archer, so immobile in sleep he looked dead, and leaned my head down to his chest to listen to his heart pump blood through his body. It was still beating.

That hadn't been a dream. It was a vision Archer had of his future. The perspective was his. He had seen me with the children in the church, and when he passed the vision to me through the touch of his body as we slept, I saw what he saw. I felt the bullet bury itself in his chest. I felt the flames ignite his robes as he fell into the fire.

If it were possible, my heart pounded even harder than it had when I first woke. I sat up and looked around the barn.

Ringo still slept in his bed near the wall, his blanket tangled around him in a way that spoke of his own nightmares. Where had Ringo been in that vision? Safe, I hoped, and not with the men in the village square. Not for the first time I wondered if knowing what would come would allow us to change it.

The sun had barely risen above the midpoint in the sky, and it was much too early for someone who kept Vampire hours to be up. My heartbeat had returned to something less frantic, and I lay down again, fitting my body against Archer's. I wondered if he would remember the vision tonight when he rose. If he didn't, I wondered if I'd tell him.

As it turned out, I didn't have to make that decision. For the first time in a long time, Ringo and I actually slept as long as Archer did, and the minute he sat up, Archer told me about the vision he'd had. He didn't ask if I'd seen it, and I didn't need to mention it because his recall was exactly what I remembered seeing.

"It was obviously at night, or neither Bas nor I would have been awake, and I didn't see Marianne or Marcel among the women and children in the church, so perhaps it was only people who lived in the village itself that had been rounded up." He ran his hands through his hair in frustration. "Can we warn them somehow?" Archer asked me. "Does it ever work that way?"

"We're going to change it," I said with conviction. "It's against the rules for you to die because you go on to live a long and happy life with me."

Archer didn't say anything, but he didn't look particularly swayed by my argument. His apparent acceptance of the vision reminded me far too much of the way Elizabeth Tudor had surrendered to the idea of her own death, and frankly, I wasn't having any of it.

We ate dinner with Marianne and Marcel in their kitchen, but conversation was a fairly somber affair. Archer warned her about spending time in the village after dark. The German patrols were too close, he said, and Marianne accepted his word without question. Marcel told him that an older brother of one of his classmates had come by the school that day. The children had all whispered that he was in the resistance, and Marcel had been afraid of the young man, whose eyes had looked so angry. After we'd helped Marianne clean up, we went back to the barn so Archer could translate the conversations for us.

"I don't like that the Maquis are openly entering the village during the day. It's going to draw German eyes to this place and foster suspicion among neighbors," he said. "Reprisals are considered a legal form of warfare, and the French resistance has

267

certainly done enough to cause action against them and anyone who harbors them."

I shrugged. "Tell Nancy to put her Maquis on a leash."

He looked thoughtful for a long moment. "We should warn her about what I saw."

"Warn her? How? You can't just walk up and say, 'Oh, by the way, I have visions of the future sometimes, and this is what I saw...' Best case, she doesn't believe you. Worst case, she thinks you're a nutjob and turns on you. It's bad enough being English in an occupied country. If we lose our credibility with the Maquis, we'll be hunted by all sides."

Ringo spoke nearly the first words he'd spoken since we woke up. "She's right. If Tom's in Limoges, we need the Frenchies to find 'im for us. I say we warn Bas, 'cause 'e'll understand, then we go find out what Nancy knows about this village. Maybe there's somethin' goin' on 'ere that we can change."

Archer nodded. "Fine, but let's go to Gaspard's farmhouse first. Bas is giving his evening mass right now and it'll be an hour before he's free to talk."

We pedaled our bikes back to Gaspard's and tucked them behind the barn where we'd gotten them the night before. Archer went to find Nancy, while Ringo and I waited outside. I was already on edge, and the idea of close quarters with any Mongers wasn't a peaceful thought.

Archer's vision had strung tension between all three of us, and it was affecting everyone's mood. After a loaded silence, Ringo finally spoke in a whisper. "Meeting Bas was good for 'im."

I wasn't expecting a conversation opener like that, and I waited for him to continue. His eyes were focused on the door to the farmhouse as he spoke. "Whatever story 'e 'ad about us—" he pointed between himself and me. "Whatever that was, it's gone now. 'E trusts us, or maybe 'e trusts 'e's enough for ye."

I appreciated Ringo's insight. I'd been feeling it too, but hadn't put it into words. "How about you? Do you trust him?"

Ringo knew what I was asking, and he took his time to answer. "It's different 'ere. When I first met 'im, 'e was gentry and I was from the street, so I was less than 'im."

I opened my mouth to protest, but shut it again because he wasn't done.

"When ye came back for me, 'e'd lived into a future I couldn't imagine in my wildest dreams, and 'e'd experienced it all. So again, I was less." He finally dragged his eyes away from the door and found my face. "In this time, 'e's still older and wiser than me, but I know things 'e doesn't, and I've seen things 'e 'asn't. It makes us equal."

He took a deep breath and returned his gaze to the kitchen door that Archer had just emerged from. "I wasn't so comfortable with that at first, but now being equal feels right. And I think maybe it was just me *making* myself less than 'im in those other times."

I gripped Ringo's hand tightly. "You're more than just about anyone I know."

He gave me a quick smile and squeezed my hand in return. Archer waved to us to follow him into the woods on foot, and when I couldn't feel any Monger-proximity anymore, I finally stopped.

"Okay, what?" I whispered to Archer.

"The Maquis are planning a reprisal for the snipers," he said grimly.

I looked at him in surprise. "Because blowing up the bridge wasn't enough?"

"Apparently not."

"What are they going to do?"

"Wait," Ringo cut in, "did anyone find trace of the Werwolves in Limoges?"

Archer answered Ringo's question first. "Yes, and no. They think they know where there's an advance SS unit of 2nd Panzer Division hidden in Limoges, and they assume the Werwolf unit is billeted with them. The unit works at night, according to Nancy, which means they'll be on the road hunting Maquis tonight."

"Awesome. Makes me feel so safe in the woods." I deadpanned.

"Their reprisal is a bigger problem for us though. They've captured a German Sturmbahnführer – a man named Kämpfe – and plan to send a ransom note for him, just so there's no confusion about who has him."

Ringo scoffed. "This isn't a battlefield. These are villages full of farmers and their families. Ye don't go stingin' soldiers like that. They'll not just swat at ye, they'll burn yer 'ive."

Archer's mouth was a grim line. "Considering the vision I've had, I'd say that's quite likely what will happen."

"Can ye get them to release 'im?" Ringo's voice sounded a little desperate.

"I tried. I'm not sure he's not already dead."

Ringo threw up his hands. "It's goin' to 'appen then, isn't it." It wasn't a question, and Archer didn't bother to answer.

Archer looked at me. "We need to warn Bas."

The village of Oradour-sur-Glane seemed deserted as we slipped along its cobbled streets. Luckily, the church was on a hill above the central square, so we didn't have to sneak past too many shops and homes to get there.

The sundown mass was long over, though candles still flickered at the entrance to the church. It was a formidable building, made of stone rising up from the top of its hill. It almost seemed more like a castle, and could have been one in another time.

I just barely held back the gasp that threatened when we stepped inside, and Archer's expression had turned to stone. This was the church from his vision. This was where it would happen.

The design was classic for a Catholic church – a building in the shape of a cross. We had entered at the bottom, and the long part of the cross was the nave, which held wooden benches with seating for about a hundred people. The main altar stood at the far end of the church just in front of a stone wall, and was topped by a simple, but elegant window. The window was about six feet off the ground inside the church, but might have been ten or twelve feet from the ground outside given how the building was perched on the hill.

There were two other altars in the wings on each side of the nave. Archer had known the wings were called the north and south transepts in his vision, just like he had known that Bas' safe place to sleep could be accessed behind the south transept altar.

It was surreal to stand in this empty room that I'd seen only a few hours ago full of women and children and soldiers with guns.

Ringo was the only one of us who strolled around with interest examining the icons on the walls. He had seen us both stop and seemed to be giving us space to deal with the aftershock of Archer's vision. He disappeared into the south transept, and then I heard Bas' voice greet him warmly.

Archer turned me to face him and searched my eyes. "You Saw it too, didn't you? Just like in 1888, when I Saw your mother, you Saw this."

I nodded, and my voice came out in a whisper. "It's happened since then – about Ringo getting tortured. It's what sent us back to Tudor England."

He pulled me to his chest and held me tightly. "I didn't want you to See it. I don't want you to see me die."

I pulled back and glared at him. "You don't get it!" My whisper was fierce. I didn't want to fight with him, but I wasn't giving in to this, because it could. Not. Happen. "Whatever you Saw, whatever horrible things might happen, you are NOT going to die! Get that through your head so we can figure out how to keep it from happening at all. Because if you give in to it, we'll be powerless to change it."

I was closer to tears than I wanted to be, and I turned away from him to get my pounding heart under control. Archer pulled me back against his chest and held me in his arms.

"Marry me and I can let go of the fear."

What?

I turned to search his face, and he saw the confusion in my eyes. He repeated softly. "Marry me, and then everything I have is yours."

The choke hold on my voice let go as anger took its place. "What does that have to do with anything? You want me to marry you so I can … what, inherit after you die? Are you insane?" Now I was yelling, and I didn't care if Bas and Ringo heard this fight. "That's the last reason on the planet I would ever marry you or anyone!"

I took a step backward, away from him, but he wouldn't let me go. His hands held my upper arms firmly, and he made me look him in the eyes. "I told you I should have married you when we first met, and you've told me that I want to in your time. So, there's intent that has nothing at all to do with assets."

I almost huffed an eye-roll, I was that mad, but he still continued. "This is about war, and chance, and opportunity, and love. No—" He shook his head, which was interesting enough that I let him continue. "Who am I kidding. It's *all* about love. I love you so much that since I woke up tonight, my soul has been screaming *Marry her!* Marry her so no matter what else happens, no matter what horrors you'll face, you'll have this moment of pure … light. Light and goodness and rightness and truth. That's why marrying you would erase my fear, because nothing can take away the peace of knowing I belong to the person who makes me feel whole, and she belongs to me."

I stared at Archer, and his eyes searched mine for some clue to what I was thinking.

Good luck with that, I thought. I had no idea what I was thinking. I couldn't actually think. My brain had gone into deep freeze shock and looking out through my eyeballs felt like seeing underwater.

"Hey, Saira!" Ringo called from somewhere over my head.

We both looked up. There was Ringo, sitting on a rafter above the altar where he had probably heard every word. He waved cheerily at us and then called out again. "I dare ye."

I had no idea if he was daring me to climb or daring me to marry Archer. All I knew is that he had given me a reprieve from my brain-freeze and I could have kissed him for it. Archer knew it too, because he smiled and released my arms. "Go," he whispered. "Show him how it's done."

I *did* kiss him, which surprised us both.

And then I ran.

I sprinted the length of the nave and bounded up the main altar. I was probably going to hell for desecration of a holy piece of furniture, but I figured I was already going for much more egregious transgressions, and I needed the height.

From there, I leapt to the window sill, which I used as a springboard to the heavy chandelier that hung over the altar. Because chandeliers actually beg for it.

The chandelier did that thing they always do when someone jumps forward to grab ahold of them – it swung. Away from Ringo's rafter, which was to be expected, so I had to use my own body weight to give it forward momentum. This wasn't a new move, or even a particularly creative one, but the rafter I was going for was higher than the chandelier. It was, in fact, the same height as the one the heavy brass fixture hung from. Consequently, I wasn't gaining momentum so I could let go, I used the momentum to flip myself forward and up onto the arms that held the lights.

The fixture beneath me now swung wildly without my weight to steady it, and I had to use my hands and feet like a monkey to make it up the chain. Then it was just a playground swing up to the top of the rafter, and a balance-beam run to the corner where Ringo sat grinning at me.

There was applause from Archer and Bas below us. I waved, and then dropped down to sit next to Ringo with my legs dangling over the edge.

"Pretty fancy," he said graciously.

"The fact that I didn't even see you get up here means you did it in stealth-mode. Which way did you come?"

Ringo pointed out his route, which was definitely less showy than mine had been, but would have taken a lot less effort too. Then we sat in companionable silence for a moment, watching Bas show Archer around the church and talking in tones too low for us to hear.

"So, are ye goin' to do it?" Ringo finally asked.

"Marry him?" I couldn't look at Ringo, so I kept my eyes on the two Vampires.

"Yeah."

I shrugged. "I'm too young."

"Hmm." He made a non-committal noise in his throat. "What's marriage mean to ye, then?"

I looked at him then, but there was nothing piercing or particularly focused about his gaze. It was like he was just shooting the breeze with his question. Somehow, that made me relax.

"It's a promise, I guess. A legal contract that says 'I promise to be your partner for life.' And after that, there's kids and a house—"

Ringo cut me off. "We're not talking about after 'cause ye can't take more than a step at a time without trippin' over yer own boots. Do ye 'ave any plans of promisin' to be anyone else's partner for life?"

I scowled. "Of course not."

He looked sideways at me. "Would ye want 'im to choose anyone else to be his life partner?"

"No." My tone of voice made it very clear exactly what I thought of that idea.

Ringo shrugged. "Ye've pretty much made the promises to each other. It seems the only thing missin' is the legal bit."

"But why does that matter?"

Ringo turned my chin and made me look him in the eyes. "Because it's the one thing no one can take from ye. Look, anythin' could 'appen, right? For 'eaven's sake, ye could get lost in time as much as either one of ye could die doin' the things ye do. And then ye'd just be … done. But with that contract, ye'd be 'is wife no matter what, and 'e'd be yer 'usband. And that means somethin', Saira."

Ringo's inhaled breath had a shudder riding on it, and I knew we weren't just talking about me anymore. "It means somethin' that ye've made that promise, because not everyone gets to."

I looked at Ringo for a long time, and I realized his face had changed since I'd known him. The angles had grown sharper, and the planes had widened. He had long eyelashes framing almond-shaped eyes, and cheekbones with the faint shadow of facial hair on them. He wasn't a street urchin anymore, and hadn't been a kid in a long time. There was something hurt in his eyes that I knew had to do with Charlie, whom he hadn't seen since she left 1429 with Valerie Grayson.

"Would you marry Charlie?" I asked quietly.

"If we were to each other what ye and Archer are – without a doubt or 'esitation."

"You wouldn't think you're too young?" My voice dropped to a whisper.

"Are ye so young as all that, then? Ye've fought in wars, ye've battled men, and ye've stayed alive when the odds were against ye. Are ye really so young as yer years say?"

I shook my head no, and he touched my cheek.

"Then do what's in yer 'eart, and tell yer 'ead to mind its own business."

I smiled at that, and he grinned back. "It was a good one, eh? Tell yer 'ead to *mind* its business?"

I burst out laughing, and the sound drew Archer's and Bas' attention up to us. We both stood to begin our descent. "You're a good friend," I said softly.

"You too," he responded.

He led the way back down his route, and we were back on the stone floor of the church in under a minute. I took a deep breath, squared my shoulders, and strode up to Archer where he stood with Bas. I gave Bas a kiss on the cheek in greeting, which somehow seemed like the appropriate way to greet him, then turned to Archer.

"I need to talk to you."

Bas took a step back. "I'll leave you, then."

I shot him a quick look, but then my eyes were back to Archer's. "Not in a church."

Archer took my hand and led me outside without a word. The night sky was blanketed with the kind of stars you can only see when light pollution is of the hand-held, don't-trip-on-the-way-to-pee variety. We walked around to the back side of the church, away from the village shops, to a small walled garden. When Archer led me inside, closed the door behind us, and sat me down on a stone bench in the middle of a patch of herbs, I finally knew what I was going to say.

I looked around the garden. "Did you know this garden was here?"

"I hoped." His voice held all the rich, deep tones of the man I'd loved for almost a year – but a year that spanned centuries and with the kind of experiences that could fill a lifetime.

"Why?" This Archer and I had never sat in my mom's walled garden. He hadn't buried Henry in one outside Orléans. He couldn't know what they meant to me.

He tilted his head a little as he considered, maybe wondering if I was testing him. I wasn't really. I already knew my answer.

"Why did I hope there was a walled garden here?" He inhaled, as if gathering his courage. "Because it's where I *should* have asked you to marry me. There is a walled garden at my father's estate. He had it built for my mother, and she planted everything in it herself. I never knew my mother's touch, or the way she looked, but I always imagined that she smelled like the herbs and flowers in that garden. After you left, I stayed with the Missus for several months, healing and learning to be … myself. My father's land borders the Wood, and often, after his estate staff had gone to sleep for the night, I sat in my mother's garden thinking of you."

He held my hand softly. "I wondered about a life together. I wondered what you were dreaming of in that moment, I even wondered what your favorite wildflowers were."

"Bachelor's buttons." My voice was barely above a whisper, so I tried again. "Bachelor's buttons are my favorites."

He smiled. "Just the blue ones, or the pinks and purples, whites and the deep wine colored ones as well?"

"All of them."

He smiled. "I called them cornflowers when I was young. They were my favorites too."

Archer got up and wandered around the church garden for a few minutes. He was wearing dark trousers and a black pullover sweater that made him nearly invisible, but his eyes were the first thing I saw when he came back. They were focused on me as he handed me a tiny bouquet of bachelor's buttons.

I smiled through the tightness in my throat that threatened to come with tears when he knelt in front of me and held my free hand. "Saira Elian, will you marry me?"

This was Archer – my Archer. He was my best friend, the first person I wanted to talk to every night, the last one every morning. His arms around me made me feel safe. His voice in my ear gave me comfort. His heartbeat matched my own in every way, and I knew that what gave him joy and peace would be the source of joy and peace for me too.

"Yes," I whispered. "I will marry you."

We asked Bas and Ringo to come with us to the walled garden. Ringo stood next to Bas, facing us and grinning with his whole body. In one hand, I held the bachelor's button bouquet, and in the other, I held Archer's hand. Bas placed his own hands over ours, top and bottom, and looked around the garden in delight.

"It is my honor to marry you under God's own roof," he looked up at the star blanket filling the sky, "and much easier to explain to those that would care that neither of you is Catholic, and I am only so until the tide of my education turns again."

We laughed, and lightness filled every space in my heart, mind, and body. For a moment, it felt like Archer's hand holding mine was the only thing keeping me on Earth, and that without it, I could have easily floated right away. I was really doing this. I was really marrying him.

"And as my education has been so thoroughly steeped in words, I shall use some of my favorites to bind you in each other's love."

Archer squeezed my hand, and I felt like my smile lit up the garden.

Bas took a breath, then began. "Archer, please repeat after me. On this day, I give you my heart."

His eyes held mine as he said the words. "On this day, I give you my heart."

"I promise to be your lover, companion, and friend. Your greatest advocate and toughest adversary, your comrade in adventure and your accomplice in mischief, and your ally in all things."

Archer grinned, his eyes never leaving mine. "I promise to be your lover, companion, and friend. Your greatest advocate and toughest adversary, your comrade in adventure and your accomplice in mischief, and your ally in all things."

Bas' voice was deep and rich. "I promise to communicate fully and fearlessly, and pledge my love, devotion, faith, and honor as I join my life to yours."

My heart filled to overflowing with his words as Archer repeated the vow to me, and when it was my turn, the voice I was afraid had deserted me came back with full confidence and volume. Ringo's grin as I spoke was utterly infectious, and by the time I got to "accomplice in mischief," we were all laughing.

Bas didn't even try to keep a straight face as he declared. "By the power vested in me, by every God I have ever served, and all the rest there still may be, I pronounce you husband and wife. Lord Devereux, you may kiss your Lady."

Archer laughed out loud with a joy I had never heard from him before, and then swooped me into a low, dramatic dip and kissed me on the nose before he set me back on my feet. Apparently the outrage on my face was hilarious, because all three guys cracked up, and then promptly shut up when I threw my arms around Archer and kissed him properly. On the lips. Like a wife kisses her husband.

I knew my eyes were shining because I saw them reflected in his when the kiss finally ended and we just stared at each other, face to face, inches apart. Time may have stopped for a while because I wasn't aware of anything at all except the man in front of me.

Ringo's voice was the thing that finally snapped me out of the blissful daze I was in.

"Ye get to kiss 'er yer whole life, yer Lordship. There's two of us 'ere who want to congratulate yer Lady."

I laughed as Ringo tugged me out of Archer's arms and pulled me into his own. He gave me a huge hug and swung me around. I shrieked in surprise, and then surrendered. "When did you get strong enough to pick me up?"

He set me down again and scoffed. "Ye suffer delusions of size, milady."

I snorted right back. "Since when do you call me milady? And seriously, I'm huge."

"Ye're tall, but I'm faster and stronger and always will be. And you became milady when you married 'Is Lordship." He gave me his cheekiest grin, then kissed me right on the mouth. "And that's the last one of these ye'll get until I'm married and ye get to give it back." My eyes must have been enormous in my head because he laughed and let me go to hurl his arms around Archer. They pounded each other's backs with the hug of brothers as they laughed.

I turned to find Bas behind me wearing the same grin as I did watching Archer and Ringo. Bas turned the grin to me, then took my hand and lifted the back of it to his mouth with a courtly kiss I hadn't seen since Tudor times. "Milady, you have my deepest admiration and warmest congratulations."

Milady again. The title felt itchy and weird, and I thought I might get used to it when I was about ninety. I hugged Bas tightly. "Thank you."

He kissed my cheek and spoke into my ear. "It is I who thanks you."

I pulled back to look at him questioningly. He smiled and took both my hands in his. "Your love makes him feel whole, and you have given him peace our kind rarely allows ourselves to feel. You may not have chosen this path yet had he not asked, and I understand and respect that in your time one does not necessarily marry so young. But I do believe in the rightness of things. And this ..." He indicated Archer and I together. "This is right."

He turned to Archer. "Devereux!" He called to him in a way that sounded like lords calling across a grand dining hall to each other. "Your wife, sir." He gave my hand to Archer, who pulled me in to his side. "Come, Ringo. Let us leave them to the small privacy of these four walls."

Bas grabbed Ringo around the shoulders, and the two guys closed the garden door behind them. Neither of us spoke, and within moments the nighttime insects resumed their chirping.

Archer pulled me into his arms and just held me close. His heart beat steadily against my chest, and his warm, spicy scent filled me with calm peacefulness.

"I forgot this," he said quietly as he pulled away. He reached into his pocket and pulled something out. I couldn't see it clearly in the darkness until he took my left hand and slid a ring onto the fourth finger. My heart thumped hard as I held my hand close and studied the ring. It was a gold signet ring – a heart with a crown that blazed with flames from the top. It was so beautiful and so instantly familiar it took my breath away, and an abiding certainty that I was meant to wear it settled into my soul.

"It's my family crest. This was the ring my father had made for me when I turned thirteen. The heart and the crown symbolize love

280

and loyalty, and every Devereux gives this crest to his bride." His eyes locked onto mine and he touched my face with gentle fingers. "It unlocks everything I have, and everything I am – to you, Saira Elian Devereux. I am yours, mind, heart, body, and soul." He smiled to release a bit of the tension in the air. "You've always owned me. Now it's just official."

I kissed him again, softly. We lingered like that for what felt like hours and was only moments, letting the sweetness feed something deeper, something that became laced with desire.

A breath caught in my chest, and his hands clutched my hair. I could feel the pounding of his heart as need for his touch swept through me.

I pulled back and looked at him, and I tried to fathom that we belonged to each other now. I had been a legal adult since my last birthday, but now, finally, I began to feel maybe I could trust myself as an emotional adult too. A sigh of contentment and peace mingled with the desire for his touch, and I leaned forward to kiss him again.

And then a scream tore through the darkness, and the nightmare began.

Tom – June 10, 1944

The scene was a nightmare, like something out of a low-budget horror film where the monster lurks in the woods to pick off the heroes as they shrink back in disgust from the tableau of dead bodies left for them in a burned out ambulance. This time, I wasn't the monster.

I hadn't seen the rest of my squad since I'd woken – except Karl, always Karl, who guarded me like a loyal pit bull while I slept. I didn't know which of us was more hated by the snipers they'd sent me to France with – Karl for his lap-dog tendencies, or me for holding the leash. Probably me, because I held all the leashes, and they felt like they were all big, mean Schäferhunde with spiky collars who should be allowed to roam the countryside terrorizing Frenchmen with impunity.

Which was probably what they were doing now.

Sturmbahnführer Kämpfe was most likely dead by now. The Maquis had taken him last night, and they couldn't know the storm that was preparing to descend on them, especially after SS Sturmbahnführer Diekmann saw this tableau of horror, set up by the Maquis for his viewing pleasure. Diekmann had gone mad at the news of Kämpfe's kidnapping. They had been friends before the war, and Diekmann had ordered the countryside searched for him. It was made clear that finding Kämpfe was the first priority, but finding Maquis, their weapons, and anyone who helped them in their terrorist activities was equally vital.

I knew there were Maquis operating in the area around Oradour-sur-Glane, and I'd followed some to Gaspard's farmhouse several nights before. I considered blending in with the rough group that had set up camp around the farm, until I heard the Australian woman's voice and realized I wasn't quite prepared to kill her if need be. I'd avoided the area since then, but an explosion at a railroad bridge two nights ago, and then Kämpfe's kidnapping, had made it impossible to stay away. Now a group of SS had discovered the burned out ambulance just outside the village, and Karl had dragged me here tonight because he'd heard the SS talking about reprisals. I wasn't a fan of the French – those Maquis were as brutal as the Germans were, and twice as hungry for it – but I couldn't stomach reprisals against common farmers.

We had arrived before Diekmann, and Karl gagged as he opened the back of the ambulance. The driver and passenger were both from the advance 2nd SS Panzer Division and had been transporting wounded German soldiers to a hospital in Limoges. All of them were dead, and the Maquis had wired the driver and passenger to the steering wheel, which likely meant they were conscious while the fire consumed them.

Karl and I moved away from the SS soldiers who stood in a loose formation around the site, and I spoke to him in low tones. "When Diekmann sees this, he will take his men straight to the village. If we can round up a couple of Maquis before he gets there, maybe the farmers won't become his target."

"Yes, sir," Karl said shakily. He really wasn't cut out for this bad guy business. He should have been home reading books or making bread for his mother. The kid had learned baking from his grandmother and had been very excited to come to France to eat real French bread. I didn't bother to tell him that the bread we got now was coarse and grainy in comparison to what I knew French bread could be. He thought it was the food of heaven.

The regular soldiers left us alone as we drove away from the site. They knew enough to stay away from the Wolfsangel armbands, and it suited me to be left alone. Self-destruction is one thing, but in war, there's always someone else to kill, and I had become alarmingly good at it.

Karl drove carefully. I hadn't learned how to yet, and didn't think it was a skill set the walking dead needed. The village seemed eerily silent as we drove past shuttered shops. When we arrived at the town square, we suddenly understood why.

We were too late. People were milling about, looking frantic and terrified, while a group of SS rounded them up with machine guns and shouts in German. I spotted one of the snipers from my unit – the short, weasely one called Oskar – and a couple of others whose names I hadn't bothered to learn. They had managed to join up with a half-dozen SS thugs led by one of Diekmann's right-hand men.

"What are they doing?" Karl whispered to me.

"Inviting them to tea." I didn't hide the anger in my voice, and Karl flinched. They had emptied the houses to search for weapons, and the square was full of farmers and shopkeepers. If there were any Maquis among them, it was purely accidental.

Karl parked the truck behind a barn just outside the town square as a transport truck came barreling into the village from the other side. SS soldiers poured off the sides, and I knew it was futile to hope any of the villagers could stay hidden in cellars and attics. With this many men, the SS could do a proper house-to-house search and find nearly everyone.

Diekmann was already likely insane, but with his friend Kämpfe dead, and the tortured men in the ambulance, I didn't think he'd be anything less than savage.

A scream came from somewhere up the hill behind me, and I turned to find Oskar, the weasely sniper, pushing a young Frenchwoman toward the church. Two others walked in front of her, and one of them was holding a baby. I sprinted up the hill behind him, my pistol already out in my hand.

"Oskar! What the hell are you doing?" I shouted at him in German. Karl came charging up behind me, carrying his rifle with both hands. If he tripped, he'd probably shoot someone.

"Major Braun believes Sturmbahnführer Kämpfe was brought here by the kidnappers, and we volunteered to come with them." Oskar's sneer diminished very slightly as he spoke to me. Despite the rest of my unit's hatred of me, they'd heard what I was capable of doing to armed men.

"Where are you taking the women?"

"Braun said the women and children would be safe in the church." The sneer was back, and it didn't bode well for the women in his care.

"Karl, go with him. Shoot him if he tries to harm the women," I said, glaring at Oskar.

"What if he shoots me first?" Karl whispered. I ground my teeth against the thought of being anyone's protector, but I smiled at Oskar anyway. "If anything happens to any man, woman, or child in that church, I will tear out your tongue and feed it to you. Are we clear?"

Oskar swallowed visibly and the sneer disappeared. "Yes, sir."

"Good. Now, where's Johann? We have a mission, and this isn't it."

Another visible swallow. "The partisans got him, sir. We heard about their plan to blow up the bridge, and set up to take them out. I got most of them, but then the bridge exploded and they got Johann before I could kill the rest."

Everything about his body language said he was lying, but on the other hand, Johann was the worst bully in the Werwolf pack, and I wasn't sorry he was dead. "Did you strip the body of identification?"

He shook his head. "No sir. There was no time."

I shot him a hard you-screwed-up look, then gestured to Karl. "See the women safely to the church, and then both of you meet me back at the truck. If they found Johann's body, our presence here is compromised and my mission is done. I'll leave that to you to explain to Diekmann and to Paris." Despite my harsh tone, I didn't care that our cover was blown. I was only there to get transportation to England, and if my unit had to leave France right now, so much the better.

Oskar looked at me through narrowed eyes, and I could see the calculations going on in his head. He knew I was right and it galled him, so he turned and shoved the girl ahead of him again with a growl. "Move!"

My finger twitched on the trigger of my pistol, but I closed my eyes and took a breath. He wasn't worth losing the English job over, and Diekmann would use any excuse he could to take me off of it.

I strode back down to the village square. The crowd of French villagers had gotten bigger as more and more groups of SS brought them stumbling in. An older man wearing a luxurious mustache was irate at having been dragged from his bed and demanded to speak to the commander. I shook my head sadly. The man wasn't likely long for this world with that attitude.

Just then, Diekmann arrived, looking grim-faced and narrow-eyed. He knew I didn't like him, and he didn't like an English traitor in their midst. It was the type of mutual admiration society that usually ends in bloodshed, so I stayed out of his sight whenever possible. The man with the mustache must have recognized power when he saw it, because he marched right over to Diekmann and began a tirade that would have made Hitler himself wince.

I turned away from Diekmann, which was much like turning away from a rattlesnake, and saw two SS guards come into the square shoving a mother and her young son in front of them, while a third held his rifle pointed at a young man who was with them. The young man seemed to be walking along peacefully, but his eyes were locked on the little boy's, and I could see he was trying to keep the boy calm.

I might have been that little boy once, but the soldiers had been my father, and the young man had been my cousin, Adam. I was just turning away from the scene when the little boy stumbled. The young man darted out to steady him, which earned him a shove from the rifle butt for his kindness. He brushed the hair back from his face and smiled at the boy to show him he wasn't hurt, and suddenly my blood turned to ice water.

Ringo.

NIGHTMARE

My heart was pounding so hard it could probably have been heard across the church. Loogie had just entered the nave, pushing three women and a baby ahead of him. A wary young soldier trailed after them and didn't take his eyes off Loogie when the sniper joined the six other soldiers arrayed in a loose formation around the edges of the nave.

My reaction was kind of ridiculous given that Loogie had never seen me, but having a sniper in a room full of women, children, and *my husband* was not comforting.

My husband. It was almost too weird to even think, and it sounded far older and more respectable than I felt. I'd been married all of about half an hour, and the peace I'd had in the garden already seemed like a lifetime ago.

The soldiers had begun bringing women and children to the church just after Ringo had slipped out to check on Marianne and Marcel. Bas had loaned Archer one of his priest's robes, and it had helped to calm the women down who came in terrified and frantic about husbands, brothers, and sons. It also meant he could stay in the church, unlike a teenaged boy who came in with his mother and was immediately escorted back out with directions to take him to the village square with the rest of the men.

When the first SS soldiers came in brandishing rifles and yelling at the women to move their prams to the sides of the nave, I had to push the panic down to somewhere around my knees. It rose when they barred the doors, and rose again with every new Frenchwoman who was shoved inside the stone walls "for their protection," the soldiers had told Bas. And now, watching the men arrayed around the perimeter of the nave holding their rifles at the ready, all I could see in my mind was Archer's vision of this exact scene.

I had to get Archer out of there.

Bas had shown me the hidden entrance to the crypt, accessible from behind the altar in the south transept, and with his help, I'd been very slowly leading a couple of women with nursing babies to the doorway and hiding them from view as they slipped into the darkness that Bas had lit with a shielded lantern. I'd gone down once, with a woman whose two-year-old was too scared to walk down the stairs. I carried her down in my arms and set her next to her mother on the cold stone floor. About ten women were huddled against the walls holding sleeping or nursing babies or quietly whimpering toddlers in their laps. The terror in their eyes was excruciating, and I was ashamed to admit I was afraid to stay down there with them. Because I was afraid their fear was infectious.

I had taken a moment to find a piece of chalky stone that I now carried in my pocket. There was a wall in the south transept that was somewhat protected from casual view, and I knew it was our escape hatch if things played out like they had in Archer's vision. I didn't like the idea of leaving the church full of women and children to their fates, but I had a way out, and I'd take it if I had to so I could save Archer.

Archer slipped up behind me, and I felt him the way I'd always felt Mongers – except not. Instead of the stomach-squeezing nausea, a feeling of warm tingles spread through my chest. Maybe it had always been there, or maybe I was imagining it, but somehow I thought that with the marriage bond had come the ability to sense his presence nearby.

I know my mate, my Cat rumbled from deep inside my head. She'd startled me, and I immediately sent apologies to her. Of course she knew her mate. I just hadn't realized mating could be affected by something like marriage.

Archer leaned in to whisper, "How are you holding up?"

"Mostly fine," I murmured, "except Loogie just came in with the ginger kid who looks like he wants to throw up."

Archer's eyes narrowed. "I saw him. I can take him out of the equation if I need to."

I slipped behind a column so we were hidden from casual view. "See that wall over there?" I nodded toward the back corner of the transept.

"Yes," he said.

"I'll spiral us out there. Just tell me when."

"We'll need Ringo."

"We'll get him from the farm."

Archer nodded thoughtfully. "I'll talk to Bas, then we'll go."

A wave of relief washed through me. He didn't need to be a hero here. He was willing to go before the events of the vision came to pass. Archer's touch left an imprint of warmth on my back as he slipped past me to return to the nave. I took my first deep breath since the nightmare of armed men had invaded the church.

And then I stopped breathing when Marianne and Marcel were shoved through the door.

I almost darted out into the growing crowd to go to them, but Archer saved me from a stupid move by calmly changing trajectory and gliding to them himself. My presence hadn't yet been really registered by any of the soldiers. They might have seen me, but since none of them brought me in, I was still wearing a scrap of a cloak of invisibility. It's what allowed me to stay in the transept and lead the few people who stumbled close enough to me down to the crypt.

Marianne looked equal parts stoic, poised, and terrified, and Marcel did too. Bas must have seen Archer change direction because his eyes followed his friend, and he saw what I saw – Loogie had noticed Marianne too. There was more than casual interest in those laser-focused eyes, and they frowned at the relief on Marianne's face when she saw Archer.

The ginger kid seemed to notice Loogie's interest too, and I wondered if he was part of the same Werwolf pack. He wore an armband of some kind, but it wasn't identifiable from where I stood. Then Loogie changed his hold on the rifle and he suddenly had all of my attention.

I was dimly aware of motion in the north transept because my eyes were locked on Loogie as he moved his finger to the trigger of his gun. He took a step forward just as Archer turned to lead Marianne and Marcel toward me. Ginger Boy readied his own rifle, and suddenly there were two too many fingers on triggers in the enclosed church for my taste. Something needed to happen. Something needed to distract the sniper and his watchdog so they would stand down from their ready position.

I stepped out from the protection of the south transept, and I saw Archer's eyes widen. I didn't look at him, but kept my gaze locked on Loogie. He hadn't seen me yet, but I needed his gaze to shift away from Archer, so I took another step forward.

That was when I saw Tom enter the church.

Loogie saw him too, and swung his rifle along with his gaze.

"Tom!"

I yelled his name without thinking of the consequences. Loogie fired, and people screamed. Tom's eyes caught mine, and he reached a hand out to me just as the bullet hit him squarely in the chest. I lurched forward instinctively.

That's when Gaspard, the Maquis leader, materialized from his hiding spot in the north transept. That's when he threw something into the nave. That's when the world exploded.

The floor seemed to burst open, and the blast of fire sent chips of glass and stone into the air like shrapnel.

Archer shoved Marianne and Marcel away from the blast toward Bas and tried to use his own body to shield them from it. Tom staggered and fell near the entrance to the church.

And then the shooting began in earnest.

Loogie's rifle swept the room before he even brought it up to aim, and Ginger Boy's finger clenched on the trigger, sending a volley of bullets into the ground. Archer had turned toward me and taken a step forward when Loogie's shot found its home in his back.

The screams of women and children were deafening, and the roar of another blast literally shook the stones of the church. Gunfire erupted from all sides, and I saw one of Ginger Boy's bullets tear the arm off a doll that had been dropped in the panic. I knew it would have done worse to the child the doll belonged to, and I wrenched my eyes back to Archer.

Blood gushed from the gunshot wound, and he stumbled forward right into the path of the flames that began licking their way along the wooden pews. Loogie's second shot hit Archer in the shoulder and spun him away from a lectern that had just exploded with fire. There wasn't a third shot. My heart had stopped, and all I could see in front of me was Archer's blood.

There was a hail of bullets that seemed to ping around the nave like a scene from The Matrix, and one of Ginger Boy's shots found its home in Loogie's throat. I saw the explosion of blood over Archer's shoulder as I reached him and grabbed his robes with both fists. I felt fire graze my thigh, but I ignored the burn and focused all my strength into hurling Archer toward the transept. He stumbled and went down, but was back up a moment later with enough forward momentum to make it out of the hailstorm of bullets.

As I turned, the world around me slowed to bullet time, and I really was in a Matrix movie. Women were climbing the altar to reach the window ledge. An older woman was shot as she jumped out, and a younger one threw her baby out before she dove after it. Loogie's body was still upright, but had filled with holes as Ginger Boy's rifle discharged everything it had into the sniper. Ginger Boy seemed barely conscious of pressing the trigger until one of his bullets hit a little boy, and then he finally stopped. He threw himself toward Tom, who struggled to get to his feet. Bas had covered

Marianne and Marcel with his body and was pushing them toward the south transept. His walk was jerky and unsteady, and I realized he was being hit by gunfire with every step.

The sound of my name finally pulled me out of my bullet-time trance, and I spun to find Archer reaching for me from the shelter of the transept. I reached back, and a bullet grazed my wrist as it embedded into the pillar near Archer's head. He grabbed me and pulled me to his body.

"Ringo—" he gasped. I Saw what he Saw through the touch of his skin. Archer's vision of Ringo was as clear as if we were standing next to him in the town square among the village men surrounded by soldiers with guns.

I didn't go back for Tom; I didn't even look back. I didn't want to see the faces of anyone I left behind as we stumbled to the tucked-away wall and I began to draw. The chalk rock slipped twice, and Archer finally held my hand closed around it as the spiral hummed and pulled us in. The one conscious thought I formed was of a barn. Not Marianne's farm, because she was in this church filled with death and pain, but a barn that housed a mechanic's garage at the edge of the village square – the square where they had Ringo.

A moment later we were in Rachel's barn, where the hulk of a half-repaired car stood in the darkness. Sounds here were muffled and vastly different than the mayhem in the church. Outside in the village square there was anger and outrage, and soldiers shouting in German demanding to know where the weapons were and who had set the fire. The dark and quiet of the barn had dampened the noise but not the fear, and it leaked in through every crack and crevice in the walls.

Archer's gasps filled the silence with something tangible, and I found him by the dim light of the moon through a rear window. He had let go of my hand and was on the floor struggling for breath.

"Archer!" I whispered, dropping to my knees beside him.

The barn door slammed open and someone – no, two people – hurtled inside. I threw myself over Archer's body to shield him, but a sob escaped my throat.

The people stilled. One closed the door carefully and silently, while the other moved closer, but stayed out of range. I didn't sense a Monger, but I was frozen in place.

And then Archer moaned, and I stopped caring who else was in the barn. "Shh, Archer."

"Saira?" A voice whispered from the dark in surprise.

I sobbed with relief. "Ringo – help me. Archer's been shot."

Ringo raced forward and knelt beside me. A candle sputtered to life and came forward too, but not in his hand. I looked up to find Rachel, the mechanic's daughter, holding the light as close to us as she dared. I darted a glance at Ringo.

"She 'elped me escape the square." His breath caught. "They took Marianne and Marcel."

"I know." I didn't say more. Archer was the only one I could hope to save at that moment. Ringo reached for Archer, and I suddenly realized how horrible Archer looked. He was pale and sweating, and his skin was freezing cold. Blood continued to seep out around his shoulder. I moved to touch it, but Ringo stopped me.

"Not you."

I stared at him, stunned. "Why not me? It's safer for me than you. At least his infection won't kill me."

"You can't touch him with that hand." He nodded his head at my right hand. It was bleeding, and I remembered the flying bits of rock from the bullet storm. I wiped the blood away, but a rock or a bullet had torn off a chunk of skin and it was an open wound. He was right.

Ringo looked up at Rachel and spoke quietly to her. "Are ye cut anywhere on yer 'ands?"

She stared at him as if he was talking nonsense, so Archer translated into gasping French. She turned her stare to him, then held up her hands and answered in English.

"I have no injuries."

"Can you help me with him?" Ringo asked her as he lifted Archer into a sitting position. Rachel handed me the candle without hesitation and helped pull Archer's coat off him. I moved the light around to his back and then nearly dropped the candle. Two bullet holes had shredded the fabric of Archer's blood-soaked shirt.

"Why is he still bleeding?" I tried to keep the frantic edge in my voice under control. "It should have stopped by now."

Ringo tore what was left of Archer's shirt away and wiped the blood away from the two bullet wounds. The one at his shoulder wiped away fairly clean, but the hole under the edge of his scapula bubbled blood.

Archer's gasping quieted a little. "My lung's torn, and the tissue's trying to close, but there's still a bullet in me. I won't heal until it's out.

"Then we 'ave to get it out."

Oh God. I quickly unsheathed one of my daggers and wiped it down as much as possible with the edge of my shirt. The germs didn't really matter because they couldn't kill him, but the tenets of modern hygiene don't just disappear in the face of reason. I offered it to Ringo, handle first, but he shook his head. "Too big."

Crap. I wasn't in the habit of carrying scalpels with me. I patted my pockets as if I was doing a key check, and realized I had Sanda's little knife tucked into my back pocket. I pulled that out and flicked it open for Ringo. He studied it for a second, then nodded and took it from me.

"Sit in front of 'im and 'old 'im upright. Keep 'is eyes on ye so 'e doesn't move."

"When did you learn to do surgery?" I asked Ringo, when what I really wanted to say was, *why couldn't Connor or Mr. Shaw have been here?*

"Saira," he said to me in a voice that brooked no argument, "do as I say."

Rachel moved into the spot I vacated when I crawled around to the front of Archer. He gave me a sort of weak half-smile with a raised eyebrow that said *when did he get so bossy?* as loudly as if Archer had spoken the words. I loved him for that.

"I think I need to straddle your lap to keep you upright. Is that okay?" I whispered to him.

"I think pain might just keep me preoccupied enough to manage it without embarrassing myself." His pulse was thready, and I could see it stuttering in his neck. I climbed onto him and wrapped my legs around either side, then used my arms under his to help support his body. In any other situation it would have been a very intimate pose, but all I could concentrate on at the moment was feeling Archer breathe and not letting him move.

"Right, now, 'old very still." Ringo moved in very close to Archer's back, and I could feel the heat from the candle against my arm as I remembered something.

"Wait! Rachel, check Archer's coat. He sometimes carries an extra torch on him for me."

I could feel Archer smile against my neck. "Anything for you," he whispered. My heart hammered in my chest. He sounded weaker and a little delirious. "Quickly," I breathed.

She rummaged around in his bloody coat then held up a small Maglite. I grinned and held my hand out for it so I could twist it on. "Nicked it from my bag, did you?" I asked Archer.

"Seemed sensible."

When I handed the Maglite back to Rachel, she was clearly fascinated by the size and modernity of the torch, but she held it rock steady as close to Archer's back as she could get it without impeding Ringo's knife hand.

"Right. Archer, I'm goin' to 'ave to cut ye a bit more so I can dig the bullet out. 'Ang on to yer wife and don't move."

He rested his forehead against mine, and our gazes locked. The word 'wife' had made him smile, but the smile became grim determination as Ringo opened the hole in Archer's back. His breathing faltered and his eyes closed against the pain.

"Stay with me, Archer. Don't shut me out," I whispered fiercely.

His eyes opened and found mine again, but he didn't speak. Ringo was focused on the bullet in Archer's back, and Rachel's whole world was holding the light for him. Archer was clenching his teeth and trying not to twist away from the pain, while I used every ounce of muscle control to keep him completely still.

Something in Ringo's face shifted. "Ah, got it." The sound of something metal pinging against the wood floor released all the tension in the moment. "I don't have a needle to stitch it— but it seems to be closin' on its own now." Ringo sounded exhausted, but I didn't break my eye contact with Archer to look at him.

Archer looked as tired as Ringo sounded, but the pulse in his neck was beating strongly again, and his breathing had calmed. "You okay?" I asked him in a whisper.

He nodded, finally allowing his eyes to close. "Thank you." He took a couple of deep breaths, then sat up straight without my help and looked at Ringo.

"Thank you, my friend."

There was a smear of blood on Ringo's cheek where he'd wiped his face, and he was trying to clean the blood smears off his hands with Archer's ruined shirt. "Ye're welcome."

"Ringo, be careful with the blood," I said, concerned that even rubbing his skin could cause an abrasion that would let the virus in.

I looked behind Archer to where Rachel was still holding the torch aimed at Archer's back. She stared at it, and I imagined that the wound would have closed itself by now. I climbed off Archer's lap, though his hand twitched as if to keep me there, and knelt beside Rachel. She seemed a little dazed when she looked at me, and I gently took the flashlight from her hand. "Do you have water?" I asked quietly.

She nodded and brought Ringo a bowl of water and a cloth. She wet the cloth and handed it to him, and then returned her gaze to Archer's back. "He will heal?"

I nodded. "Yes."

"He has already." It wasn't a question.

"Yes."

Just then, shouting rose up from the village square, and I immediately twisted the Maglite off. Rachel doused the candle and shoved the bowl of water under a table. It took a moment for our eyes to adjust to the moonlight, and when the voices came closer, Rachel whispered to us. "Come."

I kicked the bloody scraps of fabric under the table, and Ringo helped Archer to his feet. He wasn't steady, and the hard breathing came back, but resting in the middle of the floor wasn't an option with SS soldiers outside.

Rachel waited for us at a wardrobe in the back of the barn that I now realized housed the garage in front and Rachel's living space in the back. But instead of opening the wardrobe like a door, she pulled it straight down to reveal a Murphy bed. As clever as the design was, and as much as Archer needed to rest, I didn't think a bed was in any of our futures. But then she slid the headboard panel open, climbed up on the bed, and jumped down to the other side of the wall.

"She wins," Ringo said under his breath. I smiled because I knew he was talking about his collection of hidden room designs. I went next, and Ringo supported Archer as he climbed onto the bed, and came through to the other side. Rachel had Ringo grab a rope at the end of the bed and toss it to her. Then, when he had climbed through, too, they hauled the bed back into its upright position, and Rachel cut the rope so no one would find it if they pulled down the bed. Then she carefully slid the headboard closed, and the space went completely dark.

This cupboard behind the bed was only about three feet deep, and it was the length of the wall in the bedroom. Whoever had built the false wall had left enough space for two people to lie down, or four people to sit with our backs to the outer wall. I helped Archer to the ground and then sat next to him so he could use my lap as a pillow. He laid on his uninjured shoulder and faced away from me, and my hand trailed through his hair, absently stroking it off his face. Ringo sat on the other side of me, and Rachel crouched down next to him with her ear to the false wall.

298

I clutched Ringo's hand. "Thank you."

He didn't say anything for a long moment, just held my hand lightly. Then he squeezed it and let go. "Were ye still in the church when the shootin' started?"

My voice caught in my throat. "Yes," I whispered.

"It's where they took Marianne and Marcel, yeah?"

"They were alive when we left. Bas had them." Guilt punched me in the gut.

"It's where Archer got shot?"

I nodded and then realized he couldn't see me in the pitch black. "Yes." I had to swallow hard to keep the tears down where they stayed invisible.

"Just like 'is vision?"

"Mostly. Except for Marianne and Marcel. And Tom."

"*Tom* was there?" Ringo said in surprise.

"Yeah." I didn't elaborate. I couldn't. We had come here to find him and take him home, but when the shooting started, I'd left him without a backward glance.

Ringo was silent for a long moment, and when he spoke again, the bitterness surprised me. "They might 'ave been alright if I 'adn't gone for them."

Rachel's whisper surprised me. "No, they took everyone from the farms. They would have found your friends with or without you." I could feel her tense suddenly. "Sssshhh! They're in the garage," she whispered.

Rachel, Ringo, and I went utterly still as if our lives depended on our silence. Archer's breathing had gone quiet, and I knew he was out to give his body a chance to repair itself. My hand rested lightly on his hair, and one small part of me felt peace that he was here, safe, on my lap.

Something crashed to the floor in the main room of the barn, then shuffling and footsteps in the bedroom. Another crash, this time closer, and then the Murphy bed was opened.

Not even my heart beat as a tiny seam of light shone through the false wall. One of the soldiers told the others it was all clear in the room, and then he pushed the bed back into place.

My heart gave a giant thump and then settled back into an elevated and amplified rhythm I was sure could be heard in the main room.

There was more yelling in German as soldiers herded people into the room and told them to lie down on the floor. No one was talking back anymore, and the silence from the Frenchmen was more frightening than the anger and yelling had been in the village square.

After about ten more minutes of shuffling and orders to lie still, the main room was silent.

I thought the SS soldiers had made the French lie down so they could get out without reprisals. I thought the soldiers had gone, and I began to relax.

Until the shooting started.

Whatever breath had been in my body got tangled up in the horror of what was happening on the other side of the wall. My heart slammed in my chest, knocking the air out of it, and every scream of every person in the barn felt like a gut punch.

Ringo grabbed my hand and gripped it, hard, and I could hear Rachel sobbing silently into his shoulder. When the sobs began to wrack her, he let go of me and wrapped both arms around her to try to quiet her. Archer didn't move from my lap, and my fingers wove through his hair in a pattern I could repeat without thinking – so I could stop thinking. Anything to stop thinking.

I began a mental chant of every medicinal plant I knew, with all their properties and purposes. And then moved on to medicinal recipes for burns and cuts, vomiting, and fever. Since I was there anyway, I started making up my own recipes for lotions and creams, lip balm and shampoo, and even something I thought would work pretty well on a rash.

The whole time I wove my fingers through Archer's hair in the same pattern every time.

Eventually, the shooting stopped. And then Rachel's silent sobs turned into the barest gasp and sniffle. And then the footsteps faded away, and finally the noise of jeeps began to disappear. And all that was left was the sound of four hearts still beating, and four people still breathing.

I carefully pulled the Maglite out of my pocket and covered the business end with the palm of my hand before I clicked it on. The dull orange of the light shining into my skin was even too bright, and I winced away from the tiny sliver of light. Rachel covered her face with her hands, but Ringo looked right at me with dull and empty eyes.

"Yer not goin' out there," he whispered.

I shook my head. "No. None of us are."

"What if—" he began.

"No. The only thing we can do is get out alive. If we do that, we can tell the story. If we die, the truth dies with us."

Ringo looked at Rachel, then at Archer. "Do ye need somethin' to draw with?"

I pulled the bit of chalk rock I'd saved from the church out of my pocket and reached up above my head to the wall behind me. I closed my eyes and began to draw from memory.

"Move in close," I whispered. I clutched Archer with my free hand, and Ringo snaked one arm behind my back. He put the other one around Rachel and brought her to his chest.

The humming began with the second spiral, and my mind began to drift to places of safety. I thought of Archer's secret lair at St. Brigid's, and his hideaway behind the library at Bletchley Park. I thought of my room at Elian Manor, and of the Edwards' cottage kitchen where they used to live. But ultimately, the choice was all about finishing this so we could go home, and I chose the one place in London I hoped we would find safe haven no matter what.

And then we Clocked out of France.

TOM – JUNE 10, 1944

The fire still smoldered among the bits of wood around the stone church, and the smell of charred flesh hung in the air with an oily stench.

Bodies were everywhere.

They were a blanket covering the ground. Their clothes were a tapestry of blues and browns that threaded through blackened ash. A little girl's skirt was yellow. A boy's shirt was green. And through it all wove ribbons of red blood that connected the people of this village to each other after death, even if there had been no connection in life.

Saira was gone. She'd half-carried her wounded and bleeding Sucker to the side wing of the church during the chaos, and when the shooting finally stopped so the soldiers could flee the burning church, they had disappeared. All that remained of Saira's presence was a chalk-drawn spiral in the corner. I stepped toward it, and then I saw the priest emerging from behind the altar.

His eyes didn't go wide in the way a person's might when confronted by a man in a German uniform covered in blood. They narrowed. It intrigued me. He probably wasn't the only one hiding in whatever crypt he'd come from, but I had no interest in seeing more dead.

So I shook my head at him, put my finger to my lips, and waved him back to his hiding place. He hesitated just long enough that I thought he might be assessing whether or not he could take me. He was tall, older than me but not more than a decade, and he looked fit. To him, I must have seemed scrawny and weak, despite the uniform and the rifle I had to wear so the regular SS didn't start things they couldn't finish with me.

The priest's gaze was direct and unflinching, and I met it with my own. The horror of the other room was still imprinted on my eyes, and looking at him meant I didn't have to watch Karl vomit in a corner, or admit that I noticed the three SS soldiers who had returned to pick over bodies for something to steal.

After a long moment – too long for someone who wanted to stay alive – the priest reached out a hand and made the sign of the cross at me. The bastard blessed me, right before he turned and went back down the steps. The back of his priest's robe was covered in blood, so much blood I wondered at the wounds that must be underneath it. Suddenly, I wanted to go after him. I wanted to demand to know why he thought a blessing could ever matter to a murderer. I wasn't just going to hell, I was in hell. How dare he imagine he had the power to absolve *me*.

I was shaking with rage when I strode to the spiral on the wall – Saira's unintended gift to me. Had she followed me to France? Was she looking for me? Was her presence in this place and time an accident, or was it fate that she drew a spiral here for me to use?

Whatever had brought Saira, Archer, and Ringo to this war, they had given me the means to finish my own. France and Germany could duke this out without me, because now I had a way to Clock to London and do what I came to this war to do. I would find Walters on my own. I would find him, and I would kill him.

CHURCHES

I took us to the attic of the rectory where Bishop Cleary lived – or rather, would live in another seventy years, more or less. It had been Archer's and my weapons training ground and was almost as empty now as it would be then. It was a calculated risk. Whoever the current Guy's Chapel minister was, he most likely lived alone, and Archer could probably talk our way out of anything using his Bletchley Park connections and basic charm. Except Archer was still out cold and would probably stay that way until nightfall tomorrow.

When I'd made sure the attic was empty and safe, I came back to where I'd left Archer, Ringo, and Rachel. Ringo was checking Archer's wound, and Rachel looked a little shocky. I helped her to her feet, then shook her hand.

"I'm Saira. This is Ringo," I indicated my friend, "and Archer."

She looked me straight in the eyes without any fear, and I admired her for it. "You are the friends of Father Sebastien. I recognized him," she gestured toward Ringo, "in the village square and wanted to help. I am Rachel," she said in accented English.

"Thank ye for that, by the way," Ringo said.

Rachel nodded once. "You brought meat to the children," she said, as if that explained everything. She added, "We are not in Oradour-sur-Glane anymore." It wasn't a question.

304

"We're in England. At the Guy's Chapel rectory," I added for Ringo's benefit. He looked around once, then nodded and went back to tending Archer's back and shoulder. Ringo had pulled a canteen of water out of his satchel and was wiping the last of the blood off Archer's skin.

Rachel's eyes had widened and she took a step back from me. "How—?" Then she shook her head. "No, I will just have faith and leave it alone."

"I can take you home when we're done here—"

She took another step back, but I wasn't sure that it was me she was retreating from. "I never want to see what they've done, or the faces of my friends and my father's friends. I am finished there."

I nodded. "Fair enough. Thank you for hiding us."

She shrugged, seeming to accept her new circumstances, and began to wander around the room. "You are here for a reason, I think." She rubbed a clean spot in the dusty window and looked outside.

Ringo shot me a look as I glanced over at Archer, still so vulnerable. Then I turned back to Rachel and studied her as she picked up a broomstick and weighed it in her hand, maybe to find its balance, or to check on its usefulness as a weapon. We were possibly the same age, but she wasn't as tall as me. Her short dark hair and lean, wiry frame were totally functional and gave her the tools to pass for male. But if someone looked close enough, her eyes would give her away. They were wide-set, framed with long black lashes mascara companies would pay top dollar to use in their ads, and they were currently focused on me.

"It is dangerous, what we need to do," I told her.

Her gaze didn't waver. "So is staying alive."

I took a breath. "When I can, I'll take you wherever you want to go."

She turned to Ringo. "You'll come with me to find places to sleep?"

"I don't think—" I began, about to say I didn't think it was a good idea to go wandering around a guy's house in the middle of the night, but Rachel cut me off.

"The house is empty."

"How do you know?" I asked, although a sneaking suspicion was winding its way up my spine.

"I just feel it," she shrugged and pointed to her stomach, "here. I am never wrong."

I stared at her for a long moment. "When did you build that false wall in your bedroom?"

She looked back at me without blinking, and finally said, "Three months ago."

Right.

Ringo shot me a raised eyebrow and got up to leave with Rachel, and then I was alone for the first time in days. Archer's presence didn't count because he was unconscious, and I found an old blanket folded up on a dresser to spread over him.

I went to the window and looked out over the nighttime street. Southwark seemed deserted, and there were no streetlights on anywhere. There was a big pile of rubble directly below my window, and I realized that the little park I'd always assumed the city planners had left next to Guy's Chapel was really the result of a direct hit from a German bomb. Down the street, as far as I could see under the moonlight, was the same landscape: Victorian and Georgian buildings standing singly or grouped two or three together, then an empty spot where a building had once stood. The haphazardly mixed architecture of modern London suddenly made perfect sense, and based on the number of ugly fifties and sixties-style buildings that would be built in Southwark, air raiders had hit this area really hard. The bombed-out landscape was eerie, and despite the pre-dawn hour, the neighborhood felt oddly deserted.

Ringo spoke quietly from the top of the stairs. "There's a bedroom for ye one floor down. Do ye want 'elp movin' 'Is Lordship to it?"

306

I looked at Archer, still curled under the blanket, and shook my head. "No. I'll manage. Get some rest, and we'll make a plan when we wake up." I turned back to the window, more for what I couldn't see than what I could.

Ringo hesitated, but I said nothing else, and finally he went back down the stairs. When the attic was mine again, I turned my back to the window and slid down the wall to huddle against it, drew my knees to my chest, and stared out across the room with unseeing eyes.

I started shaking.

It began with chattering teeth that had nothing to do with temperature, and then turned into a whole body tremor. I didn't even bother to fight it, I was too tired. But the shaking was making it hard to breathe, and when I tried to get up, I stumbled back down twice. Tears of frustration rolled down my cheeks, and my breath came in gasps. My lungs were beginning to seize up, and I fought panic as I pushed myself to my knees and tried to stand a third time.

Strong arms lifted me, and I twisted around to find Archer helping me to my feet. I buried my face in his neck with a cry and he held me so tightly the tremors had no room to shake. He stroked my hair, and murmured nonsensical things until I could breathe again.

I kissed him then, to find the life in being alive. The last time we'd kissed was in our little walled garden, back in a time when all those people were still breathing, cuddling their children, thinking thoughts of what to plant, or clean, or build.

I kissed him for all those husbands and wives who would never kiss each other again, for the parents who couldn't kiss their children, for the children who would never grow up to find someone to kiss. I kissed him to erase the horror from my eyes and my ears, to pull back the fear so it didn't consume me, and to find a small bit of the peace that had fled the walled garden with the first scream.

My clutching grasp on Archer's skin became the anchor to keep me sane and whole and alive, and his arms held me so tightly to his chest that my shirt became the barrier to where he ended and I began.

I didn't want any barriers between us, and I stopped kissing him just long enough to tug off my shirt and camisole. The heat of his skin was like a balm to my shocked body, and I pressed myself into his chest.

"I love you," he whispered into my hair. The words sent a wave of need through me that brought my Cat up to purr with desire. I still held control, but she rubbed against the inside of my skin in a way that made me want Archer to touch and pet and hold me.

I pulled back from him just enough to see desire in his eyes, and my Cat preened in it. "I need you," I said simply.

The desire flared with heat and fire, and then he kissed me until there was nothing else in the world.

There were no visions or dreams after we made love. There was only the peace of being held by the man I knew to the depths of my soul. The room we had found to sleep in was furnished simply, but with an old, carved wood four-poster bed that had long thick curtains we drew around ourselves. We woke at sunset, in a cocoon of white linen that felt like a sanctuary, and we whispered to each other to let the peacefulness linger as long as it could.

"How do you feel?" he asked me.

"Alive." I traced the last remnants of the exit wound in his shoulder, and I realized his skin didn't yet carry the scars of the many wounds he would one day have. "How are you?"

"In love with my wife."

My heart smiled and I laced my fingers through his.

"Are ye awake yet?" Ringo's voice intruded on the cocoon and I scrunched up my face like a kid who doesn't want to eat yucky spinach. Archer laughed and kissed me quickly.

"Yes, now go away and we'll be out in a minute," he said, grinning at me.

"Right-o. Saira, Rachel found a few tins of things in the kitchen. Come down for food before we eat it all."

"Leave me anything you guys don't like. I'm so hungry I could eat tinned peas and be happy."

"You say that as if there's anythin' I wouldn't eat. Street livin' beats the picky right out of the boy."

I was tempted to throw a pillow at him, but that would burst the cocoon wide open, so I made another face and got another laugh from Archer.

"Out!" he called to Ringo. A moment later the door closed and we could hear Ringo chuckle to himself as he walked down the hall.

Archer touched my cheek. "That thing you just did with your face is why you'll win any fight we ever have."

I did the scrunchy face again. "You mean this?" Archer's laughter was infectious, and I was tempted to start a tickle fight just to prolong his playfulness.

He opened the curtains and pushed me up. "Go, or the rascal will eat all the food just to punish you."

"You come too. I don't want to face those two alone."

Archer stilled and looked at me carefully. "Are you ashamed of our lovemaking?"

I stared at him. "What? No! I meant that I'm going to blush like crazy, and I need you next to me so I don't turn into a complete idiot." I pulled him up to stand in front of me and wrapped my arms around his neck.

"I love you, and I'm crazy *in* love with you. I just want the whole war to go away so we can spend all day together somewhere sunny and deserted."

"Except for the day and sunny bits, I'm with you." Archer grinned.

My eyes opened wide. "Oh God, Archer, I'm sorry."

He touched my face gently. "Not as sorry as I am, beautiful Saira. Nothing would make me happier than to see you with the sun shining on your skin."

My stomach clenched with guilt, and I turned away to pull my clothes on. Archer watched me dress for a long moment before he finally moved to pick up his own clothes.

I went to the door. "I'll see you downstairs?"

He smiled gently at me. "I'll be down as soon as I find another shirt."

I left the room and made my way to the stairs. I had lost my appetite and lingered in the staircase while guilt churned my stomach acid into something frothy and gross. What the hell was I doing, and what had I done? I was dreaming about spending time someplace sunny with Archer when a: I had basically told my modern Archer he couldn't risk the cure to ever see the sun again, and b: I wanted to go somewhere to spend time alone with him? Which him? The one I had just married and shared the most intimate touch privileges with, or the one I would be going back to when this was all over?

I suddenly wanted to unzip my skin and step outside it, because being me was too hard. I had no business getting married – that's what adults did, and frankly, I sucked at adulting.

Archer appeared at the top of the stairs, pulling on a simple linen shirt. The smile on his face faded when he saw me paralyzed on the stairs. "What's wrong?" He said it as if he already knew the answer and was just waiting for me to figure it out. He came down and sat on the step, then patted the place next to him. I sat and leaned against him so I didn't have to meet his eyes.

"I suck."

I could feel him hold back a smile. "In general, or is there something in particular?"

I took a deep breath. I didn't need to protect Archer from myself – he was great at seeing the real stuff through the murky crap. "What I said to you about sitting out the war someplace sunny so we could just hang out – everything about that statement is just so ... loaded."

He picked up my hand and laced his fingers through mine. "You don't know how to feel about being married to me here, while I'm waiting for you in your time."

My breath caught in my throat and I finally met his eyes. "It feels so disloyal and weird to want to spend time with you here ... now. I should be doing everything possible to get back home to you, but this ..." I gestured around me with my hand. "This feels like real life, and anything in my time is just ... happening without me."

Archer lifted my hand and kissed my fingers one by one. "I am me, no matter which time I'm in. And I'll still be me, and still your husband, when you go back to your time. Whatever happens here and now between us will exist for me in seventy years, so if anything, you're giving me more to sustain me through the years we're apart." He smiled at me, and his smile untangled some of the knots in my stomach. "And if you need to go back tomorrow, I'll have your return to me then to look forward to as well."

I shook my head. "I just don't know how you can be the *you* that I met a year ago."

He kissed my forehead. "I don't either. But we'll figure that out when we get there."

I searched his eyes. "You promise I'm not screwing up?"

"Not with me, you're not. Now, or then."

My gaze was locked in his, and the last of the knots slipped free. "When the time comes, Archer ..." I took a breath. "Do what you need to do about taking the cure. Whatever you choose, I trust you."

He held my face in his hands. "I love you more than ... I love chocolate."

I barked a laugh and he grinned at me.

"That's to the moon and back, in case you were wondering."

I kissed him playfully. "Since chocolate is its own food group, I'll take that compliment."

He bit my lip. "Oh, you're definitely your own food group."

I shrieked and jumped down the rest of the stairs. "Ringo! Save me! I'm about to be dinner for a hungry Vmmph—" Archer managed to catch me and kiss me before the word came out, which was a good thing, considering the stare Rachel gave us when we came crashing into the kitchen.

Ringo looked rested. Rachel did not. She had deep circles under her eyes, and she wore sadness like a cloak wrapped around her shoulders. She picked at a bowl of tinned beans without much interest, while Ringo tucked into corn like it was his birthday and this was his favorite cake.

I sat down across from her, and Ringo shoved a bowl of peas in my direction. I stuck my tongue out at him and then took a spoonful of the grayish mush anyway.

"How much do you want to know?" I asked Rachel. She looked startled, and I shrugged casually. "We're clearly not normal, and your life just got very strange. Do you want to know the whole story, or just roll with whatever happens?"

Ringo stopped eating and seemed interested in her answer. Archer just hung in the background so it wasn't quite as obvious that he wasn't eating.

Rachel put down her fork and leaned her chair back against the wall in a move I'd seen Connor and Ringo do a hundred times. "I knew you would come," she said simply.

I nodded. "Yeah."

"You are not surprised."

"Not if you knew to build that wall."

"Why do I know things?" Rachel asked, in a tone that said she'd been wondering for a long time.

I shot a quick look at Archer. He stepped forward and spun a chair around to sit at the table. Rachel hadn't really noticed that he was moving without evidence of his injury, and her eyes widened at the sight of him. He smiled. "I'm fine. Thank you for your help, and you …" He turned a pointed look at Ringo. "That was a huge risk you took with my blood."

He shrugged with a grin. "What's the worst that could 'ave 'appened?"

"Excruciating pain and wasting death."

Ringo raised an eyebrow, still grinning. "Well, when ye put it that way, ye should probably not be getting' shot again."

"I'll keep it in mind." Archer turned his smile toward Rachel. "If I had to guess, I'd say you and I belong to the same Family."

She sent him a completely disbelieving look, and he then proceeded to give her the scholar's rundown of the Immortal Descendants, much the same way he had educated me when we first met. I watched Rachel go through the same emotions I remembered having. Fortunately, she seemed inclined to believe things she'd already experienced, like Clocking locations and Seeing the future. Having witnessed Archer's injury and miraculous recovery, she didn't fight the idea of his lineage either.

Whatever food had been opened was gone by the time we wrapped up our crash course in Descendants lore, and the sadness seemed to have temporarily lifted from Rachel's shoulders. She was intrigued and fully engaged in the conversation, and it was clear from her questions that she was not only fluent in English, but had the same kind of inquisitive intelligence Connor and Ringo had.

"Can I ask you some questions about yourself?" I said finally.

"Yes, of course." Her accent wasn't just French. There was something else underneath it.

"Why do you speak fluent English?"

She smiled. "My father taught me English and German so I could read auto repair manuals."

"Were you raised in France?"

Her expression didn't change, but her voice got a little tighter. "My mother died when I was born, and my father took me to France because my grandparents tried to buy me from him. When he refused, they threatened to take me by legal force, so he left Poland."

I stared at her. What was wrong with people? Archer asked the next question. "Is that a Polish accent beneath the French?"

She shrugged. "Possibly. My father also taught me Hebrew so he could read to me from the Torah, because the only time we could ever go to temple was on once-a-year trips to Paris. I haven't been for three years, ever since they sent him to Drancy."

"Where's Drancy?" I asked.

"Just outside Paris. But they moved him two years ago."

"Where?"

"To a camp in Poland."

"Do you know which one?" My expression must have given away the sinking in my gut, because Rachel's expression tightened even further.

"Auschwitz."

"Oh." There was no part of me that could force lightness into my voice.

"That's bad, isn't it." It wasn't a question, but I answered it anyway.

"It's not good."

Ringo stood up suddenly. "Ye know, I think we should go for a run." He looked at Rachel. "I know a place ye might like to see."

I pushed back my chair. "Do you mind if we come? I feel like I need to see what's happened to this city."

"To be honest, I'm feelin' a need to make sure London's still standin' too." His eyes returned to Rachel's. "Can I give ye the whirlwind tour of my town?"

She nodded. "Yes, please."

"Ye look strong enough, but can ye run?"

She arched an eyebrow at him, and I liked her a little more just because of that. "When you are a girl dressed as a boy, and you don't want to fight – you learn to run."

Ringo liked her for it too. "Sounds about right." He looked at us. "Ye ready? Let's go."

The run down the deserted streets of Southwark felt like something from a post-apocalyptic movie, and it wasn't until we crossed London Bridge that we saw any signs of life on the streets.

There wasn't a block that hadn't been damaged in an air raid, and some areas had more rubble than upright buildings.

The worst was a bookstore, still filled with a jumbled pile of books, missing its front wall. I decided to make a game of it so I didn't cry. Every pile of rubble was a new jungle gym to be climbed, flipped over, or jumped off. Of course, Ringo took to it immediately, and turned every new pile into a challenge for me to match his moves.

Rachel had kept up with us easily, and about five rubble piles in, she began to try some of Ringo's moves. His competitiveness switched on and off depending on whom he was talking to. With me, it was all challenges, but with Rachel, he took time to correct mistakes and give shortcuts. I hadn't seen him be a teacher before, and he was very good at it. He was also leading us toward Aldgate, and when he finally stopped, it was in front of an old, dark brick, square building.

"What is this place?" Rachel asked.

"The oldest synagogue in London," Archer said, smiling at Ringo, who nodded.

"That's right. I used to let myself in to practice chandeliers."

"To practice chandeliers? What does that even mean?" I scoffed.

He grinned. "Ye'll see."

Rachel's eyes were wide and aimed at Ringo. He smiled at her and leapt to the top of a trash container, then pulled himself up the door lintel to the window ledge above it. He pried the bottom of the window open and disappeared inside the building in under thirty seconds. Rachel turned her stare to me.

"He just entered a synagogue like a thief."

"Yeah. He's sort of an equal opportunity offender when it comes to private buildings. The first time I met him he broke into Kings College for me. He'll open the door in a second so we can go in."

She gasped. "I don't think I can enter a temple when it is closed."

"It's open now." I pointed to the door Ringo had just flung wide.

Archer held his hand out to Rachel. "Come. Your faith sees this place as *schul* to learn, and as a place of peace and worship. There are no hours for that."

After a moment's hesitation, Rachel allowed Archer to lead her inside. I shot Ringo a grin as I walked past him. "Nice one, Keys."

He wiggled his fingers at me, then pointed up as I entered the long room. I stopped in my tracks with a gasp that echoed what Rachel had just done, but for a different reason.

Hanging from the tall ceiling were seven huge brass chandeliers, three on each side of the room, plus an even bigger one hanging in the middle. "Are you kidding?" I said to Ringo.

"I'll show ye," he said mischievously, but I stopped him before he could jump up the altar.

"No!" I whispered fiercely. "I don't think she could handle that kind of disrespect. She's having a hard enough time being in here without the sight of you swinging from the chandeliers." Then I grinned at him. "But it looks like fun."

I looked over to find Rachel standing in front of the main altar at the far end of the room. She was staring up at what looked like Hebrew writing on two tablets at the top. Archer had stretched himself out on one of the pews under the biggest chandelier and was looking up at it with such a peaceful expression on his face that I went to join him. I lay down so the tops of our heads touched and our feet pointed in opposite directions. The chandelier looked a little like a kaleidoscope from that angle.

"It was good to bring her here," Archer said quietly.

I looked past my feet to where Rachel stood, still staring up at the altar, and I saw her shoulders shake.

"She's crying," I whispered.

"I'm guess she hasn't let herself mourn him."

I knew Archer meant her father, and I dropped my whisper even quieter. "Only about five or ten percent of the people sent to Auschwitz survived."

"Oh, God." His tone was horrified, and I rolled over onto my stomach to face him.

"Hitler and the Nazis murdered six million Jews – most of them in camps." Archer's shocked expression said it all, and I added the clincher. "In total, over sixty million people died because of this war."

Archer squeezed his eyes shut and rubbed the heels of his hands over them. "How did we do this to ourselves? How can we have allowed this to happen so soon after the Great War?"

"*Have you ever asked yourself, do monsters make war, or does war make monsters?*" I said. "It's a quote from a book about angels and demons, but it fits."

He was silent, and his eyes went back up to the chandelier above our heads. Ringo passed me and gave me a quiet nod as he went to stand by Rachel's side. He murmured something to her, and she nodded, and I thought about what makes monsters, and what makes men.

Going Underground

The night was clear and warm when we left the synagogue. Whatever had broken in Rachel as she stood in front of the altar had left exhaustion in its wake.

"I'm goin' to take Rachel back to Guy's if it's alright with ye." Ringo said to us in a quiet voice. I nodded, then caught her eye and stepped over to where she stood under an unlit streetlamp.

"How are you?" I asked her.

She inhaled softly. "When they took my father, I stayed in the village to keep the garage for him to return to. Now there is no village, and perhaps my father will never come home. It is as though my purpose for living was just torn out of the book, and I don't know what happens next."

I searched her startling eyes and saw her strength in them, even under the doubt and pain that clouded them. "It's your story to write now."

"Is that what you've done? Did you choose the purpose of your life?"

I almost smirked and made a joke about barely being able to choose what t-shirt to wear each day, but I realized it wasn't true, and saying it wouldn't do justice to Rachel and what she faced now. "I don't know how to choose my purpose – that sounds too big and … significant. But I know who I am, and I've chosen the things that are important to me. I think the best decisions I make

318

about what to do in my life come when I'm being true to both of those things."

She blinked, as though my answer had surprised her. "Thank you."

Ringo came up next to me. "Do ye 'ave it in ye to run back?" he asked Rachel.

She nodded. "Yes, but only if you show me some new things to try." She looked at me. "I'm writing a story, you see, and I need to learn who my main character is and what she likes to do."

I grinned at her and they took off at a sprint. I turned back to find Archer watching me thoughtfully.

"I told him we'd go up to Russell Square to scout Holborn station, and then we'd meet them back at Guy's Chapel," he said. "Although the encoded message gave the date of Tom's mission as June 12th, we've both learned that the twelfth begins at midnight tonight."

I grimaced at the reminder of my horrible mistake in Victorian London on the night Mary Kelly was murdered by Jack the Ripper. It was not one I'd ever repeat. "It *would* be nice to actually be able to make a plan, instead of just reacting to everything," I said.

We jogged through the streets of Old London, and had to move away from the London Wall down toward the river because of building damage and debris. The neighborhood around Saint Paul's Cathedral had been destroyed by bombs and fire, but the dome still rose up from the ashes like a shining beacon in the moonlight.

"Are the bombs that hard to direct to targets?" I whispered to Archer when we stopped to stare at the Cathedral. "I mean, you must be able to see that dome from miles away."

"That's exactly why they've left it standing. It's a navigational tool now, especially with so much of the city unrecognizable."

We saw no one out on the roads until we passed St. Bride's Church, but it wasn't a surprise that Fleet Street was bustling with life. Slivers of light shone through blackout curtains, and messengers darted between buildings as they ran errands for the papers that delivered each day's war news. They barely seemed to notice us as we sprinted toward the Strand, intending to cut up toward the British Museum after we'd passed the Royal Courts of Justice.

The bit of activity on Fleet Street made me happy. It was a small thing, to see people scurrying about at night, but significant in this city that had been so besieged from the air since the Blitz of 1940. I didn't know a lot about the Blitz, but running through London four years later was a major education in the damage the German bombs had done.

The silence as we passed the Bush House seemed almost absolute. Our feet pounded a soft staccato on the pavement, and Archer's pace was perfectly matched to mine. I was just about to take his hand and pull him into a doorway for a surprise kiss when an air raid siren sounded its wail above us.

I barely bit back a shriek of surprise when Archer grabbed my hand and swung me off the curb to dart across the Strand. "There's a shelter at Aldwych Station," he said with grim determination. I remembered his story about having been caught in a wave of people going underground during the Blitz, and I yanked his hand sharply to make him stop.

"Wait! When did you eat last? The buck in France?"

"I'm fine, Saira. We need to get off the street."

The drone of airplane engines was faint, and I looked around us at the buildings. "There are no landmarks here. We can hide on the surface." People had already begun streaming out of flats and houses, heading toward the Underground station. They looked grim-faced and exhausted, and most were carrying blankets and pillows. I suddenly didn't want to be stuck underground with so many grumpy people.

Archer spun me around to face him. "Saira, you can't hide from a bomb, because it's not looking for you. The only part of hide and seek it knows is *ready or not, here I come.*" He wasn't angry, just determined, and one small part of me wanted to dig in my heels and resist on principle.

320

But then the drone of the bomber engines carried a new sound under them. It was sort of like a mechanical bumble bee, with an engine that surged rhythmically.

Until it didn't.

My brain automatically began counting. In the movies, the V-1 rockets went silent for a count of twelve before they exploded. Except … this wasn't a movie.

"Ahhh!" I grabbed Archer's hand and pulled him after me. "Run!"

We wove through the people moving like lemmings to the Underground entrance, dodging the kids who decided running with us looked fun. No one else seemed to understand the imminence of the danger, and we had just made it to the top of the stairs when the unconscious count in my brain hit twelve.

BOOM!

"What was that?!" Archer shouted.

"A V-1 rocket," I shouted back over the screams of panicked people as they ran for the station. "Haven't you heard one before?"

"No!"

I didn't know how far away the explosion was – a couple of blocks, maybe – but I felt it in my teeth and bones and eardrums. A tidal wave of people running for the station entrance threatened to sweep us away with it. The stairs were completely jammed, and I leapt to the stair rail to ride it down. Archer was right behind me, and we made it down the multi-level stairs before the next bomb hit.

Underground, the explosions were like a great, angry giant thumping his club on the ground as he demanded the blood of Englishmen. Both platforms at Aldwych were filling rapidly.

"Is Central the only line that runs here?" I asked Archer.

"Yes. It's a dead end from Holborn, so it's an easy air raid shelter. They stopped running trains to Aldwych during the Blitz."

"So the track should be dead, right?" I had heard enough horror stories of people being pushed onto live rails that I stared dubiously off the platform.

Archer searched into the blackness of the tunnel for a long moment, then quickly took my hand and pulled me toward the northern end. "You're a genius."

"I am? I mean, yes, thank you, I know." I grinned at him. "What did I say?"

"Holborn is about two hundred and fifty yards away. We can get there underground."

"Yep, I'm a genius. Especially since I have this." I whipped my little Maglite out of my pocket, and Archer hid it from view as he took it from my hand.

"Undeniably genius."

Archer gave me a quick kiss on the lips. I was a little giddy from the adrenaline of running from bombs, and I kissed him back with enthusiasm. An older woman standing behind him smiled cheerily through her exhaustion.

We dodged people who were beginning to settle down in hopes of getting an hour or two of sleep, and finally made it to the far end of the platform. A very quick look around revealed no obvious watchers, so I blocked Archer's body with mine as he dropped to the tracks, then surreptitiously knelt as if I was tying my boots. I took his outstretched hand and leaned forward to slip down next to him. "Nicely done," he whispered as we crouched low and hugged the platform wall.

A moment later we were inside the tunnel, with the dim light of the platform fading behind us. I held Archer's hand tightly and used my night vision until the light was completely gone.

"Torch, please," I whispered into the blackness.

A moment later, the Maglite clicked. I stifled a scream as a headless ghost rose up in front of us, its arm raised in a warning. We both froze in place, until I realized the ghost was naked ... and not a ghost.

"It's a statue," I breathed, relief pouring out of my whispered voice.

"It's not just any statue. It's one of the Elgin Marbles." Archer shone the Maglite around the headless naked guy, and I realized he was made of marble, and he was hanging out with a headless centaur.

"From the British Museum?" I had just been to the Duveen Gallery a few weeks before and had been following the controversy about whether Britain should return the marbles to Greece.

Archer snorted derisively. "Duveen was an idiot, and Elgin was a thief."

"So, apparently, you have an opinion about whether or not to give them back?"

We had continued walking, though more slowly now as the light from the torch played over the surfaces of friezes and sculptures that had once graced the Parthenon in Athens.

"I have opinions about art dealers and preservation techniques," he said as we approached one of the wall friezes filled with horses and their riders. Archer shone the light at the carvings and pointed to clear grooves in the finish. "Lord Duveen did this a few years ago. Pentelic marble patinas to a honey color, but he thought the marble should be white, and he directed the use of scrapers and a chisel against the stone."

I held out my fingers and touched the two-thousand-year-old sculpture, feeling the ridges and grooves that should have been worn soft with age. "I didn't notice when I saw them in the gallery. But you're right."

"The museum must have moved them here after the Blitz," he whispered as we continued making our way down the tracks. The tunnel was full of the marble slabs, but the most striking pieces were the statues. The head of Selene's horse glared down at me from the top of another piece, and I wanted to blow it a kiss.

"I wonder what else they have stored down here?" I said as we resumed walking.

Archer froze and stared at the marbles. "Or if this has anything to do with the Werwolf mission with an *entrance from Holborn?*"

I peered down the tunnel in front of us, but it fell off into blackness. "You think it's a simple case of theft?"

"The Germans are looting the rest of Europe. Stealing Britain's greatest art treasures right out from under their noses would be utterly demoralizing." We had begun walking again and whispered as we picked our way past the marbles that still lined the tunnel.

It did make a certain amount of sense, except for one glaring thing. "But why would Tom steal art from his own country?"

Archer was silent for a long moment as we walked. "I don't know Tom. But I do know that if this is indeed theft, there has to be an inside man. These are priceless treasures, and there was no guard posted. Anyone could do what we just did and walk away with a beautiful horse head for their fireplace mantle. Except no one in England knows they're here. No one but the people who moved them and the people who arranged to have them moved."

"Which means museum employees?" I asked. I picked my way carefully over the uneven ground next to the tracks.

Archer sighed. "It only takes one disgruntled or greedy person with the right knowledge."

"But it still doesn't explain Tom." And Tom was the whole reason we had come to this time and place.

Archer clicked off the small Maglite, and I was about to protest until I realized I could still see the dim outline of his shape next to me. I looked ahead of us and realized we were approaching another station.

"Holborn," Archer whispered directly in my ear. He stopped and crossed the track, pulling me with him. The marbles were tucked safely into the black tunnel behind us and weren't visible at all in the dimmest of light that leaked from the platform ahead of us. I could feel Archer step over the tracks, and I followed, nearly blind, but with that extra spatial-awareness sense the darkness brings.

"Why are we on this side?" I asked in a whisper.

"We're on the branch line from Aldwych. If there's a way to cross over to the through line platform, I'd like to find it rather than use the passenger tunnels." I tried to picture what he was talking about in my mind. Aldwych station was a branch line that was closed in my own time. Before it closed, trains originating from Aldwych only went through Holborn station on their way back out to the main Picadilly line – but the track we were on started at Holborn station and was therefore a dead end.

"Tell me about the rocket that went silent before it exploded," Archer whispered as we walked.

"I'm pretty sure it was a V-1 rocket. They also called it a buzzbee. In old war movies they always went silent for a count of twelve before they exploded."

Archer was silent for a moment, then he said, "I'd heard the Germans were building something new. That must be it."

I stumbled over something that I wasn't expecting and hissed out to Archer. "Wait. Shine the light here." I back-stepped and felt it again with my foot. An electrical junction with a line running straight at the wall. I reached out to the wall just as Archer clicked the Maglite on and hid the beam with his palm.

Through the red light glowing from his skin I could just make out the edges of a metal door. "Block the light with your body if you can, but I need to see."

Archer did as I asked, putting himself between the Maglite beam and Holborn station. The door I'd found had a rigid electrical cable running through the wall next to it, which was what I'd kicked. There was no handle, just an indentation to pull it shut and a lock. Instinctually, I looked up. There was no lintel above the door – nothing to stick out into the tunnel and potentially catch on a passing train. But I reached up anyway, and felt what I'd hoped to find.

"There's a recessed shelf, just like the door handle," I whispered as I patted around, praying there were no spiders up there waiting to attack my groping fingers.

"Got it," I said, drawing the flat key from its hiding place above the door. I loved lazy people who left keys hidden in convenient places.

The lock turned fairly easily, and I pushed the door open and handed the key back to Archer to replace. Then I stepped into the narrow passageway. "Let me make sure there's a way out before you close it," I whispered.

He handed me the Maglite and I aimed it as far in front of me as it would shine. This place was a long passageway that must have been a conduit between two tunnels. The light didn't reach quite far enough for me to see the end, but from the angle of the passageway, I realized it wasn't a straight line between the tunnels, but more like the zag of a Z. I only had to take a couple of steps before the other door began to be visible. It had a lever handle on the inside, and as I had hoped, it was unlocked. I clicked off the Maglite and pulled the door open very slowly. It seemed even more quiet and still than the tunnel behind us was, and I stood there for at least thirty seconds listening to the silence. Finally, I closed the door again and clicked the Maglite back on.

"You can close it," I whispered loudly to Archer. I kept the light on, but turned back to the door to see if it would lock when we closed it from the other side. Archer's arms wrapped around me from behind and he hugged me close for a long moment. I melted into the feeling of just being held.

"I can imagine it," he whispered in my ear. "A long shower with endless hot water, a rug by the fire, and a bed with velvet drapes to shut everyone and everything else away."

"Hmm," I smiled dreamily. "Sounds wonderful. Here, hold this." I broke out of his arms and handed him the Maglite.

He laughed softly. "What are you doing?"

I had pulled a piece of chalk from my pocket. "Drawing us a spiral so we can go find that endless hot water shower." I had three segments of the spiral finished and was half way through the fourth when I looked back at him. "Aren't you coming?"

His gaze didn't waver. "An exit strategy, I understand. But to leave now? I don't believe you would do it."

I leaned back against the wall with a sigh. "When do I get to have a life that's not about jumping around in time trying to save the world, or whatever my stupid superhero cape says?" I glanced at Archer and smirked. "Sounds really arrogant doesn't it?"

He had a straight face, but I could see the effort it cost him to keep it. "A little."

"Yeah, well, sometimes the cape itches and I don't want to wear it."

He shrugged. "So don't."

I sighed again, just for drama, because the moment called for a little drama. "Whatever this is, it isn't over yet. But I promise you, that cape is going to the cleaners the minute it is."

Archer did smile then. "You have a deal."

I finished the spiral just for the aesthetics of it. "You know how I knew I wasn't going anywhere?"

"Besides the fact that you're still wearing the superhero cape?"

I rolled my eyes at him. "Yes. Besides that."

"How?"

"There was no buzz in this spiral."

That got his attention. "You mean it's not a portal?"

"Oh, it's probably a portal, but I didn't need it to open for me I guess."

Archer tilted his head and looked at the spiral I'd drawn. "So it really is an escape hatch then?"

I shrugged. "Maybe. Hopefully not. In any case, it's here if we need it."

Archer – Present Day

I thought we might need that escape route.

In any case, I intended to show it to Adam.

I'd brought him into the Underground through the old Aldwych station. It was locked, of course, but not especially secure. They had most recently used the platform for filming an episode of *Sherlock*, so it was free of debris, and once we were on the platform it was a simple drop to the same dead track Saira and I had traveled that night of the air raid in 1944.

Saira.

My wife.

That one fact overrode every other memory that had been crowding into my brain since she left. I had seen so much death and horror during that war – so much that I'd buried it as deeply as my psyche would allow – and yet one fact made all of it fade into sepia images from the long-ago past.

I had married her.

There was a profound sense of relief that came with the knowledge that she wore my ring. It was relief for her security, and because she had finally chosen me. I'd long ago given up the ring as lost. To know that in fact I'd given it, as I'd always intended, to the woman I loved more than words could ever convey gave me remarkable peace.

I no longer felt separate from myself, nor jealous of the man I'd been. My memories of being with Saira felt fresh and real, and a part of me looked forward to each night's new batch of truths. I had resented having to stay behind and lived in constant fear for her safety, but the new memories were like looking through a portal into the past to see everything we did as we did it. It created a bit of a fugue effect in my brain though, which I anticipated would only get worse as this night wore on.

Tonight, as Adam and I crept silently along the branch line track where the Elgin Marbles had once been kept safe from German bombs, the Descendant Council was meeting. If Camille Arman had her way, there would be a vote to oust Markham Rothchild as Head of the Mongers, but as far as I knew, Claire was still opposed to a move that drastic until they had a possible replacement. Adam had gotten word from Ava that Seth Walters was not in evidence, and so far, neither was the Monger ring.

Only Jeeves and the Edwards boys were privy to our use of the Aldwych station access, which we had worked out from the urban explorers' recounting of their adventures underground. I had expected more of a fight from Connor and Logan when I told them to stay behind, and their stoic acceptance still worried me. Connor could be rational – I'd seen it so often in medieval France when he'd had to manage Jehanne – but I didn't delude myself into thinking Logan had any regard for things like rules and safety. To be fair, his ability to Shift into any animal he chose made him nearly impervious to harm, but I didn't necessarily credit him with the sense or experience to know how to use that ability strategically.

No one knew about the memories that had begun to crowd my head. I supposed that if I'd been sensible, I would have waited to come down here until I remembered what had happened to us in that Underground tunnel during the air raid. But the Seer blood in my veins boiled with warnings, and I could sense the same tension in Adam behind me.

The air in the branch tunnel was as dead as the track until we rounded a bend and a breeze picked up a bit of trash. I dragged my hand along the wall until my fingers found the edge of the access door.

"Shine a light here. You need to see this," I whispered to Adam.

He allowed the penlight to flash quickly on the wall where the door was barely visible under the black grime of disuse and age.

"Now up." I directed.

His light illuminated the recess exactly where Saira had found it, and I reached up, hoping the key had never been removed. It was there, just where it had lain for more than half a century. Adam's beam of light found the indented door-pull with the lock beneath it, and a moment later, I turned the key. The lock was tight, but the mechanism still turned smoothly, and I replaced the key above the door.

"Take your light to the end of the tunnel, but turn it off before you try the other door," I said quietly.

Adam was quick and efficient, and a few moments later he flashed his light at me to indicate the other door was unlocked. He waited with the door closed and the flashlight pointed at the floor.

"How did you know about this passage?" he asked when I reached him.

"Saira and I came here during the war."

"During the ..." He stared at me. "How do you know that?"

"Memories. They've been hitting since she left."

His stare turned incredulous. "You mean you're remembering stuff as it happens to you in the past?"

"More or less."

"What are you doing right now ... then?"

"We've just left this access passage and have switched to the Central line."

"You know how to get there because you're ... going there ... then?"

"The obvious difference between now and then is that once you and I step out of this passage, the Central line track will be live."

He shrugged. "So, as long as we keep our footing, and if we can make it past the CCTV at Holborn station, we'll just have Mongers to worry about?"

"Mongers who have kidnapped more than forty people."

Adam's scoff was mocking. "We can take 'em."

My expression was deathly serious. "Be very clear, Adam. I cannot just injure or maim a Monger. If there is blood, I will have to kill them rather than risk turning even one. I will not be responsible for unleashing yet another Monger Vampire on this world."

Adam was suddenly still, and his eyes didn't leave mine. "Tom isn't dangerous," he whispered finally.

"Not here or now," I said.

"Not then, either." Adam sounded desperate.

"He's working for the Germans." It was strange to speak of something from the war in present tense, but it was still unfolding in the past.

"I know he has a reason. Do you guys—" he paused and sighed. "You and Saira, in the past, do you know about Tom's great-grandfather – George Walters?"

"No. We have realized the museum treasures stored on the tracks are probably the Germans' target, but we don't know about Tom's personal connection to the museum."

This was not a productive conversation to be having at this moment, so I took the torch from Arman's hand and clicked it off, then reached past him for the door handle. "Despite the late hour and the lack of trains, no one is ever alone in the Underground. Tread quietly and carefully, and perhaps, if we're lucky, we'll actually make it out of here alive."

I ignored his angry sniff, adjusted the knapsack on my back, and proceeded out of the passage ahead of him.

I could just hear the hum of electricity from the live rails of the Central line track, though I doubted anyone other than myself or a Shifter could. It was a curious byproduct of the mutation that kept my cell death in stasis. Without cell death, I experienced no hearing or vision loss, which actually occurred as an enhancement of my senses. Taste, touch, and scent were enhanced too, as well as strength and endurance. I hadn't felt tired in more than a century, and oddly, it was one of the things I truly missed.

As Adam had said, the CCTV cameras at Holborn station were going to be challenging, and my excursion to the station as a Tube passenger earlier in the evening hadn't revealed any secrets to getting past them. I didn't often choose to travel by Underground train, and the last time I'd gone to Epping Wood to hunt had been three days ago. I knew I was skirting the edges of advisability for a man with my need for blood, and yet, if I were truly honest with myself, the syringe in my pocket felt a little like a safety valve. I knew it was ludicrous, because what would I truly do? Throw myself in front of a train, then inject the cure and see what happened? Of course not. But I was so very tired of harming other creatures in my need to sustain myself.

I could still sense Arman's tension behind me as we approached Holborn station, but it had shifted into something less defensive and more wary. Despite my initial jealously of his friendship with Saira, I liked Arman. He was loyal and honorable, and notwithstanding his natural arrogance, he had an easy way with people I found admirable. He would become an interesting man, I thought, and I intended to see he made it through this night to get there.

A sound stopped me in my tracks, and Arman nearly walked into me before he heard it too. Something was coming from the tunnel behind us.

Something on four legs.

Damn!

I spun to face the Wolf that ran down the tracks, his silver coat just visible in the dim light from the station. Arman gasped, and then recognized the Wolf as I had. I put my finger to my lips in warning to him as the Wolf padded to a stop behind Arman and looked at us with a tilted head as if to say, *what are you waiting for?*

I wanted to yell at Connor, to chase him back through the tunnel and away from the danger that waited for us in the dark. Anger surged up at his complete disregard for my order to stay behind, and Arman took a step back from me.

And then feathery, furry wings touched my face and I bit back a yell. The wings brushed my hair as the creature passed me and flew toward the platform. When it hit the dim safety lights of the station I saw the bat, small and black and perfectly suited to the imagined horrors of underground London. I almost laughed out loud at the absurdity that I, a bat-creature of legends, had just been frightened by a bat.

The bat suddenly darted up, and I bit back my tirade at the Wolf behind me to see what had drawn the creature's attention. I crept forward cautiously, aware that according to Connor's research, there were one hundred and thirty-one CCTV cameras spread throughout Holborn station. Not all of them were on the Piccadilly line platform, obviously, nor even most of them, as these tracks were still part of the branch line to Aldwych. Still, even divided among six platforms, including the two branch ones, there were certainly eyeballs aimed in all directions.

In fact, the bat appeared to be heading straight for the camera that was aimed at the mouth of the tunnel in which we stood. It fluttered up and seemed to hover in front of the lens, as though to block its view.

And then the bat Shifted … into an even bigger version of itself, but with a bit of red-gold on its head and a wingspan of what looked like almost five feet across. Arman came up behind me and almost got punched for whispering in my ear. "What the hell is a Philippine fruit bat doing in London?"

Did everything grow larger in the Philippines? "It's Logan," I whispered back as the Bat settled its body in front of the camera. "Come on."

I stepped out into the dim glow of the emergency lights that remained on for maintenance crews. Arman and the Wolf followed close behind me, and despite the enormous Bat blocking the nearest camera, we still hugged the platform wall.

The Bat suddenly squeaked at us and we froze in place. It Shifted back to the much smaller English version of itself, then flew to a camera I hadn't seen, and Shifted back to the Fruit Bat as it settled its large body in front of the lens. We crept forward again. Logan repeated the maneuver two more times until we were finally back in the relative safety of the dark tunnel on the other side of the station. He then Shifted back into his smaller version and flitted around my head as I headed deeper into the darkness.

Finally, when it was pitch black and we were deep enough into the silent tunnel before it rejoined the main Piccadilly line coming from Covent Garden, I stopped and whispered sternly, "Shift, but watch the track."

It was cold down here, and I knew both boys would have nothing on, but I wasn't feeling very generous at the moment.

"That was cool, right?" Logan's whisper held the excitement of a boy who had just done something clever. I took a breath and reigned in the fury I had been about to unleash.

"Does anyone know you're here?"

Logan's whispered tone shifted to something defensive. "I told Connor I was going to follow you to make sure you got past the cameras. I've done it before loads of times, and it never sets off any alarms. But obviously, it's no good revealing your location if your backup follows you."

"Uncle Bob would kill me if I let you come alone," Connor murmured angrily.

"Without a doubt," I agreed, and I sensed some of Connor's tension loosen its grip on his breath.

I sighed. "You'd both be much safer at home."

"You're both much safer with us here," Logan shot back. The sad thing was, I didn't disagree.

I was silent long enough to make Logan shift his feet nervously. "I don't retain the illusion that you'll do what anyone says because you respect authority, but perhaps you'll respect my considerable experience and do what I say when I say it. Otherwise, I'd prefer you leave so I don't put myself in danger trying to protect you."

I was speaking to Logan, as I knew Connor the way soldiers know each other. His loyalty and commitment were unwavering, and I actually did feel we had a better chance with him next to us. Logan's Shifting skills were undeniable; it was his attitude I questioned.

He finally moved, and I thought it was a nod. "What do you need me to do?" he whispered.

I exhaled quietly. "Return to Bat form – the small one, please – and scout the track ahead. There's a small branch off to the right side, I believe, which is where you'll find the British Museum station. Stay off the rails – they're live – and close to the walls where motion is less likely to be detected. Look for Mongers in particular, and pay attention to numbers of people. Anyone walking around, let us know where and how many."

"Got it." He didn't even hesitate and was barely done Shifting before he was gone down the tunnel.

Every ounce of my responsible nature rebelled against sending an eleven-year-old boy into danger, and yet he was very likely the safest one of us all. I turned to the others. "Arman, when we get there, your whole focus is rounding the captives up and leading them out. Use the service passage to get back to Aldwych if you have to, but make sure you get them to safety."

"Right." Arman was all business, and I appreciated it.

"Connor, Shift back to Wolf form. You and I will provide defense as necessary." I knew how much he had come to dislike fighting and killing since our adventure in medieval France, but I also knew that his Wolf was less circumspect about bloodshed than the young man was. "Let's hope they don't need it."

I turned back to Arman. "Any chance you've Seen what's ahead?"

He hesitated. "Ava told me about … the explosion. I haven't Seen that."

Maybe that just meant that he would be away from the danger if it did happen, but I said what he wanted to hear instead. "Then perhaps it was nothing."

Just then, Bat wings fluttered in my hair and I barely resisted the urge to swipe them away. A moment later, Logan had returned to his boy form as his disembodied voice whispered from the darkness. "There's no platform anymore, just dirt. They've parked two train cars on the track, and people are sleeping on the benches in them. The far end of the tunnel is sealed – no way in or out, and there are two armed Mongers about twenty feet inside the spur, about fifteen feet away from the first train car. A handgun for each was all I could see, but they look the type to carry knives on 'em too. One's properly asleep, the other's nearly there, and most of the people in the train cars are out cold. Two are awake that I saw, Ava's green-haired guy and a girl, and they're hiding at the far end of the train. They're talking about how to take out the guards, so they could be helpful."

It was better news than I'd hoped, but I had difficulty believing there wasn't some other threat he couldn't see. Otherwise, it begged the question that always entered conversations about why concentration camp inmates hadn't risen up against their guards, and it generally involved factors unknown to the outside.

I spoke quietly to the three young men assembled around me. I couldn't see them in the pitch blackness, but I could sense their attention on me. "Logan, are you comfortable revealing yourself to Tam and the girl at the far end of the train?"

He scoffed. "A naked kid showing up in the middle of their party will obviously be a Shifter, so yeah, I'm fine."

I sensed Connor's tension beside me, but I ignored his fear for his brother. Logan would figure this out. "Okay, I need you to enlist their help. They should quietly wake all the sleepers and get them ready to leave. Tell them to wait for Arman's lead, and he'll take them out. If they know of any traps or any hidden threats, get that information back to us immediately. I don't trust that Walters would only leave two guards on forty people."

"Right." Logan's confidence was hearty.

"Wait, Logan – this is important. When you've delivered your messages, I need you to leave the ghost station and return to Holborn. This is the most likely way in for any Mongers arriving as back-up, and we need to know if they come in behind us. You are our only scout, a Bat-spy, if you will, and your information is vital to the safety of everyone down here."

"I know you're just trying to keep me safe, but I also know I'm the best spy you've got. Remember that the next time you plan something without me or Connor."

I was careful to keep the smile out of my voice in the darkness. "Follow my orders on this, and I will."

"Don't get dead, brother," Connor said quietly.

"I won't. Mum would kill me," Logan said just before he Shifted.

A flutter of Bat wings later, he was gone.

I exhaled. "Right. Connor, you'll go as a Wolf. You're faster and more agile that way. If I can get to the guard who is still awake, I'll take him out first, but I assume he won't go down quietly, so backup on the other guard would be appreciated. I expect trouble, so Arman, stay back in the shadows and be ready. The rails may not be live at the spur, but if they are and you need to push someone into them, do it. Surprise is our best weapon, so we have to be quick and decisive."

"I have a knife," Arman said quietly.

"You'd have to be too close to use it. Stay to the shadows as much as possible, and we may all get out of this alive."

I felt the air move as Connor Shifted to his Wolf form.

I spoke the words rather than whispered them. "Let's do this."

SAIRA – 1944

Archer had moved into position ahead of me, and I had every one of my senses aimed outward for signs of Mongers. At a minimum, I hoped to feel Tom Landers before I ran into him, but I assumed any of the Werwolf troops he worked with would also be Monger.

I sensed something coming from behind us. The Holborn station platform had been deserted, despite the air raid above, and Archer had explained in hushed tones about the deep-level shelter that had been built under the Goodge Street station, which was probably where all the people had gone. Since we'd left Aldwych, we'd been alone on the tracks.

We weren't alone anymore.

Archer stopped in front of me; he had just heard it too. He barely breathed the words into my ear. "Other side of the track. Hug the wall." It was good advice. In the U.S., people tend to walk on the right side of things, because it's how they drive. In the U.K., the opposite is true. We crossed to the right side of the track, tucked ourselves up against the cold bricks, and waited.

The footsteps came fast and were as silent as a runner could be. No Monger-gut, so ... what, then?

"Ye alright?" came the whispered voice close enough to me that I jumped.

"Ringo?!"

"Who else?"

338

I nearly throat-punched him.

"How'd you find us?" asked Archer.

"Rachel told me ye'd be in the tunnels. She Saw it, I s'pose. Ye said 'Olborn, so I picked a lock and 'ere I am."

"Was there anyone else about?" Archer sounded as relieved as I was.

"Streets were empty. Bloody bombs are still droppin' though."

As if on cue, a heavy *WHUMP!* resonated deep in the ground and shook the tunnel where we stood like a small earthquake. Brick dust rained around us, and Archer clicked on the Maglite. We stared at each other for exactly one second before we took off running.

The light swung in tight arcs as Archer aimed it roughly ahead of us so we didn't trip on cables or tracks. Whatever had made that sound was big, and if Tom's mission had anything to do with it, we had to find him.

The tunnels diverged, and we took the smaller branch to the right. A dim safety light shone up ahead, and the air was full of grit that hung like a cloud in the glow from the torch.

The platform of the abandoned British Museum station came into view, and it was full of people.

No, not people – statues.

They looked Roman or Greek, and they stood against the dirty white-tiled walls like sentries, or maybe more like an audience, because they were staring at two men who stood like actors on a stage.

"Tom!" I couldn't help whatever reflex drove me to call out his name. He turned at the sound of my voice, and a gunshot reverberated in the tiled corridor.

Tom was flung backward just as I surged forward to leap onto the platform.

The other man leveled a gun and prepared to shoot Tom again.

"No!"

Archer hadn't followed me up onto the edge of the platform. He had run straight down the track and leapt up behind the man, who turned to follow the motion. The man swung the pistol around to shoot at Archer, and the shot went wild as Archer tackled his legs. The gun went clattering across the floor.

I sprinted to where Tom no longer lay on the platform. He was on his feet. The bullet wound in his arm had already closed, but not before I caught a glimpse of the wound from the church and several others briefly blooming on his chest and abdomen. A part of my brain wondered how many times he'd been hurt since he left us in France. Enough apparently. The rest of my brain was trying to process what I saw beyond Tom, beyond Archer and the man wrestling for control of the gun, above the far end of the platform.

Something metallic glinted through broken tile in the ceiling. Debris lay scattered on the platform beyond it, and I suddenly realized what had made the huge *WHUMP!*

The man on the platform kicked Archer in the face and scrambled after his gun. He reached it and sent another wild shot in Archer's direction.

"It's a BOMB!" I shouted at them. I pointed up at the piece of shiny skin that showed through the station ceiling. My words had an electrifying effect, and everyone froze.

Then Tom burst through the suspended animation when he lunged at the man on the platform. Archer's face was bloody from the kick to the nose, but he had recovered and grabbed at the man's feet so Tom could wrestle the gun away.

The man fought them like a feral thing, but he was no match for the two Vampires. I saw Ringo out of the corner of my eye lurking on the track under the platform, ready to help as needed. They didn't need it. A moment later, Tom had the gun and it was pointed at the man. A Monger, I realized, when the twisting in my gut was no longer about Archer's safety.

The Monger was in his thirties, with the build of a boxer and the face of a street fighter. His nose had been broken more than once, and a tooth had been chipped, which was at complete odds

340

with the fancy Saville Row suit he wore. It was dusty and one sleeve had torn, but gold cufflinks shone at his wrists, and his shoes still had the shine of a recent polish. There were scars on his knuckles though, and even the flash of gold on one finger wasn't enough to dispel the image that he was a proper thug.

The hand in which Tom held the gun was shaking, and I instinctively stepped forward to take it from him. But Archer's look stopped me in my tracks. Though he still held the Monger's legs, all his attention was on Tom's face, and without saying a word, he let go of the Monger and slowly stood up. He watched Tom as if watching a wild predator that was wary and ready to bolt.

I shifted my attention from the Monger to Tom, and I nearly took a step back away from him. I'd seen him across the church, but I hadn't registered his appearance because of the mayhem. But now I really saw him. Tom looked so much older than when I'd seen him in medieval France. The bones in his face had been chiseled and handsome before, but now they looked razor-sharp, with the skin stretched tight over them. Tom's eyes were bleak and hard, and he glared with unfettered rage at the Monger who still lay on the ground.

"Tom?" I ventured cautiously.

"Back off, Saira." Ringo's voice was low and warning, and I shot him a quick glance. He, too, was staring at Tom's face.

Tom had eyes for no one but the Monger in front of him, and I wondered who he was and why Tom so clearly despised him.

Regardless of the answer, I couldn't back off. I wanted to take Tom out of there and go home with him, but for that I needed to reach through his single-minded focus.

I slowly stepped over to the wall and pulled my marker out of my coat pocket. Archer had insisted I carry it since we escaped from France, and I was glad to have it now. I began to draw a spiral. Ringo noticed and nodded approvingly.

"Who is he, Tom?" I used a calm tone that I hoped sounded reasonable, as if I was asking about the weather.

I didn't think he would answer me because all his effort seemed to bleed into holding the gun on the Monger. When he did, the voice that came out cracked as though from disuse.

"Meet George Walters, traitor, thief, beater of wives and children ..." He took a shuddering breath. "And my great-grandfather."

His great-grandfather? He came here to meet his great-grandfather? Something went *clunk* in my brain and instantly everything about Tom's plan became totally clear and completely, horribly wrong. There was nothing tentative in my voice anymore. "You can't kill him."

My tone of voice surprised Tom, and he looked at me for the first time. I froze, the spiral half way drawn, but he didn't seem to notice. Something softened in his eyes for the briefest moment, but then they went flinty again and he returned his glare to Walters.

"If he dies now, his son doesn't get beaten almost to death, and then he won't turn around and beat Seth Walters bloody. Then maybe Seth won't rape my mother, and I'll never be born."

"It doesn't work like that, Tom." I was harsh, but I wasn't feeling particularly generous about this. "Those things happened. They suck, and you've paid a huge price because of them, but you can't just make it all go away. If you kill him, you'll split time. One timeline will be what already happened, and the other one may look different, or maybe not. But you don't get to play God on this. Last time you tried," my voice got softer, "Léon died anyway."

He flinched at that, so at least he was listening. I finished the spiral and concentrated on keeping myself outside of it as I spoke to him.

"Don't do this, Tom. Going back and killing Hitler doesn't change the fact that he killed six million Jews, because he did and we know it. Killing your own personal Hitler won't change the fact that you were born, and it won't erase the circumstances of your birth. The only direction any of us can go is forward, Tom. We take what happened and we make ourselves into people we can look at in mirrors without flinching."

No matter what, I couldn't let Tom kill George Walters. I caught Ringo's eye, looked pointedly at Tom, and then at the spiral. He nodded once, reached into his pocket for something, and slunk up onto the platform. George watched us all with glittering eyes from his low position.

Tom's voice was steely. "Time travel has the grandfather clause. He is the grandfather, so he will die."

George lunged forward to grab the gun just as Ringo hurled his full weight at Tom. The combination was the only reason either of them succeeded. Ringo's hit sent Tom flying into the spiral on the wall, and with a last look of hatred directed straight at me as he screamed, "NOOOOO!!!" Tom disappeared through the portal.

There was a moment of stunned silence while the echo of Tom's voice still hung in the air, when time itself seemed to have stopped. The silence was infinite in its possibility, and it was shattered in a moment. The moment when George shot Archer.

Archer went down and George kept shooting wildly in a rage. Tiles shattered, and cement dust exploded on the platform. I leapt off the platform as bullets struck everything around me.

It felt like a war zone.

ARCHER – PRESENT DAY

A bullet struck the wall behind me, and a broken tile chip grazed my neck. The two guards we had disabled at the entrance to the station were still down, so this was someone new. I scanned the station to find the shooter, and I saw Connor's Wolf change trajectory and aim for the middle of the wall where the old passenger crossover had been when the platform was still intact. Another wild shot aimed at the Wolf broke tiles, and then two more in rapid succession. The last shot had been too close. The shooter was inside that passage, now a partially bricked-up hole in the wall, in a defensive position that left us exposed. The only barrier we had working for us was part of the train car that blocked the shooter's view of the left side of the station nearest the tunnel entrance. It was the side Adam was on with most of the mixed-bloods who had crawled out of the train cars. "Adam, go!" He didn't hesitate. He raised his arm and swung it in a commando signal for *let's move!*

Tam and Daisy, the two young people Logan had asked for help, were still on the right side of the tunnel near the blocked end. Daisy had been helping an older woman out of the train car while the green-haired young man waited to lift her down.

Everyone had frozen with the gunshots. "Wait there!" I called to them. I hoped they stayed out of sight – I wanted the only moving target to be me.

I burst forward with as much speed as the distance allowed, and the shooter unloaded his clip on me. One of the bullets tore through my coat, but just missed the shoulder. Good, I'd need it to climb.

The shooting paused for the barest of moments, and I knew he was reloading. "Go!" I yelled behind me. I hoped the kids would get the woman to Adam, but my focus was on that wall.

I climbed the broken bricks in the lower section that had once been the platform, but the shooting started again too soon, which meant he was aiming at the mixed-bloods. I growled and pulled a loose brick from the wall. Another shot, and I heard a Wolf yelp in pain. Rage filled me, and I flung the brick over my head into the passage. The shots went wild, and I heard them hit tile, brick, and metal.

I hauled myself the last few feet and barreled into the passage. Bullets tore into my chest, and old wounds bloomed fresh and bloody, but I couldn't feel them.

And then the buzzing began.

SAIRA – 1944

I heard a bullet ping against something metallic, and then a buzzing sound like an amplified electric transformer, or a great, mechanical bee, filled the station. I whipped my head around for the source of the sound, and then I stared up in horror.

It was a buzzbee that had lodged in the ceiling. It had been activated by a stray bullet, and the buzzing sound came from it.

Ringo had dragged Archer down onto the tracks out of the line of wild gunfire. George was still shooting the places where we'd stood until Ringo threw a brick at his head that knocked him down. No one seemed to understand that the buzzing sound was a very, very bad thing to hear, and we all needed to stop what we were doing and run.

The buzz filled my head with a sound we had to escape. And suddenly, escape was all we could do. I jumped back up to the platform and began to retrace my spiral.

ARCHER – PRESENT DAY

The shooter was young, barely out of his teens, and terrified. I didn't care who he was or why he was there. I ripped the gun from his hands and hurled it out of the passage.

"Run." I growled at him.

Blood loss made me dizzy, but I spun and leapt to the ground. I landed badly and hands helped me to my feet. "Where's the Wolf. We have to go," I said, my voice alarmingly weak.

"He's hurt and can't walk," said a voice I didn't recognize. I looked up and registered the green, spiky hair first, then a face about Arman's age with intelligent eyes and interesting features. "Jesus, so are you." His voice was awed as he stared at the blood that had soaked my shirt red.

"There's a bomb. Unexploded V-1." I indicated the ceiling above the last car and Tam's expression changed immediately.

"That explains what I've Seen. Right, we're going back up." He meant the passage and I stared at him in shock.

"No, we're getting Connor and getting out."

"We won't make it. The Wolf is hurt, you're practically dead. We can't get far enough. The whole tunnel collapses. I've Seen it."

Just then the Monger shooter dropped down behind me and bolted for the tunnel entrance. Tam spat. "He'll die. Serves him right."

347

I found I expected Ringo's voice to come from Tam's mouth, and it made me trust him. "I'm not healing like I should," I said wearily.

"No kidding." The awe was back in his voice as he surveyed the array of old wounds on my body. He couldn't see the sword slashes and stab wounds that I knew were under my shirt. "I'll boost you up and hand the Wolf to you."

I looked over to where Connor's Wolf lay curled around himself, breathing heavily and in obvious pain. His eyes watched me, and I finally nodded.

Then the room went silent.

"Twelve seconds," I whispered.

Saira – 1944

The room went silent. For an instant I thought I'd lost my ability to Clock, but then the hum and buzz of the portal began to grow with each turn of my finger, and I realized what the silence meant.

"Twelve seconds!" I shouted to Ringo and Archer. "The bomb blows in twelve seconds!"

Ringo understood my words immediately, and he helped Archer to his feet. The whole front of Archer's white shirt was red with blood. I was terrified for him as he struggled to stand, and I knew he'd been shot multiple times. I just barely resisted the urge to fling myself at him.

"Ringo, get to Saira! I'll bring Walters." I heard Archer's voice gasp the order. They were only about twenty feet from me, but dragging a wounded Monger could slow Archer down to a dangerous degree. I opened my mouth to protest, but it was pointless. Ringo would do what Archer wanted.

The buzzing in my head intensified and I could feel the portal open, so I stepped back to avoid being pulled in. Ringo stopped about ten feet away from me and turned back toward Archer, who was bent over George Walters checking for a pulse.

"Leave him! Let's go!"

The silence count had reached five and panic squeezed my throat.

George suddenly clutched Archer's shirt with an iron grip, and the flash of gold on his finger was suddenly more than just a ring – it was the Monger ring. Archer tore himself from George's grasp and rose like a phoenix behind Ringo, his eyes never leaving mine as he mouthed the words, "I love you."

ARCHER – PRESENT DAY

I could see her face clearly in my memory, hear the music in her voice as she promised to love me forever in that walled garden in Oradour-sur-Glane. I could see the love that shone in her eyes, the softness of her hair in the moonlight, and the smile that danced on her lips.

And I smiled.

The Wolf lay curled next to me, and my arm draped over him protectively. The young man with green hair crouched opposite, watching us both with concern.

And then the world outside the passage burned hot and bright.

And everything went black.

 SAIRA – 1944

A blast tore through the station, and fire consumed the air. Heat seared my lungs and concussion filled my head with dull, thudding silence. Ringo hit me so hard we went through the wall - through the spiral portal and *between* where shock hit me like ice water. I blindly grabbed for a hand that I didn't feel but knew was there, and then hit the floor with a *whump!*

LONDON – 1944

I lay there, dazed, and then staggered to my feet and stared around me. I'd landed in the bishop's attic at Guy's Chapel – the attic I'd brought us to after the massacre at Oradour-sur-Glane.

My vision cleared enough to see Ringo on the floor coughing fiercely.

But no one else.

"Archer!" I gasped, stumbling forward. "Where's Archer?"

Ringo couldn't speak through his cough, and I gripped his shoulder and shook him hard. "WHERE'S ARCHER?!" I shouted into his face. His eyes cleared just long enough to realize, and then they filled with despair.

"He pushed me," Ringo gasped for breath, "into you."

I staggered under the weight of the pain his words sent searing through me, and then shoved it off my shoulders, determined to be able to move. "I have to go back," I choked.

"You can't Clock into a bomb site."

"I have to! He's a Vampire. He can survive."

Unbelievably, the marker was still clutched in my hand, and I crouched down to draw a spiral around my feet. Ringo tried to crawl to me, but I croaked at him, "No, stay here!"

The hum began immediately, and I pictured the ghost station clearly in my mind. As I left the attic, the blackness of *between* consumed me.

And it didn't let go.

353

I frantically tried to picture a tunnel filled with debris, but the portal didn't open.

If it had been an actual door, I would have pounded on it, slammed into it, scratched at the edges until my fingers bled. I kicked out at the blackness, punched the darkness, threw myself against the nothingness where the portal should have been, but there was no door. There was just endless *between*.

Noooooo! I shrieked in my mind.

I couldn't reach Archer. I couldn't get back to the place I'd left him.

The bitter cold and dark of *between* filled me, *became* me.

Between stole the air from my lungs and I felt the blackness curling around my brain as oxygen deprivation became real. I had only a few moments of consciousness left before I was robbed of whatever choice I still had to leave the endlessness that was *between* time and place.

I could choose to let go. I didn't have to face a world where Archer's light was extinguished, where he would never smile at me, where his arms would never hold me again. I didn't have to go back to face the aftermath of his death.

A small spark of will still burned bright in me, and it pushed back against the blackness. I would not choose oblivion, because I would rather feel pain than feel nothing at all. I grabbed onto my choice for life with both hands, and I felt the dim light of the pre-dawn attic draw me like a moth to the weakest of flames. I used the last of my strength to pull myself toward it.

I didn't feel the impact of the attic floor when I finally emerged from *between*. I was alive, but Archer was dead, and the truth of it rode the breath I took and filled my lungs with searing pain. I had no strength left to stand, and I curled into a fetal ball as liquid darkness filled my core and consumed me from inside.

Strong hands pulled me up, and I was wrapped in arms I couldn't feel. "It's gone," I whispered. "I couldn't find the door." I felt hands tighten on my shoulders, and they shook me.

"Saira," Ringo said urgently. His tone snapped my eyes to his, and I saw Rachel behind him. "We can run there. Go down through 'Olborn station. We 'ave to try."

I searched Ringo's eyes and saw raw pain that mirrored my own. I would try for him, because this was what he could do, but I knew the truth.

Archer was gone.

Ringo had avoided speaking to me directly after we'd searched as far into the train tunnel from Holborn station as the rubble would allow. There was no way into the British Museum station from above or below, and even if Archer had survived the blast, it would be months before anyone could dig him free.

I was strangely reluctant to Clock forward, and I sensed the same hesitation in Ringo. There were too many unknowns in whatever future lay before us, and we were both shattered by the events of the time we were in. So we gave ourselves a day to build our courage, using Rachel as our excuse for inaction. None of us gave in to sleep though – I think we were afraid we wouldn't find any reason to wake up again.

So, instead, the three of us walked. The devastation from the night's bombing was limited to just a few neighborhoods, even so it was startling to turn a corner to find beleaguered firefighters dousing smoking ruins with water. Inevitably, the residents who had survived the bombs stood on the streets, hollow-eyed with shock as they tried to make sense of the fact that everything they owned was gone.

The exuberance with which we had run the night before was also gone, and the effort of putting one foot in front of the other took enough concentration to keep my mind blank and empty. Rachel walked between us, and I felt like she was the magnet that held us together.

We didn't consciously decide to go to the East End, but our legs seemed to lead us back to the neighborhood where Ringo's attic flat had been. The commercial building still stood, which, after the devastation of the rest of the city, was strangely ironic, given the average property value of that part of town. Ringo led us through the alley to the back door, which was locked, but in a matter of seconds Ringo had jimmied the door open and we slipped inside.

Rachel blinked only once – when Ringo opened the closet to reveal the hidden access to the attic – but she followed him without comment up the ladder. I didn't realize I'd been holding my breath until I gasped at the view from the top of the ladder. It was as though Ringo had just stepped out for bread and forgot to come back – for fifty years. Nothing had been disturbed, nothing had been changed. There weren't even footsteps in the dust until he walked across the floor to open a window. He was as surprised as I was at the fact that his hiding place – his home – had never been discovered.

Rachel studied Ringo as he moved around this space. "This is yours?"

"It was," he said simply.

She looked at me. "When?"

Ringo blew the dust off his tea kettle and turned on the gas to light the burner. After a moment of sputtering, it finally caught. "The last time I saw this place was 1889," he said. He cranked the water tap and waited while the rusty water cleared, then he rinsed the kettle and filled it.

I pulled the chipped mugs I knew so well out of the cabinet. My favorite had a hand-painted owl on it, and Ringo's mug was blue. I hesitated before grabbing Archer's green mug off the shelf, but I added it to the other two on the counter.

Rachel examined the flat with great attention. She noticed the drape around the bed, the extra bedroll against a wall, and the neat pile of blankets in a corner. She studied the drawings pinned to the walls and the books stacked against them, and when the tea was ready and I'd handed her the owl mug, she finally spoke.

"Where did she go?"

I automatically looked at Ringo, but his mouth was a thin line and he cradled his blue mug in his hands in silence.

When neither of us answered, Rachel continued. "I like her art."

"Yeah, she's good," I said. I spoke in present tense, which was pretty loaded for a Clocker to do.

"What is your art?" she asked me.

"Tagging. Street art," I clarified. "Why?" I was surprised by the question.

She shrugged. "Everyone has something. Mine is machines."

"Mine too," Ringo said quietly.

Rachel seemed surprised. "But I don't see any here."

He shook his head. "I didn't know it then. When we—" he swallowed, "when I was here, it was books … and stayin' alive."

She nodded thoughtfully. "Staying alive is a worthy art."

We sipped our tea in silence for a long time. Ringo's eyes went to Archer's green mug every time I lifted it to my mouth. He finally spoke directly to me. "I like yer ring."

I stared at the gold signet ring on my left hand in surprise. I'd forgotten it was there, and a band of pain wrapped itself around my heart that I could ever forget something as important as being Archer's wife. I met Ringo's eyes. "Me too."

I finally focused my gaze on Rachel. "What do you want to do?" I asked her.

"When you go?" She didn't mince words.

"You can come with us if you want to, or we can take you back—"

She interrupted me. "I'm not going back. I already told you."

Ringo finally seemed to shake himself awake. "The Allies will win this war. In another year it'll be over."

"Will it be really be over? Will I ever be able to trust my countrymen again? I don't see the English informing on their Jewish neighbors."

"England wasn't occupied," I said quietly.

"Occupation is an excuse to betray your friends? To send your neighbors to camps?" Rachel's voice was calm, but her hands shook.

Ringo spoke solemnly, as if it was something he'd thought about for a long time. "Fear is the thing that shows a man who 'e really is. The 'ateful ones are pointin' fingers and layin' blame because that's what they think it takes to survive. Those people 'ave always been there, but fear just shows the rest of us who they are, and because of that, they'll end up alone. Others, like ye and Bas – ye 'ide children and ye 'elp strangers. Ye'll never be alone because ye will 'ave the lives of every person ye 'elped to keep ye warm at night. Ye said there's an art to survivin'? Well, I say there's an art to livin', and 'ow a person deals with fear can be the difference between survivin' this life and really livin' it."

Rachel's gaze hadn't left Ringo's as she processed his words. She finally took a sip of her tea and asked him, "What will you do next?"

"I go where Saira goes," he said. "There are things she needs to finish, and until they're done, I'll be at 'er back."

Rachel nodded, then looked at me. "And you're going to your own time?"

"If I can, yes."

Her eyes found Ringo's again. "May I stay here, in this flat?"

He tilted his head. "What'll ye do?"

She exhaled. "I think I'd like to join the temple." There was a faint smile on her lips. "The one with the chandeliers. I'm very tired of hiding my faith, and I'd like to find a way to help where I can. Then, maybe, when the war is over, I'll look for my father."

Ringo nodded. "Of course ye can stay 'ere. We'll 'elp ye stock up on things before we go."

Which we did. Ringo had brought World War II era money with him, and we were able to buy enough food rations from various parts of the city that no one noticed the quantity. We also gave Rachel whatever we had of value from our own bags, which had become extensions of ourselves, much like the clothing we wore. When Ringo gave Rachel his knife, it was like he relinquished a piece of himself to her, and I think she understood how important his gift was.

I tried to dampen the noise of anguish in my brain with preparation tasks, but it wouldn't go quiet, and it wouldn't dull. The edges of it stayed sharp and cut me when I least expected it. Like when I first caught the silent glances that passed between Ringo and Rachel when they thought the other wasn't looking. The realization that my eyes would never find Archer's across a room again threatened to choke me. I shoved the pain as far down as I could push it and started to see the small things as an antidote to pain.

Rachel was clearly aware of him, but Ringo began to notice things about her, too. He was impressed when she rewired a broken lamp and changed a burner on the gas stove. He taught her how to pick locks in case they were changed on the door downstairs, and the two of them worked together to build a cistern for the roof in the event the water was shut off. I didn't ask him about her, and I doubted he would have known how to answer. Whatever tenuous thing it was between them gave us all a little bit of peace for the briefest of moments, and I loved them both for it.

After a day and a night, Rachel was as prepared as we could help her be, and Ringo and I looked at each other with the silent understanding that it was time to go. We had avoided our future long enough – it was time to face the consequences of George Walter's and Archer's deaths.

Rachel knew it too, and her gaze was on Ringo as he checked everything in the flat one last time. "Will you return?" she finally asked him.

His eyes held hers. "I don't know."

She nodded and looked away, so I pulled her into a hug and whispered into her hair. "If he comes back here, it'll be to find you. But don't wait for him. You both have things to do."

"I know that," she whispered back. "He's rare and special and so are you. I See greatness in you both."

I let go of her and shouldered my bag, feeling about as far away from greatness as I'd ever stood. "Take care of yourself,

Rachel. Rewrite your story and make sure it's full of hopes and dreams."

She wore a serious expression as she studied me. "Perhaps we'll be able to get through the wars and move past the deaths when we allow ourselves to dream again."

We gave each other the cheek-kisses of goodbye, and I stepped away toward the ladder to give Ringo some privacy. He hugged her, and his hand went to her hair to stroke it. Her eyes were shining as they stepped back, and when they exchanged the cheek-kisses, I thought he might have lingered on the last one. It was an image I tucked into the antidote box, to pull out the next time I felt the sharp edges of pain, and when we left Ringo's flat, the glimpse of Rachel's tears got tucked there too.

Present Day

I Clocked us to my mom's walled garden at Elian Manor in the late afternoon. The plants were rioting, but that was normal enough that I didn't give the garden's condition a second thought. The garden door was locked though, and that did get my attention.

Ringo boosted me up to the top of the wall and scurried up after me. I could barely breathe with the shock that coursed through me at the view of Elian Manor. It was deserted and in a state of decay that told of years of emptiness.

Weeds grew up through the paving stones in the driveway and paint peeled off the window frames. The door was locked and all the windows had been shuttered. Between the two of us and a long stick, we were able to lever the heavy cellar door open.

The light from my Maglite sent things skittering into the darkness, and except for spiders and whatever was attached to the beady eyes that glowed from the corners, the cellar was empty. The kitchen door at the top of the stairs was also locked, but Ringo used a brick to break the lock, and we slipped silently into the shadowy room.

"No one has been here for years," I whispered. Both the whisper and the statement were unnecessary given the emptiness of the room. Ringo went to the butler's pantry and opened a cabinet.

"The good china's gone, but the everyday stuff is still 'ere."

There were still pots and pans as well, but nothing to suggest anyone had cooked in the kitchen for a very long time.

Our tour of the rest of the house was much the same. Big white sheets covered the furniture to protect it from dust, and clothes still lived in all the closets except the ones in Millicent's bedroom. Those closets were empty and the room was bare. My mother's old bedroom, the one I had moved into, looked just the same as it had the first time I'd seen it. I unlocked the cabinet where I'd found her drawings of Bedlam and my father. They were still there.

Which meant I hadn't taken them.

As deeply disturbing as the empty manor house was, the fact that my mother's drawings were still locked in a cabinet meant that I'd never retrieved them, and without those drawings, I wouldn't have been able to meet my dad or rescue my mom.

Ringo found me in that bedroom, staring at the drawings which I had lain out on the bed. He had been exploring the rest of the house, and his simple pronouncement made everything so clear.

"The last date I could find that anyone might 'ave lived 'ere was 1967. There was an obituary for Tallulah Elian, and a notice, signed by Mrs. Millicent Mulroy, for the termination of the staff.

"Millicent Mulroy?" I breathed. "She married her pilot." I stared at Ringo with wide eyes.

He nodded, his expression more solemn than I'd ever seen.

"Time has split."

I Clocked us into Archer's cellar room at St. Brigid's School with the breath-holding hope of Christmas morning and the wincing anticipation of a horror film. But I knew what I would see even before my eyes adjusted to the dark. The air in the cellar annex was stale and musty from moth-eaten carpets rolled in a corner. Empty bookcases were stacked against a wall and tables lay inverted on top of each other with their feet in the air like giant dead bugs. I didn't even need to use my Maglite to find the four-poster bed at the far end of the space. The curtain was drawn back and the mattress was missing, which made the bedframe with its wooden slats look like the ribcage of a skeleton.

Ringo clicked on his Maglite and swept the room slowly as I strode back to where he stood at the spiral. It was the old one that had been scratched into the original plaster wall, not the chalk spiral I had drawn in this space at Archer's request.

"'E never lived 'ere after the war, did 'e?" Ringo's voice sounded hollow in the lifeless room.

"No, he never did."

"I Saw you come," Miss Simpson said when I found her in her office. School wasn't in session yet, as it was still the tail end of summer, but Miss Simpson was already there getting ready for the new term.

There was no smile of welcome when Ringo and I knocked on her door, and only the barest hint of recognition in her eyes at the sight of us.

"Do you know me?" I asked quietly.

"You're a Clocker. We don't get many of you at St. Brigids."

"Many?" I had been the only one.

"We have two Mulroys and a MacFarlane this term, so no, that's not many."

Two Mulroys. Millicent's ... grandchildren? Ms. Simpson studied me as I processed her words. "What did you See about us?" I asked her.

"You were gathering information here at school, finding allies. You won't stay long, but in the end, you'll destroy us." Miss Simpson smiled at that.

"Why does that make you happy?" I asked her with the little breath I had left.

Miss Simpson's eyes looked dreamy as she recited.

"Because out of the ashes the phoenix will rise.
The truth will be born, where before there were lies.
And one line will live when the other one dies."

The key was where I'd originally found it on the lintel above the door to the Clocker Tower, which was deserted with no sign that I had ever been there or made it my own. Ringo locked the door behind us as I crossed to the painting and drew back the drapes.

The London Bridge was just as it had always been, the Clocker spirals painted in with swirls of paint. I traced a swirl with one finger absently, as Ringo stood behind me near the desk.

"You have no history here, neither of you." A voice came from the doorway, and I didn't turn.

"I wondered if you'd come, Doran," I said, my eyes still on the painting.

"This time stream you created is not so easy to navigate. I wasn't sure I'd find you," he said with no irony at all.

"*I* created?" I stared at him, incredulous.

"Don't put this on Saira." Ringo was indignant enough for both of us. I finally turned to face my cousin, who had entered the room. Doran looked slightly disheveled, which was odd enough for him that I looked closer.

"What's wrong with you?" I asked him.

He grinned wryly. "Well, the wreckage you left behind in London was more than even I could sift through for something so small as the Monger ring."

I stared at him. "Did you find it?"

He shook his head with a grimace. "If it remains intact, it has become a needle in a haystack."

"*If* it does? You mean it could be gone? No more Monger ring?"

He looked oddly serious. "The Mongers no longer have the power to compel, and in fact, their power has been crushed."

"That's a good thing, isn't it?"

"I suppose it depends who you talk to, doesn't it?" His words were flippant, but his tone was utterly serious.

His mood seemed to match mine, and I shrugged. "Doesn't matter without Archer."

"Ah yes, your Victorian Vamp. Sadly, there was no sign of him in the rubble either."

I felt my fists clench by my sides. "He doesn't deserve your disrespect. He was a better man than you'll ever be, Doran." I ground the words out through my teeth.

"But why do you speak in past tense?"

Ringo stared at Doran. "Because 'e died in 1944."

"Yes, but time split the moment that bomb went off. There are now two time streams, and on one of them you have a history with the Vampire."

I gasped. "How do I get there? Can I just go back before the split and then Clock forward again?"

He looked pityingly at me. "Saira, you know better than that. When young Henry split time in France, you had to go back and repair the split before you had access to the true time stream."

"But we were *there* when it split! I can't be in the same time as myself."

"I suppose that's a conundrum then, isn't it?"

"And you're not going to tell me how to fix things, are you?" I could feel a very familiar anger rise up – the same anger Doran inspired every time he dropped into my world and scattered bits of information like breadcrumbs for the birds to eat before I could follow them.

"My aunt would be rather disappointed in me if I did that, but then she has already given you a clue, hasn't she?"

My eyes narrowed as I considered his words. "Your aunt is Miss Simpson? Are you a Seer too?"

"Of course not. My mix is dangerous enough to my health without adding another Family to the recipe. I'll leave you with this though, dear cousin: as with nature, everything needs a check and a balance, or a yin and a yang, if you will. Just as your Vampire gives you balance, so, too, does weakness offer balance to power, or the bad balance the good. There is no possibility for color in a world where everything is black or white. Only in shades of gray does an opportunity exist to find the rainbow."

With that, Doran stepped forward, past Ringo, to kiss me on the cheek. "Congratulations on your marriage, Cousin. I do hope you find your happiness," he whispered, just before he stepped through the painting and disappeared.

"Well, that was spectacularly un'elpful." Ringo sounded disgusted, which was my usual reaction to Doran's visits. But I was still reeling from the hope his words had ignited in me. Archer had existed on the time stream where we met and he was still there. I just had to figure out how to get back to him.

"No. For once, Doran gave me something useful." I looked my friend in the eyes and promised, "Archer's out there, on the true time stream, and we're going to find a way back to him."

Epilogue – Archer

The bullet wounds in my chest wouldn't heal without the blood my body had begun to crave. It had been too long since I'd last fed, and I knew it would require so much more than either of my companions could give without killing them.

Connor's Wolf lay in a coma next to me, his heat a balm to the chill that had begun to creep through my veins. Blood had soaked my shirt and was beginning to pool under me. I looked for Tam, who had taken my Maglite, the habit to carry one courtesy of my association with my wife, and was exploring the back of the passage.

"They stored their own food and water here. There's probably enough for about a week or two if we ration."

My voice croaked with dehydration when I spoke. "Don't touch my blood, or let Connor touch it. He'll heal better if he stays Wolf, but don't let him get thirsty."

Tam cocked his head at me like a dog does, and I wondered what the rest of his mix was in addition to Seer. "You sound like you're going somewhere."

I slipped my hand into my pocket and pulled out the little silk wrapping I carried there. My fingers fumbled with the ties as I removed the little syringe Shaw had given me.

"Tell Connor when he wakes that I tried his cure. Tell him I've lost enough blood that it may work."

I uncapped the syringe and rolled up my sleeve with trembling fingers. "Eventually I'd get hungry enough that I'd go feral and kill you for your blood," I told him without meeting his eyes. "I saw it happen to a friend of mine." The syringe slipped from my fingers twice until finally it rolled out of reach. I choked back the sob of frustration in my voice. "Can you … help me?"

He searched my eyes for a long moment, the truth of what I said sinking in. "You're a Sucker."

I nodded. He considered me another moment, then apparently made a decision, because he moved to pick up the syringe. I barked at him, "Not with your skin." Tam nodded and used the clean silk bandage to pick up the barrel of the needle. He knelt beside me.

"Let me do it," he said.

My breath was coming in ragged gasps and I nodded helplessly. "A vein," I remembered to tell him. He carefully cleaned a spot on my arm, then pushed the needle under my skin.

"If you see my wife, tell her she was the only thing I saw at the end."

He looked strangely at me, his finger already in the process of pressing the plunger on the syringe. "I thought you said this was the cure."

Fire began to crawl up my arm. It coursed through my veins with every pump of my heart, and I closed my eyes as if the sun burned behind them. I was in agony, and completely at peace. I whispered with the last of my breath.

"It is."

A burnt out car in Oradour-sur-Glane. (photo credit: TwoWings, CC BY-SA
Wikimedia Commons)

A NOTE ABOUT THE HISTORY

It may be an obvious thing to set a book about the Immortal
Descendants of War during the deadliest war in human history, and
I actually did consider other conflicts first *because* it was so obvious.
But I've always been fascinated by World War II – its causes, its
effects, and its extraordinary heroes and villains. My mother was
born during the war in a tiny German village in what is now part of
Poland. She was six months old when her mother fled the village
on foot with her three children, twelve hours ahead of the Russian
army. My mom's memories of childhood in the aftermath of war,
living in poverty, battling stomach tuberculosis caused by
malnutrition – those were stories that I grew up with.

The German atrocities are well recorded, though until I began
to research the setting for Waging War, I had never heard of the
massacre at Oradour-sur-Glane. It is a small village near Limoges,

France, and the remains of it still stand as a memorial to the events of June 10th, 1944. Accounts of the events surrounding the massacre from various sources including court records, German soldiers, and the few French survivors generally agree that a burned-out ambulance was discovered by a troop of German soldiers who had been searching for Sturmbahnführer Kämpfe, who was kidnapped and ultimately killed by the local Maquis. The Maquis had been effectively harassing the 2nd SS Panzer Division on its way to Normandy, and the journey, which should have taken four days, took seventeen, thus allowing the Allies to solidify their presence in northern France after D-Day. The massacre appears to have occurred as reprisal for this Maquis activity.

As the Germans conducted a house-to-house search of the village looking for caches of Maquis weapons, they rounded up the men into the village square and sent the women and children to the church for "safekeeping." There was a small explosion inside the church (sources disagree as to whether it was caused by soldiers or by someone from the Maquis), Germans began shooting, and in the end, nearly every woman and child in the church was dead, either from gunshots or from the subsequent fire.

The men, who had been moved into several barns around the village square, were shot to death by German soldiers. The village was then looted and burned. In the end, 642 French civilians were murdered in Oradour-sur-Glane. It is the deadliest massacre in French history.

The village was targeted when two French collaborators went to the Germans with inaccurate information that Kämpfe was being held there and would be burned to death, though apparently he was already dead by then in another village. In the subsequent war crimes trial, the German soldiers claimed that the massacre was legal under the Geneva Convention as a reprisal against the extensive Maquis activity in the area. Their commanding officer, who had ordered the reprisal, had been killed in the war.

Although there were approximately 40,000 French people convicted of collaborating with the Germans during World War II, there were also about 40,000 French resistance fighters who blew up bridges, derailed trains, rescued British and American pilots, ambushed German troops, and killed any German soldiers who surrendered to them. The British Special Operations Executive (SOE) was formed by Churchill in 1940 to wage a secret war against Germany on the continent. The SOE provided weapons, short-wave radios, money, and trained spies to the French resistance efforts.

Nancy Wake was an SOE agent whose French husband had been tortured and killed by the Gestapo in an attempt to determine her whereabouts. Nancy was nicknamed the White Mouse because she excelled in evading capture. On her first night with Gaspard, the local Maquis leader in the Limousin area, she overheard him tell his men to kill her and take her money. She survived by declaring that she was the only one with the codes for the weapons and money drops, and if they killed her, they'd get nothing from the English. She went on to lead a network of over 7,000 Maquisards as they conducted numerous attacks against German installations, and she once rode nearly 500 kilometers on a bicycle to replace codes her wireless operator had been forced to destroy. Nancy Wake was one of many extraordinary women who fought with the French resistance and were instrumental in helping the Allies win the war in Europe.

London was bombed for 57 consecutive nights during the Blitz of 1940, and bombings continued sporadically for the next five years. On June 12th, 1944 the first V-1 rocket was launched against London. The Doodlebug or Buzzbee, as it was called, made a very distinctive "whirring" sound, and my lovely neighbor Madeline remembers running out of the shelter as a seven-year-old Londoner to listen to them. Ben Aronovitch, in his fantastic book series *The Rivers of London*, describes the architecture of the modern city as the result of the air raids. There are neighborhoods where old Victorian and Georgian buildings stand sandwiched between concrete monstrosities that were built on bomb sites in the 1950s.

The eclectic nature of London's landscape is the direct result of the German bombing.

The efforts of the Bletchley Park codebreakers did, by some estimates, shorten the war by two years and saved countless lives, yet their work remained unknown outside intelligence circles until 1974. Alan Turing's remarkable work mechanizing the breaking of the Enigma code was documented in the Academy Award-winning (and excellent) film *The Imitation Game*. The film also provides tremendous insight into the lives of the men and women who worked in total secrecy and whose war efforts went largely unrecognized until thirty years later. When I visited Bletchley Park, several of the film's sets were still on display, and the props and set dressing were incredibly helpful in bringing to life the mansion and the huts as they were during the war.

The British Secret Intelligence Service did order all but two of the Colossus machines destroyed at the end of the war, but continued to use the last two to break the Lorenz cipher, which remained in use by the USSR for nearly twenty years. When that fact was made known to the Soviets, the remaining Colossus machines were broken up and "thrown down a coal hole," according to a docent at Bletchley Park. Not only was Colossus instrumental in breaking the code of the German high command, it was the world's first computing machine and would have put the UK at the forefront of computer technology if its designers had been allowed to talk about it.

Hitler's Werwolves did exist, though they weren't formed until later in 1944 when it became clear that Germany would lose the war. Himmler recruited young men from the Hitler Youth program to become domestic terrorists with the goal of disrupting whatever occupying force moved into Germany. As I was researching them, I discovered that they had trained at Schloss Hulcrath, a castle in the region where my mother grew up.

Despite the fact that the Werwolves collapsed and disbanded due to mismanagement and lack of funds, there were rumors that they were to be financed by "Hitler's gold," a stash of gold, art, and

372

other treasure that he had stolen throughout Europe. Adolph Hitler, an unsuccessful artist who had been denied admission to the Vienna Academy of Fine Arts, had a deep fascination with great works of art. When he ruled Germany, he empowered Josef Goebbels to systematically loot the great art collections of Europe with the intention of establishing a European Art Museum in Linz. I originally thought to incorporate some of Goebbels' actual art thefts into the plot of Waging War, but ultimately, Nancy Wake and her French Maquis proved more interesting, so the fictitious plan to steal the Elgin Marbles was born.

The British Museum did, in fact, store the Elgin Marbles on the unused track of the Aldwych line during the Blitz, and it is also factual that in 1937-38, Lord Duveen financed the cleaning of them as well as the construction of a new wing in the museum to house them. Acting under the misconception that the marble had been originally white, Lord Duveen directed masons to use scrapers and a chisel to remove the 'discoloration' of the naturally honey-colored marble, resulting in permanent scrape marks and considerable loss of detail. The controversy about the ownership of the marbles began when Lord Elgin first brought them to England at the beginning of the nineteenth century, and the debate over whether they should be returned to the people of Greece continues to this day.

There are more than forty ghost stations in and around London, and many of those deep level stations were used as bomb shelters during the Blitz. Aldwych station remains intact and has been featured in several movies and TV shows including *Sherlock*, which is one of my very favorites (an astute observer may sense my appreciation for Benedict Cumberbatch's work). The description of the British Museum ghost station and much of the route to get there is from an obscure blog by an urban guerilla explorer who actually did complete the very dangerous, don't-try-this-at-home journey between the ghost stations of Aldwych and the British Museum.

And finally, the Philippine eagle is the largest species of eagle on the planet. This fact was provided by my youngest son, who may or may not resemble the fictional Logan.

Thank you so much for reading *Waging War*. If you enjoyed this book, your review anywhere (at an online seller, in a book club, taped to the water cooler) would be very appreciated. You can find more information about me, my newsletter, my books, and whatever I happen to be blogging about on my website: www.aprilwhitebooks.com

I sincerely appreciate hearing from readers, and thank you, again, for joining Saira, Archer, and Ringo on their adventures in time.

~April White

THANK YOU

I have stumbled into a remarkable community of authors and readers, and their friendship and support is a rare and fantastic gift. I first discovered Penny Reid and Elizabeth Hunter when I read their wonderful books, and through fortuitous circumstances, I now count them among my dearest friends. Their support, encouragement, and message chats are a treasured part of every day I spend on this writing journey. Penny Reid also designed the new covers for the whole series, and it's a really good thing we don't keep score, and that I don't have plans for more children, because I'm pretty sure I would owe her my next-born.

Also, special thanks to Laini Taylor, an author of spectacular worldbuilding and lyrical storytelling in her *Daughter of Smoke and Bone* trilogy, for the use of her quote about monsters and war.

Alexandra Fasouliotis, Heather Kinne, and Dan Grover are the first draft beta readers every author covets – they don't pull punches and their insights are pure gold. Jennifer Beach and Fiona Fisher are graphic artists with unique vision who created the gorgeous cover reveal and book release graphics. And the success of these books is made possible by the generosity of bloggers like the amazing ones from Back off my Books, Have You Heard Book Blog, Readereater, Whatever You Can Still Betray, Nocturnal Book Reviews, The Lit Bitch, Urban Fantasy Investigations, and Bookwyrming Thoughts, just to name a few. I am deeply grateful to the many readers who have shared the Immortal Descendants books with their friends on social media and in person, and are the reason new people discover Saira, Archer, and Ringo every day.

My editor, Angela Houle, is shockingly brilliant and endlessly patient. My German translator, Anneke Vogt has eagle eyes and a stunning brain. My mother-in-law, Valerie, is one of the most generous and loving people I know. And my mother, Helga, is my hero. She showed me how to be a strong, independent, educated woman who values and fosters a community of friends, and her unconditional love and support have given me the best possible foundation to be that kind of mother to my own children.

And finally, the people to whom I owe the greatest thanks of all, each and every day, for loving me: Ed, Connor, and Logan. You three are my heart, my soul, and my reason to breathe. Thank you for being my people.

Made in the USA
Columbia, SC
27 October 2017